THE
DEMON'S
CALL

THE
DEMON'S
CALL

KIM GRAVELL

Matador
9 Priory Business Park
Kibworth Beauchamp
Leicestershire LE8 0RX, UK
Tel: (+44) 116 279 2299
Fax: (+44) 116 279 2277
Email: books@troubador.co.uk
Web: www.troubador.co.uk/matador

ISBN 978 1783064 038

British Library Cataloguing in Publication Data.
A catalogue record for this book is available from the British Library.

Typeset in Bembo by Troubador Publishing Ltd
Printed and bound in the UK by TJ International, Padstow, Cornwall

Matador is an imprint of Troubador Publishing Ltd

For my trio of Cancerians: Roger, Jeanne and Mum
— with love.

Thank you for making life special.

CHAPTER 1

It was the smell of blood that told Aidan Morgan he had arrived too late. He could taste it, like copper on his tongue, even before he caught sight of the booted foot, half-hidden in the bracken, or the impression of the sprawled body beyond. The smell stopped him in his tracks. He realised it wasn't just blood. Some ancient animal instinct understood that subtle mingling of scents and what they meant and Aidan froze, fear scalding through his body, locking his muscles rigid. Death waited on the hillside above him, crouched where the evening shadows spread amongst the lichen-covered stones. Death; sudden, brutal and violent, and as clear and certain as if His black cowled form had reared up from the darkening slope and loomed above him.

'John?'

Some small part of Aidan's mind registered surprise at how normal his voice sounded. He flicked the beam of his torch over the tumbled stones where, from the bottom of the slope, he thought he had seen movement. He supposed he must have imagined it.

'John?'

He didn't bother to raise his voice. He no longer expected an answer.

Yellow torchlight glinted on something metallic lying amongst the crushed and broken stems. Beside it was the cleated sole of a work boot. Reluctantly, Aidan played the torch back up the slope, tracing the shape he knew was there. Better not to think. Better to pretend this was a call-out for the mountain rescue team, one of the bad ones that ended as a bag and retrieve rather than a rescue. Make believe it was a stranger, not a friend. You learned survival strategies like that. Wall the pain away so you can function. Deal with it later when the other, more pressing things have been done. Aidan closed his eyes for a second.

'Oh God!'

It was a prayer rather than a blasphemy. Then he started up the last few yards of hillside, the knowledge of what he had seen like a cold stone in his belly.

He didn't doubt the finality of what he was going to find. He had done his best to ignore it, but, from the moment he had found Nan, tied to the field gate, he had known something was wrong. John's sheepdog was almost throttling herself in her attempts to get free, lunging frantically against her collar, making the galvanised gate crash against its post, but the nylon baling twine that held her resisted all her efforts. Other than the panting of her breath, Nan made no sound. In the pen beyond the gate the sheep were a silent mass. Aidan could see the amber of their eyes, the black rectangular pupils wide in the growing dark. Confined by the steel hurdles, they huddled together in a protective mass, facing the threat in silence. Given the opportunity they would scatter and run.

'Nan! Easy, girl.'

Aidan knelt beside the gate, trying to calm the sheepdog, but she seemed oblivious to him. Even when he grabbed her collar she continued to throw herself forward, the force of it jarring his arm. Froth flecked her muzzle and spattered down her sides. Whatever was driving her to get free, his presence wasn't the answer.

'John?'

Casting round him in the dusk, he could see no sign of his friend beyond the battered old quad bike, pulled off to the side of the track. John had certainly been out to check on the ewes, but something must have happened to have kept him out here. Was the same thing responsible for Nan's behaviour?

'John!'

Aidan's voice faded into the hillside, but there was no answering holler. The last time they had spoken, John had mentioned they had a possible sheep worrier on the loose. If he had seen the other dog he might have gone after it, tying Nan up to keep her out of the way. While Nan's distinctive sheepdog black and white should easily distinguish her from the coal black animal John had described to him, in the growing dark John wouldn't run the risk of shooting the wrong dog. He would be mortified if he could see the state the young bitch was in now.

'Come on, girl, it's the back of the car for you.'

There was no way Aidan was going to leave Nan throttling herself against the twine, but he didn't dare let her loose to go running off into the twilight-soaked hills after John. He just hoped she would calm down if he shut her in the back of his Land Rover. All the farm dogs he knew associated cars with the instruction to sit, stay and be quiet until they arrived at their destination and did just that. It was a shame no one had found a way to train children to do the same.

The thought brought a rueful half-smile as he pictured the eight Brownies he had been ferrying around that morning. Over-excited at the prospect of a lesson on the high ropes – although in truth he hadn't taken them on the really high sections of the rope course – they had bounced around the Land Rover like a human demonstration of Brownian motion. Kerry Goodhew, their Brown Owl, had been reduced to threats of making them stand in the forest and watch her trying out her rope work with Aidan – a double entendre that made Aidan almost choke, although thankfully the girls were either too young, or too distracted, to pick up on it – before they settled down.

'Kids,' Aidan snorted. 'Give me dogs any day.'

He released Nan's collar while he fished in his pocket for his clasp knife. As soon as he let go, the bitch resumed her battle to get free.

'Damn it, Nan, stop that.'

The sound of the dog's panting breath being choked off and the dull clang of gate on post were horrible to hear and the frantic urgency of her struggle was unnerving him. He wanted to find John, share some choice words with him about priorities for a Friday night and then get down to the Unicorn where a few beers would make the world easier to put to rights. What he didn't want to do was go clambering over a dark hillside to find John and the pellet-riddled remains of someone's dog – sheep worrier or not. He shivered suddenly, *someone stamping on your grave, son,* and put the picture from his mind, but the sense of disquiet remained.

'Come on, girl.'

He slit the twine tying her to the gate, but as he went to stand Nan lunged away from him and, taken off balance, he stumbled. His fingers raked the leather of her collar as he tried to grab her again, but he couldn't get sufficient grip to hold her and she streaked away, a blur of black and white in the dusk. Aidan watched her go, nursing his pulled fingers, surprised that the sheepdog had struck out in the direction of home and not, as he would have expected her to, up the hillside after John. The sense of wrongness settled closer about him. Suddenly the darkening hills seemed distinctly unwelcoming.

He eyed the hillside unhappily. John was out there somewhere. Even if there was nothing wrong and he had just taken it into his mind to sit in watch for the black dog, he couldn't just turn round and go back to the farm without finding out what his friend was up to.

At the top of the field the old chimney stack showed a pale column in the gloom. Part of one of the abandoned lead mines that dotted these valleys, the rubble stone walls – all that remained of the wheel house – had all but fallen down now, helped on their way by time and neglect and past generations helping themselves to the stone whenever there was need for it elsewhere. Only the chimney stack stood as it always had; impervious, its octagonal, yellow brick sides seeming to slough off weather and time alike, lending its name to the field and to the hillside from which it erupted.

In summers years past, Aidan and John had regularly climbed up to the stack and its slowly disintegrating collection of outhouses. Amidst the long evening shadows, when the farm chores were done, they would reinvent the derelict remains as castle buttresses and enemy bunkers. In later years they'd slumped against the sun-warmed stones, drinking canned lager as they watched the tiny dots of sheep grazing on the far slopes of the valley, talking of girls and rugby and the inner workings of the John Deere tractor engine.

Aidan stared again at the crumbling walls, straining to see in the fading light. For a moment he thought he saw something up there, moving. There, between the tumbled stones of the wheel house wall and the chimney, where the shadows were already blotting out the detail, for an instant there was a darker shadow. The light was too poor to make out what it was. It didn't move quite like a dog and besides, surely it was too big, but it certainly wasn't a man. Low to the ground he saw it pass in front of the lighter brick stack and then it disappeared again. There were thick stands of bracken up there, growing right up to the walls, but if it went into them he saw no movement among the stems. Could it be the sheep worrier John had talked of?

Aidan put finger and thumb to his lips and whistled, a long rising note with a short dip at the end. It was actually his 'come away' signal to his own dog, Sula, but most dogs would show some interest in a whistle, even if they weren't trained to come to that particular call. After a few seconds he tried it again, but there was no answering movement. Whatever he had seen, if indeed it had been anything more than shadows that his mind chose to assign shapes to, like finding faces in summer clouds, it seemed to have vanished. Aidan shivered again and shoved his hands into his jacket pockets, undecided as to what to do. He really didn't want to walk up to the chimney stack and that surprised him, for he couldn't think of one good reason as to why that should be. These hills were his heart's home, his sanctuary. They were where he went to regain his sanity. But not tonight. Something else was abroad this evening and it made him feel edgy and unsettled. There was a sense of otherworldliness seeping through the air. Like ground mist, rising from the valley, it wreathed the hillside and it was all he could do not to turn on his heel and go.

In their pen, the sheep pressed closer together, tightening into a single woolly mass. Aidan shook his head. This was stupid. He had been up and down these hills since he had been old enough to walk. Any ghosts were only in the minds of those who harked back to ancient glories or sought to cash in on the current fashion for the Celtic supernatural. There was history here aplenty, but it was the history of working men, of agriculture and of industry, not anything otherworldly.

In the kitchen at Cwm Broch, Friday Night is Music Night would be playing quietly on the radio while Nerys completed the crossword and Bryn studied the stock adverts in the *Shropshire Star*. The image made Aidan smile, as he usually did when he thought of John's parents.

He had barely driven into the farmyard at Cwm Broch before the door had opened and Nerys had been out to welcome him.

'Aidan, how are you?'

He let her plant the obligatory kiss on his cheek while sniffing appreciatively at the warm smells of baking emanating from the kitchen. Nerys smiled knowingly.

'Before you ask, they're apple and blackberry and yes, I have made one for you. You can pick it up on your way home tonight. It's too hot to wrap for you now.'

Aidan grinned at her.

'Anyone would think I only come here to let you spoil me, Nerys,' he teased. 'I'd be big as a house if I weren't running round these hills every day.'

'Hah, there's nothing of you. If I had a stick, I could play a tune on your ribs. You need fattening up. You should teach that girl of yours to cook for you.'

Thankfully Aidan was spared from explaining what Jane's reaction would be to that particular suggestion as Nerys continued without pause. 'Come on in.'

Aidan followed her into the big room. On the draining rack sat a pile of plates from the evening meal and Aidan made to pick up the tea towel.

'Don't be daft, boy.' Nerys shooed him aside. 'Go sit down and keep the old man company.'

She cast an affectionate glance at the figure sat in the battered armchair beside the Rayburn, one foot propped up on a stool. 'John won't be long.'

Aidan did as he was told, pulling up a chair at the table.

'How do.'

'Evening, Bryn. How's that knee doing?'

'Oh, middling, middling. Doctor says there's not much to be done with it, but what does he know, eh? Reckon I'd be better off going to the vet.'

'Any vet with sense would have you shot.' Nerys frowned at her husband, but Aidan wasn't fooled. 'It would get better a lot quicker if he'd just keep off it like Doctor Olson told him to,' she added, putting a plate of drop scones on the table in front of Aidan, followed quickly by a large pat of butter and a wedge of cheese.

'Can't do that when there's a farm to run.'

Aidan knew this was a conversation that had been rehashed many times since Bryn had twisted his knee a fortnight ago, hauling bales down from the trailer. Nerys was right, it would get better a lot quicker if he did the exercises the physio had given him and kept off it in between times, but Bryn was equally correct when he said that was impossible. The farm wouldn't run itself. Farming was a way of life that was unforgiving of illness or injury. Either way, he knew he wasn't expected to take sides. It was the familiar, comfortable banter of two people who, even after forty plus years of marriage and five children, were still the centre of each other's worlds.

'Two sugars now, isn't it, Aidan?' Nerys asked.

'Please.'

A large china cup and saucer appeared beside the scones.

'So where's John gone that's more important than getting the first pint of the evening?'

Nerys rolled her eyes.

'He took it into his head to go have a last look at the ewes. We brought a dozen of them down to the chimney stack fold. They'll be off to Welshpool tomorrow and he just wanted to make sure they were settled. You know what they're like.' She put a cup and saucer on the arm of the chair, her hand brushing Bryn's as she did so. He caught her fingers and gave them a squeeze. 'Pay more attention to their sheep than they do to their women.'

'There's more money in sheep, woman. Sheep bring money in; women just spend it for you. Now stop talking and let the boy eat in peace.'

Nerys snorted as she stacked the plates on the dresser, but made no retort. Bryn winked at Aidan.

'When I saw him on Tuesday he said he'd seen a dog hanging around and he thought you might have another sheep worrier on your hands.'

Bryn straightened in his chair, his body language conveying volumes, but he only nodded and said simply, 'That he has. I've not seen it myself like, but the boy's seen it a couple of times now. We've not had any new trouble yet, but it doesn't hurt to be careful.'

He reached for his tea, but Aidan saw the pained expression in his faded blue eyes. Like any farmer, he would do whatever was necessary to protect his stock, but dogs were in his blood too and the prospect of a renegade was always going to be painful.

'John's taken it to heart,' Nerys commented as she hung the tea towel to dry over the Rayburn. 'So much so he's even dreaming about it at night.'

Bryn spluttered into his tea.

'For God's sake woman, what are you talking about?'

'He's been dreaming about that dog.' She gave her husband a quelling look. 'I know because I've heard him talking in his sleep. I wouldn't expect you to notice, but I do. You know I wake up if one of you does and if either of you isn't sleeping right I know it. It's no different from you knowing when one of the ewes is having trouble at lambing.'

Bryn looked as though he had something to say about that, but Nerys ignored him and continued.

'He's not had one night this week when he's slept right through.'

'You shouldn't be saying things like that about the boy.'

'I'm his mother, I'm allowed to worry about him, and Aidan's not going to mind, are you, bach? He might as well know why John's keeping him waiting.'

Bryn said nothing, but Aidan could feel disapproval radiating from every inch of his stocky frame. Like most of his generation, the old farmer wasn't one to talk about feelings and Aidan guessed he was deeply embarrassed by Nerys' candour.

'Are you going to watch the dog trials on Sunday, Bryn?' Aidan asked, deliberately changing the subject. 'I hear that Phil Gower's new dog is going well.'

Bryn took the change of subject gratefully.

'They say she is, but Aled Rogers and Rock will still win, I reckon. How's that bitch of yours doing?'

'She's fine. Not so keen on the pub on a Friday night though, too many people standing on her tail, so I've left her at home in the kitchen.' He paused for a second as though thinking. 'You did mean Sula, didn't you? Not Jane?'

Bryn chuckled.

'Best watch what you say about that one or she'll box your ears for you.'

'Tell me about it. You should have seen her taking the juniors for the freestyle class on Wednesday. She scared the life out of them.'

He pulled his sleeves down surreptitiously so Bryn wouldn't see the mottled yellow and brown bruises patterning his forearms. The reactions of people outside the karate club tended towards disbelief when you explained that two hours spent punching and kicking your friends was a relaxing way to spend an evening.

Aidan glanced at his watch and was surprised to see it had already turned seven. Outside the window, dusk was closing in. Nerys followed his gaze.

'I'll clip that boy's ears when he comes back, making you wait like this. I don't know what he's got up to.' She looked at the clock, clearly weighing how long John had been gone against the time it should have taken him and frowned. 'I hope there's nothing wrong.'

'Tell you what, Nerys, I'll drive up there and see what he's doing. He might have seen that dog again and be waiting to make sure it doesn't come back, in which case he's probably not going to want to come down the pub anyway.'

'I'll come with you.' Bryn sounded as though he was just waiting for an excuse to get up from his chair, but Nerys was having none of it.

'Oh no you won't. You're going to stay right there and rest that leg. Why do you think John didn't want you going up there with him in the first place?'

'It's alright, Bryn. If you come I'll never get him away. The pair of you will be off, checking them all over, debating how much you're going to get for them. You'll be there all night.'

He winked at Nerys and she flashed him a small, grateful smile.

'I can give him a hand with anything he needs. Anyway, he's probably just having a quiet fag and watching the stars.'

Oh, if only… the ease of those words came back to Aidan as he stood with the smell of blood heavy in his nostrils and a sense of shock making his hands go cold. He desperately wanted to go back, to unknow the awful thing that he had discovered. He wanted to be in that warm kitchen where John was still going to come back through the door, cap pushed back on his head, a crumpled pack of Marlboro Lights poking out of his shirt pocket and Nan at his heels, as always, but Aidan knew that would never happen again.

John's body lay amongst the scattered stones of the old wheel house wall. In the shaky torchlight Aidan could make out the black glitter of blood across their surface. There was absolutely no doubt that John was dead, nor about what had killed him. He had gripped the shotgun's stock between his legs and used his shepherd's crook to reach the trigger. The galvanised steel was still in his hand, spattered with droplets of blood and shredded flesh in which fragments of bone showed unbelievably white in the torchlight. At such short range the shot hadn't spread much and the effects were that much more devastating. The blast had taken off the top of the young farmer's skull, ripping up through the roof of his mouth, destroying everything on the left side of his head from the top of the orbit back to the crown. The one remaining eye regarded Aidan with a fixed, defiant stare, but offered no explanation. Among the dried blood and mucous, the exposed remnants of brain gleamed wetly.

Aidan turned away quickly, but nothing could wipe the sight from his mind. He managed one step before his legs folded and he found himself on hands and knees, his stomach heaving uncontrollably. Though the evening was cool, he could feel sweat breaking out all over his body, his heart pounding ridiculously loudly in his ears, as though he had run to the point of exhaustion, and his head swam. Vaguely he wondered if he was going to pass out and he dropped his head and forced himself to take a deep breath. A mistake, that – given the combined smells of vomit and blood and the waste John's body had voided at the moment of death – but at least the dizziness eased even as bile flooded his mouth again. This time he managed to swallow it down and, after a few moments, he felt confident enough to sit up although he kept his gaze fixed resolutely on the horizon.

The far side of the valley was little more than a silhouette, black against the dark cyan of the sky. Ice white and glittering, the first stars were beginning to show, their constellations shockingly familiar in a world so comprehensively torn apart. Aidan knelt, shivering on the thin, tussocky grass, not feeling the dew soaking his jeans or the chill of the breeze rising from the valley bottom. Oblivious to the passing time, he watched as the night sky unfolded, constant and uncaring, above him and the realisation crept over him that he would be the one to have to break the news to Bryn and Nerys. Putting his head in his hands, he wept.

CHAPTER 2

It was well past midnight when Aidan finally pushed open his front gate and walked up the short path to the cottage door. The whitewashed walls showed pale in the moonlight, but no welcoming glow shone from the windows. That wasn't unusual. On a normal day, returning to a dark house wouldn't have bothered him, yet now he hesitated, wondering if the shadows had always clotted so thickly around the front door. He shivered, the hairs standing up on his arms and on the back of his neck. For no good reason the idea of stepping from moonlight into that inky recess unnerved him.

The sense of detachment, that shocked numbness of mind and body that had been his only possible refuge, allowing him to function through the nightmare events of the evening, was fading rapidly, leaving his senses stripped and raw, his emotions in turmoil. Grief, guilt and anger seethed within him until he felt he balanced on a knife-edge from which the slightest mis-step would send him tumbling down into a maelstrom from which he wasn't sure he could recover. He still couldn't believe what John had done, couldn't comprehend what it was that had driven him to take his own life. What could possibly have been so awful that the only way to deal with it had been at the end of a shotgun barrel?

Don't think about it. Not now, he told himself, willing himself back from the edge, but in his mind he could all but feel the weight of the gun in his hands and the sharp edge of the barrel digging into the soft flesh under his chin as he jammed it home.

Do it, a voice seemed to whisper from just behind him. *It's the only way you'll understand.*

'No!' The denial burst from his lips like vomit as though he would physically purge himself of the idea, denying that for one dreadful moment it had seemed to make perfect sense. Aidan whipped round. He could see nothing, but he knew he was no longer alone. Something else was there, hidden by the night; something malevolent, waiting and watching and biding its time.

With shaking hands, Aidan fumbled for his key, his heart pounding as he pushed it into the lock. For a moment it refused to turn and he twisted at it frantically, sensing as he did so that *something* in the dark coming closer. In the kitchen, Sula started barking, the sound sudden and startling. At the same time the key turned and he almost fell inside, slamming the door behind him. Blindly he slapped at the light switch and stood shuddering in the sudden glare, his skin clammy with sweat for all the night's chill, his eyes fixed on the door. Pulse hammering, he watched it, waiting for he knew not what… but nothing happened. A minute passed and finally he dared to relax.

What on earth was all that about?

He managed a shaky laugh, embarrassed by his own foolishness, and chose not to notice that he switched on every light he passed as he headed for the kitchen. Sula had stopped barking the moment he had entered the house, but she bounded round him as soon as he stepped into the kitchen, almost as though she were trying to herd him back into the light and away from the darkness outside. Aidan dropped to his knees and hugged her hard, indescribably grateful for the comfort of her warm, living presence. It was stupid that, after coping with so much, he should unravel just because he had come home to an empty house. After dealing with the police and the awful moment when they had taken John's body down from the hillside... Sula whined softly as Aidan's fingers tightened in her coat. He hadn't let Bryn or Nerys leave the farmhouse though he had had to restrain Bryn physically while the farmer had raged at him, calling him names he could scarcely believe Bryn knew. Aidan didn't care. They could call him all the names under the sun, but he would not allow them to identify their son by his clothes and his watch and the shattered remnants of his face. Let them hate him for it, but he chose for them the memory of the living man. He would not let them burn the sight of that blasted shell forever on their minds' eyes. Protecting John's parents from the brutal details of their son's death was the last thing he could do for his friend.

So it had fallen to him to take the police back to the hillside and make the formal identification. Going once more through the events that had led up to his finding John's body, he had been aware of activity out of the corner of his eye; John's gun and his crook being carefully removed and bagged, the details of the scene recorded; the Scene of Crime Officers working with quiet efficiency that suggested that to them at least the task was just part of a normal day's work. Aidan had tried not to think about it. As soon as he was allowed to he had gone back to the farmhouse to sit with Bryn and Nerys, white-faced and silent. There was nothing he could say that would help them and nothing would absolve him of the guilt of being the one to bring their world to ruin.

As the coroner's van bearing John's body pulled into the farmyard, Aidan followed Bryn as he limped outside, standing alongside him to offer what comfort he could whilst ready to intervene if Bryn made an attempt to see his son's remains. But Bryn only stood there staring mutely at the vehicle's blacked out windows as if trying to detect the presence of his son inside. He seemed impervious to Aidan standing beside him and, trapped in the farmer's silence like a fly in amber, Aidan had no words to reach him.

When Elizabeth, John's sister, had arrived from Aberystwyth – red-rimmed eyes bearing mute testimony to the tears she had cried even as she had driven there – Aidan had gratefully seized the chance to leave. Although Elizabeth had offered him a bed for the night, brutally accurate in her assessment that he was in no fit state to drive, he had pleaded the need to go home and see to Sula and had fled.

Aidan sighed and slid the empty tumbler away from him along the kitchen table. One glass of whisky hadn't helped and, tempting though it was, he doubted a second would prove any more effective. He really should go to bed, but tired though he was he hesitated. Oblivion would be welcome, but he feared what he would see when he closed his eyes. Sula looked up briefly as he shifted then dropped her head back to his knee. Surely grief must have a smell that she could pick up, for she hadn't left his side almost as though she knew how much he needed that contact.

'I don't understand it, lass.' Aidan's voice caught as he ran his fingers through the silky fringe of her ears. 'Why would he do it?'

But he could think of nothing that hinted at his friend having been in any way unhappy, let alone suicidal.

'By Christ, Aidan, you should have seen it. Bold as brass it was, sat at the top of our track, right by the lambing pens. Big too; bigger than Nan here.'

17

John rubbed absently at the ruff of grey and black hair on the sheepdog's neck and Nan crooned in pleasure.

'Nasty looking brute.' He shook his head at the memory. 'At first I thought it must be one of Jack Tŷ Gwyn's dogs, given we've had words about him letting them roam on our land, but it was no sheepdog. Black it was. Black as coal and big yellow eyes. I tell you it looked at me like it was weighing me up, judging me. Right weird it was. If I'd had my gun, I'd have had him.'

Knowing that Cwm Broch had lost two ewes back at the tail end of August, Aidan could appreciate John's concern at having a stray dog on his land. With margins as tight as they were, no farm could afford such losses. It wasn't just that, though. He recalled the pain in John's voice when he had described finding the last ewe with its throat torn out and knew it wasn't just the blow to the farm's finances that had upset him. John cared deeply for the welfare of his stock. Even so, Aidan didn't like the idea that anyone might shoot a dog so casually and though he didn't comment he felt obscurely grateful that Sula with her bright russet coat was nothing like the animal John had described. As if hearing her name in his thoughts, the bitch raised her head from where it rested beside his boot and looked up at him, her tail thumping briefly against the ground before she settled again.

Aidan leaned back on his elbows, enjoying the feel of the sun on his face. John had been brushing Cwm Broch's hedges, trimming them back to prevent them growing too wide or too high. Beyond the bright blue Massey Ferguson, and the toothy bulk of its heavy-duty cutting bar, a square cut line of hawthorn marked his progress along the field. The air was sharp with the green scent of sap and cut branches.

The lonely *kir kir* of a kite echoed down the valley and Aidan turned his gaze heavenwards, quartering the sky until he found the distant shape. He watched as it gyred effortlessly in the great sweep of cloudless blue, the *lazy tilt of its wings sliding it along the unseen airstreams, spiralling down the valley until it disappeared over the wooded bulk of Gwennol ridge and was gone.*

Next to him John fished in a pocket for his packet of cigarettes and lit one. He inhaled deeply and then blew the smoke out carefully downwind of Aidan.

'That one's been following me all morning,' he commented. 'He's looking to see if I turn up any rabbits I reckon. "Kites for cutting, gulls for ploughing," that's what they say.'

He took another drag on his cigarette then knocked the ash from its tip, carefully grinding it into the soil to make sure no stray spark was left to start a fire.

'There are some strange things in these hills, Aide, my friend. Strange things.'

He pushed nicotine-yellowed fingers through the tangled mop of his hair, bleached to the colour of the drying grass from that summer's sun, and somewhere near as coarse.

'Not if you go round shooting them there's not.'

They sat for a while, saying nothing, enjoying the warmth of the sun in companionable silence. Having known each other since their first school days there was no need to talk.

'I saw a ewe last Friday.'

Aidan was tempted to ask if it had been a casual date or something more serious, but he held his tongue. Stock breeding was one thing John didn't joke about. Personally he had heard enough versions of the Welshman and the sheep joke from the trainees on Red Kite Adventure Training's courses to have developed quite an appreciation for the genre although he had been known to suggest that the bawdier individuals consider who would be rigging their safety lines later. Still, as his partner at Red Kite hailed from a New Zealand sheep ranch, he and Matt formed a united front when it came to sheep focussed humour and the trainees got back as much flack as they gave.

Undeterred by Aidan's lack of response, John launched into an enthusiastic description of his latest ovine fancy.

'Beautiful she is, Aidan, right tidy. Her dam won best in breed at Builth, last year but one, and I think she's going to be as good. I'm thinking seriously about taking her.'

Aidan made a noncommittal noise knowing John needed no encouragement.

'You know Da's more or less turned the stock planning over to me. Now, please God, he'll be carrying on for a good few years yet, but I reckon I can make a name for the farm if I get some fresh blood into the breeding stock and this could be the one. You watch, in a couple of years it'll be us taking best in show at the Royal Welsh.'

Half-listening to John's plans for ovine world domination, Aidan's eyes wandered back to the familiar shapes of the surrounding hills; comforting as the presence of old friends. The soft, straight back of Cefnen Rise, its gradual slopes polka dotted with black-wrapped bales as they rose to the rounded bulk of Caerberis; Beris' fort. Ron Williams' tups were grazing the top pasture, scattered out like a random sprinkling of salt grains, heads down, methodically chewing, converting grass into wool and meat. Not that there was so much money to be made in either these days, but what else was there to do? And beyond those softer, lower cousins, the sudden fierceness of flat-topped Cadair Cawr, the giant's chair, its sides pock-marked with scree slopes, gaunt and forbidding. Nineteen years and he could still remember the day Gwyn and his mother had taken him up to the Fort for the very first time, could still recall the fresh cut sweetness of the grass as his new kite had found the breeze so lacking in the summer drowsing valleys and had finally taken to the sky, its red and black quadrants standing proud against a cloudless blue.

It had been after his father had disappeared from his life. Gone to work on the Scottish oil rigs from which he returned for infrequent and increasingly brief visits, until the day when he forgot to come back at all. Aidan remembered the pull of the kite strings in his hands and his own excited shrieks as he had raced up and down the broad pasture and how his mother had promised to paint a real kite on the chequered nylon. Later they had sat drinking warm lemonade and Gwyn had told stories of the old lord Beris and his beautiful and wise wife Alwyn, and how they had come to build their home in the shadow of the giant's chair. Although he knew his mother, leaning back on her elbows and listening to her friend's storytelling, was the smartest and most beautiful woman in the world, Gwyn was that most wonderful of things; an adult who would willingly take part in adventures, who told stories of wild and magical creatures as though they really existed and whose house was an Aladdin's cave of all that a young boy would consider treasure; badger skulls, fossil shells… even at that age he had idolised her. It had made what was to come all the harder to bear.

Movement beside him pulled him sharply back to the present as John stubbed out his cigarette and tucked the butt into his shirt pocket.

'So, what is it you want me to do with this latest group of yours?'

'The usual. We're going to start them off with the standard search and rescue exercise and we need someone for them to rescue. Jane's volunteered to be your fellow walker and raise the alarm, but you're more of a challenge to carry down from the hill than she is. One of the men we've got this time would probably try to pick her up and sling her over his shoulder. Then we'd end up having to cart him home for real, which wouldn't be good for business.'

John snorted in amused agreement.

'If we put you at the bottom of Ceinach Crag, there's a gentle enough slope there we can let them abseil down to you and then we'll stretcher you out down the footpath to the dam road. It'll take them a couple of hours to get you down, but we can keep them busy until you're ready for them to find you.'

'I suppose I get a suitably gory injury for them to play with?'

There was a degree of relish evident in John's voice. Aidan knew he enjoyed taking part in these little role plays, particularly when all he had to do was lie on his back and let the trainees carry him down the mountain.

'Matt was going to fix you up with a nice open fracture so you can overact all you want.'

'Overact? You're just jealous about that last group and the redhead who held my hand all the way down.'

'She certainly got into the spirit of things,' Aidan agreed. 'To be honest, by the time we got down I think she'd forgotten it was an exercise. You saw her face when you hopped off the stretcher when we got to the road.'

They both laughed at the memory.

'Well, I can't sit here gossiping all day. Some of us have proper work to do.'

John stood up, absently brushing splinters of branch from his overalls; a pointless exercise given that he was liberally covered in them from his morning's work. 'I'll be digging the footings for the new barn that week so give me a ring on the Sunday night and let me know what time you want me and I'll be there.'

Then he clambered back into the old Fergie's cab, holding the door open for Nan, who jumped in after him. Aidan had turned back to his own vehicle. How could he have realised it would be the last time he would see John alive?

'Damn it, John, what in God's name were you thinking?'

But there was no answer, just a raw, aching void. Sula whined nervously, picking up on his emotional turmoil.

'Sorry, girl.'

On the microwave the green digits of the clock showed 03:00. Aidan wiped a hand over gritty, stinging eyes and admitted defeat.

'I should hit the sack.'

In his dream John was waiting for him in the farmyard at Cwm Broch. Although there was still light in the western sky, the hills rising up behind the square, solid bulk of the farmhouse were dark and the farmyard itself was sunk in shadows. The tip of John's cigarette was a small firefly glow as he took a long drag, tilting his head back to exhale a thin plume of smoke into the cyan sky.

'What kept you?' he asked as Aidan pushed through the metal cow gate. Despite the dusk no lights burned in the farmhouse windows. An air of brooding silence hung over the yard and Aidan couldn't shake the feeling that there was something watching, waiting, just out of sight. The hairs on the back of his neck prickled, but when he glanced behind him there was nothing there, or at least nothing he could see. He shifted his footing slightly on the slate cobbles, the hard-learned discipline so ingrained that not even a dream could break it. For a moment he thought he caught a strange, acrid smell, like burning metal, as though he had shoved his nose close to the blacksmith's forge, but even as he tried to place it, it was gone and his next breath brought only the sweet, familiar scent of cattle and hay rising up from the cow barn. Yet even as he listened to the gentle rumbling and huffing of the cows, the rhythmic chewing and the soft rustle of hay being pulled from the fodder racks, as they steadily worked their way through their evening feed, he was aware that he was straining his ears to catch the slightest whisper of some other sound, something that had no place in the familiar scene.

He turned to John, wanting to say something, but found he had no words. The young farmer ran a finger under the band of his battered cap and tugged the peak down more closely over the tangled blond-brown mane of his hair. For a moment it seemed to Aidan that John was watching something in the shadows, perhaps the thing that Aidan knew was there but could not see, then he dropped his cigarette butt on the muddy cobbles, grinding it out carefully under the toe of his boot. His eyes flicked back to Aidan.

'Come on then. I've got something to show you.'

His voice was cold and flat and quite unlike John's living voice. Without giving Aidan another look, he walked past him out of the yard, turning up the track towards the sheep pens.

'John, wait!'

But in his dream Aidan wasn't sure if he had called out or if John had simply chosen not to hear him. Either way, his friend didn't pause and, not knowing what else to do, Aidan hurried up the track after him. He was surprised to see how far ahead John was and he broke into a run, trying to catch up, but no matter how fast he ran the distance between them stayed the same. On either side the trees closed in as the track cut first through the wooded valley bottom and then broke out onto the open hillside, running up between the slab-sided outcrops of granite and slate piercing up through the thin soil like bones jutting through skin.

As he came out from the trees, Aidan froze as he realised exactly where he was. Ahead of him John was already striding up the hillside, the pale bricks of the chimney stack standing out like a lighthouse against the dusk. The last of the day's light glinted on the shotgun he now carried in his hand.

Breath rasping in his throat, Aidan bolted after him, screaming John's name, but the other man ignored him or perhaps he couldn't hear him because Aidan wasn't really there. As Aidan flung himself over the final few yards of ground separating him from his friend, he saw John kneel down in the bracken. The sharp green scent of the broken stems filled Aidan's nostrils. He understood what would happen next and he knew he wasn't going to be able to reach John in time to stop him, but in his dream he could not turn away.

'John! Don't!'

Perhaps it was the utter desperation in his voice, but finally it seemed that John heard him. Aidan felt a rush of relief as, for a single instant, John looked at him, his expression puzzled above the grey steel of the shotgun barrel. Then the cornflower blue eyes widened, like those of a sleepwalker waking in panic to find himself on the edge of a precipice, and the young farmer looked down at the gun as though seeing it for the first time. His expression changed to one of utter terror, the sweat sliding down his face, the muscles of his arms trembling spasmodically as though he fought against something Aidan could not see. His eyes found Aidan's one final time.

'Help me!' he mouthed, even as he pulled the muzzle up under his chin, the blue steel digging into the pale skin. Then he pulled the trigger.

By Saturday evening Aidan was shattered. The dream had haunted him throughout the day; the terror in John's eyes, his friend's last desperate plea for help, the ear-splitting suddenness of the shotgun's blast and the smell of crushed bracken underfoot overpowered by the hot reek of blood. Each detail was there, perfect and precise, and though Aidan knew it wasn't real, that knowledge didn't stop him feeling as though he had been there, that he had stood and watched as his best friend killed himself and had done nothing to intervene. Even when he managed to push the dream aside he found little relief. He might not have stood and watched John die, but he couldn't shift the feeling that if he had got there sooner, if he had gone to find John straight away instead of staying to chat with Bryn and letting Nerys mother him, he would somehow have been able to save his friend.

The combined weight of physical tiredness, guilt and grief dragged at him, but afraid his sleep would be fractured by further images of John's death, he put off going to bed until eventually he fell asleep in front of the television and an old black and white horror film. Perhaps that was enough to account for the dream that followed, but somehow Aidan didn't think so.

The film was billed as a 'vampire classic'. With a heroine who greeted every threat by raising her hands to her cheeks and screaming piercingly – leading Aidan to wonder why on earth the undead count would want to claim her as his bride – and a lantern-jawed hero who insisted there had to be a rational explanation as one by one the minor characters were despatched in increasingly unlikely ways, the plot held enough cliché to render it more humorous than frightening. Not so the dream.

It shouldn't have been frightening, but somehow it was the very ordinariness that made it worse. He was standing in the cottage's small bathroom, the steam rising up around him from the basin of hot water. The mirror reflected back his image with brutal accuracy, picking up the dark smudges of too little sleep under his eyes. His skin was so pale that even the blond stubble stood out noticeably against his cheeks. He scrubbed one hand over his chin, feeling the scratchiness of the bristles, and sighed. Leaning forward across the basin he stared himself in the eye. *You need some rest, son,* he told himself, dropping into the familiar term of address as though he were his father giving a word or two of friendly advice. Not that his father had ever called him anything but David and then only grudgingly, as though he were somehow loathe to link the boy with his own father's name, even though he had been the one who had insisted it was given to him. But, other than to give him a direct order, James Morgan had rarely spoken to his son. Mostly the man had simply ignored him. His mother preferred to call him Dai, reserving David for instances when he was in more trouble than usual. On the day she died he had left David behind for good, opting to be known instead by his middle name.

Aidan watched his mirror self strip off the crumpled grey t-shirt, with its faded rock band legend, and lather his face with shaving foam. He could have been watching an image of himself from any morning, the routine so familiar, but as he rinsed the suds from his fingers and reached for his razor, the first prickling of horror struck him. Suddenly he wanted to wake up because he knew, with the absolute certainty of the dreamer, what was about to happen.

Inside, Aidan knew he was screaming, but the face in the mirror was inscrutable, the hazel eyes regarding him dispassionately as though, at that moment, there was someone else looking out through them. Trapped in his own body he felt his chin lift without his conscious control and he watched his image pull the skin taut with one hand under his chin before he drew the blade across his throat.

The last thing Aidan saw, as the blood turned the water crimson, was his own face screaming in voiceless terror at what he had just done.

CHAPTER 3

Aidan stared at the black earth raining down on the pale oak lid of John's coffin as, one by one, the mourners filed past the grave, each casting in their handful of soil. Already only a corner of the brass nameplate remained uncovered and, as Aidan watched, the next clod obscured it completely. So that was all it took; a few handfuls of dirt and all that John had or might have been – son, friend, husband, father – was gone, all come to nothing. And still no one could explain why John had taken his own life. Yet Aidan remained haunted by the terrified face he kept seeing in his dreams. Nor could he shake the conviction that he had failed his friend when he needed him most.

A polite murmur brought him out of his reverie and Aidan hastily threw his own handful of earth into the grave and stepped away from the graveside. He was aware of someone coming to stand beside him and looked round to see Edward and James, John's older brothers, the one in the blue of the RAF, the other in the olive drab of the Welsh Guards.

There had been a third brother; Gareth. Though Aidan had never met him, he knew him from the cluster of family photos Nerys kept on top of the television. He too had been in the Welsh Guards and had just turned eighteen when he started a tour of duty in Northern Ireland from which he never came home. John had been born the following year.

Despite their older brother's death, Edward and James never

wavered in their desire to follow careers in the armed forces. They had left the farm when John was eleven. Bryn and Nerys had never said as much, but Aidan guessed they had been relieved when John had shown no such inclination. The valleys were wide enough for him; he had no need to search for glory beyond them. Since his earliest days his joy had been in the land and the animals he could raise.

Edward put out his hand.

'Thanks for coming, Aidan. I know it's been hard for you, but he'd have appreciated your being here.' He looked sadly at the grave. 'I've not had a chance to say it before, but thanks for what you did for Da and Mum too.'

He ran a hand distractedly over the close crop of his hair; a gesture heart-wrenchingly reminiscent of John. Whereas Elizabeth had taken after her mother, the twins, like John, had both inherited Bryn's blond hair and blue eyes. Though Edward wore a regulation crew cut while James' hair was mown down to mere fuzz, looking at them was like seeing two older versions of John. Aidan swallowed down the lump in his throat.

'I've seen bullet wounds,' Edward continued, 'and they're not pretty. God knows, Johnnie must have been an awful mess. We're very grateful to you for keeping that from them.' He shared a look with his twin. 'I know Da said some harsh things to you. Things he shouldn't have. That was the shock speaking, not him. Jim and I, well, we're just grateful you were there.'

James nodded. Always the quieter, more serious of the two, he tended to let his younger twin do the talking.

'You're coming back to the chapel, aren't you?'

Aidan didn't want to, but he knew there was no polite way to say no. Certain things were expected even if Bryn had barely spoken to him since the shooting and Nerys could hardly look at him without dissolving into tears. Convention dictated that he go and convention meant a lot in such a small community. Not yet trusting himself to speak, he nodded.

'Good man.'

Edward clapped him on the arm and James gave him a brief lopsided grin that suggested he knew it would be an ordeal.

'Thanks, Aidan.'

The schoolroom at the back of the chapel was crowded when Aidan walked in. He had taken his time walking the mile and a half back from the cemetery, putting off the moment when he would be forced to join in and make polite conversation. It wasn't that he didn't know most of the people there. He and John had shared many friends, most of whom were there, and the rest he knew as neighbours or family of friends. At any other gathering he would have been trading stories for hours, but not now.

He caught Elizabeth's eye briefly, as she hovered protectively around her parents, and she smiled at him, but didn't leave their side. Aidan didn't feel it would be appropriate to go and join them. He could offer no comfort. For now he was just one more reminder of their loss. He had said a few words to them earlier, when he laid his wreath on the chapel path before the funeral, had given Nerys a brief hug and even shaken hands with Bryn, knowing the man would not make a scene at his son's funeral. Aidan felt slightly guilty for that, but, while the farmer's eyes hadn't softened, Bryn had taken his hand with no outward sign of reluctance. For Bryn too there were conventions to be followed. One day, perhaps, the farmer would accept what Aidan had done. For now he could only take comfort from knowing that John's brothers and sister understood.

Standing at the edge of the room, Aidan watched the ebb and flow of bodies as friends and neighbours chatted and mingled. The sadness of the occasion might keep the voices subdued, but it wouldn't stop people socialising. Aidan wondered if he was the only person there who didn't want to talk to anyone. How could he when each time someone expressed their sympathy about how shocking it must have been for him to find John's body, he only felt his guilt slice him more keenly? If they could see the images that haunted his nights what would they say to him then?

He was growing used to waking in a sweat-drenched tangle of sheets two or even three times a night. Nothing seemed to help; neither whisky nor staying up late nor going to bed early. The only comfort he had was from Sula for she seemed to sense when his dreams descended into nightmare and he would wake to the sound of her barking. He had started letting her sleep in his bedroom and though her presence helped, each morning the face in the mirror was a little more pinched, a little more worn. The lengthening stubble on his cheeks and chin did little to help, but he hadn't been able to pick up a razor for days. Not since the first dream of slitting his throat.

Abandoning even the pretence of mingling, Aidan took his untouched plate of sandwiches and cup of tea and found himself a seat in a corner out of the main throng of people. His head was pounding and his mind felt leaden. More than anything he wanted this to be over so he could go home. He hated funerals, hated the stream of people coming to shake hands and say their piece about it having been a lovely service as though that somehow helped weigh the balance against the pain of loss. It never did.

'They say he saw it,' someone said close by in a too loud whisper that was surely meant to be overheard. 'The Black Dog. Every night in his dreams. That's why he killed himself.'

Aidan swung round sharply, the tea slopping over the edge of his cup and onto his leg. He ignored it. A black and white magpie of a woman shushed her companion and glared at him for daring to eavesdrop on their conversation. Aidan glared back, scarcely able to believe what he had just heard. The animal John had seen had been flesh and blood. Even without a field of rip-throated carcasses to prove it he knew that, so why would anyone feel the need to embellish a suicide with mention of the Black Dog? It wasn't as though the legend was even original; a phantom hellhound said to roam the local hills appearing as a harbinger of death and disaster to all who saw it. Any area of forest and moorland might spawn such a legend.

As a member of the Plynlimon mountain rescue team, Aidan had his own views as to why people got into trouble on the hills and none of them had anything to do with the supernatural, yet for all his initial scorn a small part of him recalled the movement he had seen in the shadows under the chimney stack. Unbidden, the image of a dark snout and sulphurous yellow eyes, half-glimpsed in the corners of his dreams, came back to him and with it the sensation of malevolence that had begun to stalk him after dark. The prickle of his own fear angered him as much as the women's superstitious gossiping.

'Does that mean I'm next?' he wanted to shout at them. 'Are

you going to be saying the same thing at my funeral in a month or a week's time? Is that all this is to you – some novel piece of gossip?'

Instead he felt himself turn away, swallowing the bitter words that were rising in his throat, aware that such an outburst would only be a source of entertainment; something to bring out and pick over for years to come, like a dog bringing out a favourite bone to gnaw and worry long after all the meat had been picked clean.

He put down his plate and the half-empty teacup as disgusted with himself as he was with the attitude of the two women. It wasn't just that he was physically tired, he realised. He felt as though his spirit was foundering. Wearily he rubbed one hand over the back of his neck trying unsuccessfully to ease the tension that was building there. More than anything he wanted to be done with this, to escape from this crush of people, the sympathetic and the gossip-mongerers alike. The image of an open hillside floated seductively behind his eyes; a fresh, clean wind sweeping the clouds across the sky and scouring the fog from his mind, close-cropped grass under his boots and the grey granite bones of the hills rising above him. He could almost hear their siren song calling him upwards, upwards to the high, lonely places where a solitary kite hanging on the thermals was the only other living thing in sight. And there, on the hillside, waiting for him amidst the tumble of bracken and lichen-crusted stones, was a black dog and John with his gun.

He jolted back to reality, his pulse hammering, glad that he had already put down his plate for surely his shaking hands would have dropped it. To his relief no one seemed to have noticed his distress. The two carrion crows he had overheard were deep in conversation with another couple and he looked away quickly before his staring could attract their attention. His heart felt as though it was trying to break free from the cage of his ribs. How no one else could hear it he didn't know.

Black, leaden despair welled up inside him then. Whether it was John's death or a premonition of his own that waited for him on the far shores of sleep, Aidan knew with certainty he could no longer face it alone. Unless he spoke to someone about his fears he felt he would go mad. But there was only one person he knew who would listen to what he had to say and wouldn't simply tell him he was crazy. And he had very little reason to believe she would even talk to him.

She had been there earlier, but that was true of most of the local community. Although the crowd had thinned slightly, the room still held a sizeable number of mourners. As he scanned the mass of people, Aidan prayed that she hadn't already left. Despite the horror that rode him, he wasn't sure if he could bring himself to go and find her.

He was beginning to think he might have to do so when he spotted her through a sudden gap in the crush of people. She was standing in the far corner of the schoolroom, tucked between the cupboard that held the Sunday school books and the dustsheet-covered shape of the chapel's ancient harmonium. Deep in conversation, she had her back to him, but though he only glimpsed her for an instant before the crowd shifted and someone stepped between them, blocking his view, he would recognise her anywhere, even now.

Trying not to think too much about what he was doing, Aidan took a deep breath and pushed his way through the people separating them, only to stop dead in his tracks when he saw her fully. The realisation of what she was wearing made him go cold. Surely there must have been other times when she had worn that particular suit, other funerals she had been to in the intervening nine years, when the black wool would have been pressed into service, but to see her in it now brought all the pain tumbling back. Suddenly he was fifteen years old again and his world had just fallen to pieces around him.

Like a priceless vase, the second before it hits the floor, he had never realised how perfect his world had been, nor how fragile. His mother's death had changed that forever, wiping away everything he held dear, taking him overnight from childhood to adulthood. Though he had continued on in the shards of his old life for two years, he had taken the first chance of escape, heading for university and the flat expanses of East Anglia. It was, as he had put it to one friend, as far from the Welsh mountains as he could go without falling into the sea. At the time he had thought he would never return and it had been five years before he had done so, choosing to stay in digs between terms and travel during the long summer vacations. But he had been born in the valleys and eventually they claimed him back. *Hiraeth* they called it, an irresistible longing for home peculiar to the Welsh people. It had crept up on him unexpectedly in the badlands of Dakota, a place so unlike Wales that the fifteen-year-old Aidan would have been hard pushed to imagine it. It planted hooks in his soul and, though it had taken him another six months to get there, from that point he knew he would finally go home.

But there was one part of that old life he had never quite made peace with, one player in the tragedy of Anne Morgan's long illness he had never quite forgiven. Aidan would have turned and run even then, but she must have sensed someone behind her for she turned and in that moment he was trapped. For a second her face showed surprise, shock even, as well it might, given the last words he had spoken to her. Then she smiled and only someone who knew her well would have noticed the slight hesitation or the edge of wariness in those peridot eyes that her smile couldn't quite hide. He knew she was also remembering that other funeral and all that had preceded it.

'Hello, Aidan.'

It seemed strange hearing her say his name after so long.

'Hello, Gwyn.'

Aidan paused, suddenly unsure of what he was going to say. All the things he had thought to tell her seemed ridiculous now they were face to face. Gwyn cocked her head to one side, a gesture he remembered of old. A slight frown dinted the skin between the black arched brows as she waited for him to continue, but beyond that her face was expressionless. She was good at hiding her feelings, he remembered, at keeping grief and anger hidden behind a calm face and a level voice. For years he had thought it was because she didn't care. By the time he had realised that that might not be the case the damage had been done.

'Uh…'

He wasn't sure he could bring himself to say it, but once more Gwyn extended a hand to help him.

'I'm sorry you had to find him, Aidan. I know how close you and John were.' She paused and then added, 'Whatever was going through his mind that night, I don't think he planned it that way. He wouldn't have wanted to hurt you.'

She studied him and he realised she was waiting for him to

react, waiting for him to knock this peace offering to the ground as he had done with every other approach she had held out to him. After so many times he found it incredible that she would make the effort again.

It was that which decided him. In a rush he released the breath he hadn't realised he had been holding.

'Can I talk to you?'

Standing to one side, Jenny Harmond raised a tactless eyebrow, her expression clearly asking if Gwyn wanted her to stay. Jenny the Lamb, she was known as in the village. Not in deference to her placid nature, which in truth was anything but, but in reference to one of the stranger curios she had had under her care during her time as curator of the Llancathan museum. Although she had been retired for seven years now, the name still stuck. Gwyn turned to her friend and this time her smile was unforced, the effect brightening her face.

'I'm sorry, Jenny. Would you excuse us for a moment?' She turned back to Aidan. 'Here?'

The very fact that she asked the question suggested she knew he would want to go somewhere more private.

'No.'

That came out more vehemently than he had meant it to. Dark brows rose slightly as Gwyn registered the emotion, but she made no comment, for which Aidan felt ridiculously grateful.

'No, it's um… look, do you want to grab a coffee?'

She glanced down at the cup she was holding and the corners of her mouth twitched as she suppressed a smile, but all she said was, 'I'd love to.'

CHAPTER 4

Aidan took his coffee and Gwyn's tea to a table at the rear of the Shepherds' Rest and sat down, facing the door. Without a word, Gwyn slid into the seat opposite him, shrugging out of her suit jacket and dropping it on top of her oversized shoulder bag on the seat next to her. Short of the few words it had taken to order their drinks, they had said nothing since leaving the chapel, each being content to walk in silence. Aidan was glad of the space to organise his thoughts. Already he was beginning to wonder exactly what he could confide to Gwyn.

At least Gwyn had the sense not to push him to talk. She sat sipping her tea, elbows propped on the table, bergamot-scented steam rising around her sharp cheekbones. Wisps of dark hair were already starting to escape from the French plait she had worn for the service, curling haphazardly around her ears. She was a small, fine-boned woman. With her pale skin and gemstone green eyes, a stranger might have described her appearance as elfin, although Aidan would never have done so. Elfin conveyed a certain frailty and frail was not a word that could be used in conjunction with Gwyn's name. Her small frame held a core of tempered steel and a will to match.

She also had an asbestos throat. Aidan dumped two sugars into his coffee and stirred it vigorously. He had no intention of putting the liquid anywhere near his mouth until it had cooled several degrees. Instead he sat back in his chair and pulled at his tie, loosening what had felt like a noose around his neck all morning. For good measure he flicked open the top button of his shirt, breathing a small sigh of relief as he got rid of the unfamiliar constriction around his neck. Used to a working uniform of hiking trousers and either a fleece or a t-shirt, depending on the weather, he felt out of place in a suit. If it hadn't been for the occasional need to don one in his role of partner and co-founder of Red Kite Adventure Training, he wouldn't have had one in his wardrobe. The suit he had worn to his mother's funeral had certainly never seen the light of day again.

Aidan became aware that Gwyn was watching him over the edge of her cup, her face a study in careful neutrality. He wondered what was going through her mind, but there were no clues to be found in her face. By the time he returned to the valley from his travelling, open hostility on his part had given way to active avoidance, but there had never been a reconciliation. He had kept his distance from her and she had never tried to bridge the gap. Over the years the habit had become so ingrained that he no longer thought about it. He had not imagined there coming a time when he would approach her voluntarily.

Finally, Gwyn put down her cup, turning it on its saucer until the handle pointed directly away from her, like a compass rose indicating north.

'You look…' There was a fraction of a second pause as she weighed her final choice of adjective. 'Tired.'

Tired? Aidan nearly laughed. He could hardly imagine a greater understatement. He suspected he could find roadkill three days dead that looked better than he did.

Dear Lord, Gwyn, when did you become so tactful? He knew the answer to that; nine years ago when all their conversations had become potential minefields. He stirred his coffee again, wondering what he was going to say to her now. In the warm fug of the chapel schoolroom, with the scald of adrenalin still hot in his blood, it had seemed a good idea. Now the moment was here he was less than sure. Behind her the watery sunlight spilled in through the windows and he watched a couple with an ancient grey lurcher pause just outside the door. The girl's purple ringlets clashed furiously with the canary-coloured scarf that caught them back from her face, exposing multiple piercings in her ears completely at odds with the old-fashioned wicker shopping basket she carried in one hand. Her other hand was being held by a young man whose head was shaved down to stubble except for a straggly ponytail at the nape of his neck and a beard that made Aidan think of goats.

As he watched, Goatboy turned to his companion and said something that made her shove him in the ribs with her basket. It could only have been a token protest though, for Goatboy leaned over the top of the basket and planted a kiss on her cheek. As the kiss rapidly became more intimate, the lurcher wandered to the end of its lead as though trying to pretend it wasn't with them. Feeling slightly voyeuristic, Aidan turned his gaze away.

There were one or two more people on the street now; a few black-clad forms who had obviously been to the funeral. Not wanting to catch anyone's eye, he turned his attention back to his companion. Gwyn was still watching him, her hands wrapped around the blue china cup, her green eyes expressionless. She reminded him for all the world of a small black cat with its paws tucked in, watching and waiting, keeping its own council.

He still couldn't imagine what he was going to say to her, what he could say that wouldn't make him sound as though he was going mad. Was he going mad? The thought had crossed his mind. Probably all he needed was a good night's sleep. It was only natural that his dreams had been disturbed after the shock of finding John's body. He should tell Gwyn that he had made a mistake and leave. He reached out for the sachets of sugar in their yellow pottery bowl, but a touch on his arm stayed him.

'Even you can't want that much sugar in your coffee.' Gwyn nodded at the two screwed up sugar papers on the saucer. 'You've already sweetened it.' For a long moment she held his gaze, her green eyes thoughtful.

'If you've changed your mind about talking to me, Aidan, that's okay.'

Her voice was soft and Aidan thought there was a trace of sadness in her tone, but maybe he was just fooling himself. Either way, he didn't have an answer for her. Instead he looked past her again, out into the street, watching the people strolling past. Seven days ago he had been like that, his world untouched by thoughts of mortality. He wanted to be like that again, but with the fear that was building in his mind, he wondered if that would ever be possible.

When he didn't reply, Gwyn leaned forward in her seat and put her cup down on its saucer, pushing it to one side on the scrubbed pine boards of the table. There was an air of finality about the gesture, the decisive touch of someone moving a piece to checkmate.

'I'll go.'

She scooped her jacket from the chair beside her and stood up. Slinging her battered leather bag over her shoulder, she added softly, 'It's natural to be upset and hurt by what's happened, Aidan. Anyone would be. Don't feel it's wrong or that you're letting the side down, if you think you need help to get you through this. Most of us would.' A rueful smile accompanied her next words. 'I'm probably not the best person for you to talk to, but talk to someone about it. Please.' She paused as though wanting to say more, but uncertain what would be acceptable. 'Take care of yourself, Aidan.'

He said nothing, not looking at her. After a moment he heard her turn and walk away.

'Gwyn.'

She had one hand on the café door and for a moment he thought she would carry on through it, but she paused and then turned back to face him; even now it seemed she was prepared to give him a second chance.

'I do want to talk to you. It's just… I don't know where to start.'

Gwyn came back to the table and stood looking down at him.

'Would it be stupid of me to suggest the beginning?'

Another coffee, another tea; fetched from the counter as displacement activity while Aidan tried to sort out where the beginning was. What he was thinking went against everything he knew about the way the world worked, every belief he held, every finely tuned scientific theory he had come across. If he gave voice to it or, worse still, if Gwyn confirmed his suspicions, not only would the world cease to be the comfortable place he knew, it would also have become something very dangerous. And he knew that once that bridge was crossed there would be no going back.

He leaned back in the wooden chair, ostensibly gazing out at the autumn streets but actually watching Gwyn from the corner of his eye. She sat sipping her tea, her eyes raised to read the café noticeboard where an assortment of postcards advertising massage and Reiki healing jostled with those for rooms either wanted or available to rent, puppies for sale and gardeners and odd job men touting for business. Covering everything in the centre of the board, a lurid green poster advised that Saturday night's Music Clash would see local group Reservoir Sheepdogs battling it out against a band from Rhayader with the unlikely name of Turbo Trout. He had heard the Sheepdogs play a few times at the Unicorn's Tuesday night music sessions and even John, who preferred heavy rock to folk, grudgingly admitted they weren't bad. He might even have suggested to John that they went along to support them.

Damn it, John. He swallowed down the sudden lump in his throat and turned his attention fully to the silent woman opposite him.

'I keep thinking about it, Gwyn.'

The words did little justice to exactly how much of his waking moments were being eaten up by thoughts of John's suicide.

'If only I'd got there sooner. If I hadn't stopped to talk to Bryn about the farm, to ask him how his knee was coming on, if I hadn't sat there in front of the Rayburn, drinking tea and trying to persuade Nerys that I wasn't in immediate danger of starving to death…'

Gwyn smiled.

'I might have got there soon enough to stop him.'

'You might have done,' she agreed. She put the cup down, turning it once more on its saucer, a small fidgeting movement from a woman who could sit so still that wild birds would perch beside her in her garden. 'But I don't think it would have made a difference. He knew what he was doing, Aidan. Let's face it, he'd shot enough things in his time.'

She didn't try to keep the tone of disapproval from her voice and he remembered what she had said on the subject when he had gone to her thrilled that Bryn was going to take him and John shooting rabbits.

'He knew exactly what damage a shotgun would do at that range. This wasn't a cry for help, like taking an overdose or even putting a hosepipe over your car exhaust, knowing that someone's going to come home in time to find you. Whatever his reasons and – bless us – we'll probably never understand them fully, he knew what he was doing.'

Aidan sighed. Everything she said was true. It might even have held a grain of comfort, of absolution, that the time he had spent being neighbourly with Bryn and Nerys didn't make him responsible for John's death. It might have done but for one thing.

'I think something made him do it. No,' he cut off her protest, 'I don't mean he was so desperate about something that he felt it was the only solution. John wasn't like that.'

He struggled to find the right words, not sure how he could voice the feeling that had been gnawing at him, the only conclusion of that terrified face in his dreams.

'I think someone, something,' he corrected himself, 'made him shoot himself against his will.'

Gwyn sat back in her chair, crossing her arms.

'The police don't think it was a murder,' she pointed out reasonably. 'You were the one who found the body, Aidan. You said yourself that there were no signs of a struggle and the coroner's report said there were no suspicious circumstances. Just because we can't understand what drove him to do it doesn't make John's death anything other than a tragic suicide.'

He opened his mouth to argue, to say he hadn't meant

someone had put the gun in John's hands and forced him to pull the trigger. Instead he said, 'The stories you told me when I was young, the ones about the shrieks, were they true?'

The dark brows drew together. For a second the green eyes below them were as hard as emeralds. Then the moment passed and Gwyn asked simply, 'What do you think?'

'That I got the kicking of my life in the playground for telling the wrong kids about them.'

His mouth quirked ruefully at the memory. Unconsciously, he ran a hand over his ribs as if reassuring himself of the wholeness of muscle and bone where the kicks had slammed into him, hard and vicious and intended to do much more than just hurt.

'It was like being the last kid in the class to believe in Santa Claus. Not good if you're also the smallest kid in the class. I often wondered if that was why Griff Howell pushed me down the stairs in year two. We both got into a lot of trouble over that fight and he never let me forget it. As far as he was concerned, it was all my fault.'

He remembered Mr. Hughes' angry voice as he had pulled Griff and his two friends, Rod and Alec Owen, off him and hauled him to his feet. The concrete playground had spun around him as he had stood there, blood streaming from his nose and split lip, and he would have fallen but for the man's grip on his arm. Worst of all was the thought of what his mother would say when she saw his torn shirt and the silent reproach in her eyes. Money was tight enough without having to find more to replace clothes ruined through fighting.

Mr. Hughes' anger had been as much directed at him as at the other boys, the tall geography master holding the firm belief that both sides were equally to blame in a fight. *If you walk away there can't be a fight, now can there? You stay and you're just as much responsible for what happens.* At the time Aidan had wondered if Mr. Hughes had ever tried to walk away from a fight and had a boy almost a year older, and a lot stronger and heavier, jump on his back. *If I'd stood my ground I wouldn't have ended up on the floor with three of them kicking me… or at least not quite so quickly.*

To his eleven-year-old self, the teacher's attitude had seemed both unfair and cowardly, but later he had heard similar advice from people he knew were more than capable of standing and fighting if they chose to. Over the years he had trained under a number of different sensei, but they had all shared a similar philosophy: *if you've got the chance to run then you run. It doesn't matter what the other guy thinks; anyone who chooses to fight when they don't have to is a fool. But, if you can't run, if you have to fight, then by God you make sure you're the last one standing.*

Gwyn had also had words to say when Anne had called her that night. *I hope you gave back as good as you got, Brightboy. At least they didn't break your nose so the girls will still be chasing you.* She had held her strong hands over his bruised ribs and face and, whether from that or the cold compresses his mother had applied, the pain had soothed. Had it really be thirteen years ago?

So much had changed in those intervening years, too much for him to ever reach out to this woman for help again, or so he had thought. The pain of betrayal had cut him off from all those earlier memories. He was surprised to find they still existed. Perhaps an echo of that earlier Gwyn remained in the woman sat across from him now. It was to her that he spoke.

'But, if they were true, then what I'm about to say would make a lot more sense. It would also make it very, very frightening.'

Gwyn listened without comment as Aidan told her about the dreams, about the sulphurous eyes that tracked him in the darkness and the cold, whispering presence when no one was there.

'Jesus, Gwyn, I woke up this morning with my hand on the bathroom door. If Sula hadn't started barking I don't know what I might have done.'

Even now, in broad daylight, Aidan felt the hair standing up on the nape of his neck at the memory. In his mind was the fear that he would only have woken when the razor drew the first cabochon rubies of blood from his throat.

'I had to buy an electric razor so I could have a shave today.' He hadn't wanted to admit that, but he found himself desperate to convince her that he was serious. 'I'm out of my depth here.'

He didn't bother to add that there was no one else he could talk to. They both knew the conversation wouldn't have been happening if that weren't the case.

For a long time Gwyn didn't say anything. Although her expression had grown more serious as Aidan had spoken, not once had she looked surprised by anything he had said. Watching her now, Aidan had the sense that she was sifting through the things she might say, like a gambler sorting a hand of cards, assessing the relative risks and merits of each possible play. Finally, she sighed and shook her head, her expression a mix of emotions that made no sense to Aidan. Then she smiled a crooked half-smile.

'If I tell you the truth, I'm going to break a promise I've kept for thirteen years. Your mother had quite a few things to say to me after you came home in that state.'

Aidan stiffened, not quite ready to have Gwyn talk to him about his mother. Then he consciously exhaled, forcing himself

48

to relax, because for all that, he wanted to hear what she was going to say.

'She made me promise not to tell you any more nonsense about things that don't exist.'

A tiny shake of the head was sufficient comment to suggest what Gwyn thought of the promise she had kept all these years. 'But they do exist, Aidan. All the things I told you about; spirits and shrieks and all the rest of them, they're real. People might choose to believe otherwise, to say it's just superstition and that anyone who says that it's not is stupid, but that's not true.'

She may have said more, but Aidan was no longer listening. He hadn't really expected her to agree with him. His sane, civilised self had been waiting for her reassurance that what he feared was just fantasy. Peripherally he was aware that his face had drained of blood and his hands were suddenly icy.

'Oh dear G…' His voice tailed off as the full implications of what she had said hit him. 'You mean something really could have made John kill himself?'

The room spun.

'No.'

Aidan wasn't sure if it was her voice that grounded him or the touch of her hand, warm on his wrist.

'Aidan! Look at me.'

He did, focussing on those deep green eyes as though they were the only solid thing left to him. Surprisingly strong, her hand gripped his arm as though she would physically hold him there, relaxing only once she was satisfied he was back with her again.

'Yes, they exist, but none of those things could have done what you described. They can mislead people and trick them, make them think they've turned one way when they've turned

49

another. If someone's out on the hills and they're lost and frightened, a shriek could make them go the wrong way. In bad weather, when you can't tell where you're going, a really strong one might even lure someone off a cliff. But they're not capable of making someone do something completely against their will. Whatever your dreams, they can't make you do anything to hurt yourself. Nothing can make you do that,' she added, picking up on his unvoiced fear.

'But something made John kill himself,' he protested.

'That I don't know.' Gwyn's voice was firm, brooking no argument. 'I don't know what could. Certainly shrieks couldn't do anything like that, but they could be shaping your dreams, making you believe that's what happened.'

Aidan looked at her, wanting to believe what she had said, but not quite daring to trust. Gwyn seemed to understand his confusion.

'Shrieks are ancient creatures, Aidan. Beings, if you will, for they're certainly not flesh and blood as we understand it. They feed off emotions; good, bad, it's all energy to them. Unfortunately for us, it's the bad ones that tend to be strongest so those are the ones they've evolved to encourage. A pity really, life could be a lot better if they amplified the positive in people.'

'We'd probably all go hyper,' Aidan noted sourly, but he felt his curiosity piqued. 'If most people don't believe in them, why were you so keen to tell me about them when I was a kid?'

'Because children often see things differently and why shouldn't you know the truth about the world? Mostly though I did it because I thought you might be one of the few people who would be able to sense them and I thought it would be safer if you understood them for what they are.'

'Why me?'

But Gwyn just shook her head.

'I had my reasons,' she said enigmatically. 'It doesn't really matter now. What is important though is that I think I can help you do something about the dreams.'

'You can?'

Aidan's reluctance to let her evade his question was outweighed by his sense of relief.

'If you trust me, yes.'

She looked at him and her eyes were uncompromising, green and ancient as the heart of the forest.

'Do you trust me?' she challenged. 'I mean really trust me?'

Once upon a time he had. He would have followed her to the ends of the earth. Anything had been possible if she had said it was. Then, when it had mattered most, she had let him down. She had hurt him more than he had thought possible. Was he prepared to take that chance again? Silently he weighed the history between them. He had been a child then, trusting with a child's implicit belief. As an adult, trust meant something subtly different. Did he trust her? He wasn't sure, but he couldn't deny that he had sought her help. He supposed that was sufficient for now.

'Yes,' he said at last.

Briefly Gwyn closed her eyes. If he hadn't known better, he would have said she was fighting back tears.

'Thank you,' she said. 'That means a lot.'

Then she hit him.

CHAPTER 5

Aidan rocked back in his chair, his head snapping back and his ears ringing. Then he was halfway to his feet, reflexes taking over, before he realised that Gwyn hadn't moved. Her hands were resting on the table in plain view. Whatever had just happened – and he would have sworn someone had cuffed him hard around the head – Gwyn hadn't touched him. He froze and then carefully looked around him. The youngster behind the counter was plugged into his mobile phone. Whatever he was engrossed in it wasn't his customers' curious behaviour. There was no one else in the café to notice. Very carefully, Aidan sat down again, his eyes never leaving Gwyn.

'What,' he asked quietly, 'did you just do?'

His voice had an edge to it that few people ever heard. Tentatively he put his hand up to his cheek where he thought she had slapped him. There was no tenderness, but he felt as shaken as though she had.

'I hit you with a psychic bolt,' Gwyn said matter-of-factly, as though it should have been obvious. As Aidan opened his mouth to protest, she cut him off. 'And a fairly low-powered one at that. It's perfectly possible to kill someone doing that, if you don't know what you're doing.' She raised an impish eyebrow. 'Or if you do. Come on, Aidan, you're not really hurt. You're just a bit shocked, that's all. You'll get over it.'

Her words were so close to those he used himself in the karate dojo, the first time one of the juniors got tapped during freestyle, that he had to bite back his angry retort. It didn't mean he was happy with what she had just done, but he could grudgingly admit she was right. It had been just like catching an unexpected knock during training.

'Anyway,' Gwyn continued, choosing to ignore his discomfort. 'What I did isn't as important as why I did it and I did it to see how strong your shields are.'

If Aidan had thought this conversation had started on dodgy ground, as far as he was concerned they had just fallen off the edge of the map. A big sign with the words 'Here be dragons' should appear over Gwyn's head at any moment. It was time to apply the brakes.

'Hang on a minute, Gwyn, one thing at a time. What the Hell is a psychic bolt?'

Gwyn sighed.

'It's not important, Aidan. I can explain it some other time.'

'It's important to me. I've been training for twelve years now. I don't much like the idea that someone can knock me cold without so much as lifting a finger. I want to know what you did and how you did it.'

Perhaps Gwyn remembered how stubborn he could be because she scowled at him but didn't argue.

'Okay, but you're just going to have to accept some of the things I tell you. This is my understanding of the way things work. If you want to go and find different reasons then that's up to you, but if what you've just experienced hasn't convinced you I'm telling the truth then I'm not going to try and prove it to you.'

She glared at him fiercely and Aidan had the impression this was not something she spoke of lightly. 'Do you trust me?' she had asked him. It seemed she was now putting her trust in him.

Her decision made, Gwyn's tone lightened. 'First up, you need to understand that humans all have their own little energy field and it's something you can tap into, if you know how. You've done t'ai chi as well as your karate; you should understand what I'm talking about.'

Aidan thought about that. So far she hadn't said anything that would have generated so much as a raised eyebrow in the dojo. But it was one thing to talk about chi and meridians, or even sometimes to feel the prickly static between his hands as he held a semi-imaginary ball of energy, and something very different to experience the tangible force that Gwyn had hit him with.

'Okay, I'm with you so far.'

'Good. So, you know you can learn to move energy around. What I did was one up from that. I gathered up a handful of my energy and threw it at you.'

'Right.'

Gwyn grinned at the doubt in his voice. She made it sound very simple and, in a way, Aidan supposed it was. If you accepted that people were little walking dynamos – which he did, even though it had been a rather theoretical acceptance up until now – it wasn't that great a leap to believe that what Gwyn had described was possible, especially having just been on the receiving end of that handful of energy.

'So how come not everyone can do this? I mean, I'm assuming that is the case, isn't it? But if we all have energy fields, then why not?'

The question seemed to please Gwyn.

'Look, let me grab a piece of cake and I'll try and explain.'

'You need a piece of cake to explain this?'

The thought made Aidan laugh and the look that Gwyn shot him only amused him more. He realised it was the first time he had so much as cracked a smile since John's death.

'No. The cake is because I'm hungry.'

'Psychic energy's much the same as ordinary physical energy.' Gwyn's words were slightly muffled by a mouthful of apricot flapjack. 'Mmm, that's good.'

She finished chewing and took a long drink of tea. Aidan looked at his own cup reproachfully. He would have preferred another coffee, but Gwyn had been insistent that she wasn't teaching energy moves to someone who was hyper on caffeine so tea it had to be. At least he had held out for ordinary tea and not the perfumed dishwater she drank. He shuddered mentally. If he had to drink it, it had to be good strong builders' tea with milk *and* sugar. Not as good as coffee, but not too poor a substitute.

'If you throw it at someone, you lose it, so you have to refuel. Admittedly, the small amount I chucked at you won't do me any harm, but it's as good an excuse as any for a piece of flapjack. Are you sure you don't want a bite? It's very good.'

Aidan shook his head, slightly surprised by the speed with which the pastry was disappearing. To look at her you would think she subsisted on lettuce and fresh air, but if Gwyn had a bird-like appetite the bird in question would have to be a vulture.

'I don't think I'd dare deprive you.'

Finishing the last mouthful, Gwyn carefully wiped her fingers and then settled back into her explanation. Despite his initial scepticism, Aidan found himself listening with interest.

'There are two reasons why not everyone can do what I just did. The first is simply a matter of belief and training. There just aren't that many people who believe in the body's energy field. I mean really believe, not just accept it as a theoretical concept. Of those that do, even fewer have any sort of training in manipulating that energy. People who do martial arts, particularly the Chinese disciplines, touch on it. Certain healing systems, acupuncture, Reiki, that sort of thing, use it, but even acupuncture really only focusses on correcting energy imbalances within the patient. The practitioner isn't using their own energy to deliver the treatment and Reiki is more about tapping into a universal energy field and channelling that. So really you've got a very small base of people who have any understanding of psychic energy and virtually none of them will have ever been trained in using it the way I just did.'

'So what's the second reason?' Aidan asked, intrigued despite himself.

'Simple ability. Most people don't have the spare energy to be able to throw it around. Some naturally have more power or can build it up.'

'So you're one of the powerful ones, are you?'

There was an edge to his voice, part sarcasm, part challenge, that he couldn't help, but Gwyn simply shook her head, not rising to his bait. Her brief smile did not reach her eyes.

'I was once, or so I like to think. But then I did something stupid, something I shouldn't have done. And I did it without thinking, because there wasn't time to think. There wasn't time to do anything except reach out to her.' Her voice dropped to almost a whisper and it was clearly something other than the battered café furniture that the green eyes focussed on. Something that Aidan couldn't see. Then she raised her head, back with him again.

'It was a long time ago; the autumn before you were born. I saved one life for certain that day, probably two. In the process I ripped open every power channel in my body.'

She shrugged, dismissing her loss as though she didn't care, daring him to suggest it might be otherwise.

'That's one way that psychic energy really is different from physical energy, Aidan. Or at least it was for me.' She spoke as though this was something she had puzzled over for years. Perhaps she had. 'It just didn't heal up. Not properly. For a long time I couldn't do anything, not even the simple things I'd always taken for granted. It seemed to take forever before it started to come back and when it did it wasn't the same. I can't really describe it other than to say that it's as though my energy channels are blocked up; with scar tissue maybe – I don't know. But it's not easy anymore. It takes effort and I can't tap into energy fields like I used to. When I work with energy it has to come purely from what's within me. The sad thing is you don't really appreciate what you've lost until you need to use it again.'

The sense of desolation that had crept into her voice shocked Aidan. This admission of frailty was new to him. He had grown up thinking that Gwyn could do anything, had believed it right up until the time when she had failed utterly. If that had been her only crime he would probably – in time – have forgiven her; as an adult he had learned to accept what the child could not. But she had carried him with her, had convinced him that he could help her change the inevitable, and so he had failed too. The guilt of that had eaten at his heart for years and for that he had never forgiven her. Now, for the first time, the old bitterness didn't come.

'So no, I'm not that powerful. Not now.'

She looked up from the pattern she had been doodling absentmindedly with her finger in the spilt dregs of her tea. 'But you knew that anyway.'

Aidan wasn't sure what to say. There were some things he wasn't ready to talk about and finding his sense of outrage had deserted him left him feeling off balance. That finely honed anger had been his sole defence. He wasn't ready to contemplate what it might mean to lose it.

'Still, that's ancient history.' It seemed Gwyn was no keener to dig into that aspect of their shared past than he was and she was a master at being able to parcel up inconvenient emotions and put them to one side. 'And, interesting though it is, I didn't mean for us to get sidetracked by energy bolts. As I said, what I was doing was testing your shields. Now don't look at me as though I'm talking nonsense. You've taken energy fields in your stride. Now you just need to know a little about shielding.'

'Shielding?'

Aidan really wanted that cup of coffee now. In fact something stronger wouldn't have gone amiss.

'Yes, shielding. It's nothing out of the ordinary, Aidan. Everybody has some level of shielding, whether they know it or not.' Gwyn's face was sympathetic as though she could see he was beginning to struggle. 'It's how we keep our emotions, our energy, to ourselves, instead of sharing them with everyone we come across. It's also how we stop ourselves being affected by the energy and emotions of everyone around us. You know if you're at a party and everyone's really buzzing you pick up on that energy.'

Aidan nodded.

'In the same way, there are some people who are always miserable and just being in the same room with them makes you feel as though the sun's gone out. What's happening is that you're picking up that person's energy and letting your own be coloured by it. When you shield, all you're doing is putting up a barrier, literally a shield, between yourself and all those different energies – good and bad – so you're not affected by them. It's an idea that's creeping into some of the more right brain personal effectiveness training. I'd have thought you'd have come across it.'

'Gwyn, this is all getting a bit metaphysical for me,' Aidan complained. 'Just tell me what it's got to do with my dreams and how I can stop them.'

'I'm just trying to help you understand.'

Her reply held the faintest touch of petulance. This was probably a hard conversation for her as well. Aidan looked at her, his eyes feeling bleary. He rubbed a hand over his face. Already he could feel the first prickling of stubble on his cheeks. It would be nice to be able to have a proper wet shave once more.

'Just cut to the chase, Gwyn. I'll read up on the background theory later.'

He took a mouthful of tea and then pushed his cup away in disgust. Cold coffee he could stomach, but cold tea was another matter entirely.

'Oh alright.' Her lips pursed as she mentally changed track. 'What I think is happening is that all your emotions around John's death are being picked up and amplified and that's what's spilling over into your dreams. Your shields are pretty much non-existent, Aidan, even by ordinary standards; that wasn't a hard tap I gave you. Consequently you're broadcasting raw emotional pain and the shrieks are having a field day with you. You're effectively an eat all you want buffet for them and I think they're taking advantage.'

'So the answer is to make my shields stronger?'

Gwyn grinned at him.

'Got it in one.'

Aidan was surprised. He had meant to be sarcastic, but perhaps this was going to be easier than he had anticipated.

'Okay, so how do I do that?'

The grin disappeared, taking Aidan's hopes with it.

'Well, it's not as easy as that. You can't just snap your fingers and it's done. Or at least, not until you know what it is you're doing. Once you've got the hang of it, it's pretty straightforward.'

'Gwyn…' he warned, sensing she was about to slip into lecture mode again.

'All I'm saying is that there isn't an instant fix that will get your shields up to strength.'

'You said you could do something about my dreams.'

But you said I could have sweets now! Aidan was aware that he sounded like a small child, but the sense of disappointment was overwhelming. He had trusted her and once again she had let him down.

'If you'd just let me finish, Aidan.' The edge of steel in her voice cut across his thoughts. 'I can give you something that will do the same job until you've learnt to get your own shields up to scratch.'

He looked at her quizzically.

'Give me something?'

Was she about to offer him drugs?

'Consider it an un-birthday present.'

'I'm not going to close my eyes.'

'You don't have to.'

As she spoke, Gwyn reached under the collar of her blouse

and pulled the silver torque she was wearing from her neck. Suspended from it was a large oval of purple and pink crystal, bound with silver, which she slid off and handed to Aidan. He looked at it suspiciously. Close up he could see the pendant was made of two concentric rings of crystal, one purple and one pink, with a very fine infill of silver between them.

'It's a couple of pieces of rock,' he said, unimpressed.

'Very good. I can tell Matt's geological talents are rubbing off on you. Do you know what kind?'

'Pink and purple?'

Gwyn rolled her eyes.

'Amethyst and rose quartz.'

I'm not stupid, Gwyn.

'I can't believe you're giving me crystals.'

He made to hand it back to her, but she gestured for him to keep it.

'So energy bolts and shields are perfectly reasonable, but crystals are a step too far? If I'd handed you a lump of uranium you wouldn't be sceptical about its ability to affect you.'

'That's because radiation's measurable. Crystal rays, or whatever these things are meant to emit, aren't.'

Gwyn held her hands up.

'Let's not argue about that now. Just humour me on this. If it works you'll get a good night's sleep tonight. If not, well, what do you have to lose?'

'My street cred? You're not expecting me to wear this, are you?'

He turned the stone over in his fingers. The surface was gently rounded and flawlessly smooth. This was no cheap trinket. It would have taken a skilled jeweller to make such a fine join between the stones and the silver that they felt like one single piece. He rubbed his thumb over it like a touchstone. It felt surprisingly soothing. He thought of the countless Greek men, sitting outside the tavernas, with their tiny cups of thick black coffee, slipping their strings of worry beads through their fingers in a slow, rhythmic shuffle. He became aware of Gwyn's gaze and stopped immediately, putting the oval of crystal down on the table between them.

'Well, you could wear it, but no, you don't have to. Just take it home and put it beside your bed at night or, better still, put it underneath your pillow. You should find that the dreams stop. Or at least the only bad dreams you have will be normal ones. The ones about turning up to work naked or being chased by giant spiders I can't do anything about.'

The impish grin made her look like a young girl. 'You might like to carry on letting Sula sleep in your room as well. Some of the old breeds were meant for guarding against more than just wolves and bandits. I'd guess there's an old bloodline or two running through her veins.'

'And that's all I have to do?'

'That's all you have to do. As I said, what do you have to lose?'

Aidan looked at the crystal and silver pendant on the table and then at Gwyn. Of all the things he had thought he might get from this conversation, this wasn't one of them, but if it could stop the dreams, he was willing to give it a try, no matter how daft it seemed. He picked the pendant up and tucked it carefully into his wallet.

'Thank you,' he said and genuinely meant it.

She had shown him that the world was more complicated than he had thought, but that it was not necessarily something to be frightened of, that there was another explanation for the terrified face in his dreams. Now he just had to learn to believe it.

'You are certain nothing could have made John do what he did?' he pressed her.

Gwyn paused in the act of pulling on her jacket.

'I promise you, Aidan. No shriek could make a sane adult do something like that against their will. Now, give me a call when you're ready to do some work on shielding, okay? And please, don't leave it too long.'

'Yes, yes, I will, Gwyn.'

And to his surprise he realised he meant it. She gathered her things together and he watched her through the window as she crossed the road, disappearing from view as she cut down the little footpath towards the car park at the back of the library.

It was only much later that he realised that although she had given him an answer, it wasn't to the question he had asked.

CHAPTER 6

Despite everything weighing on her mind, Gwyn found herself smiling as she stepped into the little shop in the foyer of the Gaia Natural Healing Centre. Set in a courtyard, backing onto the Hafren River, this was Llancathan's alternative community centre. Once a woollen mill, the centre provided offices and work rooms for many of the town's established therapists and healers, while the upper floor had been converted into a large light-filled studio that was used for yoga and t'ai chi classes. On the ground floor was a small café area with seating and plants and the shop. To Gwyn the place was almost a second home.

She took a deep breath as the warmth and the mixed smells of sandalwood and patchouli incense washed over her, feeling some of the tension leaving her shoulders. Her smile broadened as she surveyed the near chaos of the shop interior. Not that Rowan, the centre's founder and driving force, would accept that it was chaos. She maintained – quite accurately – that she knew where everything was and could find any item of stock in moments. But to those uninitiated into Rowan's filing system, the shop was like some gorgeous treasure trove of alternative living. Baskets of small crystals and polished stones were angled to entice the casual browser to pick them up, while larger and more spectacular pieces were artfully highlighted with miniature spotlights.

In one corner a collection of amethyst geodes clustered around a votive statue of Isis. Dream catchers and crystal pendants hung from the ceiling and elsewhere shelves held everything from boxes and tubes of incense sticks to t'ai chi slippers, packs of tarot cards and meditation tapes. Behind the counter large screw-top jars of herbs were labelled with old-fashioned copperplate; comfrey, lavender, coltsfoot, thyme.

'Be with you in a second.'

The voice drifted out from the back of the shop. Gwyn followed its slightly muffled sound and located Rowan, or at least her feet, sticking out from behind one of the large display cases that filled the rear of the shop. The glass-fronted shelving had been pulled out from the wall just sufficiently to allow someone to crawl behind it.

'Don't rush, Rowan, it's only me.'

Gwyn moved over to the section of wall dedicated to books. There was one she specifically wanted and she hoped Rowan had a copy. She didn't have the luxury of time to order it from Amazon. With her head cocked on one side, so she could read the titles on the spines, Gwyn surveyed the crammed bookshelves. Here at least Rowan kept some sort of order. She might be the only one who understood why local history and legends should be jammed between crystal healing and past life regression, but once she had found the section she wanted, Gwyn knew that if Rowan had a copy, the book she sought would be there. And indeed it was. She slid the volume from the shelf, grimacing slightly at the book of mid-Wales love spells that sat beside it, and put it down on the counter. After a moment's thought she added a fat bundle of beeswax candles, holding them to her nose for a second to breathe in their sweet, heavy smell.

'Do you still have those nice flat crystal tablets, Ro?' Gwyn addressed the feet.

'Left-hand side at the back, just beside Ganesh,' came the unhesitating reply.

Gwyn turned her gaze to the contents of the back of the shop, hunting for the things she needed. Her eyes passed over the niches lined in rich sari fabrics holding bronze and resin statues of various gods, positioned with no particular deference to their place in the pantheon, hunting for Ganesh. Lao Tzu rode his water buffalo towards a black resin Anubis, who in turn glared down his pointed muzzle at Buddha and a collection of carved stones bearing the image of flute-playing Kókopilau dancing the world to life.

So many beliefs, so many ways people chose to explain the balance of the universe. Could any of them help her now? Last night she had sat for a long time thinking about what Aidan had told her and what it could mean. She had the sense of things falling into place, of a pattern she had not wanted to acknowledge starting to come clear, and what she thought she could see in those half-made connections gripped her, like a cold hand around her heart. She had prayed last night, kneeling alone in the darkness, had prayed as she had not for many a long year. She knew her prayers had been heard. Only time would tell how they would be answered.

Let me be wrong. Let it not be true.

For how could she keep him safe? She who had once held power in the palm of her hand and had seen it run through her fingers like water and seep away into the dust. She had drunk in full the bitter dregs of that loss, facing its consequences every day as the friend she loved died, inch by inch, and she could only watch, as futile and helpless as everyone else. A life saved, a life lost; thus was the balance maintained. Yet, if what she feared were true, that loss would be as nothing compared with what was to come. These hills would become a charnel house and the little powers she could still muster would never be enough to stop it. This was a wound she could not hope to heal, a cancer, malign and deadly, that she no longer had the power to excise. And Aidan was already marked by it. What god had she offended that Fate would mock her so?

Aidan. Gwyn bit her lip at the thought of yesterday's conversation. She had lied to him and, even knowing that she had done it with the best intentions – had done it because it was the only way she could think of to keep him safe – still she hated herself for it. The seal she had given him would shield him for now, buying her time to persuade him to learn to shield himself. Eventually she would tell him the truth. When that time came she could only hope he would understand why she had lied. She did not go so far as to hope he might forgive her. Shrieks might not be able to force a person to kill themselves, but there was something that could. If that was what had risen in the hills then none of them would be safe. In truth she couldn't say they were safe even now; not after John's death. Because his had not been the first.

Katie Thomas had been a brilliant athlete. A popular member of the Hafren Harriers, she had won national acclaim as a junior and, in her second year in senior competition, had been picked for the Olympic squad. Many had predicted a 10,000m medal would accompany her back to Wales, but an injury picked up during training had dashed her hopes of glory. Those who didn't know her might have expected her to be bitter, but, when interviewed, she refused to dwell on her disappointment, focussing instead on the future and the fact she would be coming into her prime for Rio in 2016.

Then, one wet November evening, Katie had been driving home from a training session in Aberystwyth and her car had skidded off the road, a mile or so outside Llangurig, rolling down the embankment to finish up on its roof at the edge of the Wye. Airlifted to hospital, the doctors could save her life, but Katie's running days were over. She would never walk again.

Even then it seemed that Katie wouldn't give up, declaring that if she couldn't run she would learn to race as a Paralympian. But it turned out her brave face had been a façade. On a warm summer evening, a walker discovered Katie and her boyfriend's bodies at a picnic spot overlooking the Clywedog reservoir. In a suicide pact that had shocked the whole town, they had driven into the hills where they had downed a lethal combination of drugs and alcohol before lying down together to die in each other's arms.

It was Aidan's description of his dreams that had made the connection for Gwyn. When he spoke of the sulphurous eyes that haunted the far shores of sleep she was certain she had heard that description before. The memory had taken a while to surface. When it did she had prayed she was mistaken, but every instinct had told her otherwise. That morning she had driven into Newtown to look at the back issues of the *Cambrian Times* in the library, but it was only when she had seen it there, in black and white, that the enormity of what she faced had started to sink in.

Several papers had printed extracts from Katie's suicide note. It made tragic reading. In it, Katie had spoken about her life having become meaningless and of how everything was over for her. She had despaired about the black dog coming down out of her dreams. Then came the line that Gwyn had remembered: *Sleeping, or waking, its yellow eyes follow me. Even though I turn from it I know it is there and everything I do will come to nothing because of it.* The experts had concluded she had been writing about her depression and the papers had railed at a health service weakened by cuts in funding. No one had really questioned why Ioan Bennet had chosen to die at his girlfriend's side. There had been no suicide note to explain his death. Gwyn wondered when he had started to see yellow eyes in his dreams.

Movement beside her broke her free of the bleak cycle of her thoughts. The feet began to shuffle backwards and a pair of legs clad in green velvet jeans emerged, followed by a patchwork jumper of such extravagant size and pattern that it could only have been created by an elderly, and presumably colour-blind, relative intent on using up every last scrap of wool in her knitting bag. With the sleeves rolled up to her elbows and the bright copper frizz of her hair clashing furiously with her jumper where it fell in spirals over her shoulders, Rowan Jarmon looked like a wild marsh fey dressed in the combined cast offs of Oxfam and the local theatre company. She pushed her hair out of her eyes, leaving a smudge of dust across her nose and cheek.

'Hello, Gwyn. Lovely to see you.'

She engulfed Gwyn in a hug as enthusiastic as though it had been months, rather than days, since they had last met. 'Just changing the fuse on my Tibetan singing bowls. There,' she said, in satisfaction, as the flick of a switch illuminated the display in a glow of rose and violet light. The metal bowls gleamed like living things in their nests of velvet. They almost seemed to shimmer as though they were quietly vibrating, singing softly to themselves in voices too low for human hearing. Rowan dropped the screwdriver and the dead fuse onto a convenient shelf and pushed the cabinet back against the wall with surprisingly little effort.

Many people were surprised by Rowan, mistaking her almost scarecrow thinness for frailty, but no one who had received a massage from her was left in any doubt as to the strength of her arms.

'I was hoping you might drop by today, I have someone I want you to meet.'

Rowan's face was lit with enthusiasm. Gwyn felt her heart sink. Rowan was an inveterate matchmaker, but her enthusiasm for the task was rarely tempered by anything approximating common sense regarding the suitability of the match. The last person Rowan had wanted her to meet had sweaty palms, a receding hairline and an absolute conviction that the location of the cave in which Merlin had laid Arthur and his attendant knights down to sleep for eternity had been revealed to him in a dream. It had taken a restraining order from the police and a near-fatal encounter with Bill Meirionydd and his shotgun to stop him digging holes all along the side of Cadair Cawr.

'Ro, I don't want another blind date,' she protested faintly, knowing that nothing short of an act of God would stop Rowan's matchmaking. In her heart she was already reconciling herself to an evening spent discussing ley lines and their use as marker beacons for flying saucers.

'Hah, you keep your hands to yourself, my lady. If this one's on the market, he's mine.'

Gwyn blinked in surprise. This was something new. She listened as Rowan launched into an enthusiastic description.

'He's tall; just a shade under six foot; slim; dark, floppy sort of hair; gorgeous eyes,' she widened her own periwinkle blue ones expressively, 'and eyelashes you would just die for.'

'So why are you telling me about him if he's such a hunk?

Judging by the last couple of specimens you've tried to pair me off with, you've got me marked down for paunchy and balding.' She shook her head ruefully. 'Besides, I suspect my days of attracting hunks are long gone.'

Her matchmaking friend grinned impishly. 'Why else do you think I'd let you anywhere near him?'

'Bitch.'

Rowan simply stuck her tongue out.

'He's a writer,' she said, reaching past Gwyn and imperceptibly straightening the silk scarves decorating the wall. 'Like you,' she added, as though Gwyn might not make the connection on her own. 'He's staying in Llancathan while he does the research for his latest book and I thought the two of you would hit it off.'

Gwyn wasn't so sure. Although the description was certainly more promising than his cave-seeking predecessor, she knew from experience there was likely to be some crucial detail that Rowan hadn't thought to mention. The book, if it existed at all, would probably turn out to be about Welsh fertility rituals and its author would want to be beaten with a bunch of leeks or daffodils, so he could take on the essence of Thor – *Why did they always mix their mythologies?* – before a very brief and unsatisfactory performance in bed. No doubt he would then blame his shortcomings on the fact that they hadn't consummated their relationship in the centre of a ploughed field under the full moon.

'Rowan love, I'm a technical author. I write abstracts for scientific papers and articles on urinary incontinence for medical journals. I help editors explain the difference between punctuated equilibria and phyletic gradualism in ways that make you think it's the one piece of information that's been missing from your life. I can write you anything from a sales leaflet for your new wonder drug to a sensitively worded article on dealing with prostate cancer in the over-eighties, but I don't touch New Age hippy-dippy stuff.'

Gwyn knew that Rowan wouldn't be offended by the description or her view that it would be professional suicide for a technical writer to become associated with the subject. It was a debate they had had often enough. Rowan was of the opinion that the best way to get well-written, carefully researched books on Wicca, crystal healing, mediumship or any of the myriad subjects that were lumped together under the 'New Age' banner was to get people like Gwyn to write them. While Rowan's support was undoubtedly flattering, Gwyn had no desire to wear her heart quite so openly on her sleeve. While it would never make her rich, she had a steady stream of work supported by a good reputation and a solid network of contacts in the scientific press. She wasn't about to jeopardise either by proclaiming her beliefs to the world.

'Besides, I really don't want to hit it off with anyone just now. Life's complicated enough.'

Rowan humphed and readjusted the decks of tarot cards on top of the display case, turning them so the gaudy beauty of a Pre-Raphaelite style pack would catch the eye. The Queen of Swords' long auburn hair fell over the hilt of her drawn rapier and her full, sensual lips curved slightly as she stared into the distance. *A saddened woman representing widowhood, privation, absence, sterility or separation,* thought Gwyn, the card's description as a significator rising unbidden in her mind, familiar as the lines of a well-loved poem. Who had thought to put her figure on the front of the deck?

'You're only saying that because you haven't met him.'

Gwyn rolled her eyes heavenwards, but her retort of *I don't want to meet him* remained unspoken as the shop door opened to a gentle tinkling of finger cymbals. Automatically both women turned towards the sound.

'Talk of the Devil,' whispered Rowan, nudging Gwyn in the ribs with a bony elbow. Glancing back at her friend, Gwyn was surprised to see the centre's owner was blushing slightly.

Talk of the Devil, indeed. The man who came in through the shop door, ducking slightly to avoid a dream catcher and a clutch of low hanging crystal pendants, would have made a very good Lucifer. Sharp cheekbones, arched brows and a strong, almost beaky, nose gave his face an angular, saturnine look, which the dark hair, falling straight to his collar, did nothing to soften.

Surely the Devil would have worn his hair more conventionally short?

Not handsome exactly, Gwyn thought, *but certainly striking*. He was tall, too. As he straightened Gwyn could see that Rowan's estimate of nearly six foot wasn't far wrong. He would top Aidan by a couple of inches.

Enter the King of Swords, stage left.

Yet there was something about the man that raised the hackles on the back of her neck and it wasn't simply the threat of Rowan's matchmaking. There was a cold appraisal inherent in that grey gaze and a sense of detachment, of aloofness, as though the man held himself slightly separate from everything around him. Gwyn might have put it down to the arrogance of a handsome man, but there was something else, something about him that made her deeply uncomfortable. It took her a second to realise what it was for it had been many years since she had felt anything like it. There was power there; a great deal of power if she was not mistaken. She could feel it at the very edge of her senses, prickling her as though she rubbed her skin against sandpaper. The moment she recognised it she drew back into herself, tightening her shields, grateful that he didn't appear to have noticed that light touch. She found herself wishing there was a back way out of the shop. She would take the balding Arthurian adventurer any day, sweaty palms or not. All her instincts were screaming at her that she did not want to meet this man.

But it was too late for that. Peering into the back of the shop, Lucifer's gaze lit upon Rowan and a smile broke across his face, transforming it completely.

'Rowan, hi.'

He noticed Gwyn and his smile widened to encompass her too. He inclined his head slightly, the modern equivalent of bowing over her hand.

'Hello.'

Rowan's enthusiastic description had failed to mention his voice. It was surprisingly deep and clear, a voice like granite threaded with silver, and for a moment Gwyn wondered what it would be like to hear him sing.

With that voice any choir would snap him up if he can hold a note. She stopped, horrified, as she realised that he had defused her wariness with nothing more than a word and a smile. A wolf in sheep's clothing indeed.

'I was hoping to be able to catch you. I'm not interrupting you, am I?'

'No, not at all.'

Rowan stepped forward, bridging the gap between them.

'I was just telling Gwyn that she needed to meet you.'

'Oh, really?'

His gaze came back to Gwyn. On the surface it was warm and friendly, but she felt that sense of appraisal behind the charm.

'It's always a pleasure when one beautiful and interesting lady introduces me to another.' One dark eyebrow quirked upwards as if inviting her to comment. Once more Gwyn's hackles rose, but this time for entirely different reasons.

Oh, please! Could you get any more clichéd?

At least he hadn't referred to her as young. She scowled back at him to let him know she was immune to his charm.

'To be honest I'm rather at a loss as to why Rowan thought I should meet you,' she said bluntly. 'I have no idea who you are, although I believe you claim to be a writer.'

She kept her eyes on the stranger, watching his reaction. Beside her she could feel Rowan's startled horror at her rudeness and she hoped her friend would keep quiet. She wanted to hear what the man had to say for himself. Surprisingly, he seemed to take no offence at her tone. If anything he seemed slightly amused, which only served to irritate Gwyn further.

'Allow me to rectify the situation.'

He dug his wallet from a jacket pocket and produced a card, which he presented to her with a flourish. Gwyn took it reluctantly and looked at the name embossed on it. M. Eldritch. Underneath the name, in a flowery copperplate, was the designation 'Author'.

'Eldritch?' She made no attempt to hide the sarcasm in her voice.

'I can assure you it is my real name.'

The wry smile accompanying his response suggested that hers was not an uncommon reaction.

'And what does the M stand for? Surely not *Monsieur*?'

Eldritch laughed, a short huffing of breath.

'Marcus,' he elaborated, 'but only my parents ever called me that and then, only when I'd done something wrong. *Marcus!'* The deep voice became surprisingly shrill and his whole demeanour changed. Standing with his hands on his hips, Eldritch managed to convey a wealth of disappointment and disapproval with that one word. He grinned at her. 'My friends call me Eldritch.'

'Well, Mister Eldritch.' Gwyn made a point of stressing the title, not feeling inclined to be counted as a friend. 'I've never heard of you, nor any of your books.' She held his eyes with a challenging stare.

He was either the least egotistical writer she had ever met or he wasn't a writer at all, because his only response to Gwyn's barb was a shrug. The smile turned a little rueful.

'I'm afraid that studies of folk legends from around the country rarely make it onto the best sellers list, although *Ghosts of the Fens* did get some rather good reviews from the Cambridge University student magazine. I think the idea of taking part in a ghostly pub crawl rather appealed to them. Mixing spirits with spirits, maybe?'

The expressive eyebrows rose once more, inviting her comment. When she stayed silent he continued undaunted. '*Legends of the Fells* is out of print, but I still have some copies available if you're interested.' At Gwyn's determined silence he turned back to Rowan. 'Of course, it doesn't help when establishments such as this don't stock them.'

The corners of his mouth turned down in an expression of exaggerated disappointment and he looked at Rowan mournfully. 'Perhaps I might send you a couple of copies to tempt a few new readers into the fold?'

'Of course,' Rowan murmured, blushing furiously and ducking her head like an infatuated schoolgirl. Gwyn could have kicked her. Engaging smile or not, she didn't trust Marcus Eldritch.

'Thank you.'

He turned back to Gwyn.

'Still, that's actually not why I'm here. I'm doing research for my latest book and I suspect the reason Rowan thought we should meet is because she thought you would be able to help me.'

He looked at Rowan for confirmation. She nodded in agreement and Eldritch smiled at her as though she were a pet dog that had just performed a favourite trick. Gwyn went cold. This man wasn't going to be writing some harmless nonsense on fertility rites; no one radiating that much power could be in any doubt as to the existence of the Unseen Realm.

'What exactly is the subject of your book?' she asked, surprised to hear the indifference in her voice.

'Well, it's folk legends of mid-Wales, but specifically I'm interested in appearances of the Ci Du.' He mangled the pronunciation, but Gwyn barely noticed. 'The Black Dog.'

From the look Rowan gave her, she knew she must have gone white. She felt the knot tighten in her gut like a snare. As if from a great distance she heard herself say, 'No.'

'Gwyn…?'

'No. Absolutely not.' She rounded on Rowan, eyes blazing. 'And don't even think about giving him Aidan's details.'

Even as she said the name she cursed herself, knowing Eldritch had noted it, knowing there wasn't likely to be another Aidan between Llancathan and the Scottish border.

Why couldn't you have stuck with David? she thought bitterly, but it was her mistake, not Aidan's. The fact that Eldritch could pick up the name from any one of the newspaper reports of John's death was no consolation. For a moment Gwyn considered pushing past Eldritch and walking out of the shop, but gratifying though it might be, she dismissed the idea. If she did that he would know he had touched a nerve. The last thing she needed to do was to mark herself out in any way as special.

She swallowed down her anger and turned back to Eldritch, looking contrite.

'I'm sorry,' she said. 'It's been a long week. I've been trying to complete a commission for a rather tricky technical paper and the last thing I need right now is to be interviewed for a book.'

Gwyn thought the grey eyes hardened momentarily, as though he read her lie, and then the smile returned.

'Not at all.' He held his hands up as though accepting the blame. 'I should have explained what I'm looking for. I only want to get local people's views on the legend, talk to anyone who thinks they might have seen the Dog. I understand that people might want to remain anonymous and I wouldn't dream of naming anyone without their consent, if that's what you're concerned about.'

Gwyn managed a small, grateful smile as though accepting his tacit apology.

'Even so, I'm afraid I really can't help you.'

She offered him his card back, but he waved it away.

'Hang on to it, I've got plenty. I'm staying in the area for a couple of weeks so if things calm down for you and you change your mind you can always give me a call.'

Gwyn slipped the card into her bag, knowing there wasn't a cat in Hell's chance that she would phone him but realising it was the best way to stop him pressing her further. She would come back later and complete her shopping when she and her purchases wouldn't be observed, but, as she turned to take her leave of Rowan, Eldritch stepped across to the counter. Moving the bundle of candles to one side, he picked up the book, flipping it over to read the synopsis on the back.

'*Dark Places of Powys.* A study of the occurrence of demons and other supernatural phenomena in central Wales,' he read. 'This could be just the sort of thing I need for my research.'

'I'm sorry.' Gwyn resisted the urge to snatch the book out of his hand. 'But that's my book. I'd just chosen it when you came in.'

The corners of Eldritch's mouth hardened slightly, but all he said was, 'I don't suppose you have another copy, Rowan?'

Rowan shook her head.

'I'm afraid I don't have the room to keep more than one copy of anything. I can order you one if you like.'

The tall man turned back to Gwyn.

'Could I borrow it from you? I'd stay in tonight and read it so you could have it back tomorrow.'

'No.' Gwyn felt obliged to give a reason. 'It's for a gift, you see,' she improvised. 'I'm sure you'd take good care of it, but I can't really give a second-hand book as a present. I'm afraid you'll have to get your own copy.'

Black brows drew down over eyes that had turned colder than the Atlantic, but even though she was sure he knew she was lying, there was no way he could challenge her. Gwyn couldn't resist a dig of her own. 'I'm surprised you didn't come across it when you did your initial research on the area.'

From the look in his eyes she knew she had caught him, but he recovered his composure almost immediately.

'I'm rather embarrassed I didn't. If you don't mind I'll take the ISBN number and see if they have a copy in the library.'

Gwyn could have told him not to waste his time, she knew they didn't. Instead she smiled encouragingly. 'Maybe. It's local interest so they may well do. If they haven't got a copy in Llancathan you could try Newtown library; they have a far wider selection,' she added helpfully. Let him waste his time in the library. At least he was unlikely to cause trouble in there.

'I'll do that. Thank you.'

He bowed his head slightly, like an old-fashioned courtier, the light picking out threads of garnet and bronze in the dark fall of his hair, and Gwyn knew it wasn't her help he was acknowledging. Then he straightened and the wolf smile was back in place as he turned to Rowan. 'I'll leave you two ladies in peace for now. I'll drop in sometime during the week, Rowan, when I'm not interrupting business. Nice to have met you, Gwyn.'

Gwyn winced at his use of her name. *Conjure with it at your peril, wizard.*

'Give me a call if you change your mind about having a chat.'

'I'll do that, Mister Eldritch.'

When Hell freezes over.

As the door closed behind him, Gwyn turned to confront Rowan. Her friend might not like what she was about to say, but Gwyn knew she had to warn her away from Marcus Eldritch. But Rowan cut her off before she had even started to speak.

'Gwyn.' Rowan's voice was contrite. 'I'm so sorry. I didn't think you'd mind talking to him.'

She held out her hands to Gwyn and, after a second's hesitation, Gwyn took them and let Rowan draw her into a hug. There was no point in being angry with her. Gwyn knew she genuinely hadn't meant any harm.

'I should have realised it wasn't the sort of thing you'd want to get involved in. It's just that he seems such a nice person and I know you'd be able to help.'

That was Rowan's failing and what made her such a delightful friend. She simply couldn't stop herself helping people. Besides, power could be very persuasive. Gwyn thought of what she had glimpsed behind the gentle self-mockery and winced. This was not a man she wanted Rowan getting involved with.

'Gosh, no wonder you snapped at him. You've got knots the size of marbles in your shoulders.'

Gwyn stood still as the strong fingers moved lightly between her shoulder blades.

'I've got a free slot at eleven on Monday morning and you're coming in to have this worked on properly. What's been bothering you?'

Before Gwyn could think of how she could possibly reply, Rowan continued. 'Is it Aidan?'

She must have felt the stiffening in Gwyn's muscles for she didn't wait for a response. 'Jenny told me that he came up to you at the funeral yesterday. What did he say that's bothering you so much?'

Gwyn snorted.

'Can anything happen in this place and not be public knowledge the next day?'

'Probably not.'

The fingers probed a particularly hard knot. Gwyn winced and leant back into the massage, wondering what she could say without breaking Aidan's confidence in her.

'He's been having trouble sleeping since it all happened. Hardly surprising really, but he thought I might be able to help him.'

Rowan's fingers came to a standstill.

'Good heavens. No disrespect intended, but I'd have thought he'd have reached for the sleeping pills first.'

'Believe me, I was as surprised as you are.'

'Surprised' hardly did justice to the way she had felt when she had turned round to find Aidan standing there, plainly wanting to talk to her. She had known immediately that something had to be desperately wrong to drive him to do so. She just hadn't realised how desperate things were.

And then there was Eldritch. Only a fool would believe it was coincidence that he had turned up when all the signs screamed that a demon was manifesting somewhere in the local hills. A person could wreak havoc, in such a situation, if he had the power and the desire to do so and Marcus Eldritch certainly had the power. As for whether he had the desire, well, she would just have to find out and be very careful in doing so. There had been a cold ruthlessness in those flint grey eyes that suggested he was not a man to cross. So now she had two threats to deal with and very little idea as to what she could do about either of them.

CHAPTER 7

The first thing Gwyn did, when she got home, was to switch on her PC. She scooped up Kali, who had been drowsing on top of a pile of papers on endocrinology that she still hadn't found time to read – let alone précis – and deposited the brown Burmese on the floor, ignoring the indignant yowl of protest. She paid even less attention to the flashing red light on her answer phone, which she dropped into her wastepaper basket, reasonably confident that she would notice it again when she emptied out the contents for recycling. The papers she pushed into a random pile to one side of her keyboard while she typed in the Amazon website address with the other hand.

Somewhat to her surprise, a search of the book section revealed that she owed Marcus Eldritch a small apology; his books did exist. *Legends of the Fells* was out of print, just as he had said, and there were no copies available second-hand, but *Ghosts of the Fens* was listed, so she ordered a copy and paid the extra for express delivery. It wouldn't get to her until Monday, but reading his book would give her one level of insight into the man. Unfortunately, if anyone else had purchased a copy they hadn't bothered to fill in the online survey, so there were no comments from other people for her to read. Privately Gwyn doubted that anyone had bought it. Certainly no helpful 'people who bought this also bought…' suggestions popped up on her screen after she had placed her order; a reasonable indication that no one had ever purchased the book online. However Eldritch earned his keep, it was unlikely to be through royalties from his writing.

Well, she would have to wait to find out what secrets she could divine from his book. In the meantime she was interested to see what else she could find out. Gwyn was just typing his name into Google when her email alert popped up at the bottom of her screen. This one was a small green troll waving a placard on which the legend 'Duty calls' appeared to have been written in blood. Gwyn swore softly under her breath. That particular alert was reserved for a select group of business contacts all of whom were important. At one time or other, each person in that group had taken a chance and given her work when another editor might have chosen a more experienced, or more familiar, contact. Now they formed a solid core from which much of her regular work came. It might be the weekend, but, as a freelance writer, Gwyn had learned early on that it was best to keep on the good side of editors and agents. Besides, no one in that group was likely to send a message at the weekend unless they needed a favour from her.

Gwynyfa, my green-eyed goddess,

I tried to call you earlier, but could only get through to your voicemail so I do hope you pick this up. There's new research just been released showing that the use of hormone therapy is as effective as chemo for women under forty. Alistair Wainwright at Oncology UK wants a lead article on the topic despite the fact that they go to print on Tuesday! I know it's a subject that's dear to you so will you help a poor man out? Give me a call by 3pm and let me know if you can do it and I'll send you the papers, otherwise I'll have to find someone else or fall upon my sword in Alistair's office come Monday morning (very messy and it would absolutely ruin his carpet).

I will be yours for all eternity if you can help me.
Mal

Gwyn rolled her eyes heavenwards as she read the text, but she couldn't stop herself smiling. Only Malcolm Dickinson could get away with sending a business email phrased like a declaration of love from an over-the-top historical romance. The man had a mind like a razor although, for reasons known only to himself, he mostly chose to hide it behind a rather foppish dress sense and a vocabulary to match. Yet, for all his theatrical flamboyance, he was a solid friend, as well as a steady source of commissions and nothing demonstrated that more than his giving her a second chance to take the work, instead of going straight to the next writer on his list when he couldn't reach her by phone. Part of the reason for doing that was cold business logic. Mal was right about it being an area she was interested in and he knew as well as anyone that an interested writer makes for a more interesting article and a better satisfied editor. Already Gwyn's mind was recalling snippets of other research that might be woven in to support the overall article and she hadn't even seen the new research yet. Mal would understand that, but he would also know that she would want to write this article and that would hold equal weight with him. It was just a shame that the news had broken today and the *Oncology UK* print deadline was so tight, but sometimes one just had to do the right thing. Gwyn rummaged through the papers on her desk, trying to find her phone, until she remembered it was in the wastepaper basket. As she bent to retrieve it she acknowledged to herself that Marcus Eldritch would just have to wait.

The room at the top of the Llancathan View Guest House was small but neatly laid out. Tucked into the eaves of the terraced house, its single bed took up much of the space with a single chest of drawers and a bedside table taking the rest. There was no room for a wardrobe; a simple peg rail, on the wall opposite the bed, provided hanging space for clothes. At the moment it held Marcus Eldritch's jacket and a faded denim shirt. The rest of his belongings were stowed neatly in the small duffle bag tucked under the bed. He made it his habit to travel light.

Eldritch himself stood at the window, looking out over the town's slate roofs. Half an hour ago they had been hunched under the onslaught of a sudden autumn shower, the rain sheeting down the slate tiles and inundating the gutters. Now the sky was a pale blue again, the roofs sleek and shiny, like the backs of so many seals, in the bright sunshine.

Through the glass the sun was strong enough to warm his face, but when he threw the window open there was a chill in the air that the sunshine could not fully dismiss. The leaves of the plane trees, marking out the start of the High Street with its splendid Victorian frontages, were still mostly green, but the odd flare of red and yellow showed that autumn was pushing at the door. Eldritch stood, breathing in the sharp, wet smells of the town. Even after heavy rain London smelled of exhaust fumes and diesel, of discarded rubbish and the reek of too many people crammed together. Here he could smell the rain itself, could fancy that the air contained the essence of the high, wild mountains, the dark brooding stands of pine and the brown, fast flowing river. Wood smoke rose from a few of the nearby houses and he could smell it, mingling with the faint oiliness of damp tarmac, like a foretaste of Guy Fawkes' Night, still a month off.

Before the bonfires though, there would be Halloween. Not the trick or treat variety of orange plastic pumpkins and black witches' hats, which the shop windows were already sporting, but the ancient festival marking the passing of the old year. Soon the new year would begin, not with the promise of spring and new life, but in blood and encroaching darkness. And here, in these quiet, unsuspecting hills he intended to see to it that blood was indeed spilled.

Eldritch took a deep breath drawing the scent, the very essence of the town, down into his lungs and holding it there. Eyes closed he tilted his face to the caress of the sun and allowed himself to relax. Here, in the privacy of his rooftop room, he did not have to pretend to be that which he wasn't. Marcus Eldritch, author of little read texts on regional folklore and legends, was a useful disguise, a way of teasing out information from people who might otherwise be reluctant to talk to him, but it was tiring, forever being careful of what he said, of never revealing what he knew or thought. It was good to let the mask drop and to be his usual self.

He had been surprised at how readily his story of researching local myths had been accepted and how willing people were to talk to him. It helped that Mrs.Vaughan, his landlady, appeared to know everyone in Llancathan, even those she wasn't related to – and they seemed very much in the minority – and had insisted on introducing him to a host of people who might help him. She seemed delighted by the idea of the old stories being written down.

'Even if they are only cobwebs and moon dreams,' she had told him, wagging a finger as though daring him to disagree with her. 'They're as much a part of our heritage as the tales of the shepherds and the farmers. They deserve to be preserved.'

Even with such introductions he had expected a degree of reticence from those he approached, but Mrs. Vaughan's seal of approval seemed to wield a magic of its own, breaking down barriers and encouraging people to open up to him. The first exception to that rule had been the woman who had been with Rowan this morning; Gwyn.

Eldritch let his breath hiss out between his teeth as he contemplated that morning's encounter. He supposed he had been naïve not to think he might come across someone with power, but it was so rare and there had been none of the little telltale remarks that might have given him warning. No one had said to him, 'Gwyn's the one to talk to, she knows about these things' or 'Old man so-and-so, he had the Sight. You should speak to his daughter, Gwyn'. Even Rowan, he guessed, had thought to introduce them purely on the basis that they were both writers. He shook his head, finding it hard to believe the coincidence. Even he might not have realised they had other things in common but for the fact that she was so well shielded she was almost invisible to his inner senses. He wondered how much she had guessed about him.

He didn't think she could read his power, but something had made her wary. Either that or she was naturally hostile, but somehow he didn't think that was the case. Otherwise why would Rowan have been so surprised by her attitude? She certainly knew about the demon though, however much she had tried to cover her reaction, and that complicated things.

A spattering of heavy raindrops against the slates shook him from his reverie. On the street below, the cars already had their windscreen wipers and headlights on as the leading edge of the rain swept in from the west, drenching the town. Reluctantly Eldritch ducked his head back inside and closed the window. One way or another he would have to deal with the witch. He couldn't afford to let her interfere with his plans.

Then there was the small matter of the young man she was so protective of. Aidan. Eldritch had recognised the name instantly. The papers had reported that one Aidan Morgan, a close friend of the latest suicide, had found the body. Eldritch was not a gambling man, but he would bet good money that the Aidan Gwyn spoke of and the late John Evans' friend were one and the same. He was a vital link in the chain for he would be able to show him where Evans had taken his life. Eldritch needed to know. He needed to stand in that place and send his senses scanning out over the hillside, feeling where the demon had been. Only then could he hope to be able to track it back to its lair and his ultimate goal. His pulse quickened at the thought of how close he might be. The papers had mentioned a place called Cwm Broch. Though Eldritch had consulted various maps he could find no such name; he presumed it must refer to Evans' farm. No matter. Aidan Morgan would be persuaded to show him what he needed. Here, where there was no one to see and comment, Eldritch smiled coldly. The Unseen Realm had woken again. A demon was rising and he intended to greet it. Under such circumstances he could be very persuasive indeed.

Andrew Holmes was unbothered by demons, but he was interested in the supernatural. A slightly chubby man, with thinning sandy hair that was fast turning to silver, he propped his elbows on the table and leaned forward to address his audience enthusiastically.

'These old stories, they're fascinating, aren't they? I had an old chap used to come to my practice; best set of teeth I ever saw – I never had to do a thing for him right up until the day he died and he was ninety-five then – anyway, he used to swear blind he had a ghost in his house. He lived in one of the mill workers' cottages in Chapel Street. That was before they knocked them all down and built flats. He said he'd hear him early in the morning, the sound of someone moving around downstairs and then the back door opening. You'd think that would make anyone want to move, wouldn't you, but not Gwilym. He seemed quite fond of him. Old Dai he called him. Said it was as good as having an alarm clock. When he heard Old Dai go out he knew it was time to get up for work. Brilliant, eh?'

'Amazing.' Eldritch made a note on his pad. 'Did he ever see Old Dai?'

Andrew straightened up and took a sip from his pint. He shook his head.

'No. I did ask him once if he'd ever thought of going downstairs to see who it was making the noise, but he said no. I got the feeling he didn't want to frighten Old Dai away.'

'It's unusual to find someone quite so comfortable with the idea of a ghost,' Eldritch mused. 'Most people tend to be uneasy about anything that could be described as supernatural. The vast majority of the stories I hear are about ghosts that were seen before some terrible accident or that appear as a harbinger of doom. Every rural area seems to have its own legends of supernatural creatures that lead travellers astray. In the Highlands, for example, they have kelpies that lure passers by into the lochs and drown them. Now you'd think that one kelpie would be much the same as another, but, if you research them, each area has its own variation. In fact every body of water bigger than a puddle seems to have its own specific kelpie. Some of them appear as beautiful women, some as spirited horses, and woe betide anyone foolish enough to try and ride them, but they all have their own individual features that people can say, "That's the kelpie from the lochan not the river kelpie". It's that level of detail that makes you think there has to be something more to these tales than just people's imagination.'

Eldritch paused, judging his moment. 'I believe you have something similar locally.'

'Ah, you mean our Black Dog.' Andrew nodded almost as though he approved of Eldritch's logic. 'Well, this is a mining area, you understand, and the miners were a superstitious lot; rather like sailors in that respect. They had all sorts of strange beliefs; corpse candles, Knockers, all sorts. The sight of a black animal anywhere near the mine would have them quaking in their boots; dogs especially.'

'Hence the Black Dog?'

'Hence the Black Dog,' Andrew agreed.

'It's strange…' Eldritch picked up his pint, turned the glass round a couple of times and set it down again. 'A couple of people have mentioned it, but they seemed rather uncomfortable about it, as though it's very real to them; not so much like a legend as a real – albeit a supernatural – beast.'

'Well, around here it is.'

'In what way?'

Eldritch was careful to convey the right degree of interest and curiosity. Andrew was the first person he had interviewed who had volunteered information on the Black Dog. Despite what he had told the dentist, no one he had spoken to had brought it up and, when he had asked them directly, they had all shied away from the subject.

'Well, it's exactly the sort of thing you described with the kelpies; a cursed creature – see it and something awful is going to happen to you.'

'And have many people seen it round here?'

'Oh, not actually in Llancathan. I don't think anyone's seen it sitting on the corner of Bridge Street say, but there are plenty of stories of sightings round the Clywedog area, round here.' He indicated the area north of Llancathan on Eldritch's OS map. 'It doesn't seem to be associated with one particular spot – not like your kelpies – but it's very definitely the same animal, there's never been a suggestion that there's more than one.'

Eldritch made another note on his pad.

'Fascinating,' he breathed. 'So when exactly did people start seeing it?'

'Well, that's what's interesting.' Andrew was clearly warming to his subject. Eldritch suspected it was rare that he had the opportunity to talk about his pet interest, at least not to an appreciative audience. 'Like I said, the miners had their superstitions about black animals and black dogs in particular, but for all that the tradition of *the* Black Dog seems to be quite a recent phenomenon. There are stories of incidents that were associated with a black dog going back some twenty-five, twenty-six years or so, but nothing before that. I've never found any reference to a specific beast, to *the* Black Dog, in local histories or talking to the older folk. It just seemed to appear.'

Eldritch was impressed. Andrew Holmes was proving to be an excellent source of information.

'You're obviously very interested in the local legends.'

The Llancathan dentist stared down into his pint. When he raised his head he wore a distinctly sheepish look, as though he had been caught doing something that wasn't quite appropriate for a professional man of his age.

'I suppose you could say that,' he said, his tone apologetic. 'It's been a hobby of mine ever since I came to live here, back in the sixties. It gives me something to talk to my patients about. Something that's more scary than the dentist's drill.'

Eldritch laughed appreciatively and, after a moment, Andrew grinned back at him, relaxing in the presence of a fellow enthusiast.

'I should be encouraging you to write this book instead of me.'

'Me? Good grief, no. I'd never find the time. It's fascinating to talk about these things, but I have no interest in writing them down. I'll be retiring next year and I intend to spend my days testing my wits against the trout in Llyn Clywedog, not hunched over a typewriter. Although I suppose you use a computer these days?'

Eldritch nodded. 'It's a lot easier.'

'That's what my receptionist keeps telling me, but I'm not convinced. So I let her get on with it and she keeps me on the straight and narrow.'

The two men sat for a while in companionable silence.

'It's rare to find a legend like the Black Dog starting up so recently,' Eldritch mused. 'Do you have a problem with feral dogs in the area?'

'You mean like the big cats in Cornwall, the Beast of Bodmin and that sort of thing?'

'Yes, it's the sort of thing that might trigger a legend, but you mentioned accidents associated with the Dog. What sort of things?'

'Oh, there was a woman who swore she had been attacked by a giant dog while out riding. Very sad really; her horse bolted out onto the road and straight in front of a car. Had to be destroyed.'

'Surely a normal dog could have been responsible?'

'Well, yes, I agree, but that seems to be the first time a black dog was mentioned. After that it starts to crop up more regularly. A forestry worker reports seeing a black dog seconds before the tree he's felling falls wrongly and crushes his legs; the sole survivor of a car crash says the driver came off the road because he swerved to avoid a black dog – that sort of thing. It's almost as though the idea has entered the local psyche at that point and the presence of a black dog has become associated with accidents. Then over time the idea matures until you reach the point where, when something tragic happens, someone says, "He must have seen the Black Dog."'

Seeing the look on Eldritch's face, Andrew added, 'Now don't misunderstand me, I don't mean that everything gets blamed on the Black Dog obviously, but it's developed its own presence.'

'So you don't believe in it?' Eldritch queried gently.

Andrew laughed. 'No, of course not. I mean, it's interesting that people claim to have seen a huge black dog and then something terrible has happened – and some of them are very insistent that that was the case – but really? No, it's a local myth, a story. "Be good or the Black Dog will get you." These things add colour to everyday life. Good for tourism too – especially if your book takes off – but I'd have to see it myself to believe in it.'

The dentist grinned widely as if he had made a huge joke.

Pray that you never do, thought Eldritch, but he kept the words to himself, returning Andrew's grin with an entirely false one of his own.

'It's interesting that you say it's come to be associated particularly with tragedy. One of the people who mentioned it to me said there had been a suicide recently. That the young man had seen the Black Dog before his death.'

The smile disappeared from Andrew's face.

'John Cwm Broch, yes.'

'Cwm Broch?'

'Oh, I'm sorry, it's a local habit – I suppose I've fallen into it over the years – calling people by where they're from. John Evans was the lad in question. Cwm Broch is the family farm. A terrible tragedy.' Andrew shook his head sadly. 'No one knows why he did it, there was no suicide note, you see, and he certainly had everything to live for. It's things like that, when there's no explanation, no logical reason for something awful happening that people – certain people anyway – attribute them to the Black Dog. The Dog's become a metaphorical scapegoat for the senseless tragedies that life throws up. Perhaps you should write about that in your book.'

Andrew applied himself to his pint in a determined manner. Eldritch was aware he was in danger of the other man backing out of the conversation. He reached out with a tendril of power, touching the edges of the man's aura with empathy and compassion.

'It must have been a shock to the whole community,' he said, keeping his voice carefully neutral. He mustn't let Andrew think he was after sensational details.

Andrew looked up from his pint with a sad smile and nodded, his prickliness eased by the writer's obvious understanding and sensitivity.

'It's ripped the heart out of his parents. Damn shame.'

'I can't imagine anything worse.'

Except perhaps knowing what had done this to their son.

'The person who mentioned the Dog to me said I should speak to someone. Hang on a second.'

Eldritch flipped back through the pages of his notebook, making a show of checking his notes for the name. 'Yes, here it is. Aidan Morgan.'

He looked at Andrew as though seeking his guidance on the matter.

'Aidan?' The shock was apparent in Andrew's voice. 'No, I don't think that would be a good idea. Not a good idea at all. He's taken it very hard. You do realise he was the one who found John's body?'

'No, I had no idea,' Eldritch lied, radiating shock and just the right touch of embarrassment.

'There's no reason why you would have known, but I'd have thought whoever you spoke to would have had the sense to mention it. I mean, I know you wouldn't be prying about John's death, but it just wouldn't be appropriate.'

Eldritch was gratified to note that Andrew Holmes' indignant tone was aimed wholly at his fictitious source. The dentist was actually being protective towards him.

'No, of course not. I'm very glad you told me. I certainly wouldn't want to upset anyone at a time like this.' Eldritch paused as though weighing something up. 'I wonder, would you mind pointing Cwm Broch out to me on the map? I was going to plot out some of the sightings to see if there was a pattern to them. Not that it would be appropriate to include Mister Evans' death in that, obviously, but I am a little curious as to whether or not it fits with any other sightings.'

'Of course, it's far better that you've asked me.' Andrew put his pint to one side and turned the OS map so both he and Eldritch could read it. 'You won't find Cwm Broch marked on the map. It's part of this area here; Tair Fferm. It means "three farms". There's Cwm Broch, Tŷ Gwyn and Foel Dywyl.' Andrew pointed out the little clusters of buildings shown on the map as he named each one. 'Of course, Foel Dywyl hasn't been a farm for some time now. Now, there's a story if you're after tragedy. Thom Hughes came home drunk one night and murdered his wife and their baby daughter. Then he went out into the yard and turned his shotgun on himself. The land went to a cousin out Pant-y-Dawr way. He's let some of it as grass keep – in fact the chimney stack field where John died is one of his – but the rest's going back to the wild. Why he doesn't sell it, I don't know.'

'The chimney stack field?'

'Part of one of the old mine workings. The hills round here are littered with them; you'll see them on your map. You need to be careful if you go wandering off the footpaths. Not all the shafts are properly capped. You might fall down one of them.'

Interesting, thought Eldritch, *and where one thing might fall down, something else might climb out.*

97

CHAPTER 8

The clock above her desk reminded Gwyn it was one o'clock when she finally looked up from her PC. Other than a short break to feed the cats and to make herself a large pot of Earl Grey, she had not moved from her desk since she had spoken to Mal. Absentmindedly she reached across the desk for the teapot and then remembered it was empty. It had been empty the last time she had surfaced from her writing for long enough to admit that she could do with a cup. That had been eleven o'clock and she had fully intended to get up and make one. She had just wanted to jot down an idea first. Two hours later and the tea was still nothing more than a wishful concept, but the idea had developed into a satisfying conclusion to the article.

Gwyn yawned hugely and rubbed the back of her neck, her fingers disturbing the haphazard braid she had pulled her long hair into when she had grown tired of pushing it out of her eyes. Except for the pool of light from her desk lamp and the blue glow of the computer screen, the room, and indeed the entire house, was dark. On the battered armchair Kali and Yard Away Cat were curled together, a Yin-Yang of brown and grey fur, waiting for her to decide to go to bed; Kali, so she could assume her rightful position, stretched out full-length at Gwyn's side, and Yac so that he could sleep right at the end of the bed where she would know he was ignoring her. Two sets of green eyes regarded her as she stretched.

It had been a long stint, but the bones of the article were now in place, with a structure that would position these latest findings in the context of existing knowledge before leading the reader through the research and on into a discussion of its possible implications for future treatments. Gwyn saved the file and shut down her PC. She was quite used to writing into the small hours of the morning and, although now she had stopped she had to admit she felt tired, she could have continued quite happily through the night. However, she had reached the point where she needed to leave the writing alone for a while, to return to it later when she could review it with a fresh eye. Ideally she would leave it for a couple of days, working on another commission, if she had one, to give herself the perspective of distance from what she had written. Given Mal's deadline she did not have that luxury, but she had thought of another paper to review, which would bring an additional level of perspective. She would get some sleep and then on Sunday – later today, she corrected herself, shaking her head at the clock as though it were in some way to blame for the passing hours – she would start by reviewing that, after which she would look over some back issues of *Oncology UK* to re-familiarise herself with their house style and then she would come back to her own writing, ready to flesh out the skeleton she had painstakingly created.

However, before she did any of that she had another task to perform, one that would be best done in the still and quiet of the early morning. Even as she had been writing, a small corner of her mind had been thinking about John. There was one thing she could do that might, just might, tell her whether she was right to fear the coming of a demon. It wouldn't be pleasant, but it was less risky than trying to call an image in her scrying mirror. Gwyn felt her heartbeat quicken at the very thought. It might yet come to that, but she would not go down that route just yet.

As she padded across to the window to draw the curtains, she paused, glancing at the sky. The afternoon's rain had passed and the stars stood out like chips of ice. She thought wistfully of what it would be like to be out there, walking in the cold, damp night air, passing like a wraith through the sleeping world. Briefly she wondered whether she should go now and then common sense reasserted itself. What she was going to try needed a clear head and a ten-hour writing stint was not a good base from which to start. Besides, being spotted in the cemetery in the small hours of the morning would probably lead to her being arrested.

A fine mist was rising, like milk, from the water as Gwyn crossed the river and walked out of Llancathan towards the cemetery. The houses petered out just past the War Memorial Hospital and so did the pavement, so she walked in the road, her trainers barely making a whisper of sound on the dew-dampened tarmac. Had she wanted to she could have parked in the lay-by beside the main cemetery gates and saved herself a fifteen-minute walk, but she wanted that time to attune herself to the morning. As she walked she let her senses sink into the grasses and the hedgerows, feeling within them the delicate traceries of energy formed by the myriad lives of the small creatures that lived therein. She reached out to the wind, tasting the rain lying on its western edge… *nothing good comes from the west*… and to the clear cerulean sky, as yet innocent of any cloud. All the subtle accents of power and energy she drew close around her, weaving them round her shoulders like a cloak, cobweb fine and yet strong as the bones of the mountains. This would be her standard, her benchmark, against which she would gauge the taint of the demon.

But, even as she reached the green, wrought iron gates of the cemetery, Gwyn paused, her hand drawing back from the latch as her outflung senses warned her that there was someone else within the hallowed ground. Automatically she stepped back from the gates to where the laurel hedge would hide her and a second later the tall form of Marcus Eldritch materialised between the neat rows of gravestones.

Damn you, damn you, damn you, she whispered in her mind. What was he doing here? She couldn't do what she had intended to while he was hanging around, in fact she daren't so much as go through the gates, for as soon as she did he would see her and she would not risk tipping him off to what she planned. Through the leaves she watched him walking along the gravel path, his head down, hands pushed deep into the pockets of his jacket. He seemed to be thinking rather than reading the gravestones, for he kept to the middle of the path and, though he walked slowly, he did not pause at any of the graves. The path would take him straight past John's grave and from there to the cemetery gates.

Gwyn made her decision. There was no car parked in the lay-by so Eldritch must have chosen to walk here, as she had. The road ran straight for the first half-mile; as soon as he came out of the gates he would see her. She glanced down at her trainers. She could pretend she was out for a morning run, but the rest of her clothes would give her away, even if she weren't carrying a satchel stuffed with things she had no wish for Marcus Eldritch to see. She ghosted back along the hedge until she could cross the road without being seen from inside the cemetery and then slipped over the stile giving onto the footpath to Bwlch y Foel. As she cut up the hill, keeping to the lee side of the hawthorn hedge to stay out of sight, she couldn't help feeling she had had a lucky escape.

Gwyn had to wait almost half an hour before she saw Eldritch come through the cemetery gates and start walking back along the road towards Llancathan. Sat pressed against the trunk of the old oak that marked where the footpath turned right to follow the contours round the slope of the hill, she knew she would be all but invisible to anyone looking at the hillside from the road, but Eldritch did not even glance her way. He walked as he had in the cemetery; head down as though lost in thought. Gwyn would have given much to know what he was thinking and more to know what he had been doing at the cemetery. Had he sought, as she had intended, to read the energies that might yet remain around John's body, hoping to pick up the faintest resonance of the Unseen Realm that might tell that he had been demon touched? Gwyn brushed her fingers absently across the canvas satchel, tracing the shape of the things within; salt and candles, water and incense. She would rather face the risk of scandal should she be seen creating a sacred circle for herself at the graveside than try for such contact unprotected. Would Eldritch do such a thing?

As she watched the tall form disappear from view, cut off as the road curved round towards the town, she wondered again what he wanted. She scrambled to her feet, brushing bits of bark and leaf from her jeans, and made her way back down to the stile. A car drove past, heading towards Llancathan, and Gwyn knew she had missed her opportunity. Even so, she walked back towards the cemetery rather than heading straight back to town. One thing was bothering her about Eldritch's visit. Standing by the gates it was obvious which were the most recent graves; the grass around them was muddy and flattened while their flanks were still bare earth. If Eldritch had wanted to visit John's grave he would not have had to look far to find it. But when she had seen him, Eldritch had been walking up from the far corner of the graveyard. To get there he would have had to have walked past John's grave, so what was it that he had wanted to see down there? Gwyn walked along the gravel path to where she judged she had first seen Eldritch. Standing a little apart from the other graves, rather as though they had all pulled back from it, was a small black marble slab. Gwyn crouched down to read the simple inscription. *Katie Thomas.*

CHAPTER 9

When Aidan knocked on her door at seven o'clock on Monday evening Gwyn had to remind herself that the meeting was his idea. Although three decent nights' sleep had done much to erase the charcoal shadows that had been so prominent under his eyes on the day of the funeral, there was still a pinched look to his face and, when she opened the door, he simply glared at her balefully as though laying all the woes of the world squarely at her feet.

'Aidan,' she said brightly, wondering for a second whether the message he had left on her answer phone had been some kind of joke. But, if that were the case, surely he wouldn't have bothered turning up. He had admitted he had thought Friday night's lack of dreams to be a fluke, but a second night of sound sleep had persuaded him that he needed to talk to her about this shielding lark. Gwyn forced herself not to smile as she remembered the tone of his voice. He had sounded as though he were caught between relief and irritation, almost as though he might have preferred the dreams not to have stopped if the alternative meant admitting she was right. His expression now suggested he was having second thoughts about the whole idea, but it wasn't as though she had forced him to come to see her. Despite his appearance of reluctance, deep down he must want to learn.

'Go on through.'

Gwyn moved to one side to allow Aidan to step through into the cottage's tiny lounge. No matter how fierce tonight's scowl it was a sheer delight compared with the blank mask she had been forced to deal with in the years between Anne's death and Aidan's leaving to go to university. She closed the door and turned to find him standing awkwardly in the middle of the room.

'You are allowed to sit down,' she chided him gently. 'But not there,' she added hastily as he moved to drop into the nearest armchair. 'Not unless you want to get covered in cat hair. Oh, sorry.' Realising that the other armchair was sporting a selection of textbooks, the crewelwork shawl she had wrapped round her during Saturday evening's mammoth writing session and a pile of clean washing that hadn't quite made it upstairs to be put away, Gwyn scooped up the offending items, looked round fruitlessly for a clear space to put them, gave up and settled for dumping the whole lot onto her desk.

Aidan muttered something that might have been a thank you and dropped into the armchair as though his bones had melted, long legs sprawled out in front of him. Gwyn picked up a t-shirt from the jumble sale chaos of her desk and made a play of folding it, surreptitiously watching her guest from the corner of her eye. Aidan might not look as tired as he had on Friday, but there was no hiding the fact that he had lost weight in the last two weeks. He had never carried much spare flesh, but Gwyn was shocked by how prominent his collar bones were. She hadn't noticed at the café, they had been hidden by his suit and shirt, but now, as he lounged across the armchair, in his baggy surfer t-shirt and jeans, she could see how they stood out under the pale skin of his throat, so close to the surface, so vulnerable.

From the way he sprawled there he might look as though he didn't have a care in the world, but Gwyn had no need to extend her senses to feel the tension rolling off him. Something had upset him, but she was reasonably certain it wasn't the prospect of a lesson on shielding or else he wouldn't be here. She put the folded t-shirt on top of her PC monitor, where it promptly slid off, causing a pile of CDs to cascade across her desk. Gwyn turned her back on the lot and focussed on Aidan.

'Bad day at the office?' she asked, deliberately keeping her tone light, almost teasing.

'Don't ask.'

He didn't even bother looking up. *So much for the direct approach.* Gwyn shrugged and pulled a face. She hadn't really expected him to tell her what it was.

'Okay, I won't. Do you want a drink before we get started?'

'I could murder a beer if that's what you're offering.'

This time he did look at her and there was a challenge in those cinnamon-coloured eyes. Gwyn sidestepped it neatly.

'Maybe later, but for now it's tea or nothing. Oh don't look so worried. I called in at the Spar and picked up a box of PG Tips when I knew you were coming round. You can even have sugar.'

Aidan snorted, but Gwyn hadn't missed the faint twitch at the corner of his lips. Nothing she would go so far as to call a smile, but it gave her hope that he would come out of this mood. 'Make yourself at home. I'll be back in a minute.'

'There you are.' Gwyn handed Aidan a mug filled with liquid the colour of wood stain. 'I know you like it strong so I only put a little milk in.' Aidan shot her a look and sniffed his tea suspiciously. 'Relax, it came out of a cow. The cats don't drink soya. If you don't believe me the carton's in the fridge.'

Slightly mollified Aidan took a sip, immediately screwing his face up and pulling back from the cup as though he had been poisoned.

'What happened to the sugar?'

'Nothing; you can put that in yourself. I'm not being held responsible for the state of your teeth.'

She passed him the bowl, trying not to wince at the amount he spooned into his tea, but Aidan picked up on it anyway. That or he knew of old what her reaction would be.

'You'll give yourself wrinkles if you keep frowning like that, Gwyn.'

'I may have wrinkles, but at least I'll still have my own teeth.'

Gwyn took her own tea – Earl Grey, black, unsweetened – and perched on the windowsill, drawing her feet up so she could rest the mug on one knee. A stranger hearing their words might think there was real friction between them, but Gwyn knew better. It was when Aidan stopped talking, when his only response was a scrupulously polite 'Yes, please' or 'No, thank you' that you knew there was cause for concern. He might be in a foul mood, but he wasn't cutting himself off from her, which was good, because if she was going to teach him about the Unseen Realm there could be no barriers between them.

'Have you eaten?'

Aidan jumped slightly as the question jerked him back from wherever his mind had drifted to. He didn't answer immediately. Instead he looked at her as though trying to judge the reason behind her question.

'You're not about to offer me some of your cooking, are you?'

Gwyn ignored the implied slur on her culinary skills.

'No, I simply want to know if your charming demeanour this evening is down to your naturally warm personality or whether you're suffering from low blood sugar. If it's the latter then there's a bar of chocolate in the pantry, ready to make your acquaintance. I wasn't joking the other day when I said energy work takes energy. As a beginner you don't want to be doing this on an empty stomach.

'Of course,' she added, unable to resist giving him a dig back, 'if it's just your sunny disposition getting the better of you then I suppose I'll just have to get used to it.'

'Looks like you'll just have to get used to it then. I had a takeaway earlier.'

'Ah, so it's MSG overload that's the problem. Has no one ever told you that you need to eat a more balanced diet?'

'That's rich coming from the woman who taught me to eat sardines out of the tin because it saved on cooking and washing up.'

Gwyn – whose dinner that evening had consisted of a can of baked beans and bread that had never quite made it as far as the toaster – had to smile. It was easy to forget that Aidan knew her habits as well as she had once known his. Her memory supplied her with several images of the two of them sat at her kitchen table with a tin between them and one or more of Kali and Yard Away Cat's predecessors, watching carefully for any morsels that might go astray.

Gwyn had never expected to spend her time helping to raise her friend's child, but when Anne and James had separated and Anne had had to return to work, Gwyn had stepped in to help. Articles could be written at any time of the day or night, not just between nine and five, so Gwyn had become a childminder and fish dinners for two had become a not infrequent occurrence in her kitchen.

'They were pilchards, not sardines, and they were a perfectly nutritious snack. Anyway, you can't complain that it stunted your growth.'

Aidan shook his head and declined to comment, but Gwyn could see he was on the verge of smiling, the tension easing from his shoulders as he too remembered those evenings when getting up to the sett in time to watch the badgers emerge for their evening's foraging was infinitely more important than the temperature of one's food.

'So, what happened today?'

'I told you not to ask.'

But this time there was no venom in the words. All of a sudden Aidan sounded tired, his voice flat as though he had run out of energy. He wiped a hand across his face, a habit he had when he wanted to shut the world away, and Gwyn thought he would say nothing more on the subject. But then, almost as though he hadn't just told her to mind her own business, he began to talk.

'We're running a management training course this week. We do it three or four times a year. Companies send their graduate trainees and we teach them about teamwork and learning styles, that sort of thing. It's pretty popular.'

Aidan managed a small smile. Even fatigue couldn't completely deaden his pride in the business he had set up.

'One of the first exercises we have them do is a mock up of a mountain rescue. The idea is that they have to organise themselves so the team can handle all the different elements of the rescue. So between them they need a couple of people who can map read, others need to be able to abseil so they can get down to the casualty, then someone has to handle the first aid, coordinate the rescue, you get the idea. Matt and I take them through the skills in the morning and then, in the afternoon, we go out and rescue our casualty. It's a good exercise. You'd be surprised how the team dynamics change when they're actually out in the hills and they're using these things for real. We keep an eye on them to make sure they don't get into real trouble and Christine – she's the HR manager for this bunch – makes notes on who's working effectively and how they're all interacting as a team so it can all be fed back to them when we review the exercise with them later.'

He stared out of the window at the growing dusk, his eyes distant as though he were watching a replay of the exercise in his mind.

'The thing is,' he continued softly, 'John should have been our casualty today.'

Gwyn heard the slight stumble over his friend's name and felt a surge of compassion; no wonder he had been upset. But Aidan hadn't finished. 'So Jane did it instead. We made her up with an open fracture and all this blood and face paint so she looked the part and had her lying at the bottom of Ceinach Crag. But seeing her there, crumpled in amongst the rocks and then on the stretcher like a real casualty…'

Aidan swallowed. Even now, seeing the picture in his mind's eye, he looked shaken. 'I don't know why, but it really freaked me out. I was meant to be supervising them, making sure they did everything we'd told them to, and I just couldn't do it. I had to walk away.'

His hands twitched in his lap and he balled them into fists. 'How stupid is that?' he asked her, his eyes suspiciously bright.

Gwyn sighed. More than anything she wanted to gather him up in a hug, as she would have done when he was little, and tell him that the world was alright. But he was grown-up now and, much though she might wish it otherwise, the world was not alright and no amount of lying to him would change that. Still, she could tell him that it was never wrong to grieve for a friend and that it was natural for that grief to spill over into fear for other loved ones. She let all of those things show in her eyes as she met his stare.

'I don't think it's stupid at all. In fact, I think you'd be pretty unusual not to be upset given everything that's happened. Cut yourself some slack, Aidan. You're not Superman.'

For a moment she thought he would argue with her, but then he let out his breath in a long sigh.

'I suppose you're right. Half the reason we do exercises like that is because the trainees get so caught up in them they forget they're not real. Then they stop acting the way they think they're meant to and you get to see their real personalities.'

'It's powerful stuff make believe,' Gwyn agreed. 'Ask any child.'

Aidan shook his head ruefully. 'And I was acting like a spoilt brat earlier, wasn't I?' He didn't wait for her to speak, didn't need to hear her answer, to know that that was the case. 'I'm sorry.'

'Apology accepted, but don't do it again or I'll slip foxglove in your tea. You'll never taste it over all that sugar.'

He looked at her as though he wasn't quite sure if she was joking. Gwyn looked inscrutable.

'You would, wouldn't you?'

She winked at him. 'Never doubt it.'

CHAPTER 10

Aidan sat cross-legged on the floor and watched while Gwyn went round the room lighting candles until the small space was filled with a flickering, golden light and the mingled scents of beeswax and vanilla. He inhaled the familiar scent and felt himself relaxing as the associated feelings of warmth and comfort washed over him. He couldn't consciously say why those scents meant calm and safety, but as he breathed them in, he couldn't help smiling. He leaned back slightly against the armchair and closed his eyes.

Something nudged his knee and he looked down to see a small brown cat had appeared beside him. It looked up at him with bright emerald eyes very like Gwyn's own.

'Hello, cat.'

The cat butted its head into his leg once more, quite a solid push for such a delicate-looking creature, and began purring loudly. Despite a stated preference for dogs, Aidan couldn't help but be charmed by this display of unsought affection. He reached down and ran his hand over the silky body. The purr volume increased dramatically.

'Ignore her, she's a slut,' Gwyn commented, not bothering to look round. 'Aren't you, Kali?'

Aidan assumed the latter must be addressed to the cat.

The cat looked up briefly at the sound of her mistress' voice and then wound herself deeper into Aidan's caress, her whole body vibrating with pleasure.

'She treats everyone as though they were the long lost love of her life.' Gwyn looked over her shoulder and rolled her eyes heavenwards. 'The way she behaves you'd think she was a dog.'

'On behalf of dogs everywhere I take offence at that. Sula doesn't fawn over everyone she meets.'

'I think you'll find that Sula comes from quite a distinguished bloodline. You'd do well to pay attention to who she likes and dislikes. This one, however,' Gwyn bent suddenly and scooped up a bundle of grey fur that had been sat between the legs of her office chair, 'doesn't like anyone.' She turned the cat on its back, holding it in her arms like a baby. Surprisingly it didn't struggle, but lay there with what Aidan could only describe as an air of resignation. 'Actually, that's not strictly true. He likes to be somewhere where he can watch what you're doing, but sufficiently out of reach so he doesn't have to put up with any undignified human affection stuff. Isn't that right, Yac?'

She kissed the cat on top of its head and Aidan fancied he could almost see it shudder with distaste, even if it made no attempt to escape from Gwyn's arms. 'That's why he's called Yard Away Cat. Yac for short.'

She ruffled the cat's fur affectionately before putting it down. Aidan watched with some amusement as the cat stalked to the other side of the room where it sat, back turned, pointedly washing itself. If he stretched out his arm he would be just a few, carefully judged inches shy of touching it. Yard Away Cat indeed.

Gwyn finished lighting the last of the candles. She shook out the match and then licked her fingers and damped the head down thoroughly before dropping it into the wastepaper basket beside her desk. Satisfied, she came and joined him on the floor, sitting comfortably cross-legged and close enough that their knees were almost touching. Aidan wasn't sure whether that was a necessary part of what they were about to do or just a symptom of the lack of available floor space. He had forgotten how small Gwyn's lounge was and it didn't help that large portions of it were given over to overflowing bookcases, stacks of magazines, some rather sinister-looking houseplants and boxes of what appeared to be miscellaneous junk.

'It's a good job the Child Protection Agency didn't exist when you were young,' Gwyn reflected as she made herself comfortable on the floor. Aidan blinked and tried to work out where that comment fitted in with the evening's proceedings.

'You were quite right,' Gwyn continued unabashed, as she rolled her shirt sleeves up over her forearms, revealing a thick silver and turquoise cuff on one wrist and an assortment of bead and thong bracelets on the other. 'I'd probably have been done for neglect or for child cruelty, some of the things we ended up doing; never taking you to McDonalds, letting you try Ian's homemade sloe gin.' She chuckled. 'Sweet Lady, your mum was mad at me for that one, but I suppose she had good reason to be. You were sick as a dog the next day. Do you remember when I threw you in Don and Mary's duck pond?'

Aidan frowned at the memory.

'I thought you said I'd slipped and fallen in and that was why I ended up in casualty with concussion.'

'Hmm, I probably did. Truth be told, you were being such a pain that evening that I threatened to throw you in if you didn't behave. I don't think you believed I'd do it.'

'You mean you really threw me into their pond? Fully clothed?' Aidan wasn't sure whether to be horrified or amazed at this revelation.

'It certainly taught you not to call my bluff. Or at least it did for the two minutes before you slipped trying to climb out and knocked yourself senseless on the ducks' nesting box. I ruined a perfectly good pair of leather trainers having to jump in after you.'

'Serves you right, I reckon,' he said, but with no malice.

Gwyn grinned back at him and shrugged. 'I suppose it did. They'd have had a field day though. Not just with things like that, but telling you stories of the Unseen Realm and some of the other things I'd started to show you.' She shook her head. 'All very dodgy, in fact, a definite case of child abuse.'

'I don't remember you showing me anything unusual,' Aidan queried.

'Oh well, you might find that some of what we do tonight is familiar. Are you ready?'

Aidan nodded and sat up straighter, resettling his weight so he would be comfortable for whatever Gwyn had planned. Kali gave his knee a last nudge and jumped onto the chair behind Gwyn, tucking her paws underneath her until she resembled a small brown cushion. Aidan could envy her apparent ease. He was aware now of a slight butterfly feeling of adrenalin tightening in his stomach and that his pulse had increased. Not nervousness exactly and not quite excitement. He took a deep breath, drawing the air down into the bottom of his lungs, consciously feeling his belly swell and his ribs lift, grounding himself in the solid feel of muscle and bone. These were the things he knew. These were the things he could be sure of, not Gwyn's tales of shrieks and arcane powers.

Yet they were real too. On one level he accepted that. After all, he would never have approached Gwyn if he hadn't believed something in her stories to be true. But now that the chilling power of his dreams had been broken, he wanted to dismiss the whole idea that what he had felt had been anything more than a natural reaction to a harrowing set of circumstances that would have upset anyone. He was like a man who believes in ghosts only when he finds himself alone at night in a strange house. Yet nothing would have convinced him to remove that small piece of crystal that warded his bed.

He exhaled slowly, accepting that dichotomy of belief and scepticism. To go forward he had to prove to himself that these things existed or that they did not. Belief was one thing, but tonight Gwyn would guide him on his first step towards knowledge. He licked his lips nervously.

'Can I ask you something before we start?'

Gwyn smiled. She had gathered up her long, dark hair into two haphazard braids that meandered across her shoulders. The effect was something akin to a schoolgirl's pigtails, which should have looked ridiculous and yet somehow didn't. The ease with which she had spoken of his childhood, of their shared past, surprised him; it had been a no-go area for so long, but Gwyn seemed more open now, more approachable than she had earlier that evening. Most likely, he realised, with an inward wry smile, she hadn't changed at all but was simply reflecting back his own improved mood.

'Of course. What is it?'

'You know that...' He paused, trying to remember the words she had used. 'That psychic bolt thing you hit me with at the Shepherds' on Friday.' The words felt strange and uncomfortable on his tongue, as though he were reading the part of a character in a science fiction novel. 'Will you teach me how to do that?'

Gwyn had a delightful laugh. It was light and playful and surprisingly full of mischief for a woman who could no longer call herself young. It was certainly not the reaction Aidan had expected.

'What? What is it?'

Gwyn made a credible effort at straightening her face, but her eyes still twinkled.

'I'm sorry, Aidan, I shouldn't have laughed. It's just… well, what's the most difficult kata you know?'

The question took Aidan by surprise, stemming the wash of irritation that, for a second, had threatened to sour his mood. His brows pulled down as he considered what she had asked, weighing them one against the other. When he answered, his voice reflected his puzzlement at her question.

'Gojushiho,' he said slowly. He nodded, confirming his selection. 'But why?'

She didn't answer him directly, just said, 'Okay,' and then posed another question. 'And how many years have you been training? Eleven? Twelve?'

'Twelve.'

He was beginning to get an inkling of where this might be going.

'Right. So, how would you feel if a beginner saw you practising that kata and came up to you on their first lesson and asked you to teach it to them?'

Aidan didn't need to think about that. He shook his head and then laughed too, feeling foolish and slightly embarrassed. Her point was well made. Gwyn said nothing more. There was no need. She could read in his face that he understood.

'Okay, sensei.' His choice of that simple honorific was deliberate. He inclined his head. Had he been standing, he would have bowed. 'I get your point.'

'Good.' His teacher smiled, but there was a firmness in her voice that brooked no disagreement. 'Because you have to understand that you're a beginner at this and things that I can do and make look easy are going to be beyond you. In fact, you should realise from the start that there may be some things I can do that you will never be able to, simply because you don't have the power. However,' she added, 'we're a long way off doing any of those and fortunately, shielding isn't one of them.'

Aidan nodded to show he understood. It felt surprisingly natural to think of this in terms of the discipline he would adopt in the dojo. Knowing Gwyn she had already planned on using that approach with him. Her next words suggested he was right.

'You might have been joking just now, but when we're working together I want you to think of me as your sensei.' Her voice was light, but Aidan knew she was deadly serious. 'At times you might not understand what I'm asking you to do or why I want you to do it. I will try and explain, but I've never taught this before. Sometimes you'll just have to be patient and accept that, even if I can't explain it, there's a reason I'm asking you to do things in a certain way and that I'm not just being awkward.'

'And if I don't, you'll give me press-ups?' Aidan couldn't resist a little teasing.

Gwyn shot him a wicked grin. 'Believe me, Aidan, by the end of tonight you're going to wish it was as easy as doing press-ups. So, no last questions?'

Aidan shook his head.

'Okay, let's get started.' Gwyn paused as though gathering her thoughts. Then she nodded to herself. 'The first thing I do is ask the Powers That Be for guidance and protection. Before doing anything like this I always place myself in their keeping. You can invoke God, Allah, the Great Spirit, the Highest Good… whatever best suits your belief in how the universe is constructed. You can invoke The Force for all I care.' She raised her eyebrows impishly and he grinned back at her, glad that however serious this was, there was also room for humour. 'You're the only one who knows what's right for you and whatever that is, use it. The exact words you use aren't important; you'll find your own way, your own voice, but it's the intention behind them that counts. So, I start like this…'

She sat up straight, closed her eyes briefly and took a deep breath. This Aidan recognised; it was much the same as the short breathing meditation that preceded each karate class, focussing the mind and body on what was to come. Then Gwyn opened her eyes and began to speak. Her voice was light and clear and a faint smile lifted the corners of her mouth.

'Gatherer of Souls, Watcher on the far horizon, you who stand against the darkness, I ask your help this night. We place ourselves in your protection.'

As she spoke Aidan felt the hairs rise on the back of his neck and the prickle of goose flesh spreading along his arms. If the words she used were unimportant then there must be power indeed in the intention behind them for Aidan felt the energies in the room shift. Gwyn, however, carried on speaking as though nothing untoward had happened.

'Hold us and our endeavours within the circle of your light, this night and every night. Amen.'

The green eyes bored into him.

'Amen,' he added uncertainly. He hadn't thought of Gwyn's words as a prayer until that final Amen, but now he wondered uneasily who or what it was that she had invoked. Whatever it was, something had come at her calling. He looked at the woman who had been his mother's best friend as though seeing her for the first time. With her half-plaited hair spilling over her shoulders, her bare feet and her wrists full of bracelets, she could have been anything from an artist to an internet entrepreneur. A free spirit certainly, but there was nothing about her to suggest the sort of arcane power he had just experienced. This was streets away from what they had discussed in the Shepherds' Rest. It was one thing to talk of humans as being little walking dynamos and being able to channel energy, but at some basic level he understood that what he had just felt came from no human source. It was different, unimaginable… and Gwyn had called it. A hundred different questions rose in his mind, but before he could ask any of them, Gwyn spoke.

'You felt that, didn't you?'

'I felt something,' Aidan agreed reluctantly. He was conscious he didn't have the understanding to describe what he had just experienced. Nor was he sure he wanted to develop that understanding, but it was too late to back out now. Gwyn must have registered his discomfort for she reached out and squeezed his hand briefly, the touch gone almost before he registered it. She smiled reassuringly.

'It's nothing to be scared of, Aidan. Can you sense that?'

That last comment wasn't so much a question as an instruction.

'Take a moment and just feel the room around you. Does it feel uncomfortable in any way? Can you smell anything out of place? Or hear anything? Just close your eyes and go with your gut instinct. Ask yourself if you feel safe in this room.'

Aidan did as she asked. Even with his eyes closed he was aware of Gwyn's presence so close in front of him. He strained his senses trying to hear any noises that were out of place or to catch any unfamiliar scent. He wondered briefly what scent it was that he was trying to detect, but all he could smell was the honey sweetness of beeswax and vanilla.

'There's nothing,' he said, not sure whether that was because there genuinely was nothing to sense or because he simply couldn't pick it up.

'But you don't feel uncomfortable? Or threatened?'

'No, nothing like that.'

'Okay, that's good. Just bring your focus back and open your eyes.'

She paused, waiting for him to come back to her.

'They're not just words, Aidan. When you invoke a higher power, when you make that connection with your intention, with your desire, then there's meaning, there's power in what you do. What happened just now is proof of that. You won't always feel anything – maybe you'll get a sense of calm or peace – but never doubt that that connection is being made and by tapping into it you're placing that protection around you. Now, I want you to put that aside for the moment. Just accept it and we'll carry on.'

Aidan would have liked to ask more questions, but he reminded himself that Gwyn was the teacher here and he had agreed to follow her instructions.

'The first step to being able to shield is being able to feel your own aura, your own energy field if you prefer. What I'm going to do is talk you through a simple meditation and then some exercises to help you to become aware of your aura and maybe to be able to manipulate that energy a little. Is that okay?'

Aidan resisted his initial impulse to make a joke, to ask what would happen if it wasn't okay. He knew he was fooling himself if he thought that Gwyn wasn't aware that he was outside his comfort zone and feeling edgy. She didn't need him to play the joker in an attempt to cover that up. She was prepared to teach him. Now he had to be prepared to learn.

'Close your eyes and take a deep breath.'

He did as he was told, focussing on the sound of her voice. It helped that he had done some meditation before. As she talked him through a simple relaxation exercise, tensing and relaxing the muscles from the crown of his head all the way down to his toes, he gradually let go of his apprehension, allowing it to seep from him along with the tension in his muscles.

'As you sit there, perfectly relaxed, I want you to imagine that your body is made entirely of golden light. The shape you know as Aidan is like a glass shell, filled with beautiful, honey-coloured light, warm and bright and perfect.'

Gwyn's voice was easy to follow, her words clear and rhythmic, and Aidan found it quite simple to imagine his body being filled with light. What surprised him slightly was that the light was not a constant, uniform glow; which is how he thought he would visualise such a thing. Instead it swirled and pulsed, almost as though it were liquid, surging and receding as it answered the pull of the moon. For some time he was content simply to watch the ebb and flow of the light, mesmerised by it, for it was beautiful, one of the most beautiful things he had ever seen, but gradually the truth stole over him that this light, this energy, was him. As an energy being he felt light, almost weightless, buoyant. He knew the shape he occupied, but, even before Gwyn's next words reached him, he knew also that he was not constrained by it.

'Now, as you feel that light within you, you begin to notice that it doesn't quite stop at the edges of your body. It actually extends beyond that shell. Just a little way, just half an inch or so, all the way round. So when you look at yourself now, in your mind's eye, you can see this light extending beyond the tips of your fingers, coming out of the top of your head, out of your shoulders, your back, out of your chest and your legs, even out of the soles of your feet.'

Aidan held out his hands and watched, fascinated, as golden light spread from his fingers. Slowly he brought his palms towards each other, feeling the resistance as the two energy fields pushed against each other and the prickly tingling feeling it caused, not just within his palms, but throughout his body.

'Now I want you to take that light, that golden energy, which is your real body, and pull it in, squeeze it in tight, as though you're trying to pull yourself into a tiny little ball, into a pearl of golden light right in the centre of your body. And once you're as small as you can be just notice how that feels, how you feel very strong and grounded.'

Aidan pulled his energy body in tight around him, condensing it down until he was not so much a pearl but more like the grain of sand around which the layers of nacre formed. He was aware of a feeling of weight that he had not been conscious of in his expanded form. He was dense and heavy like the core of a mountain. Nothing could move him, nothing could disturb him. He was powerful, immutable, unchanging. He could stand in the heart of the furnace and remain untouched. But, just as he determined he would stay that way forever, Gwyn's voice sought him out urging him to transform once more.

'And now you're going to uncurl and let that energy flow

back out into that shape that you're familiar with, that glass shell that you call your body, and that being of energy, that light, that you know is the real Aidan, is going to flow right back to the edges of that shell and then slowly and gently you're going to extend beyond that shell once again. It's perfectly natural, perfectly safe. You know that as soon as you want to you can pull yourself back in, but for now you're going to let that energy which is you spread out and feel wonderfully light and unconstrained.

'And as you do that you become aware of the things in the room around you, be they other people, animals, plants or just the everyday objects around you; a chair, a table, whatever is there in the room with you. And you can reach out now and touch those things with this expanded body of yours. You can let your energy flow round them and over them and, as you do that, you can feel each object and you know the shape and the colour of it and the taste and the texture and what it smells of. You can pick up all these things just by letting your energy touch these things. It's so simple, so easy.'

Aidan followed the commands of that disembodied voice. He found there was a limit to how far he could extend his energy self, that perhaps a foot from his body his energy seemed to thin and dissipate, like mist. It wasn't lost to him, but he couldn't reach out any further than that. His mind logged the fact, but there was no disappointment. He could still experience things through his energy body, brushing them with tendrils of golden light.

'Now I want you to pull back in to the edges of your glass shell.'

Aidan heard Gwyn's words, but he chose not to obey them. He was getting the hang of experiencing things through his energy body and the world had been remade, fresh and new and exciting. Gwyn he could 'see' as a bright blue column of energy burning steadily in front of him. The two cats were smaller flames of shifting colours. He could feel the chair his other body leaned against, let himself sink into the wood and the fabric and taste the echo of other people who had sat there over the years.

'Slowly you find yourself drawing back, back into your centre.' If he chose not to listen he could carry on exploring this new world. The thought was appealing, but Gwyn's voice was insistent. It pricked at him, setting little hooks throughout his body that drew him back to her. How could they catch in his flesh when he had no flesh, only glorious golden light? But they did and reluctantly he followed her voice, letting it bring him back into his body.

He had thought she might end the exploration there, pulling him back into what he had previously thought of as the real world, but the voice encouraged him to stay in his energy state.

'So now you know that you are a being of light and of energy, I want you to feel the edges of your energy body. At the moment you can feel that it's open; that you can touch and feel with it. But the reverse is also true. While you're open like this anyone can touch you, can sense you. You can feel what they feel; their joy and delight, but also their sadness or anger and fear. You're safe, here in this room, in this circle of light and love that we have created, no one can hurt you, but I want you to reach out now, to the edges of your energy body and just change it slightly. In your mind I want you to make those edges impervious to anything outside. However you want to do that is up to you. You can make those edges shiny and slippery, so nothing can gain a hold on them. Or you can think of yourself as wearing armour or building a wall, right at the edge of your body, whatever comes to mind.

You're going to do that now. Easily and comfortably you're going to create a shield around you that will keep you safe.'

Wings, thought Aidan. *How weird is that?*

A moment ago he had been listening to Gwyn's voice, speaking of creating a barrier at the edge of his energy body, the shielding, he realised, that he had come to her to learn. Then suddenly he found himself standing in the dark here; wherever here was. It felt like a cave or a great underground chamber, although it must be vast, for he couldn't sense walls around him, yet he didn't have the feeling of being outside. *Besides*, he thought, *there would always be stars.* The air was cold against his face and smelled, in some indefinable way, old, although it was perfectly breathable, and he was standing on sand for he could hear the sibilant whisper of the grains under his feet as he shifted his weight slightly. Beyond that, there was little he could tell. Except for the fact that, wrapped around him, were two huge wings.

Other than a feather cloak, that was all they could be and, as Aidan could see the great sweep of the primary feathers merging seamlessly into the secondaries and the coverts, it would have to be a fabulously detailed cloak. But somehow he knew it was not. These feathers belonged to no inanimate garment, no matter how beautifully made. They did not simply drape; there was power and strength in every line of them. They were like the wings of some great raptor. He could imagine them spreading out to either side of him. The wings flexed slightly, as though responding to his thought, and then settled again.

Now that was curious. It was dark and yet he could see the feathers as though they shone with their own inner light. At first he had thought them white – *like angel wings* – but as he looked more closely he began to pick out the subtle shading of colours over their surface. The contour feathers at the top of the wing blushed with the softest fauns and greys, like a dove's breast. Below them, on the secondary feathers, the colours were repeated more strongly while the primaries were edged with a gilding of amber and gold, stolen from the wings of a barn owl, which brightened into iridescence where their tips swept the floor.

Aidan reached out tentative fingers, noting as he did so that he was very definitely back in his physical body, and touched one of the great primaries. It was like oiled silk beneath his fingers, beautifully smooth and supple. He felt the tiny ridges of the barbs, so tightly meshed together, and wondered at the perfection of its design. The whole wing was magnificent. It would cut through the wind in flight or mantle the bird on the nest. Even in the foulest weather, rain would simply slide off it. It was the perfect shield.

He froze. Surely not. The idea was preposterous and yet... Aidan turned, trying fruitlessly to see over his own shoulders. The wings moved with him. He stopped, muscles locking rigid. Then very slowly he reached over his shoulder. His fingers encountered the cloth of his t-shirt, but nothing more. He swept his hand down over the scapula and then across to his other side. Still nothing. He withdrew his hand and laughed shakily. Okay, so he hadn't actually grown a pair of wings. *That's good*, but he couldn't escape the conclusion that they were connected to him in some way.

Now extend your shield out. The thought came to him like words whispered on a far off breeze. Even as he contemplated the words the wings moved away from him. As they did so he expected them to part, but they did not. Instead the feathers seemed to spread, the gaps between them filling with that shimmering iridescence that he had seen glittering along their edges, and in that moment he was aware that they were actually encircling him. It was as though some winged being stood behind him, closer than breathing, enfolding him in its wings.

Yet the wings seemed to be under his control. He willed them further away. *How far can you move it away from you?* the distant voice seemed to say. The wings were just short of an arm's length away from him, but that seemed to be as far as he could move them. Not only was there a resistance to that movement but the wings themselves seemed to change becoming gauzy and insubstantial, their iridescence dimming. Alarmed he pulled them back towards him, even as the instruction to do so seemed to form in his head, and felt relieved as they returned to their earlier solidity.

'Feel yourself protected and safe.'

Yes, he thought.

'Now come back into your body.'

The words were loud in his ears, as though the speaker stood right beside him.

'Know that you are an energy being, but for now you will reside in your physical body.'

No!

'As I count backwards you start to become aware of your body. Five… four…'

The wings and everything around him faded and Aidan was conscious once more of the leg of Gwyn's chair pressing into his back. A sense of unbearable loss crashed over him, threatening to swamp him.

'Three. Come back fully into your body now.'

Then it was gone and he couldn't quite remember what it was that he had lost.

'Two. You're back. Have a stretch and prepare to open your eyes.'

He straightened and pulled his shoulders back, feeling the crack and pop of stiffened muscles.

'One. You're feeling wonderful and refreshed. Open your eyes.'

CHAPTER 11

Aidan blinked owlishly at Gwyn, waiting for his eyes to remember how to focus after the darkness. The room was a patchwork of amber candlelight, mottled with Stygian shadows, and her pale face floated ghostlike in the cloudy frame of her hair. As he finally managed to focus, she asked, 'So? How did you find that?'

Judging by her tone, something of his experience showed in his face. Aidan considered his answer, trying to find the right words, something that would do justice to what he had just undergone. The best he could manage was, 'That was weird.'

Amusement and curiosity warred briefly in Gwyn's face.

'Is that good weird or bad weird?'

'Oh, good weird.' Of that he was certain. 'But weird nonetheless.'

He frowned in concentration as he picked through the glittering memories for things that he could express. Already the sensations were fading, the bright clarity he had experienced slipping from his grasp. It was like trying to call the memory of extreme pain or pleasure. You knew you had experienced it, but you couldn't quite recall the actual intensity of the sensation.

'I could really feel it when you asked me to push myself out beyond the limits of my physical body. It was like I was able to touch things in the room, all at the same time, and I could see you and the cats.' An expression akin to wonder crept over his face. 'They were glowing like little energy flares and you were a column of blue flame.'

130

The eyebrows raised in that thin, pixie face. It seemed he had managed to impress her. A childlike glow of pleasure washed over him. There had been a time when the very thought would have made him burst with pride. Aidan turned aside from the memory, refusing to let it spoil the moment.

'That's very good going for a first time. Have you done much meditation before now?'

'Some,' he admitted. 'One of my third year subjects was sports psychology. We did quite a lot of relaxation and visualisation techniques; Mohammed Ali and his future histories, visualising winning each fight for months before he stepped in the ring, that sort of thing. It's pretty standard stuff now in all competitive sports.'

But what he had just experienced was very different.

'I've never done anything where I've had to visualise something that doesn't exist, though.'

'Whereas winning an event that's going to take place in the future is something that does exist?' Gwyn challenged. Her voice was light and teasing, but Aidan shook his head.

'No, that's not what I meant. When you're doing that you're drawing on your own experience. You know what it's like to win a fight or, if you've never managed to win one, you've got a pretty good idea of how the other guy's feeling when he beats you.'

His expression was one of rueful amusement. He knew both scenarios well. 'So you use that.'

He paused, once more trying to find the right words, and his voice grew serious again. 'What I mean is that I've never tried visualising something I've never seen or experienced before. How do you know that your brain's not just making it all up?'

Gwyn cupped her chin in her hands and looked thoughtful.

For a long time she said nothing, but just sat there, seeming to draw the stillness of the room around her. Outside, the first spatter of raindrops against the window was loud in the deepening silence.

Finally, she spoke.

'To some extent the brain is just making it all up,' she said. Seeing the look of disillusioned hurt on Aidan's face, she continued. 'But not in the sense of it not being real. Think of it as the brain trying to interpret a reality that you have no reference points for. It cloaks the things you're experiencing in images and sensations that it feels make sense. It's what it does with everything. How do you know that what you see as a teapot and what I see are the same?'

Aidan was about to try and answer that, but Gwyn raised a hand, cutting him off.

'You don't. You just assume that they are, that our brains have put the same pattern in place, but you can't *know*.'

'Yes, but I can pick up the teapot, I can describe it to you in terms of its weight and dimensions, its texture, what it's made of.'

'And if you really thought about it you could do the same with the things you've just experienced. It's simply a matter of getting used to them and developing your own sense of reference points.'

She regarded him quizzically for a moment and her voice was gentle when she spoke again. 'Are you worried that you were imagining everything?'

It was Aidan's turn to sit in silence, mulling over the answer to that question. Eventually he marshalled his thoughts into something approaching a coherent summary of the tangle of desires and fears and strange longings that the exercise had woken in him.

'I want to know that what I saw, what I think I felt, was... real.'

'Hmm... you described seeing me as a column of blue fire. A nice image by the way; thank you. If I'd asked you beforehand how you thought you might see someone if you were looking at their energy self, do you think that's how you would have imagined them?'

Aidan considered that and then shrugged.

'I don't know. The word "energy" could be associated with flames, gas flares, that sort of thing. It's not that strange an image.'

Gwyn nodded, accepting the point. 'So what about shielding? What images did you have in your mind when we spoke on Friday?'

'Well... I guess armour, for starters, or some sort of protective barrier, kind of like bullet-proof glass, coming down round me, or a force-field or something.'

'And when you visualised your shield today did you see it as any of those things?'

Aidan couldn't help the grin that spread over his face, nor could he keep it from lighting his voice.

'No. Nothing like that.'

From Gwyn's expression he could see she was intrigued, but when he offered no further details, she didn't pry. Aidan was glad. For one thing he lacked the words to explain the intensity of what he had felt and the more he tried to pin it down the more it seemed to slip from his grasp. If he tried to describe the experience to Gwyn he felt he would lose it completely. Yet, more than that, he was reluctant to commit it to words because it was too intimate to share. It had been... well, the nearest he could come would be describing it as a religious experience and he baulked at such a comparison, even in the privacy of his own mind. Yet it had that quality of having revealed to him something, if not of the Divine, then certainly beyond what he had, until then, considered to be the boundaries of the real world. The thought was at once intriguing and frightening. Like the knowledge that Gwyn's tales of shrieks were true. In some ways the world made a little more sense, as previously unseen pieces came together, but what was revealed was more complex. Was something more frightening when it was just a story, endowed with limitless powers by your imagination, or when you knew it was real?

Aidan pushed that line of questioning away. He didn't want to get sidetracked into thoughts of ghoulies and ghosties and long-leggedy beasties, nor anything else that might go bump in this night or any other. What he wanted to do was go back into that dark, still place and see what more he could do with those wings.

He rubbed his hands together and looked at his teacher expectantly.

'So, what do we do next?'

Gwyn's response was like a bucket of cold water thrown on the fire of his enthusiasm.

'Nothing. That's enough for one night.'

'But we've only just started!'

Earlier, when he had stood outside having one final debate with himself as to whether to knock on her door or simply go back home and sit in front of the television with Sula and a beer, Aidan would never have believed how disappointed he now felt. Worse than that, he felt cheated, as though Gwyn had held out to him the promise of something wonderful and, just as he had reached for it, had snatched it away. A small, cold voice in the deepest recesses of his consciousness whispered to him that she had done that once before.

'Do you know what time it is?'

Automatically Aidan glanced at his watch and then at the window for confirmation. Outside the world had been reduced to the velvety blackness of full dark.

'Your perception of time is very different when you're meditating,' Gwyn commented matter-of-factly. 'It probably didn't feel anything like it to you, but you were working for over an hour. That's quite long enough for a first session.'

Aidan disagreed. What she said might be true of other people, but he was used to pushing himself. He knew where his limits were and he knew he was nowhere near them. How could Gwyn know what he was capable of? Hell, the last time they had shared anything more than the most basic conversation he had been barely fifteen. Irritated, he realised she was still thinking of him in terms of that child; someone who had to be guided and protected, not an adult capable of making his own judgements.

With difficulty he reined in his frustration, knowing how easy it would be to snap at her and having the sense to realise that that would put an end to the evening's lesson and, quite possibly, the likelihood of any further lessons.

'Come on, Gwyn, I'm fine. You'd be surprised how much mental discipline there is in karate at my level; I'm used to it. You're the one who was so keen for me to learn how to shield.' He couldn't resist throwing her words back at her. 'So let's do it.'

Gwyn was unmoved.

'No, Aidan, you've done more than enough for one evening.'

'Rubbish. Just let me stretch and then I'm ready to do some more.'

He got to his feet quickly, too quickly, he thought later, and was taken by surprise when the world jinked sideways under him and his balance went with it. Gwyn, it seemed, was not. She had her shoulder under his arm with practised ease, for all the difference in their heights, and guided him down into the armchair with a strength and sureness that was surprising in so small a woman.

'That,' she said, in a tone that brooked no argument, 'is exactly why we're not doing any more tonight. Stay right there,' she commanded, her look threatening dire things should he choose to disobey her again. There was little chance of that, thought Aidan, and it had nothing to do with any concern for what she might do. His fear was that if he tried to move he would find himself getting reacquainted with everything he had eaten for the last week. He sat still and concentrated on taking slow, deep breaths, eyes focussed tightly on a spot on the wall above Gwyn's desk so that he didn't move his head and inadvertently start the room spinning again.

Gwyn was back at his side moments later.

'Eat some of this. You'll feel better in a minute.'

In her hand was a family-sized bar of chocolate. Aidan took one look and felt his stomach heave. He clamped his hand over his mouth and nose; even the smell was nauseating. Gwyn, never slow on the uptake, dropped the chocolate and offered him the contents of her other hand. Aidan regarded it suspiciously.

'Beer?' he queried faintly.

'Well done.'

From the sarcasm edging into Gwyn's voice, Aidan determined that he must be looking slightly less green, even if he didn't feel it.

'Don't just look at it. Take it and drink some.'

When he made no move to comply she muttered something under her breath, which Aidan felt sure he must have misheard, took a long swallow from the bottle herself and then offered it back to him.

'If you can't stomach something sweet, beer's a good way of getting sugar into the body, alright? Orange juice would do the trick quite nicely too, but it's a bit acidic if you're feeling sick, and I don't have lemonade or coke.'

Aidan gave in and took a cautious sip. When his stomach didn't rebel he ventured another, slowly relaxing as the fear of embarrassing himself faded. He continued to sit quietly, taking the occasional swallow of beer.

'Better now?'

Because he was feeling better, Aidan scowled at Gwyn, waiting for the lecture he felt certain was coming, but Gwyn just shrugged, a small gesture, barely noticeable.

'I wasn't joking about the amount of effort you'd be putting in.'

Gwyn settled down in the other armchair, scooping Kali off the seat and into her lap with practised ease. As the cat began to purr loudly, she tucked her feet up beside her and regarded Aidan thoughtfully, the candlelight reflecting in her eyes like chips of golden fire.

'What are you doing with your trainees tomorrow?'

Understanding that he had been let off the hook, Aidan was prepared to be more forthcoming than he might otherwise have been.

'We're taking them on the high ropes in the morning and then after lunch we're down at the sailing club doing some raft building. Should be an interesting day.' He grinned, warming to his subject. 'We've got one who says she's terrified of heights. She's not the one who worries me though. By lunchtime we'll have her up to the Crow's Nest and throwing herself off onto the Tarzan slide. No, I reckon the problem's going to be one of the lads, Martyn. Big guy, real tough nut, he got quite stroppy when we mentioned the rafts. I've got a sneaking feeling he can't swim and I don't think he wants to admit it. Mind you, the whole idea is to build a good enough raft that you don't have to swim, but we might have some fun with him. Why do you ask?'

'I was wondering if you were going to have any time to practise what we've done today.'

She paused to break a piece of chocolate from the bar she had brought in earlier and then tossed the remainder across to Aidan. It was not something he would normally consider eating with beer, but he dutifully took a few squares. Thank heavens the regulars at the Unicorn couldn't see him now.

'It's going to take some time before you can shield yourself effectively,' Gwyn continued, nibbling at her chocolate. 'So I want you to keep the seal I gave you, for the time being at least. What you need to do is practise what we did this evening. Get used to the feel of your energy field, play around expanding and contracting it, but then concentrate on your shields.

'Do the exercise we did tonight; find the edge of your energy field and then put your shields up.'

'Okay.'

Aidan wasn't sure when he would have the time, but he would just have to make it somehow.

'It doesn't have to take long,' Gwyn added, almost as though reading his mind. 'But ideally you should do it every day. Just think about making your shield thicker and stronger each time. Then, when you're ready, I'll take you through some more exercises and you can start to learn how to do it at any time you want, not just when you're meditating.'

She paused to finish her chocolate. 'That's another thing you should be aware of. You might find that it's not as easy when you try and do this on your own. It does make it simpler if you've someone guiding you through the meditation, but don't worry. Just do what you can. It all helps.'

'But how do I know if I'm doing it right, Gwyn? I could spend hours practising and then, when you come to take me through the next stage, find out that what I've been doing has been wrong.'

'Well, you could come up here and we'll work on it together, but I wouldn't have thought you'd have the spare time to want to do that and, to be honest, you do need to get the hang of doing this yourself. If you repeat what we've done this evening you won't go far wrong. I know it must feel strange to you, but trust me, you were shielding tonight. I could feel it.'

'But how do I know?' Aidan persisted.

Gwyn frowned. 'I suppose at the moment you have to take my word for it,' she said slowly. 'You will get a feel for it, I promise you, but you can't expect everything to fall into place after just one lesson.' Seeing the look of disappointment on Aidan's face, she laughed. 'What do you want me to do? Hit you with another energy bolt?'

'Yes.'

'You're joking?'

The look on Gwyn's face was priceless. At any other time Aidan would have derived great pleasure from breaking through that seemingly impenetrable aura of calm, but for now all he wanted was to find a way of proving to himself the reality of what he had experienced.

'No, I really want to know, Gwyn.'

Gwyn shook her head. 'Absolutely not.'

Aidan straightened up, goaded once again by her flat refusal to discuss the issue, but, as he prepared to argue, she cut across him once more. It took Aidan a moment to register that she was giving him an explanation.

'I could do it now, but there'd be no point. You don't have the discipline yet to strengthen your shields at will and you're tired. If anything your shields are probably lower than they were when I hit you on Friday so it wouldn't prove anything. Next time you come,' she continued, with the air of someone offering a treat, 'I'll get you to put your shields up and then I'll hit you and you can see the difference, but not tonight. Is that a deal?'

For a moment Aidan looked faintly mutinous, but then he relaxed, perhaps remembering the consequences of his earlier attempt to override Gwyn's instructions. He raised the bottle of beer to her in a silent salute.

'Deal.'

They lapsed into companionable silence. Aidan sat back in the armchair, cradling his beer. Having drunk little more than half the bottle he was feeling surprisingly sleepy. *It's been a long day,* he reminded himself, smothering a yawn, *but a good one.* Even by his own high standards, the first day of the course had gone well, despite his over-reaction to seeing Jane playing casualty, and the group had begun to gel. The next four and a half days would be an interesting mix of physical and mental challenges, not just for the trainees, but for him and Matt as well, as they worked with the mix of personalities. By the time the course finished on Saturday afternoon they would all be shattered, but they would have learnt a lot and, hopefully, had a reasonable amount of fun in the process.

'I met someone in town on Saturday.'

The sound of Gwyn's voice intruded gently on Aidan's thoughts. 'Rowan introduced me to him. His name's Eldritch.'

'Odd name,' Aidan commented, just to show he was listening, despite his eyes being half-shut.

'Odd person.'

There was a strange note in her voice.

'That goes without saying if he's one of Rowan's friends.'

That made her laugh. *She should do that more often*, Aidan thought. He leaned his head back against the wing of the chair, listening to the whisper of rain on the window. He was warm and relaxed and the glow of the candles made the small room seem cosy in a way that electric light could never manage. He let his eyes slide closed again.

After a moment Gwyn's voice continued.

'He's writing a book on local legends.'

Her words conjured a mental picture for Aidan of a small, wizened man in his late sixties, resplendent in tweed jacket with leather elbow patches, which he couldn't quite match with the distaste apparent in Gwyn's voice. Aidan cracked open an eye and looked across at her, wondering what was wrong.

'You'd think, given John's death, that people would be a bit more sensitive, but someone's mentioned the Black Dog to him so, of course, now he's poking around, wanting to build it into a juicy piece of gossip-mongering to help him sell more books.'

Gwyn sighed, twisting one braid around her fingers, until it was so tight that Aidan thought it must surely hurt.

'I thought you should know in case he comes and starts asking you questions.'

Aidan considered this. He felt that he should be irritated. The last thing he wanted was for an interfering stranger to start asking questions about something so raw and emotionally charged as John's death, but the beer had gone to his head in a way that would be truly embarrassing if he were down at the Unicorn and here, in the candle-flecked warmth of Gwyn's lounge, it hardly seemed worth getting worried about.

'He'll have a job finding me,' he said, reasonably. 'I'm going to be busy all week with this course. I won't be going anywhere near town.'

The look of relief on Gwyn's face was almost comical. *She really is trying to protect me,* Aidan thought. Somehow he found that amusing rather than irritating – that must be the beer's doing too. He felt a tiny spark of sympathy for the author who had inadvertently risked Gwyn's ire. She must have rounded on him like a cat protecting her kittens.

'I'm glad. He's a real pain. He wanted to talk to me, but I told him I was too busy with work. The last thing I want is to spend time with some crackpot author just looking for scandal and gossip to make his book saleable.'

She scowled ferociously then added, almost as an afterthought, 'If he does find you, for goodness' sake, don't mention the shrieks or anything of this to him. You'll never get rid of him if you do.'

Aidan laughed. 'Trust me, Gwyn, I'm not going to be mentioning this to anyone, but thanks anyway.' And once again he was surprised to realise he meant it.

Eldritch stretched out full-length on his bed, fingers laced behind his head, and stared through the darkness at the ceiling. It was amazing how much it was possible to discover about a person using the internet. Aidan Morgan might be quite restrained in his personal use of social media but the website and Facebook page set up for his training business both offered a summary of his background while the archives of the local paper provided a wealth of further information. In a small community like Llancathan it seemed that even the minutest details of people's lives were held up for public scrutiny. In the space of little more than an hour Eldritch had found articles on Aidan's business, his links with the local karate club, even his mother's obituary. With all of that he would have no difficulty working out an approach to the young man that would let him get inside his defences. Even if Gwyn had warned Aidan against him, Eldritch knew there were ways he could gain the young man's trust and persuade him to give up the information he needed.

It would have to be soon. Each night he could hear the demon yammering in his dreams, its presence burning at the edges of his brain, like a migraine building before a storm, and yet he was still no clearer as to where it was going to break through. Even scrying at John Evans' grave had provided only echoes of the demon's influence, fragments that proved its existence, but gave him nothing to follow. Lying alone in the dark, Eldritch conceded he had run out of options. The only route left to him was to trace the avatar – the creature that had become known as the Black Dog. Yet he could take a week walking over the hillsides and still not cross its tracks. He needed to start from the spot where Evans had died and to do that he needed Aidan Morgan. Eldritch's lips tightened grimly as he acknowledged what he would have to do. There was too much at stake to think of one person's sensibilities. Aidan Morgan was going to help him whether he wanted to or not.

CHAPTER 12

'Excuse me, are you Aidan Morgan? From Red Kite Adventure Training?'

Aidan glanced up at the sound of the voice. He was tempted to ask how many other people might be clearing a load of blue plastic oil drums from the sailing club jetty or indeed whether or not the RKAT logo, emblazoned on the side of the old Land Rover, might not be enough of a clue, but he bit his tongue. It would not be the first time that an unexpected enquiry led to a serious amount of business. Nor was it the other man's fault that it was the end of a long day and Aidan was looking forward to nothing so much as a hot shower and a cold beer, not necessarily in that order.

It had turned out that he had been wrong in his assumption that Martyn couldn't swim. In fact the management trainee swam very well, something that hadn't prevented him from coming within a hair's breadth of drowning when, as teenagers, he and his sister had flipped the hobby cat they had been racing and he had ended up trapped underneath the hull. It had been less than a minute before his sister had reached and freed him, but those seconds had left him with a terrible appreciation of just how badly things could go wrong, hence his pointed comments about the safety of amateur raft building.

Aidan smiled inwardly as he thought of where those comments had led. With its emphasis on team dynamics, the course encouraged the group to deal with problems by drawing on the skills and strengths of each member, even when those were being expressed in a way that seemed to run contrary to what the team was trying to achieve. With a degree of guidance from himself and Matt the trainees had eventually settled on the idea of assigning Martyn the role of safety control officer for the raft construction and its maiden voyage. Perhaps Matt's initial gambit, that drowning trainees was considered to be bad for business so, of course, the exercise was safe, while truthful, had been less than sensitive, but once they had briefed Martyn on the safety measures Red Kite deployed, not least the fact that the two trainers would shadow the raft in one of the sailing club's boats, with Matt in his wetsuit ready to go to anyone's assistance in the event of an emergency, Martyn had eventually taken to his role with enthusiasm.

It had resulted in the building of the most impressive raft that Aidan had seen in three years of running this exercise. The downside had been that it had also turned into one of the longest raft building exercises they had run, so Aidan had volunteered to pack up on his own while Matt took the trainees back to the centre for the day's debriefing with Christine. He could have done without anyone showing up to make the process any longer, even if they turned out to be a prospective client, but none of that showed on his face as he stuffed the last of the life jackets into the kit bag and turned to greet the newcomer.

Sula he noted had already introduced herself. Her new admirer gave her head a last rub and straightened up, a broad smile on his face.

'Lovely dog,' he said.

'She's a bitch actually,' Aidan corrected. 'Gender that is, rather than temperament,' he added for clarification. 'Her name's Sula. I'm Aidan. What can I do for you?'

The man took a moment to push the long, dark hair back from his eyes.

'I've been told you might be able to help me.'

Aidan raised a quizzical eyebrow and shrugged noncommittally. 'Maybe.'

He picked up the kit bag and slid it between the seats in the back of the Land Rover. 'It depends what you want.'

'You do training for outdoor activities, climbing and that sort of thing?'

'Yes, we can do. Either for groups or individuals.'

Aidan grabbed the nearest of the little herd of oil drums and, working round Sula, manhandled it into the trailer. 'Is that what you're interested in?'

The other man pursed his lips and looked thoughtful.

'Sort of. I'm not sure if it's training I need exactly or at least, it's not just training.'

He paused as though remembering something and added, 'I'm Marcus, by the way.'

'Nice to meet you, Marcus.'

Aidan shook the proffered hand. A good strong grip, he noted, without any attempt at alpha male hand crushing. Not that Marcus gave the impression of someone who would go in for such behaviour. He seemed genuinely pleasant and Aidan, who thought of himself as a good judge of character, felt himself warming to the man.

'So, what is it that you're wanting to do?'

The smile on Marcus' face grew a little tentative, as though he already guessed the likely response to his next words.

'I want to go into one of the local lead mines. Yes, I know,' he added, reacting to Aidan's incredulous look. 'They're not the sort of places that it's safe to go poking around in unsupervised. That's why I wanted to talk to someone who knows what they're doing. It's not as though I want to go far into one. I just want to get a feel for what they were like.'

He watched Aidan load another drum. 'Can I give you a hand with those?'

Without waiting for an answer he caught hold of the nearest drum and swung it over to the trailer.

'They're wet and muddy,' Aidan warned, but Marcus seemed unbothered.

'It'll wash off,' was his only response. He manoeuvred another drum into position for Aidan to load. Aidan took it from him and lifted it into the trailer.

'Why on earth do you want to go down one of the mines?'

His normal reaction to such a request would have been outright refusal, especially from someone whose experience of caving was almost certainly non-existent, but the fact that Marcus seemed to recognise the difficulties inherent in his proposal made him curious.

'It's for a research project I'm doing.'

Though the other man's back was turned, Aidan could hear the self-deprecation in his voice. When Marcus turned back with the next drum he was wearing a wry smile, as though he knew the response his next words would bring and had grown to accept it.

'I'm doing a Ph.D. in Social History at University College. Not everyone's idea of fun, I know, but it's really interesting… if you like that sort of thing,' he added. His tone spoke volumes about just how enthralling most people found his pet subject. Aidan couldn't help but smile. He couldn't think of many things he had found more tedious at school than history, but the passion in Marcus' voice was obvious. 'I'm studying the impact of lead mining on the social make-up of mid-Wales. When the mining took off here it was just at the end of the tin mining boom in Cornwall and there were mass migrations of Cornish miners into Wales, searching for work.'

He must have read the look on Aidan's face, for he broke off his enthusiastic explanation looking slightly embarrassed. 'Er, yes, well, that's beside the point really,' he conceded.

Aidan smothered a grin of his own. Here was a man who could probably talk for hours about his interest, but thankfully he could accept that not everyone was going to share his fervour.

'What I want to do is go into a mine and experience it for myself. There's too much research these days that relies on nothing more than reading through records and old texts. It doesn't touch the reality of what went on. Not that I'm advocating trying to work in a mine or anything daft like that. It's one thing recreating life on a mediaeval homestead for a year. The worst thing that's going to happen to you is you're going to get cold and wet and lose a few pounds in weight. I know mines are dangerous places, but I want to get a feel for myself of how narrow the tunnels were and just how little the miners must have been able to see, working by candlelight. I mean, I've been down Big Pit at Blaenavon, but that's a modern coal mine and it's not the same.'

He stopped, his hands resting lightly on the rim of the last drum, and looked at Aidan, his expression an odd mix of hopefulness tinged with the expectation that he was asking the impossible. Aidan sighed.

'I'm sorry,' he said, and he genuinely was. Having known the man for only a few minutes, still he felt as though he was letting down an old friend.

'Most of the local mine workings were capped when the mines were closed. Those that weren't,' he added, seeing Marcus pick up on that 'most', 'you wouldn't be able to get down anyway. Over the years they'll have had all sorts of rubbish tipped down them; old cars, dead livestock, building rubble, you name it. Especially since the landfill taxes started shooting up.'

'So there aren't any that you could access?'

'Oh, there's probably the odd forgotten ventilation shaft out on the hills somewhere, but all the ones I know of are either capped off or blocked up.'

Marcus picked at the barrel rim with his thumbnail, not looking up. When he spoke Aidan could hear the bitterness of frustration in his voice.

'It's a damn shame, really. It's work that should have been done thirty, forty years ago, but no one was interested back then. Now we're reduced to talking to the second generation; the men whose fathers or grandfathers worked in the mines and who are remembering the stories they were told. There's no one left with firsthand experience of being down there. That's one of the reasons I want to experience something of it for myself.'

'Isn't there some industrial heritage society you could get in touch with? There must be someone who's responsible for the old mines.'

'There is and I tried contacting them before I came down here, but they never came back to me. Too busy preserving old sites, I guess. That's why I thought I'd try you. I thought they might be the sort of thing you'd use on your courses.'

Aidan snorted in amusement. 'Only if we had a group of trainees we were really fed up with.'

He nodded at the grey waters lapping at the end of the jetty. 'Usually we try drowning them first.'

Marcus followed Aidan's gaze and a ghost of his earlier smile returned.

'Oh well, looks like I'm back at square one again.'

As he swung the final drum towards the trailer, he paused, a curious expression on his face.

'I know this might seem a strange thing to ask, but do you do karate?'

Coming out of the blue like that it certainly was an odd question. Slightly non-plussed, Aidan answered cautiously, 'Yes. Why do you ask?'

'Two years ago, you took…' The dark brows drew down in concentration as Marcus searched his memory for a scrap of information. 'Second, no, third place in the senior kata at the Shotokan Nationals in Crystal Palace.'

Aidan looked at him in amazement. 'How the Hell did you know that? Do you train?'

He had noted the ease with which Marcus moved the barrels around. He was clearly strong enough, but he didn't move in quite the way Aidan associated with most martial artists. And yet, when he thought about it, there was a subtle air of power about the man, a quiet confidence in the way he held himself that suggested he could take care of himself if the need arose. But Marcus shook his head.

'Me? No.'

He seemed genuinely surprised at the suggestion.

'I knew I recognised your name from somewhere and it just

came to me. My wife had just taken up karate and we went along to watch the tournament. It was very impressive.'

'You've certainly got a good memory.'

Aidan felt both embarrassed and – and this embarrassed him further – slightly proud. 'Does your wife still train?'

He knew it was the wrong thing to ask the moment he said it. The other man flinched as though he had been struck and a shadow darkened his grey eyes. He swallowed and then said softly, 'No, she passed away.'

'I'm sorry.'

It was the only thing Aidan could think of to say.

Marcus looked past him, staring out at the pewter-coloured water and its ring of encircling hills. The light breeze ruffled the surface of the water into small ripples that slapped against the silvered timbers of the jetty. His face grew still and his voice dropped almost to a whisper. Aidan did not need to hear his next words to know that he was seeing something other than the dinghies bobbing gently in the evening sun.

'She got a knock in training, nothing much, but for days afterwards she couldn't seem to catch her breath. The doctor thought she'd bruised a rib so he told her to go away and take painkillers. After two weeks it still didn't seem to get any better so he sent her for x-rays. That's when they found the tumour. Lung cancer.'

Haunted grey eyes turned back to Aidan.

'She was dead within five weeks. She had no family history of cancer, she didn't smoke. There was no reason why it should have happened to her. It was just one of those crap hands that life deals out and she happened to be the one who picked it up.'

'That must have been awful.'

Oh, brilliant understatement, Aidan, well done. What will your next revelation be; that the surface of the sun is hot?

Marcus shrugged and looked away. 'It was eighteen months ago. It's ancient history now.'

That in a voice that said it was anything but. He bent his head, fingers twisting the copper bracelet on his right wrist. 'I shouldn't have mentioned it.'

'I don't suppose it helps much, but if it was untreatable, it was probably better for her that it was over that quickly rather than dragging on for months. Or years.'

In case that seemed like one-upmanship, Aidan added quickly, 'Either way it still sucks.'

Marcus looked at him, his dark brows arching an unspoken query. He must have seen something in Aidan's eyes for he said, 'You too, huh?'

Now it was Aidan's turn to shrug.

'Even more ancient history.'

'Ah.'

They stood in silence, each wrapped in his own thoughts. After a moment Marcus ventured, 'They say that pain is nature's way of letting you know you're still alive.'

Despite himself, Aidan laughed, shocked out of his dark memories.

'Yeah. Growing old sucks, but it sure beats the alternative.'

The two men looked at each other. There was no need for further comment; each knew what the other had been through.

Marcus glanced at the trailer and back at Aidan. 'Anything else need to go in?'

'There are some paddles lying around. If you can round them up while I get the barrels tied down that would be a real help.'

'There should be eight of them,' he called as Marcus started down the jetty.

An idea was beginning to take shape in his mind as he wound the first webbing strap round the barrels and cinched it tight. The idea surprised him, but once it had formed, it seemed the right thing to do. Down at the water's edge Marcus straightened up, his arms full.

'There's only seven here.'

His head dipped as he made a mental count of the jumbled yellow and white plastic blades and aluminium shafts. A change in the breeze blew dark hair across his face and a couple of the shafts slipped through his arms as he put a hand up to push it back out of his eyes. He glanced round the jetty again.

'No, hang on, there's the other one.'

Aidan paused to watch as the tall man bent to retrieve the last paddle, waiting to see the whole lot tumble from his arms and into the water. It wouldn't matter – they were designed to float, after all – but they'd have to be quick getting them out before the on-shore wind took them under the jetty, but this time Marcus had them balanced and he managed to retrieve the stray paddle without losing the others. As he came back up the jetty, Aidan was ready with his proposition. Taking the paddles from the other man's arms he asked, 'Have you been to look at any of the old mine workings above ground?'

Marcus shook his head.

'I know there are some marked on the map, but I didn't want to trespass on anyone's land to go looking for them, I didn't think it would go down too well. It would be good to see them though.'

One by one Aidan slid the paddles down between the oil drums and the side of the trailer.

'If you wanted to I could take you to see some.'

He hadn't thought of it before, but he could take Marcus up to the chimney stack. It would do him good to go back there, to see it again without the crumpled body and the reek of blood and death. It might even help to lay John's ghost. He nodded to himself. It would be better to have company when he went. Someone who didn't know what had happened there and so wouldn't be watching him surreptitiously, waiting to see if he could cope with the memories or if he would break down. They could go on Friday morning. The trainees had a night exercise on Thursday so the next morning would be free. Mind made up, he looked at Marcus.

'Well? How about Friday morning?'

A slow grin spread over Marcus' face.

'That would be brilliant, thank you. I'd really like that. I'll pay you for your time, obviously.'

Aidan shook his head.

'Don't be daft. I've got a half-day off and Sula could do with a decent walk. You can buy me a beer at lunchtime.'

He walked round the trailer testing the straps. Satisfied, he turned back to Marcus.

'Are you staying in town?'

'In Llancathan? Yes, I'm in a B&B on Oak Street.'

Aidan knew the road. It was one of the narrow streets that ran along the back of the market hall.

'Okay, I'll need to check that it's alright to go up there first, but I can pick you up at nine o'clock from the library car park, if that's okay.'

Marcus had the look of a child whose Christmases had all come at once. He nodded enthusiastically. 'Marvellous. I'll give you my mobile number in case there's any problem, but nine o'clock Friday would suit me fine.'

He fished a slip of paper from his wallet. 'I don't suppose you've got a pen?' he added hopefully.

Aidan rummaged for a moment in the chaos of the glove compartment before producing a rather battered biro, which he handed over. After a bit of scribbling, Marcus managed to get it working.

'There you go. Give me a call if there's any change of plan, but if not, I'll see you in the car park on Friday morning.'

CHAPTER 13

Eldritch was waiting, sat on the low brick wall that bordered the edge of the car park, when the Red Kite Land Rover pulled up alongside him just before nine o'clock on Friday morning. He had pulled the collar of his jacket up against the damp cold sweeping down the alley between the red brick cube that housed the library and the slate-clad end wall of the terrace that stood beside it. Though the mercury in the thermometer showed no change over the previous day it seemed colder than it had been. There was a chill in the waterlogged air that made the slowly stirring town seem miserable and he was glad that Aidan was slightly early.

He pushed himself off the wall and walked round to the passenger door. Water had puddled in a dip in the tarmac, old petrol brightening its surface like a fallen rainbow. As his feet splashed through it the reek caught in his throat, bringing with it memories of wasteland, pockmarked with puddles and rubbish. In his mind he could see the shadow twisting and burning amongst flames of Levin fire, could hear his own voice screaming, tight with the mingled adrenalin rush of fear and anger and, over it all, binding everything together into one hellish nightmare, was the stink of petrol. Resolutely he clamped down on the flow of images, bringing his mind to heel like an errant dog, and turned his thoughts to the task in hand. Soon the hunt would be on again.

The thought should have brought him a certain grim satisfaction. After all, he had worked towards this from the moment he had been alerted to the demon's rising. Yet instead of triumphant, Eldritch felt flat and curiously sullied. He knew it was stupid. There were too many lives at stake to be concerned with one person's feelings. Aidan was an adult. He would get over it. Irritated with himself, Eldritch pushed the thoughts away. He was here for a reason and nothing could be allowed to get in the way of what he had to do.

Low clouds filled the dark sky, grey as ashes and heavy with the threat of rain. As he slung his small rucksack into the back of the Land Rover a few heavy drops spattered across the windscreen.

'I hope you've got something more waterproof than that to put on,' Aidan said, by way of a greeting. From his hiking boots to his own clearly waterproof jacket, Aidan looked set for a day in the hills. Eldritch shrugged. It had been a choice between the felted wool he was wearing or none at all. Packing for the great outdoors hadn't been his primary consideration when he had set out for Llancathan two weeks earlier.

'It's pretty waterproof.'

Aidan gave him a look that said *on your own head be it*, but he made no further comment. Sliding into the front passenger seat, Eldritch was surprised by an uncharacteristic urge to make conversation.

'You've not brought your dog, er, bitch I mean,' he corrected himself.

'No, not today.'

'Oh. I thought you said she'd enjoy the walk?'

'Change of plan.'

157

Aidan didn't seem minded to offer any explanation and after a moment's hesitation Eldritch decided it was best not to pry. The younger man seemed unusually quiet this morning – the word withdrawn hovered on the edge of Eldritch's mind – his mouth set into a thin, tight line. Sat behind the wheel of the Land Rover, his whole body spoke of tension and a certain edginess that was a world away from how he had been at the sailing club. Glancing across at him, Eldritch wondered how much of that was a subconscious reaction to the prospect of returning to where he had found his friend's body. Once more he brushed the inconvenient thought to one side. It was too late for regrets now.

They drove out of Llancathan along Bridge Street, crossing the Hafren in silence. Over the stone balustrades of the bridge Eldritch could see the heavy brown waters, swollen with last night's rain, rushing beneath them. As the last few houses dropped away behind them and Aidan had still not spoken, Eldritch asked carefully, 'Are you alright?'

'What?'

The question seemed to startle Aidan, but, after a moment, he recovered his composure. 'Yes, I'm fine.' He smothered a yawn behind one hand. 'I had a bit of a late night last night, well, an early morning if I'm honest. We were running a night exercise and I didn't get to bed until almost three.'

'Three o'clock?'

'That's five hours' sleep. It's not bad. I thought you students were out to all hours drinking and running riot?'

'That's the undergraduates.'

Eldritch's tone suggested he was a little put out being lectured on student behaviour by someone who must be at least fifteen years his junior.

'You don't get quite so much time for that when you're doing a Ph.D.'

'I see.'

Aidan looked sideways at his passenger and smiled knowingly and Eldritch thought there was scepticism there too. Whether it was lack of sleep, half-suppressed grief or a combination of the two, there was definitely a harder edge to Aidan this morning. Changing the subject he asked, 'You were out in all that rain?'

Even in the depths of his dreams he had heard it sheeting down the slate roof above his head.

'Sounds like a fun way to spend the early hours of the morning.'

Aidan shook his head dismissively. 'It wasn't too bad in the forest. Anyway, there's no such thing as bad weather, just the wrong clothing.' He looked again at Eldritch in his wool jacket and jeans. 'If this lot comes down,' he raised a finger from the steering wheel to indicate the louring sky, 'you really are going to get soaked.'

They sank once again into silence and this time Eldritch made no attempt to break it. He let his mind settle, gathering his senses, preparing himself for the hunt to come. Focussing on that he hardly noticed when Aidan turned off the main road onto a single track lane dropping steeply between the trees. The narrow ribbon of tarmac curved round to the right and, with the bulk of the wooded slope quickly cutting them off from sight of the main road, they could have been deep within the heart of the forest. On either side the pines stretched up, towering above them, like dark green fingers clutching at the sky. Eldritch was aware of a sense of age here and yet also of timelessness as though the weight of years was measured in ways that had nothing to do with the mortal span of men. It was just the sort of place he could imagine the boundaries between the Unseen Realm and the Mortal World wearing thin.

Ahead of them the tarmac ended in a small rectangle of gravel, just sufficient for two or three cars to park and still allow turning room for anyone else coming down from the main road. Its edges were already blurred under a carpet of pine needles and leaf litter, fading back into the forest. It looked to be little used, but Aidan swung the Land Rover round before carefully parking on the very edge of the gravel. As he switched off the engine and the silence returned to the forest, he nodded towards a gap in the trees to their right that Eldritch now realised marked the start of a path.

'That's where we're going.'

Eldritch followed Aidan along the path as it zigzagged down the slope. The surface was slick from last night's rain and scattered with fallen leaves for, despite initial appearances, the woodland was not solely pine. There was a fair mix of deciduous trees here as well, judging by the variety of leaf shapes underfoot, although Eldritch could not have said what types they were. He trod carefully, mindful of his footing on the sodden, slippery ground, dropping behind Aidan who strode along confidently, seemingly unconcerned by the mud or the prospect of a fall. What it must have been like to have been out in the forest during the storm Eldritch could hardly imagine. Despite Aidan's rather blasé earlier comment he couldn't believe it had been pleasant. He stopped for a moment to let the net of his senses spread out through the trees. So far he could feel nothing but the small energies of the creatures that lived out their lives largely unnoticed amongst the canopy of the trees or deep within the thick carpeting of leaf mould underfoot. He wondered how far they were from the spot where

John Evans had died and when he would feel the first traces of the demon.

Conscious that Aidan had continued walking and was now some way ahead of him, Eldritch hurried to catch up. Following the path he became aware that the trees were opening up in front of him as the ground dropped away sharply into a narrow gorge, the sound of running water rising to him from its depths. Spanning it was a narrow timber bridge, its weathered timbers darkened and slimy with age. In the middle Aidan had stopped and was leaning on the balustrade and staring up the valley.

It wasn't until he had stepped clear of the overhanging branches that Eldritch could see what had caught Aidan's attention. When he did, he too stopped and stared. Quarter of a mile away the valley was blocked by an immense bowed wall of concrete. Even at this distance it seemed to tower over them and Eldritch realised that the torrent racing below their feet was the controlled overspill from that huge edifice. Water was cascading down between the buttresses all along the face of the dam, white against the storm grey of the concrete. If that vast curtain wall failed there would be no chance for anything in this valley. Running for the high ground would be futile; nothing would escape the maelstrom that would be unleashed. Ridiculous though it was, Eldritch felt his heart beating faster at the thought. With some effort he tore his gaze away. Leaning on the timber guard rail, Aidan was watching him, seemingly well aware of the view's impact. He pushed himself upright and his smile seemed less forced than it had earlier.

'Impressive, isn't it?'

'It certainly is.'

'It was the tallest mass concrete dam in Britain when it was built. But that's not why we're here. Come on.'

Below the great concrete slab of the dam the far side of the valley was criss-crossed with low stone walls, none more than waist high. As they walked up the slope, on the springy, close-cropped grass, Eldritch could see they mostly formed neat rectangles and it dawned on him that these were the remains of buildings. As they got closer he could see metal railings fencing off parts of the structures and, here and there, were plaques giving information about them. Nowhere was there anything that could even vaguely be described as a chimney stack, nor he realised, despite the odd pile of droppings indicating that the occasional sheep did wander through here, was this an area you would let out for grazing. In fact, nothing about this place matched anything he had gleaned of where the suicide had taken place. He stopped and looked around, scanning the valley with more than just his eyes, but there was no trace here of the demon's avatar nor the bitter residue of sudden, violent death. Something was wrong.

Aidan came strolling back towards him, hands hooked in his trouser pockets. Ignoring the written injunction to stay off the ruins he perched himself on a wall, leaning back on the iron railing that prevented the unwary from falling into the pit below.

'Is this what you were hoping for?'

'I... well, yes.'

Whatever was going on here, Eldritch knew that he had to maintain the pretence of being interested in the mine workings. There might be a perfectly good reason why Aidan had brought him here. Perhaps he had decided to show him this site first before taking him up to Cwm Broch.

'It's just that I didn't think it would be such a public place. When you said you needed to ask if it was okay for us to come here I thought you meant we were going to a site on someone's private land.'

As he spoke he reached out with a tendril of power to touch the younger man, to subtly reinforce the influence he had placed on him when they had met at the sailing club, and recoiled, shocked. Whereas before Aidan's aura had been more or less open, today he was tightly shielded. For a second Eldritch thought he must be mistaken. He tried again with a more focussed effort, but it was like brushing his senses against polished glass. There was nothing there for him to catch hold of, no way he could manipulate the other's perceptions. Without applying a level of force that would bring Aidan, quite literally, to his knees, Eldritch knew he had no way of breaking that barrier.

Pulling back his senses, Eldritch became aware that Aidan was watching him and there was an oddly knowing look in the back of those wide, cinnamon eyes, almost as though he understood what Eldritch had just tried to do. Eldritch dismissed the thought as ridiculous. The young man had a potential for power working, but it was essentially untrained – something that confirmed his view of how amateur the witch was if this was indeed her protégé. Certainly he had shown no awareness of the influence Eldritch had used on him at their first meeting. No, Aidan's shielding now was most likely an instinctive reaction to revisiting the site of his friend's death. Even so, the young man's next words were not reassuring.

'So, how's the book coming on?'

'It's a thesis,' Eldritch said slowly, sensing the trap, but keeping to the pretence that nothing was wrong. 'Although sometimes it seems as long as a book. It's taking shape though.'

'Oh.'

Aidan picked a piece of moss from the top of the wall and studied it as though it were the most fascinating thing he had ever seen. Then he carefully pushed it back into place.

'It's strange that,' he went on after a moment. 'I called round to see a friend the other night and I happened to mention what I'd be doing today. She said she'd met a writer in town who was researching a book on local folklore.'

He looked at Eldritch and Eldritch's casual 'Really?' died unspoken in his throat.

'It seems that his name is Marcus too, only he prefers to go by the name of Eldritch. Isn't that a coincidence?'

Under the unruly thatch of brown hair, Aidan's eyes sparkled with an almost malicious delight.

Eldritch said nothing, knowing what was coming next.

'And guess what? When we checked his business card, he has the same phone number as you.'

Eldritch let out his breath in a long sigh, his shoulders slumping a little beneath the charcoal wool of his jacket, as he recognised the pretence was over.

'It's not what you think,' he began.

Aidan was off the wall in one fluid movement, his face pressed close to Eldritch's before Eldritch could continue.

'Oh, I think it is.'

There was steel in Aidan's voice now. It was low and tight, like a clenched fist, and Eldritch did not have to be sensitive to feel the anger radiating from him. 'You lied to me.'

Backed up by the force of Aidan's anger the accusation was like a slap in the face. Eldritch recoiled slightly. 'You're not interested in mines or miners. All you wanted to do was to find out more about John's death. What did you want – to see the bloodstains for yourself? To imagine what he must have looked like, lying there with his brains blown out over the stones? Was it just detail to tempt people to buy your sick little book?'

Aidan was almost shouting, his voice uncomfortably loud in the still morning air. His hands came up, seemingly of their own volition, the fingers clawed as though straining to reach round Eldritch's throat and throttle him. For a heartbeat Aidan stared at them as though seeing them for the first time, seeming torn over what to do next. A look of pure loathing contorted his face and he flung his hands wide in disgust, dismissing the very thought of fighting someone so contemptible.

Turning on his heel he stormed away, but stopped after only a few steps, standing, hands balled into fists at his side, his turned back eloquent in fury. In the silence Eldritch could hear the heavy rasp of the younger man's breathing as he fought for control. Finally, Aidan turned back to him.

'By God, you knew which buttons to push.' There was grudging admiration in his voice. 'You must have done some digging. Ask him about karate; that'll soften him up. Tell him your wife died of cancer; he lost his mother the same way. Ancient history now, but he'll understand.'

That part was true, Eldritch wanted to say, *except it wasn't cancer,* but Aidan hadn't finished. He shook his head slowly as though he could not quite bring himself to believe that their conversation on the jetty had been so completely stage-managed. His lips compressed into a tight, thin line.

'You bastard.'

'It's not like that.'

Eldritch was aware how feeble that sounded in the face of Aidan's righteous disgust. 'Whatever Gwyn told you, she's got it wrong.'

Aidan looked at him as though he had crawled out from under a stone. 'I don't think so.'

His voice had dropped back to a more normal volume, but Eldritch was not fool enough to think his anger had abated. There was nothing remotely friendly about Aidan now. 'If it wasn't for the fact that I know the team who'd have to drag your worthless carcass down off the hills I'd have taken you up to the top of Plynlimon this morning and left you there. As it is, I hope you like walking. It's about four miles back to Llancathan.'

Aidan glanced at the sky over the dam and then back at Eldritch. The ghost of a smile twisted the corners of his mouth, but there was no warmth in it. 'Looks like you're going to find out just how waterproof that jacket is. Turn left when you get up to the top and that'll take you back to the main road. It's signposted from there.'

And without another word he turned and walked away down the gentle slope of the valley.

Eldritch stood silently and watched him go, striding easily across the weathered timbers of the bridge and disappearing into the trees beyond. There was nothing he could have said, no explanation he could have offered, that would have made a difference. Even if he had told the truth, Aidan would never have believed him and not simply because very few people in the twenty-first century were going to believe a story of demons.

The wind was building, whipping at his hair and he pushed the long strands back from his face absently and then, a few moments later, did so again. He turned and surveyed the valley, a tall, solitary figure, his black jeans and shiny city-wear boots, fit for London streets but clearly out of place in this land of wood and water and wild brooding skies. Aidan was right. It would rain soon and it would be a long walk back to Llancathan when it did.

For a moment he cursed Gwyn and the boy for not simply telling him what he wanted. If they only knew why he needed to know, if they could only understand what it was that he was trying to keep them from... but they didn't; they couldn't, and so they had reacted as he might have done in their place. His thoughts as black as the storm clouds massing behind him, Eldritch turned his back on the dam and began walking.

He dreamed of Helen that night. She was sat on the end of the bed, her long legs tucked up, elbows resting lightly on her knees and her chin cupped in her upturned palms. Seeing her there the memory returned, unbidden, of how he would tease her, saying she looked like a flower fairy, strayed from her woodland bower to experiment with a mortal's existence. Though she could never see it herself, with the short corn-silk fineness of her hair tucked back behind her ears and her wide, pansy-blue eyes, she had had an ephemeral beauty that invited comparisons with the Fair Folk. Like her namesake, Helen's was a face that men would fight over. Now, with his heart thudding hard against his ribs, Eldritch was conscious that already one man had died for it.

In the bright spill of moonlight he could see her gazing at him as he pushed himself free of the constraining bed clothes. He could feel her amusement as she drank in his fear and it was not the chill of the night air that prickled his bare skin, raising the hairs on his arms and the nape of his neck. He forced himself to meet her eyes, steeling himself to see the yellow fire burning within.

There was nothing enchanting about her now. Her face bore a calculating, vicious look as though she were weighing up exactly what it would take to make him scream. It was the look she had had after the coming of the demon, the expression that had been there every time she had turned away from him, every time she stood where he could not see her face. Even in his dream he wondered how he knew this to be so, for in waking he had never seen the demon exposed like this. It was only that, when he turned away from her, he would sometimes feel that her face changed, that if he could only turn around fast enough he would catch her with that greedy anticipation naked in her eyes. Now, as she sat on the bed, watching him, he was grateful he had never managed to do so.

'You're going to kill them, aren't you?' Her voice was soft and throaty and as sweet as strychnine-laced honey. He tried not to listen.

'The witch and the boy. You're going to get them involved and when you do my demon-brother will have them.'

She lunged at him suddenly, with a viper's speed, and he found himself pinned against the bedstead, unable to move. He was aware of the cold metal scrollwork digging into his back and of his breathing, high and in his throat, as his nerves sang with adrenalin and terror. The door was barely four feet away yet he knew he would never live to reach it.

Holding him there the demon ran her fingers slowly up over his stomach and across his chest, tracing the tautness of muscle, in an obscene parody of a lover's caress. Where her fingers trailed he felt his skin burning. He fought down the impulse to look, knowing he would see his flesh blistering away, the edges blackened and curling and weeping with straw-coloured fluid.

You're making this up, he told himself. *This is just a dream.* But his body knew that this was real.

The pain was agonising. Sweat slid down his skin, stinging in the raw wounds across his belly and chest. Part of him registered that he was going into shock and he fought to stay conscious, fought too not to flinch back from her, aware that she was drinking his fear and the more he reacted the worse it would get, knowing too that she understood his struggle and was amused by it.

'Will you watch as he rips the souls from their bodies while you just stand there, too pathetic, too impotent, to do anything to save them? Just as you were when I took your little she-wizard.'

Eldritch willed himself not to hear her.

'What fun it will be.' The demon's voice was vitriol, flaying him open with her words. 'Your little she-wizard didn't put up much of a fight. She left herself wide open trying to save her precious brother.'

The demon nuzzled her head against his chest and looked up at him with those deep, velvety eyes. 'How I laughed when I killed him,' she purred, running the tip of her pink tongue over neat, white teeth. 'It was delicious.'

Eldritch woke in a tangle of sweat-soaked sheets and blankets, with the pain of the metal bedstead biting into his back. For an instant he panicked, twisting frantically to free himself before his mind took in the reality of where he was and what was happening. Moonlight lay across the end of the bed like a gauze shawl, but no figure watched him from within its opaline brightness. His eyes darted round the room seeking where a denser shade might lurk within the shadows, but found nothing. For now, at least, he was alone.

It's not true. It's not true. He breathed to himself, slowly feeling the horror subside and the frantic pounding of his heart begin to lessen. *You drove the demon out. Helen was gone, but you destroyed the demon that took her.* He dared to look down at his chest, where her touch had seared him, half-expecting that the intensity of his dream would have left him branded, but there was nothing to see except the wholeness of muscle and skin. He pushed the sweat-soaked spikes of his hair back from his forehead and let himself relax, sagging sideways down onto the pillows, the sheets still twisted around his hips like a rope.

Could he do that again? If he went to Gwyn and told her what he planned to do, she would never be content to stay on the sidelines. She would either come with him or come after him and, when she did, the demon would have her. His throat tightened at the thought of what he would then have to do. Would driving a demon from a woman he barely knew be any easier than what he had had to do to Helen? He doubted it. Yet, if he did nothing, if he relied on his ability to track the avatar back to that point where the boundary between the Unseen Realm and the Mortal World had grown thin, if he took the time he sensed he would need to find it unaided, then he might well be too late. Every instinct told him that the demon was increasing in power. All it needed was one susceptible person to be drawn to it and it would have the host it wanted. Eldritch swallowed, his mouth suddenly gone dry. When that happened all Hell would, quite literally, be free to break in.

He lay in the darkness, his mind racked with indecision. If he could find a way to keep Gwyn from becoming involved, or if he could be sure he could find the demon before it took a host, then the choice would be simple. But how could he balance the risk of bringing one vulnerable individual to the demon's notice against the likelihood that delaying would allow it to summon a victim of its own? And if the demon took an unknown host it could be weeks before he managed to find it. How many more innocents would suffer as a result? However he looked at it, there was no easy answer. Havoc and destruction lay down either path. It was simply down to him to choose where that suffering would fall. He was still wrestling with his conscience when sleep finally took him.

CHAPTER 14

'Do you normally stalk people?'

There was cold anger in Gwyn's voice as she addressed the man who had just walked into her garden. Her initial impulse, when she had seen exactly who it was coming through the gate, was to slip back round the side of the cottage and away. The house was warded well enough, he could do no mischief there, but the thought had passed in a second. She refused to be intimidated by him. Briefly she considered the secateurs in her hand. Not much of a weapon against a man who stood close to a foot taller than she did, and especially one who had enough power to knock her senseless, but she wasn't exactly defenceless herself. Besides, there were things she could happily do to Marcus Eldritch, for which a pair of secateurs would be a reasonable weapon of choice, albeit these ones were neither as blunt, nor as rusty, as he deserved.

Gwyn was gratified to see her unwanted visitor start at the sound of her voice; he hadn't known she was there. Not surprising, given she was half-hidden in the shadows of an overgrown thicket of honeysuckle and well shielded, but it was satisfying to disconcert the man. He turned, still looking for her, and she stepped onto the path in front of him. For the space of several heartbeats they stood there, the tall man and the slender woman blocking his way, facing off like opponents in some arcane contest. Framed in those improbably long lashes, Eldritch's eyes held the same look of appraisal that had raised Gwyn's hackles a week before, but this time he made no move to conceal it from her. Gwyn stared back at him. Interestingly he looked as though he hadn't slept well the previous night. Under his eyes the flesh was dark, almost bruised-looking, accentuating the angles of his face. Gwyn didn't delude herself that his conscience might have kept him awake, but she wondered what had and whether it had anything to do with his turning up on her doorstep.

'I need to talk to you.'

His voice was as beautiful as she remembered, but Gwyn was in no mood to be swayed by something so simple. Nor was he going to be able to influence her through other means.

'I told you that I don't want to talk to you,' she said, crossing her arms, her face like thunder. She gave him the sort of look she might have turned on one of the cats had it done something particularly disgusting in the middle of her bed, but without any trace of underlying affection. 'And turning up uninvited at someone's house is pretty much stalking, as far as I'm concerned. How did you find out where I live?'

Eldritch took both the stare and the anger surprisingly well, neither retaliating in kind nor trying to charm her with the wry humour he had wielded so lightly at their first meeting. His answer was both direct and honest.

'Rowan told me.'

Her disbelief must have shown on her face because he held up his hands to forestall her denial and added, 'I told her I'd not heard from you so I wanted to send you some flowers to make up for upsetting you last Saturday. She thought it was a lovely idea.'

Gwyn's eyes rolled. *Oh Rowan!* Even having known her for years, sometimes it was hard to believe that her friend could be so gullible. She was a successful business woman, for goodness' sake! Yet Rowan had an appalling tendency to believe that everyone had the same natural inclination to goodness that motivated her. Gwyn could only believe she must have amassed an impressive stock of good karma in a previous life because none of Rowan's misplaced trust ever quite backfired onto her, but it certainly kept her friends on their toes, reining in the more extreme of her altruistic leanings and keeping an eye out for those who would exploit her. Gwyn might have made it clear to Rowan that she wanted nothing to do with Marcus Eldritch or his book, but if said author turned up at the Healing Centre, asking for the opportunity to apologise, Rowan would bend over backwards to help. It was a miracle she hadn't driven him up here herself.

'It's not her fault. I persuaded her.'

The granite and silver voice cut across her thoughts almost as though he could read them.

'You probably didn't need to.' Gwyn muttered, venomously. Then she shook her head, reminding herself who it was who truly deserved her anger. Rowan had simply been being helpful. Irritatingly naïve as well, it was true, but helpful none the less. It was Eldritch's sly manipulation that warranted her disgust.

'Just as you persuaded Aidan to take you to Cwm Broch?'

Gwyn's hand tightened around the secateurs at the thought of what this man had tried to do. Coercing Aidan into going back to the site of John's death! She took a deep breath to steady herself, knowing she could not afford the distraction of anger, not in the presence of someone so powerful. Even so, it was lucky for Marcus Eldritch that he had been nowhere near when Aidan had told her he was going to go back to the chimney stack.

For the barest second she thought she saw a flicker of regret in those dark-lashed eyes.

No, she thought, *if you regret anything it's only that we found you out. I hope the walk home gave you blisters!*

'It's not something I make a habit of.'

There was no defensiveness in his response, nor did he sound as though he was trying to make light of what he had done. It seemed a simple statement of fact.

'Only when it suits you, you mean.'

Eldritch merely shrugged, the saturnine brows raising slightly, acknowledging her point.

'You're unbelievable, you really are. Literally,' she added as the irony of that statement hit her. 'Do you ever tell anyone the truth?'

'Not when doing so might get them killed, or worse, no.'

The bluntness of that statement stopped her, hanging in the air between them.

'That's quite a claim to make.'

Eldritch's lips tightened and there was a touch of irritation in the deep voice, as though the conversation were not progressing quite to his liking. 'We both know it's true.'

Gwyn eyed the tall man thoughtfully. 'Do we?'

'Stop messing around, woman! You know what I am; why I'm here.'

For the first time the façade of affability slipped and Gwyn sensed the dark currents of anger and rage held in check beneath that calm masquerade. She stood her ground. Instead of scaring her, his flash of temper actually made her calmer, that glimpse of seething emotions rendering him more human than the cold, dispassionate creature she had feared him to be. She could understand the violence of rage and pain and the aching void of loss. They were things she could deal with. It was those who were without emotion, who held themselves remote from everything and everyone around them, taking and using without thought or care for the consequences, save only that they got what they wanted; those were the people she feared. And such a one with power; he might be worse than the demon itself.

'Do I?' she countered. Her voice was steady and unflinching, not giving back rage for rage, but refusing to back down. 'In reality I know very little about you. You claim to be an author and yes, your books exist, but you've lied to me, to Rowan, to Aidan. In fact you've probably lied to everyone you've met so far. You have a huge amount of natural power,' there, she had said it, 'more so than just about anyone I've ever known, and you seem to have a fascination with the Black Dog, but also, I think, with demons. So, Marcus Eldritch, that's what I know of you. I can think of several reasons, good and bad, why you might have chosen to come to Llancathan, but as far as knowing for certain...'

She shrugged eloquently, letting the gesture finish the sentence for her. 'And I'm similarly in the dark as to why you've tricked your way into coming to see me this afternoon. Although,' she added with a barbed smile, 'I don't believe for an instant it was to apologise for your behaviour last week.'

Eldritch opened his mouth as though he would speak and then shut it again, visibly reining in whatever comment he had been about to make. Gwyn stayed silent, watching him closely. His face darkened and she could sense the fierce argument raging behind the King of Swords' cold façade. He barely seemed to notice her as that internal battle waged and she wondered what conflicting desires he was trying to balance.

Finally, he turned back to her and she knew that, however reluctantly, he had made his decision. There was a subtle difference in the way he looked at her, nothing she could give voice to, but something had changed. For a second she was reminded of Aidan when he had asked her if her stories of shrieks and spirits were true. She bit back the thought immediately; Aidan would be less than happy to hear he had been compared to this man, but there was that same air of having decided to trust, albeit because it was the only way out of an intolerable situation.

She heard the echoes of Aidan's hesitation in the depths of his voice now.

'I'm here because all Hell is about to break loose and a lot of people are going to get hurt if I don't stop it happening. Unfortunately,' and he glared at her as though what he was about to say was somehow her fault, 'I can't do that without your help.'

That last admission seemed to hurt him. Gwyn wondered when he had last been forced to ask for help. She suspected it was not something that came naturally. She weighed him up, this tall, enigmatic man, with his cold grey eyes and rich, velvety voice, considering what he had said and all that he had not. Finally, she made her own decision.

'I think you'd better come inside so we can talk about your "book".'

Aidan slowed as he approached the turning for Schoolhouse Lane and glanced at his watch. It was half past five now. If he carried straight on he would be in Llancathan in ten minutes and picking up a takeaway soon after. Home, fed and showered by seven, he could easily make it down to the Unicorn to join Matt, Christine and the two trainees who were staying in Llancathan for an extra night. Not that their journeys home were likely to be any easier in the morning, certainly not if the plan that Matt and Christine had been formulating at last night's course meal was anything to go by. Aidan winced at the thought. Martyn and Becky would be heading for Cardiff while Christine herself had to get back to London. The roads south over the Brecon Beacons were wonderful, but not with the sort of hangovers they were likely to be nursing come Sunday morning.

Three weeks ago Aidan would automatically have joined in with whatever post-course revelry his partner and the HR manager had planned. Tonight, however, there was someone else Aidan wanted to catch up with first.

'What do you reckon, girl? Do you think Gwyn would fancy a Chinese tonight?'

Sula's tail thwacked enthusiastically against the passenger door at the sound of his voice. He grinned and reached across to ruffle her ears. 'I think so too. She could do with some real food.'

So that was that. Decision made. He would eat with Gwyn, amuse her with the full details of yesterday's encounter with Marcus Eldritch and still have time to get into Llancathan to join the others at a reasonable hour.

Aidan turned the Land Rover into the narrow lane, driving up past the old stone building, with its tall arched windows and grey slate roof, which had lent its name to the road. Those walls held such a wealth of memories for him, good and bad, for he had attended both infants and junior school there. No children had played in its yard for a long time now. The school had closed in 2001, followed soon after by Caeglas' Post Office and then, two years ago, by the village shop. Now the old school was home to Gwyn's nearest neighbours, Chris and Kathy Edwards. Kathy was out in the garden, raking the first of the autumn leaves from the lawn, which flourished where the infants had once lined up before assembly. She looked round and waved as Aidan drove past.

Gwyn's cottage stood in splendid isolation, half a mile further along, at the top of the lane. Still part of Caeglas, Gwyn's home was officially the furthest point of the village. As a child Aidan had thought it a magical place, out on the edge of the wilderness. 'Swn-y-gwynt' it was called – Sound of the Wind – and it was well named, bearing the brunt of any bad weather sweeping in down the valley. *Nothing good comes from the west.* That was the local saying. Sometimes, when she heard that, Gwyn would rub her hands together and cackle evilly, pretending the saying had been coined because of her. Mostly though she would smile knowingly and say how fortunate it was that she lived there, guarding the village's western approaches; a lone sentinel standing between the village and whatever ill might one day come creeping down from the mountains. Then she would settle down and tell him stories of the Wild Hunt and the shrieks that lived in the bones of the hills and twisted and pulled at the minds of men unlucky enough to encounter them. Driving up the hill now, Aidan found himself wondering how much truth lay beneath Gwyn's stories.

The road widened out slightly in front of Swn-y-gwynt, allowing parking space for two cars. Aidan was pleased to see Gwyn's ancient hatchback was there and he pulled in carefully behind it.

'Stay,' he told Sula. 'I won't be long.'

Gwyn's gardening gloves and secateurs were in the middle of the path and a pile of wilting greenery marked where she had been pruning back the thug of a honeysuckle that was making a concerted attempt to escape from the border and breech the cottage wall, but there was no sign of the gardener herself. *Probably in the kitchen sharing a can of sardines with the cats,* he speculated, but he called out anyway.

His holler raised exactly the response he had been expecting, which was to say none at all, so Aidan stepped over the abandoned gloves and knocked on the front door. When a second, harder knock also elicited no response he tried the handle. Stepping into the tiny lounge he called out, 'Gwyn?'

It felt strange to be standing there on his own, without the sound of Gwyn making tea in the kitchen or moving around upstairs. Aidan had once considered this to be his second home, but now he was aware that he was a guest and, at this very moment, an uninvited one. Not that he thought that Gwyn would mind his being there. He glanced around for some indication as to where she had got to and had to smile as his gaze fell on her desk. As always, it was covered with stacks of paper piled haphazardly on and around her PC. Today a much thumbed copy of *Black's Medical Dictionary* dominated the arrangement, sat on top of a small bundle of scientific journals, with its pages held open by a large chunk of rose quartz while several more were marked with yellow post-it notes. His curiosity getting the better of him, Aidan walked over to take a closer look. Judging by the notes mind-mapped out in Gwyn's spidery scribble, she was researching an article on blood pathologies. For no reason he could name, it pleased him immensely to see she still wrote in shocking green ink.

He looked at the titles of some of the other books littering her desk. Intriguingly there seemed to be a number on folklore and the occult. He picked one up at random and looked at the cover. It bore a picture of a large black crow perched on top of a knotwork roundel and underneath the title *A Celtic Demonology*.

Perhaps Gwyn had been asked for a Halloween-themed article, 'Did Dracula suffer from Porphyria?' or something of that ilk. He put the book down and scanned the rest of the desk.

There were no clues there as to when Gwyn might return, but something else caught Aidan's eye propped beside a multicoloured pot that overflowed with an assortment of pens, rubber bands, rulers and other stationery. Carefully Aidan reached out and lifted it free, his breath catching in his throat. Holding it in both hands, as though it was a precious piece of art rather than an old Polaroid in a plain wooden frame, he stared down at the slightly faded image.

Three faces, suntanned and laughing, each poised with a dripping ice cream cone ready to be licked, stared up at him while, in the background, the pastel quayside houses of Aberaeron marched up the hillside. Aidan swallowed, recalling the thick, buttery taste of the vanilla ice cream, mingling with the coconut smell of suntan lotion. He had been seven that summer and his mother and Gwyn had taken him to stay at a B&B in Aberaeron for a week of the summer holidays. An ice cream on the harbour wall had been the highlight of each afternoon.

It struck him then that, if he had been seven, his mother must have been twenty-eight. Not so much older than he was now. He looked again into his mother's face, seeing how the planes and angles that had been hers were now his own. They had only been hinted at in the tousle-haired boy with his stuck out tongue and freckled nose. His finger traced the sweep of her sun-bleached hair as though he could push it back out of her eyes and for a second his own eyes swam. There were good reasons why no photographs adorned the walls of his own home.

On Gwyn's PC the screensaver morphed into its next cycle,

building endless multicoloured pipes across a black screen, and the flash of movement broke him from his reverie. If her PC was on then Gwyn wouldn't have gone far. She could well have been in the back garden when he arrived and not have heard him. Aidan's stomach growled, reminding him of the reason he had called. He gently returned the frame to its place on the desk and went through to the small kitchen at the back of the house.

'Oh dear God… No!'

Gwyn was not in the back garden. She was slumped at the kitchen table, her head resting on her arms, her hair spilling over the bleached pine like a mass of shadow. For a second Aidan froze in the doorway. The crumpled figure was so still that he hardly dared bring himself to step over to her side, to touch her, for he was sure she was dead. A dozen stories of seemingly healthy people who had been found dead in their homes crashed over him. Then he saw a tendril of her hair stir and realised she was breathing and he took a breath himself, the knot of fear loosening just slightly from around his heart.

'Gwyn? Gwyn!'

Aidan shook her shoulder, gently at first, and then a little harder. 'Come on, Gwyn! Wake up, you're scaring me!'

Perhaps it was the fear in his voice that reached her for her eyelids flickered open and she raised her head slightly, peering up at him blearily as though she were having difficulty focussing.

'Aidan?'

He relaxed further, starting to feel sheepish as he realised she must only have been deeply asleep.

'What are you doing here?'

She straightened slowly, rubbing one hand over her forehead and eyes.

'Oh, do I have a headache,' she complained, circling her head carefully and then twisting it from side to side to loosen off the cramped muscles in her neck. Finally, she looked at him directly, her dark brows drawing down as she frowned. 'Where's Eldritch?'

The question took Aidan by surprise.

'Eldritch? I've no idea.'

Belatedly he realised the implication of her words. 'You mean he was here?' he asked, incredulously. 'Why? What did he want?'

Some of the fear he had just felt transformed instantly into anger. He knew exactly what Eldritch would have wanted – to pump Gwyn for any juicy facts he could include in his book. The man was a ghoul, intent on seeking out personal tragedy and misfortune with an eye for nothing but his own personal gain. 'When I find him I'm going to take that wretched manuscript and shove it—'

'What time is it?' Gwyn's voice was like a guillotine, slicing through his angry tirade.

'Quarter to six.'

Aidan felt obliged to add an explanation as to what he was doing in her kitchen. 'I was on my way to the Dragon Garden for a takeaway and I thought you might like me to get you something.'

His explanation trailed off as Gwyn stiffened perceptibly, dark anger suffusing her face.

'Oh, you stupid, chauvinistic bastard.'

Aidan took a step backwards, hands raised, half placating, half ready to fend off an attack, such was the venom in Gwyn's voice.

'Hey, I was only offering to pick you something up. It's not like I was actually going to buy it for you. Hell, you can even pay half towards the diesel if you're that touchy about it.'

Gwyn looked at him as though he had suggested she focus her writing on 'chick lit' instead of science. After a second she took a deep breath, her nostrils flaring.

'I wasn't referring to you, Aidan,' she said slowly, enunciating each syllable as if to ensure that even the dimmest listener might understand, 'and yes, a takeaway would have been lovely, but I haven't got time for that now. He's gone to find it.'

Ordinarily Aidan would have given short shrift to anyone using that tone on him, but now he found himself wondering whether Gwyn might have suffered some kind of blackout after all. She seemed to think she was making sense, but he was damned if he could understand what she was on about. He propped one hip on the edge of the table and gestured helplessly.

'Who's gone to find what?'

For a moment he thought he was going to get more abuse, but Gwyn seemed to realise that he wasn't being deliberately obtuse.

'Eldritch,' she said. It surprised Aidan to hear exasperation had replaced the note of disgust that would normally accompany that name. 'He's looking for the demon. He's been plotting incidents and sightings on an OS map, trying to work out where it's breaking through so he can go after it. The likeliest place seemed to be over on the far side of the reservoir, up beyond the forestry land, but there wasn't enough of a focus to be sure. We were talking about the easiest way to get up there, but instead of being sensible and agreeing to let me help him, he comes over all gallant, whacks me one and clears off. He's gone up there on his own, I just know he has.'

'Hang on, Gwyn, slow down. I know he's a creepy son of a... but why on earth is he going to go searching for a... a "demon"?'

Aidan baulked at using the word. 'On a Saturday night, out on the hills? And what did he whack you with?'

He stood up. This could explain why Gwyn was acting so oddly.

'Don't bother.' She batted away his attempt to look at her head. 'You won't see a mark on me. He hit me with a Levin bolt – it's pure psychic energy. Same thing I did to you in the Shepherds' only more focussed and he put a lot more power behind it. He did this to me through full shields. Marcus Eldritch isn't a writer, or at least it's not all he is. He's a warlock.'

Gwyn must have seen the blank look on his face because she added, 'A warlock. A sorcerer. A wizard, if you prefer. The name doesn't matter; they're really one and the same.'

'A wizard?' Aidan tried to keep his tone neutral. Gwyn really must have banged her head. 'As in Harry Potter?'

Despite his good intentions the words dripped scepticism.

'No, not as in Harry bloody Potter.'

The look she gave him would have melted the lead from the chapel roof at fifty yards and gone on to scorch the tiles underneath. Aidan winced and did his best to look apologetic. It was a long time since he had seen Gwyn quite so livid and he had forgotten how formidable she could be.

'We're not talking wands and games on broomsticks; we're talking real power, real magic.'

With her blazing green eyes and her cloud of dark hair foaming around her shoulders she looked like an angry cat with its fur all bottle-brushed up, ready to fight. Then, as suddenly as it had arisen, the anger passed and with it, it seemed, the flare of energy that had animated her. She slumped in the chair as though the outburst had left her exhausted, and put her head in her hands.

Wordlessly Aidan fetched a glass of water from the sink and handed it over.

'Thank you.'

She took a sip and then tilted her head back and closed her eyes. Aidan stood there for a moment, looking down at her. Normally pale, Gwyn's skin seemed almost translucent now. Her dark brows were drawn together and the vertical line between them looked as though it had been etched permanently into her skin. He wanted to ask her if she was alright, but he guessed what her reaction would be and another outburst wouldn't help either of them. Uncertain what else to do, he opted for the only practical thing he could think of and put the kettle on. He had a suspicion that it was going to be a long explanation and he figured they could both do with a drink.

CHAPTER 15

'Wizards exist, Aidan.'

Gwyn cradled the teacup in her hands, the saucer balancing forgotten on the arm of her chair. At Aidan's insistence they had decamped to the lounge and she was now sat in what Aidan privately referred to as the 'human' chair, remembering from his first visit that the other armchair was reserved for feline usage. Gwyn fidgeted slightly, tucking her feet up underneath her. Some of the colour had returned to her cheeks, but Aidan fancied she was moving just a little too carefully. One hand kept creeping up to knead the back of her neck, leaving him with the suspicion that she was nursing the mother of all headaches, but he knew better than to ask her about it.

Still, her voice was steady and her tone matter-of-fact when she spoke, so that Aidan found himself putting aside his concern to consider what she was saying. His first instinct had been to treat it with outright disbelief until Gwyn had reminded him, rather pointedly, that not only had he experienced her using power but he was also learning to use it himself. But shielding he felt was one thing. What she had just described was something very different. Besides, when they had spoken before, she had always used the term power. He would have run a mile if she had called what she did magic. But now she was saying that the two were, broadly speaking, the same.

'It's not a name you'll hear many use for themselves; witch, wizard, magician.'

Gwyn's words brought Aidan back to the present. She spoke quietly, almost reflectively. 'Yours isn't an untypical reaction, but perhaps it's better that way. Better to meet with disbelief, even contempt for being soft in the head, than with fear and loathing. "Thou shalt not suffer a witch to live." Did you know it was Winston Churchill who repealed our anti-witchcraft laws? That's not so very long ago.'

She raised her cup from her lap as Kali leapt up and settled herself down, purring loudly. On the windowsill, Yard Away Cat regarded them through slitted green eyes, while Sula lay stretched across the front door, safely away from both cats, her nose on her paws, like a cross between a draft excluder and a drowsing sphinx.

'Given the choice, there are parts of this country that would probably reinstate them tomorrow. There's a lot of God crammed into these mountains, but scratch the surface and the old beliefs aren't so far buried. Closer than some are comfortable with, as you should know. But, whatever you call them, there are people in this world who wield magical power. And I don't mean they can do silly party tricks. What Eldritch intends to do, well, if you have to have a literary metaphor, it's more like Gandalf fighting the Balrog above the Deeps of Moria.'

Her face tightened, but this time Aidan thought it had nothing to do with her headache. His mind helpfully conjured the scene in which Tolkien's wizard had faced the fiery monster from the depths of the earth, although the image that came owed more to Peter Jackson's film trilogy than to his memory of his mother reading the books to him when he was little. There was one thing about Gwyn's chosen metaphor that disturbed him.

'Er, Gwyn, the Balrog almost killed Gandalf. Didn't it?'

Gwyn raised her head, but did not speak. There was no need to. The look in her eyes said all that was necessary.

'Oh.'

For a minute neither of them said anything. The only sound in the room was Kali. *The world might come to an end and that cat would purr through it,* thought Aidan uncharitably. Given what Gwyn had said was happening, she might well get the chance. He shifted unhappily, his feeling of discomfort nothing to do with being perched on the arm of the cat chair.

'But demons, Gwyn, I mean, surely if they existed we'd know about them, wouldn't we?' Aidan's logical twenty-first-century mind wasn't prepared to surrender to this new world order without one final fight. 'There'd be half a dozen cases of people being disembowelled or having their heads ripped off and everyone would say, "Ah, we've got a demon on the loose" and they'd send in a SWAT team of exorcists, or something.'

For a second the corner of Gwyn's mouth turned up in a small, lopsided smile, but it slipped away and her voice was serious as she answered him.

'But we do know about them, Aidan,' she insisted. 'It's just that most people choose to believe it's nothing more than superstitious nonsense. As for demons ripping people limb from limb, well, that might make for good horror films,' she wrinkled her nose, 'if there is such a thing as a good horror film, but demons have far more subtle ways of causing suffering than that. Despair and grief are just as potent a source of pleasure for them as physical pain.

'I'm not saying that demons can't, or won't, hurt you physically,' she added, as though she had guessed from his quizzical look where her words had taken him. 'Because once they've broken through into the Mortal World they certainly can, whether you believe in them or not. But, once they've taken a human host, who's to know that the man running amok with a machete is demon-ridden? Childhood abuse, broken marriage or just another lonely soul gone off the rails; they're all perfectly reasonable explanations, but demons?' The black eyebrows quirked upwards and she shook her head. 'I don't think so. Can you imagine what would have happened if the police had stood up after, say, the Hungerford shootings, and said, "We believe this man was possessed."? There'd be a public outcry.'

Gwyn pushed the dark swags of hair back from her face. Watching her, Aidan did not miss the slight tightening of her lips or the way her hand lingered, rubbing briefly at the nape of her neck, but she returned his stare with innocent green eyes as though she could not read the unvoiced query in his face.

'How do you think Eldritch knew there was a demon starting to manifest here?' she asked. It was a valid enough question even if, as an attempt to keep the conversation away from how she was feeling, it was as subtle as a brick to the head. Or a Levin bolt. Even if Eldritch hadn't meant to hurt Gwyn seriously – and to Aidan's surprise he found he wanted to think that much good of the man – he had made very certain she would be in no state to follow him.

'It wasn't just luck. He has a whole list of what he calls "indicators" that he tracks through an internet news feed. If too many show up in one area, there's a good probability that there's a demon involved.'

Aidan snorted and shook his head, caught somewhere between extreme irritation and grudging admiration of the Englishman's inventiveness. He hadn't quite come to terms with the fact that Eldritch's presence in Llancathan had nothing to do with researching a book. The man hadn't simply been in the right place at the right time... *or should that be the right place at the wrong time?*... he had come here deliberately, because of the demon, which raised another question in Aidan's mind.

'What about you, Gwyn? You know these things exist. You're here at ground zero. Didn't you guess what was happening?'

Aidan wasn't sure what he wanted to hear from her. He felt she should have known – after all, she knew about other supernatural creatures like the shrieks – but at the same time he was reluctant to find out she had kept something like this from him. It seemed that Gwyn was equally torn for she did not answer immediately. She stared down at her cup as though she could find the right words there in the dregs of her tea. Finally, she sighed and raised her head. Though she met his gaze, her eyes were troubled.

'Looking back I realise I should have seen what was happening before I did. I suppose I was like the proverbial frog in boiling water.'

'What?'

The relevance of that particular analogy was lost on Aidan and he made no pretence otherwise. There were times when it was nigh on impossible to follow Gwyn's thought patterns. In a more uncharitable moment Aidan might have said she did it deliberately. This time his outburst met with a raised eyebrow as though the inference should have been clear.

'The frog in boiling water. If you drop a frog into boiling water, it will jump straight out, but if you put it into cold water and then heat it up it doesn't notice and it will swim around quite happily until it cooks.'

Aidan made a face. 'Yuck! You learned some weird things at school.'

Gwyn rolled her eyes. 'We didn't actually do the experiment, Aidan. I'm not sure anybody has ever done it; it's allegorical. The point I'm making is that it's not always easy to see how bad things are when you're right in the middle of them. But yes, to answer your question, I realised what was happening just before Eldritch showed up. What I hadn't figured out at that time was what I could do to stop it. Demons are powerful, Aidan. They're not something to go up against lightly, no matter how powerful you are.'

Aidan heard the concern in her voice and he knew it was not for herself. He felt a surge of irritation.

'But that's what Eldritch has done, isn't it? He thinks he can find where this demon,' again he hesitated slightly over the word, 'is – what do you call it – breaking through?'

'From the Unseen Realm into the Mortal World. Yes.'

'And then what?'

'If he can find where it's happening, he'll try to stop it. It may still be possible to strengthen the boundary so that the demon can no longer reach through to influence this world. If he can do that, he can stop it gaining energy and it won't be able to break through.'

Aidan considered this for a moment. 'Why do I get the feeling that it's not as simple as it sounds?'

Gwyn managed a small laugh. 'That would be your naturally sunny disposition kicking in again.' But the laughter died from her voice as she continued. 'That and the fact that you're right, it's not simple at all. There are two problems. The first is that it will take an enormous amount of energy to seal a breach between the two worlds. Eldritch is good, but I don't know that he's that good, which is why I was going to go with him. I may not command the power I used to, but two people together would stand a better chance of creating a lasting seal.'

'And the second thing?' Aidan prompted when Gwyn seemed reluctant to continue. She looked back at him, worrying her lower lip with her teeth. If Aidan hadn't known better he would have said she was frightened.

'The demon has already managed to create an avatar. That's a manifestation of itself that can function in this world,' she added, knowing the term would mean little to him. 'An avatar extends the area of influence the demon has so it can draw more energy back to itself. Because avatars are part of both worlds they can come and go freely between the Unseen Realm and the Mortal World. Eldritch is going to have to destroy the avatar first or drive it back into the Unseen Realm. He can't seal the breach while it's on this side.'

Aidan scowled. 'Suddenly that doesn't sound quite so simple.'

Gwyn nodded, a small movement, and shut her eyes briefly as though doing so could shut out the reality of what was going on. She looked beaten.

'An avatar can be destroyed in this world, but it takes a lot of power to do so. And, of course, it's not going to just sit there and let you destroy it. Avatars have a physical presence in this world and they're more than capable of defending themselves.

'Ideally you want to destroy the avatar rather than just drive it back into the Unseen Realm. Otherwise – if you can't seal the breach – it will just come through again when it's regenerated and you're back where you started. But really you need someone to anchor it, to stop it leaching away, while you destroy it. Powerful though he is, I don't think Eldritch can do that on his own. The best he can hope for is to hurt it so badly that it has to escape back into the Unseen Realm. But that's going to take so much energy I don't know that he'll be able to seal the breach as well.'

She swallowed and her eyes were bleak as she looked at him. 'That's if the avatar doesn't kill him first.'

Aidan had no answer to that. He sat in silence, perched uncomfortably on the arm of the chair, while he considered Gwyn's words and the undercurrent of emotions that tinged her voice. He supposed he should feel more concerned. While he might not like Marcus Eldritch, if what Gwyn said were true, the man was facing serious danger, but all this talk of demons and avatars, of wizards and magic, it still seemed a little too far-fetched, just a little too distant from reality to be truly frightening. He shifted his weight, leaning back into the wing of the chair. It was ridiculous, here in the twenty-first century, to believe in demons.

And yet... like a scene from an old movie, an image rose up in his mind of those things that had so recently haunted his dreams; the dark, wrinkled snout and the cold, yellow eyes watching him from the shadows, hunger and an otherworldly avarice burning in their sulphurous depths. With the image came the memory of the terror that had reached out from the night, weaving cold tendrils of poison into his waking hours, until fear for his sanity – indeed for his very life – had driven him, in desperation, to seek the help of a woman he had despised. He had no time to question those feelings for other thoughts came to him, rising up on the back of those memories, crowding in on his consciousness; John's casual description of a coal-black dog, the stiffening carcass of a ewe with its throat torn out and the suggestion of movement amongst tumbled stone where there was nothing left alive to move.

Disbelief warred with cold certainty that had nothing to do with logic or the rationalisation of what could or could not be real. An awful suspicion gnawed at Aidan's gut. He licked his lips.

'What form does this avatar take, Gwyn?'

From the look she gave him she must have guessed he already knew the answer. Indeed, he barely heard her reply, the look of sad understanding was all the confirmation he needed.

'I'm sorry, Aidan.'

There was compassion in her voice and regret that this last piece of innocence had been stripped from him. She reached out a hand towards him and he flinched back, not wanting her false comfort.

'You mean…' He could not bring himself to continue, to put into words this thing he had feared most.

'That John was under the demon's influence when he committed suicide. Yes, I believe he was.' In the aching silence, Gwyn's words were as merciless as a surgeon's blade, cutting away all possibility of misunderstanding, yet there was worse to come. 'He wasn't the first, Aidan. There was reference to a Black Dog in Katie Thomas' suicide note and Eldritch turned up a couple of others. Thom Hughes was one of them.'

About to launch into a tirade of angry recriminations, Aidan froze, the idea of other victims like a bucket of iced water flung in his face shocking him out of his anger and grief. For a moment he could not speak.

'Why didn't you tell me?' He felt bewildered, overwhelmed by the implication of what she had said. Gwyn leaned forward and this time he made no move to avoid her. Her fingers were strong and warm against his as she took his hand.

'You asked me about shrieks, Aidan, and I told you the truth. No shriek could make a sane adult harm themselves. But when you described your dreams and you mentioned the Black Dog, I began to realise that something else was at work.'

He could sense the sorrow and yes, regret, behind her words, but she offered the facts as an explanation, not as an excuse. She did not ask his forgiveness for the path she had chosen.

'But that afternoon I wasn't sure and there wasn't anything to be gained by telling you. Fear is a powerful emotion, Aidan. Knowing about the demon would have made you more vulnerable to its influence. I'm sorry, but I wasn't prepared to risk that until you were able to shield yourself properly. Then Eldritch came along.' She shrugged slightly at the way fate had played itself out. 'I knew he was powerful from the moment I met him and it was too much of a coincidence to think that his arrival wasn't in some way connected to the demon, but I didn't know what he was planning. It never occurred to me that he was here to try to stop it.' Under other circumstances her look of exasperation would have been comical. 'I admit I was afraid of what he might do. I felt it was safer for you not to know anything about demons.'

When he made no response, she asked, 'Would it really have made any difference for you to know before now?'

Aidan wanted to say yes; he would rather face the consequences of knowing the truth than be misled for his own safety. Instead he said, 'That's what Eldritch did to you, isn't it? Decided to keep you safe whether you wanted it or not.'

Gwyn did not look pleased at the comparison. In fact, if looks could kill then Aidan reckoned his obituary would have been appearing in the morning papers, probably alongside Marcus Eldritch's, if Gwyn ever caught up with him, but Gwyn had to concede the point. Another thought occurred to him.

'You're worried about him, aren't you?' he asked, incredulously. After all that Eldritch had done, he could scarcely believe it.

'I'm worried that I can't deal with this thing on my own and the one person who could help me is going to get himself killed in a fit of chauvinistic gallantry.' The disgust in her voice almost covered the concern. 'If I thought it would do any good I'd go after him, but it was a wide area we were looking at and he could be anywhere by now.'

'Assuming he can actually read a map that doesn't have street names on it.'

Aidan couldn't help himself. Eldritch might have turned out to be one of the good guys, but he wasn't so ready to change his opinion of the man, even if Gwyn seemed prepared to accept an alliance of convenience.

'Besides, it will be dark soon.' Gwyn sensibly refused to be drawn into a discussion of Eldritch's map-reading capabilities. 'There's more chance of falling over and breaking a leg than of finding him. It kills me to say it, but he's got away with it. The stupid –'

'Wait, what did you say?'

'What? That he's got away with it?'

'No, before that; about breaking a leg.' Aidan was on his feet, a strange, wild look in his eyes. 'This isn't about breaking a leg,' he said, the certainty in his voice suggesting it should be obvious what was happening. 'It's about breaking his neck. I know where he is.'

Now it was Gwyn's turn to look confused at the direction their conversation had taken.

'How? How do you know?'

He chose not to answer her question, focussing instead on what had just become clear to him.

'They're going to drive him towards the Bite.'

He was conscious that Gwyn was watching him closely, her green eyes wary, but wisely she chose not to interrupt him. 'The shrieks. They won't need to get too close, just harry him enough so that he turns their way and not his own.'

Aidan doubted that Eldritch would realise exactly where he was until it was too late. The footing up there was treacherous. Most years laid claim to at least one fall for all that there were warnings and the cliff edge itself was fenced off. Like a cold hand on his shoulder the realisation came over him of exactly how the trap had been laid. Dark clawed shapes pulling up the posts, chittering excitedly as they threw them over the edge of the cliff. Not all the magic in the world was going to save Eldritch from a broken neck if he went over that drop.

'Aidan.' Gwyn's voice snapped him back to the present. 'How do you know this?' she repeated her question. From her tone it was clear she did not consider this sudden knowledge to be a good thing. Aidan gazed at her with a look that was somewhere between wonder and confusion.

'I dreamt it last night,' he said slowly, confusion gaining the upper hand as that fact registered fully.

'Aidan?'

Gwyn had pushed Kali off her lap and was halfway out of her chair before Aidan belatedly realised why the revelation that he had been dreaming so worried her.

'Ah, it's okay, Gwyn,' he said, sitting down hurriedly and trying his best to look normal and unthreatening. After a moment Gwyn returned to her chair. 'I was at Jane's last night. It was the first time I've… er… felt like staying over since the funeral.'

Aidan knew he was blushing and the realisation only made it worse. 'I didn't think about not having your crystal with me.'

That wasn't quite true. There had been the briefest moment, just before he succumbed to sleep, when his mind had wandered to the talisman that normally warded his nights and the fact that it was not beside him. But, lying stretched out in the bed beside Jane, relaxed and sated in the warm aftermath of their love making, it hadn't seemed anything to concern himself with. The recollection of that languid interlude made the blood scald even hotter in his cheeks.

If Gwyn guessed where his thoughts had taken him she had enough tact not to comment. Instead she asked dryly, 'And the dream?'

Aidan frowned. 'To be honest I hadn't given it any thought until now. It seemed like it was just a normal dream. I mean it wasn't scary, it was just, well, weird. I was in a forest and there were shrieks in the trees all around me, dozens of them, on the branches and clinging to the trunks; the place was crawling with them. The strange thing was I could see them. Not just as a glimpse of movement out of the corner of my eye, but really see them.'

He could picture them now, those hunched, compact forms with their grey, leathery skin, sheened all over with a seeping corpse-wight phosphorescence. Their long, hooked claws tore into the wood and their blunt muzzles split open to reveal a multitude of small pointed teeth. Aidan's shoulders hunched in disgust, even the memory of them making his skin crawl. Yet, thinking about it now, that was one of the strangest things about his dream. He looked at Gwyn, wondering if she would understand.

'I could see them, but I wasn't scared of them. They knew I was there, although as far as I could tell they didn't have eyes. I think you're right, they hunt by scent; that somehow they scent our emotions. Anyway, they were chittering and whispering to each other and I had this sense of understanding what they were saying because I was the one who had told them what to do.'

'What had you told them?'

Aidan frowned, running a hand absently through his hair as he struggled with the memory.

'I don't know. But then I was watching them tearing at something. There were masses of them. It didn't make any sense at the time. Now I know what they were doing. They were taking the fence posts out above the Bite.'

He could see that clearly now and he shuddered again at the thought of those small, powerful forms.

'Do you know when this was?' Gwyn prompted him, not letting him lose the thread of his dream.

'It was happening last night, I'm sure of it.' Aidan couldn't have said why he was so certain, but he knew it for a fact. 'But that's another odd thing. It wasn't dark. Or rather I could still see, but the colours were all wrong; it was more like I was seeing things almost in black and white. The perspective was distorted too. It was as though I was seeing things from lower down than normal.'

'Seeing it from a dog's point of view?' Gwyn asked innocently.

'Well, I was going to say a child's, but...' Aidan faltered, his brain catching up with what she had just said. 'Oh no. No, no, no, no, no. No way, Gwyn!'

'It's the only explanation that makes sense, Aidan.'

And the horrible thing was that it did.

'I am not connected with that thing, Gwyn.'

Aidan wrapped his arms protectively around himself and glared at her. He would not even consider the idea.

'I'm not suggesting you are,' Gwyn said placatingly. Somehow she managed a smile, which made Aidan glower even more. Given her reaction when he had announced he knew where Eldritch was, she seemed to be taking this new twist surprisingly calmly, but then she wasn't the one who had developed an inexplicable link to the creature responsible for her best friend's death.

'But something happened last night.' Her tone became thoughtful. 'You were out for a meal, weren't you? How much did you have to drink?'

Aidan regarded her suspiciously.

'A few pints. I was staying at Jane's so neither of us had to drive, but I wasn't drunk if that's what you mean,' he added, slightly prickly. 'I was working this morning and I don't do hangovers on work days.'

'Hmm, but you were relaxed, you didn't have the extra warding from the seal and I'll bet you weren't shielding. Not by the time you went to sleep anyway.'

Gwyn looked at him and raised an eyebrow pointedly. Although she did not say so out loud, her meaning was clear.

'Gwyn…' Aidan warned. He felt his blush rising again. *Damn the woman*, he thought. She was doing this deliberately. The twitch at the corner of Gwyn's lips confirmed his suspicions, but before he could take her to task over it, she continued in a more serious vein.

'Alcohol lowers the resistance to psychic influence. So does taking drugs, although I'm not suggesting you did,' she added, heading off his indignant protest before it could be made. 'I think the fact that you'd had a few drinks, combined with everything else,' the corners of her mouth lifted again, 'meant that, in some way, you linked to the demon, or rather to its avatar, in your dream.'

Gwyn must have known what his reaction would be for she gave a lopsided shrug, a small gesture of defeat, and continued on before he had time to ask the obvious question.

'I have no idea how. It's not something I've ever heard of happening before, but to some extent the how doesn't matter. For the moment we should probably just be grateful that you did because now we know that Eldritch is walking into a whole lot more trouble than he could ever expect.' Even as she spoke she was untucking her feet and pushing herself out of the chair. 'Come on. We have to get up there and find him before he walks off that cliff.'

Aidan, already on his feet and about to suggest the same plan of action, took one look at her and shook his head.

'*We* are not going anywhere,' he said firmly. 'I know where he is, I'll go and find him, but *you* are going to stay right here.'

Though she had done her best to conceal it from him, he hadn't missed the way Gwyn had had to steady herself on the arm of the chair as she stood up. For all she might try to pretend otherwise she was in no state to go anywhere. He said as much and was rewarded with one of her best basilisk glares.

'For God's sake, Gwyn, you can barely stand up straight.'

Gwyn took her hand off the chair. 'I'm fine.'

'No, you're not.'

A small part of Aidan's mind registered amusement at the fact that he should get to play the responsible adult to Gwyn's truculent teenager. He looked down at her, this small, fragile-seeming woman with her talk of fighting demons, suddenly aware that the top of her head was barely level with his chin. The devil in him wanted very much to pat her on the head and tell her to sit down. The part of him that wanted to survive the night told him that it would be a very bad idea indeed. *Perhaps another time...*

'Gwyn,' Aidan tried to sound reasonable. 'If I have to I can carry Eldritch off the hillside on my own, but I can't manage if I have to carry you down as well.'

He looked into the venomous green eyes and felt a stab of relief as he saw he was getting through to her. She looked angry and frustrated, but there was a glimmer of sense there. Gwyn might be many things, but she was not stupid. 'Besides,' he asked seriously, 'who's going to come to the rescue if we both get into trouble?'

Gwyn sighed and her shoulders sagged as the tension drained out of her. She shot Aidan a look too complicated to read as she sat back down again, but all she said was, 'Make damn sure you keep your shields up while you're out there.'

'I will.'

He would, too. Having just argued that he could handle this alone, he was uncomfortably aware that he was no more than a novice in this deadly game. A tendril of fear knotted itself at the base of his spine. He had no real knowledge of what he might have to face once he got up onto the hills. His plan, such as it was, consisted of finding Eldritch, somewhere above the Bite, and convincing him to leave his demon hunting for another day or at the very least warning him of what was happening. What he could do if he encountered the avatar he had no idea. All in all it would be best not to let it sense him in the first place. He could only hope that his shields were good enough to do that.

He was aware that Gwyn was watching him. From the look on her face she shared his concerns. She was also pragmatic enough to know they had no other options. No advice she could give would help him now. He would have to rely on what little he knew and his own instinctive caution. Refusing to go any further with that train of thought, he called Sula to him.

'You're staying here, girl.'

Crouching down he put his hands on either side of that long, domed skull and addressed her in mock stern tones. 'Now don't go bothering the cats or you'll get your nose scratched.'

He rubbed the base of her ears fondly and she gazed up at him with liquid brown eyes.

'Stay,' he cautioned as he straightened up. Sula's eyes followed him as though looking for confirmation that he really was abandoning her here and then she stretched herself out alongside the chair with what sounded so much like a sigh of resignation that Aidan couldn't help but smile.

He stepped over to the door and then turned back to Gwyn, feeling as though he should say something more before he left, but nothing meaningful presented itself. At that moment his stomach growled loudly. Gwyn laughed, the tension broken, and he glared at her and then at the offending piece of his anatomy.

'So much for my dramatic exit. That never happens in the movies.'

'Hang on a moment, Aidan.'

Still smiling, Gwyn got to her feet. This time she did not try to disguise the slight pause as she found her balance or the fact that she kept one hand on the wall to steady herself as she rummaged in the chaos of papers and books on her desk. 'Here we are.'

How she found anything on that desk was beyond Aidan, but when she turned back to him she was triumphantly brandishing the tail end of a bag of chocolate-coated raisins. Knowing Gwyn, it was the remains of her lunch. He raised an eyebrow.

'And you nag me about my eating habits?'

Gwyn gave him a withering glance. 'It's fruit.'

She wrapped an elastic band around the bag and tossed it over to him and Aidan plucked it from the air without thinking.

Unbidden he remembered the games she had devised and the hours she had spent throwing things for him to catch, trying to rebuild his coordination after that catastrophic fall down the school stairs. Perhaps the same thought had occurred to Gwyn for she grinned at him, the unguarded gesture rewriting the lines of her face and wiping years from her.

'Nice catch, Brightboy.'

The raisins dropped unnoticed from Aidan's hand.

A terrible silence fell over the room. Neither of them moved. Then, in a small voice, Gwyn said, 'Aidan, I'm sorry. I didn't mean that.'

It occurred to him that she must be more shaken than he had realised to make a slip like that. With a curious sense of detachment he registered the shocked white of her face and the slow flush of mortification staining her cheeks. To look at her you would think the world was about to end. Aidan wondered if it just might. Like a fairytale's long forgotten curse, invoked by accident, hearing the sound of that name again, after nine years unspoken, seemed sufficient to bring the world to its knees. Nine years! It was half a lifetime. He had been, almost literally, a different person then.

On the other side of the room, Gwyn looked as though she would give anything for the last thirty seconds not to have happened. She stared at him, green eyes wide with horror at what she had just said, waiting for him to say or do something. She herself seemed frozen. It was as though the gulf of the last nine years had reopened at her feet and she feared to make the slightest movement, lest their fragile reconciliation be swallowed up by it and destroyed. Mechanically Aidan bent and picked up the bag of raisins, his eyes never leaving Gwyn's as he shoved them into his pocket. He swallowed uncertainly, not sure if he could reach out across that gulf between them, not quite sure if he wanted to. He started to speak and then stopped.

After long seconds of silence he said, 'Look after Sula for me, Gwyn. I'm going to bring Gandalf back.'

And he turned and fled into the gathering dusk.

CHAPTER 16

Brightboy. The name followed him as he drove, ringing in his head. The cattle grids along the road through Cwm Biga shook the Land Rover on its springs, rattling his teeth, for Aidan made no attempt to slow down for them, but did nothing to dislodge the circling thoughts from his mind. Dimly he knew he should be thinking of the path up through the forestry plantation, of the best place to leave it to strike up the side of the Bite to give him the most chance of intercepting Eldritch, but every time he tried to focus, to think of what lay ahead of him, his mind spiralled back to the cold, dark nugget of that name. Brightboy.

He no longer remembered how the nickname had come about. It was just one of those odd pet names that children, like animals, seem to acquire and eventually grow out of. It was not something that should have been so overloaded with emotions. Except that it had been the last thing his mother had said to him. The last word she had spoken to anyone as she slipped into her final morphine-shrouded sleep.

There had been little left of Anne Morgan by that time. Fourteen months of cancer had spared her little. First, it had taken her breasts, then her bowel, before spreading throughout her body, eating her away from the inside. Yet she had fought it to the last. Through the first skirmishes of surgery and the tortuous slog of chemotherapy, the brittle three-month armistice, when everyone had held their breath and dared to hope that the cancer might have been beaten, followed by the heartbreaking eight-month slide into that final defeat. Every inch of the way she had fought it. And Aidan and Gwyn had been there beside her all the way.

While the doctors had wielded all the conventional weapons in their arsenal, Gwyn had sat for hours by Anne's bedside channelling healing energies into her friend's increasingly frail body. She had encouraged Aidan to do the same and, although he had never been able to sense the powers she said were there, he had believed her when she said that together they could make a difference. After all, Gwyn was special. Hadn't she helped him after his accident? If she said that they could help his mother then he knew it was true. Even when the doctors had shaken their heads and talked in terms of 'palliative care only', he had not given up that trust, knowing that the miracle would come if only he could pour sufficient energy into that healing. Gwyn would never lie to him. Oh, how wrong he had been. Wrong to trust and wrong to hope, for, in the end, it had all been for nothing.

'Gwyn will take care of you, love.'

His mother had been sliding fast into sleep that could be nothing but a merciful release for her, yet, even though he was aware of that, Aidan had fought to keep her with him.

'I don't want her to take care of me. I want you.'

He held fast to his mother's hand, feeling the bones like so many brittle sticks beneath the greying parchment of her skin. He had made no attempt to hide the tears that had slid down his face, unable to be brave in the face of such an awful loss. The twig-like fingers moved fractionally beneath his own. Faint as the scratching of leaves on the window, his mother's voice had barely had the strength to carry to him.

'I can't, love… I'm so sorry.'

For a second she struggled, the effort of speaking almost overwhelming her. 'Be strong for me… Brightboy.'

Eighty-seven minutes later, with her son and her best friend holding her hands, Anne Morgan slipped free of the earth. Her chest fell as the breath left her body in one final exhalation. It did not rise again. For a long moment there was no movement in the little bedroom, Aidan and Gwyn both frozen, waiting, and then, still holding her friend's hand, Gwyn had leant over and kissed her forehead. As she straightened up, she looked across the bed at the gangly teenage boy who was now her ward.

'She's at peace now, Brightboy. It's just you and me from now on.'

Aidan had sprung up, flinging his mother's lifeless hand from him as though by doing so he could reject everything that had just happened.

'Don't you call me that!' he shouted, unheeding of the look of shock on Gwyn's face. 'Don't you ever call me that again. I'm not Brightboy. I'm not Dai. I'm Aidan,' and he had run from the room.

That had been the last time he had shown any emotion to Gwyn, the last time he had spoken to her at all, except in response to a direct question. For the next two and a half years Gwyn had been his legal guardian and, in all that time, he had never forgiven her. She was accountable not only for her failure to heal his mother but for all the misplaced faith that he had held in her. Every time he thought of his mother's death he was reminded of the hours he had spent copying Gwyn, blindly willing life into that failing body. How stupid he had been. It was not a mistake he would make a second time. Gwyn had tried her best to reach out to him and then, when every attempt to do so was rebuffed, she had given him space to grieve and heal in his own time. His response had been to use that space to build the wall between them ever higher until university had given him the chance to escape for good.

The memory swirled around him as he drove, called back by Gwyn's unthinking use of that old nickname. It nagged at him like toothache and, just like a bad tooth, now the awareness of it had been reawakened, he couldn't help prodding at it to see if it still hurt. There was no question that it did, but once he was over the queasy sense of displacement the initial shock had given him, Aidan was surprised to find that the wave of grief he had been expecting to crash over him did not materialise. It seemed impossible that it could be such an anticlimax so he kept poking at the memory, unwilling to leave it alone until he had managed to unlock the emotional maelstrom he knew was waiting for him. But, for all his very real regret that he had been too caught up in his own loss to tell his mother how much he loved her, the raw emotional charge that scene had carried through the years had somehow faded. He kept running back over the memory, each time waiting for the pain to hit him. When, to his intense surprise, he finally realised that it wasn't going to, he no longer knew what to think.

By the time Aidan had climbed out of the managed plantations of the Hafren Forest nature reserve, leaving behind the woodchip-surfaced hiking trails and the weathered, silvery-grey picnic benches, and onto the steeper slopes that were the property of the local Water Authority, the last lingering traces of light had faded from the western sky and the cindery dusk had turned to full dark.

Ten miles away the friendly warmth of Llancathan's street lights might spill out over the lower Hafren valley, but here it was dark enough so that even the Milky Way was visible, standing out like a dusting of powder across the night.

Aidan allowed himself a brief moment to drink in the splendour of that sight. He could scarcely have asked for better conditions to be out on the hills. Though the trees here were old and densely packed, the slopes around the Bite being too steep for frequent felling, sufficient moonlight filtered through to the forest floor for him to be able to pick his way through without using a torch. For that Aidan was very grateful, for he had no wish to draw any additional attention to his presence. Before he abandoned the Land Rover at the end of the rutted forestry track, he had sat for a minute as Gwyn had taught him, calming his mind until he could find that still, quiet place where he could gather his shields around him. He had wondered at first if he could bring himself to follow Gwyn's teaching, confronted as he was with the renewed memory of her fallibility. He had thought about it for some time, sitting in the car, conscious that the sky above him was darkening through dove grey to lilac and then to the colour of ash, the light leaching away with the coming of night, but in the end he had made a conscious decision to do so. Part of that decision had been the realisation that he had little choice and yet, while he had never been able to feel the healing energy she swore was there, he did at least feel something when he shielded, even if he could not yet lay claim to understanding it. So, with that in mind, he had focussed his thoughts and his breathing until he could feel the soft grittiness of sand underfoot, could draw the chill, cold air of that other place down into his lungs, the slightly musty, ancient scent of it tickling the back of his nose as he

211

wrapped the image of those encircling wings around him and hoped to God – and anyone else who was listening – that they would see him safe through the night.

Aidan would have liked to have been able to question his newfound acceptance of the world of demons, to treat it all as a joke or a scary story for Halloween, but out here alone, in the dark stillness of the forest, he was distinctly less inclined to do so. Here he had stepped beyond the reach of logic and the innocent belief that the world was ordered by science and was well understood. He had crossed into the realm of belief and primitive fear and nothing would convince him now that what he had seen in his dreams did not exist. So he skirted the areas where the shadows lay thickest and trod carefully, as though he were out stalking badgers in the woods above Swn-y-gwynt, frequently stopping to listen, though he could not have said what it was that he listened for. Yet the further into the woods he went the clearer one thing became: the normal sounds of the nocturnal wood were noticeable by their absence and he had little hope that it was his presence that had silenced them. Somewhere in the dark soaked forest, evil was abroad. And he had to find Eldritch before it did.

Even now Aidan was in two minds about Eldritch. For all Gwyn had said they were going to need his help, Aidan wasn't sure it was help they could trust. As he worked his way between the trees, scrambling up the steepening hillside, he weighed up what he knew of the Englishman and the picture he came up with wasn't particularly attractive. He couldn't quite bring himself to forgive the practised deception or the powerful manipulation involved in trying to get him to return to the scene of John's death, even if he had outfoxed Eldritch on that one. Gwyn said it was because Eldritch had been trying to track the avatar, but to

Aidan's mind that did not excuse the way he had gone about trying to get the information. Nor was he about to forgive what Eldritch had done to Gwyn. She might believe that he had done it out of some misguided sense of chivalry, and Aidan had to admit that it was probably the only way the wizard – he scowled even as he thought that word – could have stopped her accompanying him on his demon-slaying expedition, but it still made him angry to think of the casual attack and how vulnerable it had left her.

Aidan paused in the darkness to catch his breath, standing close against the trunk of an old pine so that his own shape blended with that of the tree. He was above the Bite now and beyond him the trees thinned out into one of the odd clearings that peppered these woods. For a dozen yards in front of him moonlight picked out the desiccated stems of bracken and rosebay willow herb, edging their leaves with icy white light. Looking out at that floodlit arena, Aidan pressed himself a little closer into the shelter of the pine's trunk. The bark was rough under his fingertips and the resiny sweetness of it filled his nose, pungent and familiar as his own name. Yet the scent held no powers to soothe him tonight. He was conscious of his heart thudding against the wall of his chest, even as his breathing slowed and steadied, and he knew it wasn't just the fast climb that had set it beating so wildly. Ever since he had crossed onto the rump of hillside that ended in the Bite he had felt it. The edge of stillness and fear that had been missing from his dream was all around him in these darkened stands of pine. Hidden behind his shields he could not feel their individual presences, but he knew, as surely as he knew the scent of pine, that not far away there were shrieks, clotting in the branches, waiting and watching and that somewhere beyond them, further still, a far more ancient evil brooded. Aidan's skin prickled and he felt a sudden urge to glance over his shoulder to ensure that nothing was creeping up behind him. He fought the instinct down, knowing that it was ridiculous, for he would not be able to see anything. Besides, he also knew that it was in front of him that the worst danger lay.

He shifted the straps of his rucksack, felt the cold of sweat drying along his back and tried to convince himself he was letting his imagination get the better of him. *You're just being paranoid,* he reasoned, but he could not ignore the little voice that whispered back, *Just because you're paranoid it doesn't mean there's nothing out there.* At some level, deeper than logic or conscious thought, he knew there was good reason to be afraid.

I shouldn't be doing this. I teach outdoor skills and personal development. The only demons I'm qualified to deal with are the ones in people's minds that make them afraid of heights or enclosed spaces! But Gwyn would have been pushed to walk as far as her garden gate, let alone go clambering around in the dark on some of the steepest hills in mid-Wales, and there was no one else. Aidan sighed and told his mental voice to take a hike. Whether he liked it or not he was here. The sooner he found Eldritch the sooner he could get off this godforsaken mountain and go home.

He pushed himself upright, but, even as he started to step out from under the pine's branches, he froze as the sound of movement came to him from the far side of the clearing. Immediately he pulled back into the safety of the shadows. It was a habit he retained from those long ago nights when Gwyn had taken him to watch the nocturnal denizens of these woodlands, like the almost subliminal awareness of the wind and of moving to keep it on his face so no telltale trace of his scent would reach his quarry. But it was no badger or fox coming towards him now.

For some time he had been listening for the whispered almost-sound of a man slipping from shade to shadow, for he guessed that Eldritch, for all his lanky height, could move almost soundlessly when he wanted. What he heard now was not the sound of a man trying to move quietly through the woods. The noise was uneven, the rhythm broken and halting; slurred movement, then silence, then movement again, but with no attempt at concealment. Whatever was making that noise, it did not care if anything heard it coming.

And whatever it was, it was drawing closer. Aidan shrank back as far as he could into the concealment of the pine until he was jammed up against the trunk. It crossed his mind to be grateful that the muted colours he was wearing would be all but invisible in the darkness. If he did nothing to draw attention to himself, if his shields really did cloak his presence from those that hunted by otherworldly senses, there was a chance that he would go unnoticed.

There's no one here but us chickens, he whispered in his mind, forcing himself not to focus on the approaching *thing* lest the act of doing so should somehow alert it to his presence, slowing his breath to the merest murmur and hoping that the frantic pounding of his heart was audible only to himself. Could the red scalding heat of the blood in his veins give him away or the acid notes of adrenalin that strung his nerves like harp strings? He did not know, but he knew he would find out soon enough. The far side of the clearing was a patchwork of shadows and opaline moonlight. Whatever was coming, it would have to cross that space to reach him.

He caught the flicker of movement from the corner of his eye. There was a change in the shadows under the far trees as something

215

moved and then paused. Aidan fought the urge to turn his head and look directly at it, knowing he would lose its shape as soon as he did so, knowing also that the movement might give his presence away. Something was there, in the darkness; waiting, judging. Aidan could almost feel the shifting net of senses probing the air around him, sliding over him, finding nothing. Perhaps as tall as a tall man, it was difficult to make out the shape from the greater darkness. There was a pale blur where the face would be, if face it had, but the shape was wrong for it to be human. It was broken up, irregular, a spattering of white amongst glittering darkness. In the shelter of the pines, Aidan held his breath as the fragments of shadow came together and a figure stepped forward into the moonlight.

But the shape that emerged from the shadows was no monster. It was Eldritch. Or at least it was someone wearing Eldritch's clothes. The charcoal grey jacket and jeans were the only things immediately recognisable about the man. A diagonal spatter of some dark, viscous fluid ran from forehead to jaw, bisecting his face like some ancient tribal marking, breaking its angular planes into random patterns of shadow. Against that mask what little of his skin that remained unbranded seemed drained of all colour, bleached to bone whiteness by the moonlight, while around his face tendrils of dark hair hung in long rat tails, pointy with sweat or gore.

Aidan's breath caught in his throat. Even the man's posture had changed. Aidan was sure Eldritch was standing slightly crooked, more so than the uneven hillside warranted, his right arm tucked protectively into his body as though he was favouring either it or his side. But it was when Eldritch moved again, stepping forward across the moonlit scrub of bracken and willow herb that Aidan really knew there was something wrong. Eldritch moved as though something had broken deep within him, as

216

though nothing but grim determination was keeping him on his feet. Something had happened, something that tangled like lead around the marrow of his bones, sucking the strength from him until each step was a battle between plain stubbornness and the desire to sink to the ground and never move again. Looking at him now, Aidan wondered if the shrieks might not have to throw Eldritch off the Bite; he seemed barely capable of walking the last hundred or so yards on his own.

Even as he thought that, Eldritch stumbled and Aidan heard the sharp gasp of his breath as he caught himself on the rough ground and saw the way he clutched for a second at his shoulder. He was stepping out into the clearing to help before reason could catch up and remind him that Eldritch had no idea he was there. Surprising him probably wasn't a great idea.

For all his appearance of a man on the verge of collapse, Eldritch's reflexes were preternaturally fast. Before Aidan had taken a full step Eldritch had whirled to face him, grey eyes wild and fey. The arm he had been cradling came up and, for a second, Aidan thought he could see a pale blue haze forming round the outstretched fingers, the air crackling like a storm before a lightning strike.

He froze, some primitive instinct telling him that no matter how fast he moved it wouldn't be fast enough.

'Eldritch! No!'

For a moment he knew that the other man hadn't heard him, that he was going to die where he stood. Then the madness faded from the wolf-grey eyes and Eldritch stared at him as though seeing him for the first time. Slowly the outstretched hand lowered, the foxfire glow already gone from around the fingers as though it had been nothing more than a trick of the moonlight. For a moment

Aidan couldn't move. His mind was stalled somewhere between the thought that what he had just seen was impossible and the absolute certainty that he had been milliseconds from death. His knees loosened and he put a hand out to steady himself as his head swam. When he looked up again Eldritch was still staring at him. The grey gaze raked him like an almost physical touch.

'Aidan.'

Eldritch's eyes were as cold and as hard as sea ice among the gore splotches that mottled his face. A hard, brittle anger edged his voice. 'You stupid fool! I could have killed you.'

Aidan had the feeling the other man was asking himself why he hadn't. That perhaps, just for a second, it might have seemed simpler if he had. 'What in God's name are you doing here?'

There was an expression close to hatred in the glittering eyes and Aidan felt his own temper rising, reacting to the anger in the other man's voice. He hadn't expected to be greeted like a long lost friend, not after their confrontation beneath the Clywedog dam, but, even so, there was no reason for hatred. Given the state Eldritch seemed to be in, Aidan would have thought he would be relieved to see him.

'I came up here to help you.' His voice was quiet, but anyone who knew him would have recognised the danger signs and backed off. He stepped fully clear of the pines, but made no attempt to close with Eldritch. Instead he stood eyeing him up, squared off as though they were about to fight. Aidan's voice was as hard as Eldritch's as he continued. 'Gwyn seems to think you're worth helping though, for the life of me, I can't think why. Not after what you did to her.'

The image of Gwyn's slumped form came back to him,

218

surprising him with the surge of emotion that came with it. He glared at Eldritch, letting his eyes convey the full force of those feelings. Anger met anger under the dark trees.

'I didn't do her any harm.'

The negating gesture was cut short as a spasm of pain crossed Eldritch's face and, for a moment, he clutched at his shoulder again as though doing so could force the pain away. Aidan was too angry to care.

'I found her unconscious!'

His gut clenched as the words brought back that first rush of fear and the sudden overwhelming sense of helplessness he had felt as he stood in the kitchen doorway. It was a timely reminder that he could not trust this man.

'I hit her with a Levin bolt. She wasn't in any danger.'

Aidan bridled at the dismissive tone in Eldritch's voice.

'She was still unconscious and you just left her there. Anything could have happened to her.'

'I warded the door. No one was going to be able to get in there and hurt her.'

'I got in,' Aidan pointed out, unconvinced.

Eldritch rolled his eyes.

'And what exactly did you want?'

Aidan glowered.

'I was going to offer to buy her a takeaway.'

'Hah! Well that's hardly evil intent, is it? Not unless she's allergic to monosodium glutamate. You may not like it, but she was a lot safer there than if she'd come up here with me. A lot safer than you are now.'

With his left hand he pushed the sticky rat tails of hair back from his face.

'Why couldn't you just mind your own business and stay out of it?'

A curious weariness had crept into his voice; a suggestion that he had been here before and had suffered the consequences. Aidan chose to ignore it as he had ignored the way Eldritch's earlier gesture had made his face tighten in pain.

'In case you hadn't noticed, John was a close friend of mine. Or didn't your research mention that? If this Black Dog, this demon, whatever it is, was responsible for his death then I'm going to help track it down and get rid of it. Whatever it takes.'

He wasn't sure what made him say it, but he added, 'You can't just swan in here from London, asking all your questions, tricking people into helping you, and then expect everyone to just move out of your way. The English haven't ruled here for a long time, you know. This is a Welsh demon. What makes you think it's your job to tackle it?'

Incredibly Eldritch made a noise that, under other circumstances, might have been a laugh.

'This isn't the Loch Ness Monster that we're dealing with. It's not a bloody tourist attraction. Believe me, you're going to need all the help you can get. Do you think you're the only one who's lost someone they loved?' Eldritch didn't wait for an answer. 'You don't have any idea what you're facing here. If you knew what you were getting involved in you'd run a mile.'

'Well maybe it's a good job I don't know,' Aidan countered. 'But Gwyn seems to and she's not running.'

Eldritch snorted. 'She should be. As a healer she should know how vulnerable she is. How vulnerable you are.'

His eyes bored into Aidan's as though searching for some

understanding of the danger they were facing. Disgusted, he half-turned away. 'I can't believe she sent you after me.'

'She didn't. She was going to come herself, but she wasn't in any fit state to after what you did to her, so I said I'd come. It was the only way I could get her to stay at home.'

'And she just let you?'

This time it was Aidan's turn to laugh.

'How was she going to stop me? Besides, I knew where you were going to be.'

Some of his anger subsided as he remembered the strangeness of his dream and his horror at finding out that his mind had somehow been linked to the avatar. He paused, remembering also that Eldritch had come up here to face that evil. The two of them were meant to be on the same side.

'I had a dream last night.'

Aidan scuffed at the carpet of pine needles with the toe of his boot, avoiding meeting Eldritch's eye as he waited for the ridicule he felt sure would come. Yet Eldritch said nothing. Aidan was unsure whether to take that silence as encouragement or disbelief, but he ploughed on before he lost his nerve.

'By recent standards it was nothing to write home about.'

His mouth twitched in self-mockery, but the humour came nowhere near reaching his eyes.

'In fact, I didn't even remember it until Gwyn told me you'd been talking of coming up here. Then it came back to me.'

He shivered. The images of towering trees and the dark chittering shapes that flitted amongst them were uncomfortably similar to the reality of the night-shrouded slopes where he now stood. But running over the top of that memory was the sound

221

of Gwyn's voice, her teasing carefully judged, he realised now, to counter his horror. He fingered the memory like a talisman.

'I didn't come up here just to help you. I came up here to save your life.'

He held up a hand to forestall Eldritch's angry retort and, for once, the other man subsided. 'You probably haven't realised, but the shrieks have been herding you, snapping at you, driving you. Not too much, not so you'd notice, but just enough to make it easier for you to come this way and think you were avoiding them, rather than force you and maybe make you decide you'd stand and fight.'

Aidan glanced at Eldritch, watching him weighing this up, fitting it with what had happened to him that night and he knew he was right. There was, however, one final piece of evidence he could bring.

'Where were you heading for?'

'I was going back to my car.'

'Which is where?'

'I left it at the red kite feeding point.'

Aidan winced. 'That's on the other side of the mountain. You're going in almost completely the wrong direction.'

'That's impossible.'

The certainty in Eldritch's voice was impressive for someone so well and truly off track.

'Okay, so which way's west, then?' Aidan challenged.

An expression of irritation crossed Eldritch's face. He started to turn and then stopped. As he swung back, Aidan caught the momentary look of confusion in those grey eyes. But instead of looking at the sky, as Aidan would have done on such a clear night, or even a compass, Eldritch closed his eyes. Once again Aidan had the sensation of a net of senses being cast out over the hillside. When Eldritch opened his eyes again he said nothing, but Aidan could sense his shock. He already knew that he was right. The direction Eldritch had been about to point to was a good ten degrees out. More than enough to get anyone very lost indeed or, given the nature of the terrain, very dead.

'So the shrieks have been having their fun with me,' Eldritch conceded, his tone irritated but unrepentant. 'So what? Saving me a long walk home hardly constitutes saving my life. Besides, I seem to recall it was you who felt I was in need of some extra exercise.'

Aidan ignored the dig. There was too much at stake to revisit that now.

'The walk wasn't going to be much longer. The shrieks weren't just trying to get you lost; they were actively driving you. You don't know these hills, but there's a cliff just the other side of these trees. Another hundred yards or so and you'd have walked right off it before you even knew it was there.

'It's known locally as the Bite,' he continued. 'It used to be that every few years there'd be someone killed trying to climb it. The rock face isn't very stable; it makes things dodgy if you're not roped on.'

He didn't add that that was half the attraction of tackling such an ascent as a free climb.

'But, even after they stopped the climbers, there would always be someone who wanted to look over from the top and got too close to the edge. Awful slippy, slate is, when it's wet, and the stuff around here seems to hold water. Eventually the council got frightened of someone suing them or maybe they just got tired of fishing the bodies out of the res, but they put up a fence and warning signs to keep everyone off this part of the hill.'

'So if it's fenced off, don't you think I might have noticed?'

Eldritch didn't need to add *I'm not that stupid*; the comment was clear from his voice. Aidan gritted his teeth. If Marcus Eldritch didn't change his attitude he might join the shrieks in throwing him off the Bite. Throttling down his irritation, he said carefully, 'That's what I'm trying to tell you. The fence isn't there anymore. The shrieks pulled it down last night. That's what I saw in my dream.'

Eldritch digested this in silence, his face stony. After a moment he said, 'Shrieks don't normally work together like that.'

The comment was delivered as a fact but not as though he was contradicting Aidan. Aidan took a deep breath and let go of his irritation.

'That was the scariest part. They were being organised by the avatar.'

'And you saw this in your dream?'

Incredibly there was still no note of scepticism in Eldritch's voice. Aidan nodded unhappily. Eldritch glanced at the forest around them and swore softly.

'You didn't manage to destroy it, did you? The avatar, I mean.'

There was no malice in the question. Earlier Aidan might have taken a certain satisfaction in Eldritch's failure, he would certainly have berated him for his arrogance in refusing Gwyn's help, but now he held his tongue. There was no need to point out that their lives might hang in the balance because of that error of judgement; Eldritch must have known that better than he did. No wonder the man had been less than happy to see him.

Eldritch did not answer immediately. It seemed he might have developed Gwyn's habit of sorting words before speaking.

'I thought I had. I hurt it badly enough, but I couldn't hold it to finish it off.'

Eldritch's voice was soft, but there was no hint of excuse in his words. He stood there, a tall but somehow insubstantial figure, fading into the shadows in his dark jacket, the spatters across his face like camouflage. Even the restless glitter of his eyes was still. 'It faded back across the boundary before I could stop it.'

He pushed the ratty strands of hair back from his face again. His encounter with the avatar presumably explained the gore and his earlier air of exhaustion. He seemed to have overcome that, but Aidan wondered just how much further Eldritch was capable of pushing himself. 'If it's still capable of controlling the shrieks, by now it will know that they've failed,' Eldritch continued, his tone pensive, like a man thinking out loud. His gaze came back to Aidan and now there was a grim set to those storm cloud eyes. 'I'm worried about the avatar. I hurt it, I know I did, but there are ways the demon could get more power, power it can then pour into the avatar to regenerate it…'

His voice trailed off and Aidan could see him running through those different scenarios in his head. After a moment he visibly pulled his attention back, but Aidan did not miss the echo of old pain in his eyes and he knew he did not want to be privy to those thoughts. 'Let's just say it's not a theory I want to put to the test tonight.' He straightened imperceptibly. 'We need to get out of here.'

Even as Eldritch spoke, a gust of cold wind shook the trees. Aidan glanced up and cursed under his breath. Where minutes earlier the moon had been standing clear in a cloudless sky, now a boiling mass of cloud was streaming in. At some point since he had met Eldritch the wind had changed, swinging round to the west. *Nothing good comes from the west…* Even in the clearing it was becoming noticeably darker as the first clouds pushed in front of

225

the moon. Amongst the trees it was worse, the shadows clotting together, thick and impenetrable. Aidan frowned and unhitched his rucksack, pulling his torch from the side pocket. After a second's thought he dragged out his jacket as well, just as the first spatter of icy rain reached him. Shrugging it on, he noticed Eldritch had turned up the collar of his coat and it crossed his mind to wonder just how waterproof that grey wool had proven to be. Chances were he was in for another soaking tonight.

Aidan checked the fastenings on his rucksack uneasily. He had the feeling that the situation was beginning to slip away from them, that the good luck that had held so far was fast running out, like grains of sand through an hourglass. They weren't that far from safety, but there was rough ground to be covered and a simple slip on wet rock or a misstep in the dark could prove as lethal as the demon. He glanced at Eldritch and wondered again just how close to the edge of his endurance the other man was. In the torchlight his face was ghastly, the contrast between the pallor of his skin and the crusted black gore even more pronounced. Gwyn had said that tackling the avatar would be dangerous and when Eldritch had first emerged from the shadows he had certainly looked like he had been in a fight. He had been in pain too, though he had moved fast enough when he needed to, but tonight was not a night for taking chances. Unfortunately, Aidan had a feeling that Marcus Eldritch subscribed to the 'leave me alone, it's just a scratch' school of over-zealous independence. *Ah, well.* Aidan took a deep breath and leapt in.

'You may have hurt the avatar, but how much damage did it manage to do to you?'

There was no change in Eldritch's expression, but, watching for it, Aidan did not miss the slight stiffening of his shoulders. Even so, the grey eyes were level and direct as Eldritch answered him.

'Fortunately, it didn't.'

Aidan snorted.

'Don't give me that crap. Every time you move your arm you wince. What did it do to you?'

Eldritch's eyes glittered angrily.

'We don't have time for this,' he warned.

'I know we don't,' Aidan agreed sweetly. 'So tell me what's wrong and we won't waste any more time arguing over it.'

Eldritch said nothing, but his lips compressed into a tight, thin line, the muscles along his jaw clenching. He looked furious and for a second Aidan thought he was going to turn on him for the man's whole body tensed. As he prepared to fling himself to one side it occurred to him that a fight would suit the demon's purposes just as well as having the avatar destroy them and he wondered if it were only the shrieks that were being manipulated that night. Perhaps the same thought occurred to Eldritch for in that moment he sighed and the tension drained from him. With barely concealed ill grace he addressed Aidan.

'It wasn't the avatar. I slipped and fell coming down the slope back there.'

A small nod of his head indicated the hillside behind him. Aidan looked at him dubiously although it would explain the wet smears of mud on his jacket and over the knees of his jeans.

'I jarred my arm trying to catch myself. From the feel of things I've pulled a muscle. Stupid of me,' he added, disgust evident in his voice. 'And yes, it hurts, but it's hardly life-threatening. I certainly don't need healing, if that's what you're thinking.'

The casual assumption went through Aidan like a knife.

'I'm not a healer,' he ground out, his voice sounding strange in his ears. Before Eldritch could make any comment he added hastily, 'I was thinking basic first aid. I can do without you keeling over on me halfway down the hill.'

Eldritch shrugged one-sidedly.

'I've been better,' he admitted. 'But I'm just tired. I'll live.'

Aidan eyed him sceptically, but held his tongue, suddenly disinclined to push the matter further. Instead he resolved to keep a close eye on Eldritch. Another gust of wind blew sleety rain across the clearing.

'Come on then, before the weather really closes in.'

But Eldritch was no longer listening. He was looking around him, turning his head like a dog questing for scent.

'What…'

Aidan's question died on his lips. He could feel it too; the creeping cold that had nothing to do with the weather. All the hairs on the back of his neck stood on end and for a moment he thought the wind carried an odd, acrid scent, like overheated metal. He looked at Eldritch, eyes wide, wanting reassurance but expecting none. Eldritch shook his head. There was an animal wariness about him, but Aidan realised he wasn't braced for an immediate attack.

'My car's nearest, but it's still going to take us an hour to get down there.'

'We don't have that long.'

Aidan managed a small smile.

'Why was I afraid you were going to say that?'

He felt surprisingly calm, as though the surge of adrenalin had scoured the fear from his system. The rain had started to fall in earnest now, but Aidan ignored it. By comparison it was a minor inconvenience. 'What can we do?'

'I can't fight it again, not tonight.'

The admission sounded as though it had hurt Eldritch as much as his pulled shoulder.

'Are there any buildings nearby? Mine workings, forestry huts, anything that we can get to? If we can get some kind of walls around us I can hang a shield on them.'

'How about a cabin? Six inch thick, split log walls. Would that do?'

'Tell me you're not joking.'

Aidan shook his head. 'We have a high ropes course laid out near the top of the forest. There's a hut at the far end that we use for storage, but there's plenty of space in there. We use it as a base for some of our night exercises. In fact Matt and Kerry were there last week with half a dozen Brownies doing a sleep-over for an adventure badge.'

'How far is it?'

That depends on how fast you can walk, thought Aidan, but what he said was, 'Maybe half an hour.'

'And there's nowhere nearer?'

'Not that I know of.'

'Then we've no choice. Let's go.'

CHAPTER 17

'Hang on a minute.'

Aidan shone his torch over the hillside and then looked once again at his compass. He knew these forest tracks well; he had roamed them with Gwyn as a child and run on them, half-wild with grief, after his mother had died. During the spring and summer scarcely a week went by when there wasn't an orienteering exercise to be run or a treasure hunt to be laid out. He would have said he could find his way through these trees blindfolded, yet tonight he checked and checked again, only too aware that the shrieks that had misled Eldritch could be altering his perceptions too. It was slowing their progress, he knew, and with the memory of that chill terror he had felt in the clearing, constantly prickling at the edge of his senses, it was difficult not to push blindly on, but he felt that this was the lesser risk. If Eldritch disagreed with him he had made no comment.

Not that Eldritch had said much since they began their retreat from the clearing. Plan B, as Aidan had started to think of it, had meant a diagonal traverse across the hillside, cutting away from the Bite and back up the slope towards the forestry plantations. It was a steep climb and not one that Aidan would normally have recommended in the dark with the rain sheeting down around them. Neither of them had had breath to spare for idle conversation. In fact, Aidan suspected their frequent stops while he checked their bearings were the one reason Eldritch was able to keep up. It was clear that the exhaustion that had weighted his steps earlier was creeping over him again, but when Aidan asked if he was alright Eldritch's only response was, 'I'm fine. Just keep going.'

Aidan pushed the sopping hair back from his forehead so that – for a few moments at least – the rain wasn't running into his eyes and attempted to ignore the steady trickle of water that had found its way down the back of his neck. He valued his peripheral vision too much to even think of putting his hood up, so there was nothing he could do about it except grit his teeth and focus on the job in hand. Satisfied that he had his next landmark imprinted on his mind, he turned back to Eldritch.

The man stood with his head bowed and his shoulders hunched against the rain. He looked a picture of misery, but he only asked, 'How much further?' in a voice devoid of any inflection.

'Well, it's such a nice night I thought we'd stop by the viewing point. You get a marvellous view of the reservoir from there. It's an extra half-hour's climb, but it's well worth it.'

Aidan couldn't stop the grin twitching the corners of his mouth; Gwyn had always said he had a warped sense of humour, but the grin died when Eldritch's only response was a barely audible, 'Okay.'

With his dark hair plastered flat to his scalp the angular lines of his face looked positively skull-like, but he started forward with the grim determination of a man steeling himself to walk until he dropped. Aidan frowned as he hurried to fall into step beside him.

'Perhaps we'll pass on the viewing point after all.'

It was another twenty minutes before Aidan's torch beam

finally picked out the shape of the cabin, half-hidden amongst the sentry-like ranks of the forestry's Douglas firs.

'Home sweet home,' he said, encouragingly, turning to his companion with a grin that was equal parts satisfaction and relief. 'Well, hut sweet hut, anyway.'

Eldritch murmured something, his words lost in the rain and the dark, but Aidan took it that he was equally thankful. That or irritated it had taken them so long to get here. Either way, here they were. As they picked their way carefully down the slope, feet slipping in the morass of mud and pine needles, Aidan felt his spirits lift. They had made it. And with that thought his sense of mischief resurfaced.

'There's just one problem.'

Schooling his face into a look of frustration – the sort of expression a man might wear on realising he had overlooked a small but essential detail – Aidan turned to where Eldritch leaned wearily against the cabin's log wall, waiting for him to undo the padlocks and let them in. The tall man raised his head, but made no other response and Aidan guessed he was hoarding what little of his strength remained. He certainly chose not to waste any by indulging in unnecessary questions.

'I don't have the keys with me. I was hoping you could do some sort of magic on the locks.'

Eldritch closed his eyes and swallowed convulsively, his Adam's apple bobbing in his throat.

'Can't you just kick the door down?' he asked, his voice hoarse. He did not open his eyes.

Aidan laughed.

'I'm flattered, but we're talking six inches of pine. What do you think this is; a Bruce Lee film?'

The grey eyes opened and Eldritch looked at him with quiet desperation. The rain had washed much of the demon gore from his face, leaving only smudges where he had been pushing the hair out of his eyes. Apparently he had given up on that particular battle, for the long strands clung across his face and he made no effort to smooth them back. Either he no longer noticed them or, if he did, he was past caring.

Seeing that utter weariness, Aidan relented.

'You know, you just can't rely on anyone these days,' he said in mock-aggrieved tones. 'It's a good job they're combination locks. No keys required.'

Very clearly and precisely Eldritch told Aidan what he could do with his padlocks.

'Just helping you conjure up a bit of energy,' Aidan grinned, unrepentant. 'Can you hold the torch so I can see what I'm doing?'

Eldritch took the torch, but his hand was shaking so much he nearly dropped it. Carefully Aidan took it back from him.

'It's alright, I'll manage.'

Jamming it between shoulder and ear he turned his attention back to the door, leaving Eldritch clinging to the wall of the cabin like a half-drowned bat.

The rings of the combination lock were stiff and for a moment Aidan couldn't remember the numbers he needed. *Don't be daft,* he told himself, fighting down the momentary feeling of panic. *It's 2512 and 0101. Christmas Day and New Year's Day – not exactly difficult. And don't forget to grease these next time you're up here.* He rubbed his hands together to get some feeling back in his fingers and applied himself once more to the recalcitrant metal. This time the digits lined up obligingly and the padlock sprung open. Seconds later the second lock was similarly despatched.

'Right, we're in.'

Aidan pushed the door open and stepped inside to clear a path through the assault course of equipment littering the floor. There was plenty of room in the cabin, it was true, but somehow the floor still ended up being used as a random storage area as well as space for sorting ropes and laying out harnesses. Not a problem if you knew, but a definite hazard for anyone too tired to notice where they were putting their feet. Yet as he turned from dumping two stray helmets and an armful of assorted climbing gear with his rucksack in the far corner, Aidan realised that Eldritch had not followed him inside. The thought crossed his mind that perhaps Marcus Eldritch had to be invited inside, like a vampire, before he could cross a new threshold. The idea was rather appealing.

'You're more tired than you thought, son,' he muttered to himself, rubbing a hand over his face, but he could come up with no better reason as to why Eldritch had chosen to linger outside in the rain. He shook his head and sighed, knowing he had better go and find out what was keeping the man. But, when he went outside, he could only stare around him in disbelief. Eldritch was no longer there.

At first Aidan simply couldn't believe it. He blinked and looked again, thinking he must be mistaken, but there was no dark shape leaning up against the cabin wall or even slumped at its base. Yet nor were there any signs of a struggle, although surely nothing could have happened in the brief moments he had been inside the hut. Could it? Even if it had, Aidan told himself, he would have heard something. It was inconceivable that the avatar could have taken Eldritch without the man making some sort of noise.

Besides, he was sure he would have sensed it. Aidan cast around the clearing for some sign as to what had happened, but the torchlight revealed nothing untoward. Ridiculous though it seemed – especially given the state Eldritch had been in – the only conclusion Aidan could come to was that Eldritch had chosen to walk off into the night.

But why? Had he been lured away by some trick? And, if so, what could be done? Aidan stood racked by indecision, the rain running unnoticed down his face. *What the Hell do I do now?* He turned the torch on the surrounding trees, but there was no sign of Eldritch and nothing to show that he had passed that way, voluntarily or otherwise. Fear tightened his throat. These weren't the conditions to start searching in, even without the additional complication of the shrieks and, in all likelihood, the avatar somewhere out there in the darkness. Possibly they were waiting for him to do exactly what he was now contemplating; to plunge back into the night and search for a man who might already be dead. And if Eldritch had simply chosen to disappear, with no idea which way he had gone it was pointless striking out into the forest to try to find him. There were any number of snags or hollows where the man could lie unseen and Aidan could walk within a few feet of him and not know. Yet he couldn't simply abandon him. He wondered about the sense of calling out, but surely if Eldritch were capable of answering he would have made some sound already; if, of course, he had been abducted. If he had left of his own volition then – with a sinking heart – Aidan realised he was wasting his time.

Something moved behind him and he whirled to face it, hands coming up automatically in front of him although sense might dictate that any such defence would be useless against the things he feared that night. Then he saw who it was and he lashed out verbally instead.

'Jesus Christ! I thought the avatar had got you. What the Hell are you doing?'

Eldritch flung up a hand as the torchlight caught his face, flinching back from the sudden glare, but if the anger in Aidan's voice bothered him he chose not to show it.

'Making sure we're safe for the night.'

He dropped his arm as Aidan lowered the torch and turned back to the cabin wall as though that were all the explanation Aidan needed. Torn between relief that Eldritch was safe and feeling disgruntled by this casual dismissal, Aidan toyed briefly with the idea of retreating into the cabin and leaving Eldritch to be mysterious in the rain on his own. Yet, while he might not admit it, he was curious as to what Eldritch was doing so he stayed where he was to watch.

Eldritch seemed to be drawing something on the side of the cabin, his long fingers brushing over the timbers as though he were tracing some design upon them. There was a look of intense focus on his face as he paused, his outstretched hand hovering over the design he had just wrought, and then he moved two steps to his left and began again. Aidan stepped back to give him room, not wanting to break his concentration. He had seen the fine tremor in Eldritch's arm as he propped himself against the wall, but the fingers of his right hand were steady as he traced out his interlocking patterns of curves and lines.

As Eldritch finished the next glyph, Aidan asked quietly, 'Do you have to do this?' His tone carried a tacit apology for his earlier outburst. 'You're dead on your feet.'

Eldritch glanced at him briefly, his face a chalky blur above the dark shadows of his clothes.

'Better that than dead in our sleep.'

He moved along the cabin wall and then paused as though waiting for Aidan's next question.

'Will it come to that?'

'Tonight? Yes, I think so.'

He raised his right hand once more.

'You don't have to stand out in the rain. I won't be long.'

This time there was no sense of dismissal behind the softly spoken words. Instead Aidan realised that Eldritch was simply being thoughtful. There really was little to be gained from his standing there, certainly there was no practical help he could offer, so why not go inside. But piqued by that unexpected kindness, Aidan's conscience would not let him leave Eldritch to stand in the rain alone. He was wet already, he reasoned. A few more minutes would make little difference.

As he watched Eldritch's fingers move across the wooden wall, Aidan fancied he could almost see the glyphs forming underneath them. It was like trying to see the same rainbow auras he saw when Gwyn talked him through a meditation, but this time with his eyes open. Yet if he let his mind unfocus, slipping sideways until it felt as though he had peeled away from the shell of his body and was now standing inside it, looking out, he could see them. They glowed for a second on the wood, silver blue, as though Eldritch had written them with fingers dipped in quicksilver and then sank, fading from sight like stones dropping through dark water.

Stepping back once more Aidan found that he was again at the cabin door. He watched silently as Eldritch drew a final glyph hard against the door frame and for the second time that night he thought he saw the faint glimmer of phosphorescence edging the other man's fingers like a stray flicker of starlight. One final time Eldritch held his palm out over the wall then his hand dropped and he turned slowly to face Aidan. He stood for a moment as though gathering his thoughts or possibly his strength.

'Once this is done we won't be able to leave the cabin, not until daylight, so is there anything you need to do, anything you need to get, before we go inside?'

Aidan shook his head, a half-seen movement in the darkness. 'No.'

'Then we should go in.'

Eldritch pushed the cabin door shut and slid home its single bolt. Around him, in the darkness, he could feel the sigils he had written along the walls like a trail of little hooks, each dragging at the edges of his power. He had realised he was spent from his fight with the avatar, but the writing of them had taken more effort than he had expected. Worrying for something that should have been as easy as breathing and a sobering thought indeed given what was still to be done. He ignored the small thrill of fear that curled around his spine at the prospect. He would manage, he told himself. He pinched the bridge of his nose, rubbing the skin between thumb and forefinger and wishing away the dull ache behind his eyes, but neither made any difference. The headache was lodged too deep in the bones of his skull to respond to either measure. He would manage, he repeated. There really was no other choice.

A flare of light behind him sent his shadow looming huge and distorted over the door. He turned to see Aidan tying a battery lantern to what he had taken to be a central post but which was now revealed as a vertical ladder giving access to a loft running across the width of the hut. The cold, blue-white light glittered like diamonds on the water beading the shoulders of Aidan's jacket and tipped the blond-brown stubble along his jaw with platinum, incongruously aging a face that had yet to settle fully into the planes of adulthood. *What was it that Helen used to say? You know you're getting old when even the policemen start looking young.*

Unaware of Eldritch's thoughts, Aidan looked at him curiously. 'Now what?'

Now what, indeed.

'I'm going to draw a veil – a shield if you will – around these walls. It's the one thing I can do to keep us safe from the avatar. Once it's done, nothing from the outside can cross it. Nothing with evil intent can get in.'

'Like the one you put on Gwyn's house?'

To his credit Aidan kept the scepticism from his voice, but Eldritch could feel it underlying the question. He was, however, too weary to take offence.

'No. This is different. This is,' he searched for the words to describe something he had never tried to explain before, 'more absolute. Nothing can cross a veil until it's opened and it can only be opened from the inside. But once it's been opened, once you or I cross it, that's it, it's gone.'

Aidan digested this information in silence for a moment. 'So that's why we can't go back outside.' His teeth worried at his bottom lip as he thought this over. 'Is it okay to touch the walls or are you going to draw out some kind of circle that we have to stay inside?'

To Eldritch's surprise he found himself struggling with an unexpected rush of amusement. He supposed there was no reason why Aidan should understand such things and, for a newcomer to magic, it was a reasonable enough question.

'I am going to make a circle,' he confirmed, 'but not in the sense of one that's drawn out on the floor. You won't be able to see it… and it won't actually be circular.' He winced slightly, realising how strange that must sound. 'A circle, in the magic sense, is just a way of defining a space and yes, usually they are circular. It's easier that way. But because the one I'm about to create will be part of the veil effectively it's going to be the same shape as this room. That is, the perimeter of the circle will be defined by the walls. It will go up over our heads and beneath us too, through the ground.'

Eldritch paused and rubbed his forehead again. He should save the theory for later. He had all night for explanations once the circle was formed and the veil in place. What he needed to do now was to set those protections while he still had enough energy left to do so.

He opened his eyes, not quite sure at what point in the conversation they had slid shut, and focussed on Aidan once more.

'There's no problem with touching the walls, but don't open the door. Or any windows,' he added, realising he could not remember if he had seen any in the walls. That did scare him. He hadn't realised he was so tired that he could miss something so fundamental. He glanced around, but the pool of lamplight did not reach to the furthest walls and it was impossible to tell what lay in the shadows beyond it.

'There are two skylights in the roof,' Aidan supplied. He could hardly have known the reason for Eldritch's concern yet something made him add, 'You wouldn't have seen them.'

Eldritch sighed, but he held tight to the rush of adrenalin that had flooded his system. He dared not relax now.

'Fine. Just don't open them.'

'Okay.'

Aidan nodded his understanding of the instruction, if not the reasoning behind it. Now only one last thing remained to be done, though it galled Eldritch to have to do it.

'Do you have your compass handy?'

The raised eyebrows spoke volumes, but Aidan made no comment as he handed it over. For his own part Eldritch was simply relieved to see the compass needle tallied with his own innate sense of direction. He looked around once more, marking the cardinal points in his mind. Resignation tightened the corners of his mouth as he did so. There was no reason why the cabin should have been built square to the four directions, but he would have preferred to have the door aligned to one of the cardinal points, to give that fraction more protection where they would be most vulnerable. But a circle was a circle, after all; it would stand or fail in its entirety. It was up to him to make certain it was strong enough.

Wordlessly, Eldritch passed the compass back to Aidan and stepped into the centre of the room. Taking a deep breath to steady himself, he removed a small bag from his pocket. Beside him he was aware of Aidan's bemused look. Perhaps the young man had expected a pouch of black velvet or maybe ancient leather – no doubt encrusted with runes and other archaic symbols – but zip-lock plastic was a lot less obtrusive and had the added benefit of keeping things dry, even on a night as foul as this one. Eldritch retrieved the first item he needed and then stopped, contemplating the bag and the likelihood that, if he bent to put it down the dizziness lurking at the edge of his senses would overwhelm him and he would end up on the floor himself. After a second he looked at Aidan.

'Here, hold this for me, will you?'

Aidan took the bag cautiously, although the Lord alone knew what he thought it was going to contain; eye of newt and toe of frog perhaps, if Shakespeare still featured on the national curriculum. Well, he would find out soon enough. Turning to face north, Eldritch opened the small sachet and poured its contents into his upturned palm. Focussing his mind on the essence of what it was he held, white salt, the combined representation of the direction north and of the element of Earth, he drew the glyph for Earth over the little pile of crystals. He heard a sharp intake of breath as he did so. *Ah, another one who associates pentacles with Devil worship.* Perhaps they would both live long enough for him to correct that particular misunderstanding, but there was no time to do it now. Ignoring the weight of Aidan's stare burning into his back, Eldritch carried his palmful of salt to the most northerly point of their refuge and tipped it into a small pile on the floor. Then he turned and retraced his steps to the centre of the room.

Aidan was watching him carefully, his hazel eyes wary and suspicious, but as Eldritch approached he held out the plastic bag without being asked.

'Trust your feelings,' Eldritch said quietly as he retrieved a second sachet. 'You know enough to tell black from white.'

Aidan said nothing, but Eldritch could feel him watching like a hawk as he tipped the crumbled incense and canary bright flowers of sulphur into his palm and turned to face the east. Yet the sweeping lines of the glyph for Air brought no reaction from him and as Eldritch blew softly on the mix, the gentle exhalation barely stirring the fine powder, he thought from the corner of his eye he could see a softening in that defensive stance. Once more he walked to the very edge of the room and poured out a little pile of crystals onto the floor.

Returning to the centre of the room, Eldritch was pleased to see Aidan had indeed relaxed. That was good because he suspected what he was going to do next would unnerve the young man. Perhaps it would be best if he offered a brief explanation. As Aidan held out the bag again, Eldritch shook his head.

'No, not this time. I'd normally use a candle to mark the southern cardinal point. South is represented by the colour red and by the element of Fire; hence that red nightlight and the matches.'

Aidan looked at the contents of the bag.

'It all seems dry enough,' he commented. 'But there's a tin of matches in my rucksack if these don't light. Unless they have to have been blessed or something first.'

The raised eyebrows gave away the fact that Aidan was teasing.

'There's no need for that. So long as you bought them on a full moon they should be okay.'

Aidan sighed theatrically.

'Ah, I knew there was a reason why they don't light properly.'

Eldritch couldn't help smiling. It felt strange to do so, given the danger they were in, but Aidan's banter was a reminder that they might yet come through this. It was the sort of comment that Paul would have made. The thought of his brother-in-law tightened his throat. *Damn it, Paul, it's hard to do this on my own.* Aidan must have read the change in his expression because his voice was carefully neutral as he asked, 'So why can't you use a candle?'

Eldritch swallowed and refocussed. 'Because it will only burn for eight hours and by my reckoning it's not going to be light for another ten.'

Aidan glanced at his watch.

'More or less. Dawn is about 6:45, but it won't be light enough to see for a good half-hour after that, longer if it's still raining like this.'

His expression said all that was needed about the weather outside. Something else must have occurred to him for he turned back to Eldritch and asked quizzically, 'You can't see in the dark, can you?'

'No, that's just in stories.'

'Ah.'

'So, I'm going to use an alternative to mark the south. Which is why I have to do this.'

As he spoke, Eldritch pulled the knife from his pocket and stabbed it into the ball of his thumb.

'Blood is an acceptable substitute for fire,' he said, trying not to wince as he watched the first red droplets welling up.

'Fortunately, it doesn't have to be a virgin's,' he quipped for the benefit of Aidan who, as Eldritch had suspected he might, was looking utterly horrified, transfixed by the blood now pooling in Eldritch's palm. It was a lame joke, but it broke the tension. Aidan swallowed, still looking a little white around the lips.

'That's a good job. There aren't many of them around here.'

With the glyph for Fire drawn and the south marked with a dribble of blood already drying to rust on the floor, only the west remained to be sealed. *Not much longer*, Eldritch told himself as he returned to the centre of the room. He could feel the muscles in his legs trembling and he locked his knees against it. He was so very tired. Tired and cold. The sodden wool of his jacket weighted his shoulders and his jeans clung wet and heavy to his legs making him feel as though he might never be warm again. He just hoped that Aidan might have some trick up his waterproof sleeve to warm the cabin once this was done, otherwise it was going to be a very uncomfortable night.

There was also the small matter of his shoulder to contend with. Once the veil was in place he might have to risk Aidan taking a look at it, though the thought of anyone touching it made him queasy with apprehension. He was no longer sure what would be best. It hurt so much it was hard to focus through the pain and through the numbing effects of cold and exhaustion. *Later,* he told himself. There were things that had to be done before he need think about that. With shaking fingers, Eldritch reached into the bag one last time, withdrawing a flat disc of what looked like black glass.

Obsidian, he named it in his mind as he held the disc in his fingers, careful not to smudge the shiny surface with blood. Black for the west combined with the glyph for Water. He licked the tip of his right middle finger, flinching slightly as he raised his hand, and carefully drew the flowing lines of Water on the obsidian disc. For a moment he watched the lines sinking like fishes into the glassy blackness. They sank down and down, far beyond the thickness of the disc he held in his fingers. It was as though he held his eye above some great pool of black water into which the glyph was receding.

He could almost lean forward and touch those depths, trail his fingers in the inky darkness, slide into them and follow the glowing tendrils of light down into oblivion. With a start he jerked back from the image, his heart pounding as he realised how close he had come to losing himself in his own power working. With utmost care he carried the black disc to the edge of the circle and set it down in its appointed place. Almost stumbling with exhaustion, he came back to the centre and faced Aidan. Now came the final test.

'I'm only going to be able to do this once,' he warned. *If I can do it at all*. For a second his vision blurred and he swept a hand across his eyes again, wondering, as he did so, how much longer so simple a remedy would work. He had already pushed himself to the boundaries of what he was capable of. Now he had no choice but to step over them. Eldritch took a long breath, pushing such thoughts to one side, as he locked his gaze with Aidan's, intent on impressing on him the deadly seriousness of what he was saying.

'So whatever you see, whatever you hear, no matter who or what you think is outside that door, for God's sake don't cross the veil until daylight.'

The implication of those words must have hit home for Aidan looked as though he suddenly had a dozen questions to ask, but Eldritch did not have the strength to spare. *Later*, his eyes promised. Out loud he said, 'Just trust me on this, please, and don't open the door.'

With fingers made clumsy by cold and exhaustion he reached under the sodden collar of his shirt and carefully pulled a thin gold chain over his head. A paroxysm of shivering racked him and the lantern light caught in the facets of the antique sapphire ring that spun at the end of the links. Fumbling slightly, Eldritch unfastened the chain's catch and let the ring slide into his cupped palm.

'It's a power sink,' he heard himself saying in response to Aidan's quirked eyebrow and querying look. 'Crystals, precious metals, all sorts of things can be used to hold power. Not many of us do it; it takes power to create them, power to access them, you put more in than you get out, but sometimes, just sometimes, they can save your life.'

Eldritch looked at the ring nestled in the palm of his hand, a curious thing for a man to own, to wear, like a talisman, on a chain around his neck. A single midnight blue sapphire circled round with tiny chips of diamond; a month's wages for the man who had bought it. The rose gold band was worn thin where it had rubbed for sixty years against a wedding ring, fifty-nine years longer than the man who had bought it had lived. The band, which would barely fit his smallest finger, had been loose on hers when his grandmother had told him it was to be his. It had been her final gift to him. A week later she had died.

The ghost of a smile touched his lips, sweet as a half-remembered love song, as he thought of that tiny, wispy-haired old lady. Even at the end she had been powerful, her spirit seeming to burn ever more brightly, even as the body that held it had failed. The events of the last two years would have broken her heart, but never her resolve. She would have had a lot to say about the choices he had made. He wondered if she would have understood them.

'Eldritch?'

With a start, Eldritch lifted his head, realising several minutes had passed.

'Are you okay?'

'Fine. Just fine.'

It was a lie and by now they both knew it, but this time, mercifully, Aidan let it go.

'Can I do anything to help?'

It was in his mind to retort that the most helpful thing Aidan could have done was to have stayed out of this. *You and the witch, both. I really didn't need civilians along for the ride.*

Instead he shook his head, a mistake that, for the room didn't quite stop moving when he did.

'This will take some concentration. Do me a favour and don't disturb me, okay?'

Eldritch raised the ring to his lips and kissed it. *For luck, Grandma. We surely need that now.*

Then, focussing his awareness on the ring, he reached for his own power, not the little traces he had used to write the sigils and glyphs of the veil and circle, but the deep core of power that lay within his bones. He reached for it as he would a familiar tool… and recoiled with a gasp of pain, as though he had thrust his fingers into an open wound.

He flung up a hand as Aidan lunged forward to steady him.

'No!'

And the younger man froze, caught between instinct and his promise not to interfere. For a second it seemed that instinct might win, but then he raised his hands in a silent gesture of submission and stepped back a single pace. He said nothing, though it was clear from his expression that he was far from happy, but for now he would trust that Eldritch knew what he was doing.

Fool, thought Eldritch, but he couldn't have said which one of them he meant.

Taking a slow, deep breath he closed his eyes, consciously willing his body to relax as he exhaled, finding the point of no breath, the quiet space between one heartbeat and the next. He felt some of the tension within him ease, as his body responded to the age-old discipline. Then he reached within. It still hurt, still felt as though he was touching flesh that had been flayed raw, but now that he was prepared for it he could deal with it, focussing on his breath, choosing not to hear the small scared voice whispering in the corner of his mind. Never before had he drained his power to this extent. Not even on that awful day when

248

Paul had fallen fighting the last demon and he and Helen had battled to drive it away from him, pouring bolt after bolt of Levin fire into its body, almost blasting it apart in their combined rage. It had been a long time before he had realised it was only the physical body that had been destroyed, before he understood how readily a new body could be taken if a person's shields were down. He brushed the thought aside as he reached deeper, not acknowledging the raw, aching emptiness of life without Helen or the strangeness, even now, of turning to find she was no longer beside him.

The quicksilver core of his magic, that energy that ran like fire through his bones, had sunk to embers, but it was still there, would always be there, while breath moved in his lungs. He could not comprehend life being possible without it. Carefully now Eldritch gathered it to him, like a miser sweeping together flecks of gold dust in the hope that they would form an ingot. Finally, once he was sure he had it, he touched the matrix of the ring.

The energy stored there was like cold fire, hard and somehow brittle, and very different from the power that naturally lay in his bones. It hurt to touch it, hurt as though the joints of his hands had been filled with ground glass, but he called it and little by little it answered him. He was aware of it as a soft blue glow spilling out from the ring to fill his cupped hands and of Aidan, his face torn between disbelief and wonder, as though he too could see it. A corner of Eldritch's mind registered surprise; there was a raw talent to the young man, something as yet largely untrained, but he had not expected him to be able to See. It was an interesting conundrum, but Eldritch had no time for such thoughts now. As the light spilled through his fingers he channelled it, reaching out for the first of the sigils he had marked on the cabin walls, feeding power into it until he could feel it, solid and tangible with the power he gave it. Holding it in his mind he reached for the second symbol, joining it to the first like beads upon a string.

As the power flowed through him, Eldritch reached for each sigil in turn, linking them in a chain of unearthly light, until he and Aidan were almost surrounded. At each of the cardinal points he bound the veil to the circle, tying the power into the physical markers he had created, grounding it with the marks of direction and element so that its shape was fixed and linked to the physical reality of the cabin. Carefully, aware of how fine the thread of power was, how easy it would be to break it and how unlikely it was that he would be able to pick it up again, he reached for the final sigil. His hands, holding the ring, were trembling, the fingers numb with cold and fatigue, but his mind was steady and calm. Finally, the last sigil was linked to the first, the chain completed. Eldritch allowed himself a brief moment's satisfaction as his mind traced the chain, testing for weakness and finding none. It was stretched to almost impossible thinness, but it would hold.

Gradually Eldritch increased the flow of power into the nascent veil, shaping it, setting its pattern in his mind, knowing that the energy would follow his directions. He was aware of how thinly he was being stretched, but he held fast, letting the power drain out of him into the link. The reserves in the ring were exhausted; this final part would be down to him. He watched the pale nimbus sink into the ground and, at the same time, rise above their heads and for a brief moment the sigils he had drawn could be seen glowing through the timbers of the walls as the separate arcs of power met and closed around them. At each of the cardinal points a column of coloured flame; white, yellow, red and black, sprang up, burning within the glowing nimbus of blue light as the veil took its final shape. For an instant the combined elements of veil and circle were visible and then they vanished and the cabin was once again lit solely by torchlight. Eldritch, however, saw nothing. Conscious only of the need to drive the final dregs of his power into the link, he was blind and mute. As the veil was completed and the link snapped shut, he crumpled. He never even felt the floor as it rushed up to meet him.

CHAPTER 18

As the last of the power glow faded, Aidan started as though waking from a dream. What he had just seen had been beautiful beyond words. Although he had heard nothing, it seemed to him as though Eldritch had in some way spoken to the ring and while he couldn't make out the words he felt his body knew them, that he had heard that summons long ago and ever since had been waiting for it to be spoken again. Something deep within him responded to the shimmering, quicksilver beauty and he was overcome by a desire and a heartfelt longing for something he could not understand. For a moment his whole being was one aching loss, then reality snapped the world back into focus and he realised what else had happened.

'Eldritch?'

Kneeling beside the wizard's body, Aidan put a hand on the other's shoulder and shook him gently. There was no response, but then he hadn't really expected one. It had been clear that Eldritch had been on the verge of collapse, even before he called up the power needed for the veil, and Aidan had set himself ready to catch him when he did go down, not expecting to be caught in the glamour himself. He scowled at the unconscious man as though Eldritch had bewitched him deliberately.

'It's your own fault if you've cracked that thick skull of yours on the floor,' he muttered, running his hands carefully under Eldritch's head to make sure there was no injury there. Satisfied, he settled back on his heels and contemplated his patient further. The pulse in Eldritch's neck was feeble and slow, but at least he had one and though his breathing was shallow it was unlaboured. Beyond that, however, there was little good to be found in their situation. Eldritch might be alive, but he looked far from well. Framed by his dark hair, his face was ashen, the skin waxy and dead-looking. Spots of white had blossomed on his cheekbones and his lips were colourless. Aidan frowned and picked up one limp hand. The last joints of Eldritch's fingers were yellow-white and as cold as a corpse's.

'Oh great. Gwyn is going to kill me for this. In fact, when she hears about everything that's happened tonight, she's likely to want to kill both of us, so don't go thinking that hypothermia's going to get you out of it.'

He supposed he shouldn't be surprised. The combination of physical exhaustion and freezing, wet conditions was a classic recipe for disaster, especially when coupled with inadequate clothing and Eldritch could hardly have chosen less suitable clothes for the conditions if he had tried. With wringing wet jeans and a jacket that must have been soaking up water like a sponge, the surprise was that Eldritch had kept going for as long as he had. *You could do with being a bit warmer too, son,* a small part of his mind pointed out. He was aware that the cold was creeping into his own body. It had been a relief to get out of the wind and rain, but there was no escaping the fact that the cabin was far from warm. Aidan shivered and rubbed his hands together. He could always resort to a few dozen press-ups to warm himself up, but that wasn't a remedy that would work for Eldritch. He looked at the crumpled figure beside him and sighed.

'First things first, we need to get you out of those wet clothes.

And while we're at it I'm going to take a look at that shoulder and this time I'm not taking no for an answer.'

The buttons on Eldritch's jacket were stiff and Aidan struggled with the sodden wool and his own half-frozen fingers.

'Now would be a really good time to wake up and help, you know,' he addressed the unconscious man. There was little chance that Eldritch could hear him, but venting his frustration, even in a one-sided conversation, made him feel better as he persevered with the task. As the last of the buttons yielded, Aidan paused to consider the best way to proceed. Peeling unconscious people out of their clothing wasn't something he had had much practice at and while cutting Eldritch's clothes off was an option it might lead to some embarrassment in the morning when they came to leave the cabin. He didn't relish the idea of having to explain to the wizard why he had nothing to wear but a sleeping bag. So, what did they say on the first aid courses? Work with the uninjured side first. Okay, left sleeve it was then.

Eldritch's body was as limp as if he had been filleted, but even so it took a surprising amount of tugging and bending for Aidan to get his arm free. *To Hell with the press-ups*, he thought as he moved round to Eldritch's right side; this was proving quite effective as a way of getting warm.

'How do people manage to do this with babies?'

Getting the jacket out from beneath Eldritch proved easier, a simple case of dragging it free, but as Aidan pulled the sleeve down Eldritch's arm he stopped, too shocked to do more than stare in disbelief at the rust-like stain covering the shoulder and sleeve of Eldritch's shirt.

'Oh dear God.'

He reached out a tentative hand to touch it and then pulled back.

'Of all the jumped up, idiotic… I asked you what was wrong. Why the Hell didn't you tell me?'

But Aidan could guess why Eldritch had downplayed the extent of his injury. He had done something similar once. It still ranked as one of the stupidest things he had done in his life.

He had been starting with what he had assumed was a cold and was already feeling rough when the shout had gone up for two teenage girls who had become separated from a school hiking party. He knew he was running a temperature and wasn't really fit to be on the mountain, but it was getting late and the weather forecast was bad. For those reasons alone he should have had the sense to stay at home, but he had ignored them. Partly it had been because he had been asked to go and because he felt he would be letting the team down if he didn't, but more than that it had been because two lives were at stake and he judged that to be more important than his temporary discomfort. Also he felt he could cope. He hadn't thought he was endangering his own life or lining the team up with another casualty to take down from the mountain; he wasn't that ill. So he had taken two aspirin, told himself not to be a wimp and headed out. Five hours later, when his legs had given out and he had found himself lying in a bog near the top of Plynlimon, with no idea how he was going to get out again, let alone get down off the mountain, he had realised how stupid he had been. By then, of course, it was too late.

As it turned out, the girls had done the sensible thing. On finding themselves lost and with bad weather closing in, they had found as sheltered a spot as possible and set up a bivouac for the night, following their training to the letter; a fact that the journalists conveniently ignored when the story broke in the national press the following day. Contrary to all the hysterical ranting, when Hazel and Murphy, her Labrador-cross, had found the girls, they had been quite capable of walking off the mountain on their own, which was more than could be said for Aidan. He had had to be carried down and had spent the next two weeks in hospital with what had turned out to be flu complicated considerably with pleurisy. It had been several months before he had fully lost the tightness in his chest when he exercised. It had been even longer before the team had let him forget.

So he had an inkling as to what might have driven Eldritch's behaviour. He recalled the self-effacing humour of the man he had met on the sailing club jetty and how easy he had been to get along with. Later he had put that down to the glamour that Eldritch had cast over him to persuade him to go back to the site of John's death, but perhaps there had been less manipulation than he had thought. The real Marcus Eldritch might not be so different from the character he had pretended to be. For all their assumptions, he and Gwyn knew very little of the truth behind the man. Shaking his head, Aidan looked again at his unconscious patient.

'When this is over, you and I are going to have a long talk.'

He stood up and untied the lantern, setting it down next to Eldritch's shoulder where it would give him a better light. Then he retrieved his rucksack from the corner. The sight of the tiny pile of salt on the floor beside it made him pause. There were other things he wanted to know more about, but they too would have to wait. Right now there were more important things to concentrate on.

There was no time for subtlety now. With his penknife Aidan

slit Eldritch's shirt from collar to cuff and then did the same with the t-shirt underneath. Both were stiff with blood and Aidan found himself having to peel the cloth away from the skin.

'Sorry,' he muttered, wincing as he felt the shirt pulling at the crusted scabs. He gritted his teeth, steeling himself to pick it free. He could only be grateful that Eldritch was oblivious to the process. 'Forget what I said about now being a good time to wake up, okay?' He didn't think he could stomach doing this if the man were conscious.

Finally, the last of the cloth came free revealing the mess that had been made of Eldritch's shoulder. Aidan's teeth dug into his lip. Three gouges ran vertically across the shoulder and biceps, roughly a handspan apart. The first two formed a pair with one running from the top of the shoulder down towards the collar bone, while the other ran up across the collar bone to meet it. The third ran across the top of the biceps. Knowing this must be the work of the avatar, Aidan could guess what had happened. He turned the arm carefully and sure enough there was another gash, slightly shallower, where the bottom tooth had grazed the flesh rather than ripping into it.

A scene formed in his mind: the avatar crouched, snarling in the darkness, where Eldritch had brought it to bay, all but invisible save for the pale sulphur of its eyes. Trailing along its flanks, like a shimmer of ghostly light, the lines of power that held it were just visible; a gossamer-fine net of runes and witchlight, shaped by the power of the man's mind. The moonlight caught on the avatar's wrinkled snout, glinting on ivory teeth and the long drooling strands of saliva that trailed from its muzzle as it sank to its belly as Eldritch closed with it. It cowered away from him, but, as the wizard's hand came up to deliver the coup de grace, the avatar launched itself at him, uncoiling from the ground like a snake, all pretence of submission gone.

The speed with which it moved was terrifying and Eldritch seemed taken off guard, but at the last moment he twisted so the teeth closed about his arm and shoulder and not his throat. As the beast collided with him, the wizard went backwards under the impact, the two of them falling together. Even as they went down, the doglike form was tearing its head back and lunging again for his throat, but Eldritch somehow wrapped his arms around the beast, crushing it to him while he drove fire into its body.

With a shudder Aidan jerked his mind back, unsure if what he had seen had actually happened or if it was just a too vivid fantasy. Either way the wounds Eldritch carried were real enough. Aidan thought of the span of Sula's jaws and how hard she could bite when she chose to, but the spread of these wounds was greater than anything Sula could inflict. With his fingers splayed Aidan could just cover them. The avatar was a far larger animal and with that size came power. Under the dried blood Eldritch's shoulder looked not so much bruised as crushed, as though the whole joint had been caught in a gin trap. No wonder he had flinched every time he moved that arm; the whole shoulder must be one screaming mass of pain.

Aidan's stomach clenched at the thought, but he forced himself to remain objective. A little fresh blood oozed up where he had peeled the shirt back from the wounds, but mostly the bleeding had already stopped; probably some time ago judging from the look of Eldritch's shirt. Nor had the wounds bled as badly as he had first feared. If he thought of the blood in terms of how far a pint of beer would have spread it was easier to judge and Aidan reckoned that there was much less than a pint there. The wounds would need careful cleaning, especially the deep punctures where the teeth had first punched through the skin, but there was little for him to do now except cover them with clean dressings and concentrate on making Eldritch as comfortable as possible.

CHAPTER 19

'Aidan?'

It was the barest whisper of sound, but Aidan jerked awake from the half-doze he had fallen into, his heart pounding. For a moment he couldn't remember where he was or why there was a body cradled in his arms, but then it came back to him; the encounter with Eldritch and their flight across the dark hillside then Eldritch's warding of the cabin and his subsequent collapse. Moving carefully, Aidan squirmed his way out from under the weight of Eldritch's body and sat up. In the lantern light he could see the other man's eyes were open, but they didn't seem quite focussed and Aidan wasn't certain if Eldritch knew he was there or if he was simply saying his name.

'It's alright. I'm here.'

Eldritch turned his head slightly at the sound of Aidan's voice, moving an arm feebly as though trying to find the strength to lever himself upright. Aidan caught the hand as it fell back onto Eldritch's chest and tucked it back under the flap of the sleeping bag. The flesh was cool, but it had lost the corpse-wight chill that had marked it earlier. Eldritch plucked vaguely at the material under his fingers as though trying to make sense of the unfamiliar surroundings.

'Where?'

Aidan had to lean close to catch the question.

'We're in the Red Kite hut,' he explained. 'You put a veil

round it and then flaked out on me, remember?' He pulled the bag back up around Eldritch's bare shoulders. 'You were soaked through and I'm afraid this was the only way I could get you warm.' Aidan wondered if the sleeping bag and the lack of clothes had fully registered with Eldritch.

'Oh.' Eldritch's eyes slid closed and some of the tension seemed to go out of him. His head dropped slightly to one side. Alarmed, Aidan closed his hand around Eldritch's good shoulder and shook it gently.

'Come on, don't you dare pass out on me.'

Eldritch's eyes flickered open again, the pupils huge in the dusk and shadows of the lamplight. Only the barest thread of iris showed round them, like two silver-grey moons in eclipse. Framed in the sweat-stiffened points of his hair, his face was deathly pale, but for an instant a brief sweet smile lit it.

'I don't normally sleep with someone on a first date.'

Aidan let out a short bark of laughter, more from relief than anything else, and patted the shoulder through the sleeping bag.

'Blame it on my animal magnetism. I'm hard to resist.'

He had decided to leave the matter of Eldritch's evasiveness regarding his shoulder for another time, but he took advantage of their momentary rapport to ask a question he needed an honest answer to.

'How are you feeling?'

'I'm...'

Eldritch's eyes closed and a brief tremor ran through him. Aidan waited for the lie he was sure was coming, but when the silver-grey eyes opened again there was no deception in them.

'I'm not feeling so good right now.'

The honesty of the answer shocked Aidan. Pleased though he was that Eldritch was being sensible, he was also alarmed that the wizard thought their situation so serious that he had no choice but to trust him.

'Were you hurt anywhere else? Anywhere I don't know about?'

Eldritch's body carried a number of old scars – curious semicircular marks over his ribs and shoulders and what looked for all the world like claw marks across one side of his chest – but except for his shoulder Aidan had found no sign of recent injury. What concerned him now was that Eldritch might have sustained injuries that weren't visible.

Eldritch shook his head, a tiny gesture, barely visible in the dim light. In a voice barely more than a whisper he said, 'Only the shoulder.'

Even that much conversation seemed to exhaust him for his eyes half-closed. After a moment he forced them open again, but it was clear that this was a struggle he was already starting to lose.

'Just tired.' Even Eldritch's voice sounded weary, the words slurring together. 'Had to use a lot of power against the avatar.' He paused to gather his strength and Aidan waited anxiously for him to continue. 'Lost more when you surprised me. Not much of an option.' The faintest trace of Marcus' wry smile quirked the corners of his lips. 'Either had to drop the power or fry you.'

The smile faded and his eyes slid closed.

'The veil took everything I had left.'

'Eldritch…'

Even on the edges of exhaustion, Eldritch must have

registered Aidan's concern for though he didn't open his eyes he somehow dragged up a smile again and murmured, 'It'll be alright... just need to rest... 'll be okay in the morning.'

It was much later when Aidan woke for the second time. The luminous dial of his watch showed it was 2:30am and he suppressed a groan. Back in Llancathan even Matt and Christine – die-hard revellers though they were – would have called time on their post-course celebrations and headed for bed, whether separately or together. He wondered briefly if tonight would be the night they finally reconciled considerations of professional detachment with their increasingly obvious mutual physical attraction. Having watched them eyeing each other up for nine months now, Aidan thought it might well be, in which case his absence would probably have been counted as a blessing by both parties. He sighed and rubbed a hand absently along his jaw. He might not be the only one getting less than a full night's sleep, but he would lay bets that Matt and Christine were having more fun.

Aidan turned his gaze on his own companion. In the lamplight Eldritch's profile was tipped with a blue-white sheen, the planes of his face highlighted, gaunt and unforgiving, but the lamplight also showed the steady rise and fall of his chest as he slept. Aidan smiled. Sleep was probably the best thing for Eldritch at the moment. He should try some himself, but, although he was tired, he felt disinclined to shut his eyes again. He was cold and his muscles ached where he had drawn himself up into a ball for warmth. He needed to move around for a minute, get the blood flowing, before he tried to settle again.

He got to his feet, stumbling slightly for his legs had gone stiff, but instead of running through some stretches as he had intended, he wandered over to the door. The night was quiet, the rain having stopped at some point while he had been asleep. Even the noise of the wind had died away. Outside, the forest would be damp and still, the ground exhaling the fresh green scent of pine into the darkness. It was one of his favourite times to be out on the hills, when everything smelled fresh and newly made. He looked at the door, recalling Eldritch's stricture against opening it before dawn and shifted restlessly. He was becoming increasingly aware of the fullness of his bladder. In fact, now he was conscious of it, he realised he really needed to pee. He let out his breath in a small huff of irritation. When Eldritch had said they wouldn't be able to leave the cabin until daylight he hadn't thought about this. It crossed his mind that he could open the door anyway. It was too close in the hut, the air was too stale. It would be good to stand outside in the moonlight, breathing in the cold fresh air with its smells of rain and wind and pine.

A sharp pain jolted him from his thoughts. He looked down, shocked to see his hands on the door's black iron bolt. It was only the fact that he had barked his knuckles on the metal as he had slid the bolt back that had stopped him opening the door. Hastily he slammed the bolt home and thrust his hands behind his back as if by doing so he could deny what he had done. In the silence the rasp of his breath seemed horribly loud, but, for a second, Aidan could have sworn he heard something else as well, a sound that did not belong in the depths of the night.

He froze, startled, not even daring to breathe, but though he strained his ears he could hear nothing beyond the frantic pounding of his heart. His eyes darted to the door latch, half-expecting to see it rise, but when, after long seconds, nothing happened, he gradually allowed himself to relax. *You're losing it, son.* He was being stupid he realised, his mind conjuring noises from lack of sleep to populate the silence. There had been no sound, no soft slur of movement, no feeling for a second that there was someone standing just the other side of the door, but as he turned away he heard it again. Aidan swung back, eyes wide and staring. This time there was no disputing that the noise was real. This time there was a voice as well as that faint scuff of footsteps, a voice he would know anywhere. Gwyn!

'Aidan?'

Her voice was pitched to carry this far and no further, almost as though she knew he would be standing there. Rooted to the spot, he listened as she called again, the sharpness of desperation edging into her tone, but still she kept her voice low, afraid perhaps of what other ears might hear her. Aidan swallowed, fighting every instinct that told him to fling the door open and pull her to safety inside. What in God's name was she doing out there? He gripped the cross brace of the door, fingers clenching white on the wood, torn by uncertainty. He could not imagine how she should come to be out there or why, but he could hear the muffled sound of her moving and the fear underlying her voice as she called again cut his heart in two. He had a picture of her then, standing with her hands on the cabin door, pale and white, her head bowed against the wood as she listened anxiously for any sound from within, her long hair tangled in a wild cloud around her face, fey and wild like a woodland spirit.

'Aidan?'

Without conscious awareness of having moved, he found his hands pressed against the wooden planks, flattening against the door as though they could cup against hers through the thickness of the wood. Was it only in his mind that he felt the connection between them?

'Aidan.'

Perhaps she shared that sense of connection for there was certainty in her voice now. She did not question that he was there, listening to her, any more than he doubted that it was her standing outside in the darkness.

'Thank the Lady I've found you in time.' The relief in her voice was palpable. 'You've got to get out of there.'

'Gwyn?'

His hand strayed towards the bolt and he jerked it back. No! This was ridiculous. She couldn't be out there. He must be dreaming, dreaming that he was standing there in the cold, frigid depths of the night, listening to her voice. But what dream could conjure that barely suppressed sense of terror in her voice or mix it with that peculiar tone of exasperation that was pure Gwyn as she spoke again?

'I'm not joking, Aidan. You have to get out of there while you still can. Eldritch is in league with the demon.'

Now that surely had to be the product of his imagination. The idea was madness, more ridiculous than the fact that she had been able to find them here, but the solid reality of her voice told him otherwise.

He looked again at the black iron bolt, catching from her the sense that time was running out. He knew he should stop this charade and open the door. Instead he asked, 'How did you find us?'

He heard her draw breath to argue with him, to tell him there was no time for this haggling, but she must have realised he needed to know, to understand this missing piece of the puzzle so that he could be sure it really was her stood in the darkness. In a softer tone she continued.

'I tracked Eldritch through his magic. When he knocked me out with a Levin bolt he left a trace that I could follow.' A note of stubbornness crept into her voice, reminding him of her tendency to pare her explanations to the bone, as though details were an unnecessary extravagance. 'I can explain the technical stuff later, but for now it doesn't matter. You've got to get out of there before he realises what's happening.'

'I can't believe it, Gwyn. You must be wrong.'

Without consciously thinking about it he matched her soft whisper, keeping his voice low so it would not reach the cabin's other occupant. He glanced over his shoulder, but there was no sign of movement from the muffled shape on the floor. His hand dropped a little lower.

Again there was that little catch of breath, that pause as she sorted through what she would and would not say, searching to find the words that would convince him.

'Sweet Lady, I wish I was, Aidan. I wanted to believe in him.'

He heard the tear in her voice as she said it and for a second Aidan wondered what else Gwyn had wanted to believe about Marcus Eldritch, but her voice continued and the thought was lost.

'But that's what he plays on, that's what he does. He makes you want to trust him. Listen to me. What did he tell you; that he was putting a shield around the cabin? That you mustn't cross it until daylight?' She didn't wait for him to answer. 'That was to keep you there without questioning him. To keep you there until the avatar arrives.'

'No, that's not right.'

Aidan shook his head, but his voice was bitter as the taste of betrayal. There was an awful logic to the picture Gwyn was painting and it fitted uncomfortably well with Eldritch's previous manipulative behaviour, too well for him to dismiss it out of hand. Yet still he found himself wanting to believe in the man he had begun to think of as, perhaps not yet a friend, but certainly not as an enemy. Gwyn seemed to understand the conflict he felt.

'Aidan, what can I tell you to convince you? He'll have a knife. Somewhere he'll have a knife with him that he'll use when he needs to raise power.'

No… He wasn't sure if he spoke aloud. The mounting weight of evidence staggered him like a punch in the gut.

'He used blood in his circle, didn't he?' Gwyn's tone was quieter, almost sad. It was as though she had heard his thought and could feel his sense of shock as he realised the truth of what she was saying.

'Yes, but –'

She cut across him and there was anger in her voice now, anger that he knew was not directed at him.

'No buts, Aidan. Have you ever seen me use blood in a circle? Or draw a pentacle?'

Again that thrill of fear as he wondered how she could know these things.

'Please, Aidan.' Her voice was gentle again, but insistent. 'If you've ever loved me, trust me about this.'

He could almost see her closing her eyes, drawing on that core of strength that resided within her, steeling herself to tell him the things he had to hear for his own good.

'He's a blood mage, Aidan. I hadn't realised it before, but as I tracked him through the link it became clear.'

Aidan had no idea what a blood mage was, but from the tone of Gwyn's voice there could be no worse an accusation. Yet no matter how evil such a creature was, there was one thing about the situation that Gwyn could not realise, one thing that surely limited the threat posed by Marcus Eldritch.

'He's hurt, Gwyn,' Aidan said softly, glancing once more at the still form behind him. 'Badly hurt.'

If Eldritch was in league with the demon why would its avatar have torn his shoulder apart?

'The only person he's a danger to right now is himself. If I hadn't found him, he'd be dead by now.'

'Aidan, you don't understand. Yes, he's already met with the avatar this evening, I know. That's how he got the wounds on his shoulder.'

That shocked him, for how could she possibly know that? But her voice continued, ruthless and undeniable, not giving him time to think.

'It's part of his pact with the demon. He feeds the avatar with his own blood, with his own pain and it becomes his to use.' She paused and then continued in a softer voice. 'When you met him, did he tell you he was injured? Any normal person would have asked for help, but he didn't want you to know, did he? Don't you think that's a bit strange? He uses his blood to bind the avatar. Then, when it takes the victim that he has chosen, he gets the energy from that death, from your death, Aidan.' She choked slightly on the words and he heard her swallow and steady herself. 'And he'll use some of that to heal himself. If you look you'll see other scars on his body. This is what he does. This is how he gets his power. It's evil, Aidan, pure evil, and he's going to use you tonight.'

Aidan clenched his hands around the door brace until the wood bit into his palms. He could almost see the anguish on Gwyn's face as she pleaded with him, the frantic dart of her eyes as she watched the forest around her while she tried her best to make him understand.

'Aidan, it's coming. We have to get away now before it finds us. I can't fight it, Aidan, I don't have the strength.' Her voice slipped again and he realised she was deathly afraid.

'When did you realise?'

He knew he was delaying, stalling, trying to find a flaw in her argument before he gave in and opened the door to her. He hated himself for doing it, knowing he was endangering the pair of them with this foolish prevarication. He knew also that she understood what he was doing and yet, being Gwyn, she gave him the time he needed, not trying to force him into action. Though she must be frantic with desperation, still she answered his question calmly as though their doom was not about to fall upon them.

'It was a couple of hours after you'd gone. It took me a while to work it out, but the magic he used on me didn't feel right. It's hard for me to explain it to you in a way you can understand, but it felt dirty, as though it was tainted somehow. That's when I realised he'd lied to me. Oh, he wanted to find the avatar alright, but not to destroy it. He wanted to find it so he could bind it to him.'

A sob broke the edge of her voice then, as she tried to convince him, to save him from what was about to happen. As she had always tried to save him, he realised, with no thought for what it might cost her. His hands moved towards the bolt.

'You have to trust your feelings, Aidan.'

Trust your feelings. In Aidan's mind the picture of Gwyn was replaced with a different image: Eldritch standing at the centre of

270

the room, his grey eyes level and direct. There was no evasiveness in them, no hint of deception. 'Trust your feelings,' he had said. Nothing more, no attempt to explain or justify what Aidan had seen him do, nothing but a simple request that Aidan use his own judgement and the implicit trust that he would make the right decision. *You know enough to tell black from white.*

Not daring to think about what he was about to do, Aidan stepped back from the door. He did not answer the voice outside. Instead he did something that only days ago he would have thought ridiculous; he focussed his mind and visualised the great wings of his shields wrapping around him. The voice outside continued to plead with him, but, while it still sounded like Gwyn, in his heart he knew it was not her; that it never had been. Freed from the beguiling touch of the avatar's power, his senses could register the cold, deathless presence outside the door. The memory of a scent like scorched and burning metal brushed across his mind. Aidan took another step back into the cabin and focussed more energy into his shields, visualising the wings wrapped around him even tighter, the golden light radiating from the great primaries. As he did so, even the voice faded from his mind.

For a moment there was silence and then a hammer blow of rage struck the cabin. Even through the veil Aidan felt it lash him, overwhelming in its intensity; ferocious and inhuman. He could do nothing against it, his shields buckling underneath that tidal wave of hatred, his shoulders hunching, his hands coming up to protect his head as though he was under a physical attack. He cowered, feeling fear rising up from some primal source within him, and with that fear the knowledge that he was in the presence of something from beyond the Mortal World, something that was the deadly and implacable enemy of all his race.

Behind him he heard Eldritch cry out and he turned, even as his knees were buckling, to see the other man twisting as though trying to free himself from the sleeping bag, his eyes closed but his face contorted in pain.

'No!'

Aidan wasn't sure whether he screamed aloud or if the rebuttal was only in his head, but something rose within him at that moment, something that came in answer to this terror in the dark. It was as if some tiny fragment within him knew this enemy of old and had stood against it, refusing to be driven into the abyss. In that moment of clarity he understood that this agony of terror and helplessness was only real if he allowed it to be so. Kept at bay by the veil, the avatar was unable to reach them physically. It might manipulate his emotions, his thoughts and his feelings, but that could not harm him unless he chose to let them overwhelm him.

Yet knowing what was happening was one thing. Finding the mental strength to focus on his shields and rebuild them whilst enduring that psychic pounding was quite another. But even as his mind quailed at the enormity of that challenge, once again there came that strange feeling that he had done this before, that he could do it again. It was akin to calling up the final dregs of energy at the end of a karate grading to perform one last, perfect kata or having the resolve to go down fighting even against the biggest and strongest opponent. As his body reeled under another blow, from some deep well of resources he hadn't known existed Aidan summoned a renewed sense of focus and for a second he could have sworn there was someone else standing behind him, lending their strength to his own. The sensation was gone almost as soon as he registered it and he couldn't spare the energy to think about it further. Though the pressure building in his head seemed enough that his brain must surely burst, he pushed back against it. He was vaguely aware of his own voice rising in a scream of effort, the muscles of his arms and chest locked rigid as if he tore at invisible shackles and then those glorious feathered wings wrapped themselves around him like a fabulous cloak.

The difference as his shields surrounded him was immediate and intense, like slamming a shutter between him and the psychic pounding that was the avatar's wrath. Lightheaded with relief, Aidan let himself sag forward, unable to do anything more than kneel there, sweating and shuddering, scarcely able to believe that he had come through that holocaust of shock and fear alive. He took a shaky breath, slowly accepting that, though it had felt as if his mind and body were being shredded, he was essentially unharmed. The shields he had feared were nothing more than his imagination had saved him. *Not bad for an amateur.* He almost managed a smile. Yet even as he allowed himself that moment's relief the sound of flesh striking wood jerked his head round and he realised that the nightmare was far from over.

He might have escaped from that terrible inhuman rage, but it seemed that Eldritch had not. As Aidan watched, the wizard's body twisted, trembling and jerking like a man on the edge of a fit. Eldritch's eyes were closed as though he were still asleep, but the corded muscles of his outflung arm stood out in tension and in the pale glow of the lamplight the skin of his arms and chest was sheened with sweat. Any remaining conceit at his own prowess vanished as Aidan scrambled over to the wizard's side.

'Put your shields up, you idiot.'

He couldn't understand why Eldritch was still suffering. If he had managed to shield himself against the avatar surely it was a simple enough thing for the wizard to do. But maybe he couldn't.

He had said the veil had taken the last of his power; perhaps he simply didn't have the strength to shield himself now. Or perhaps, thought Aidan, it was because he had been asleep when the attack came and now he was trapped in the avatar's grasp as though in a nightmare. Acting on instinct, Aidan grabbed that outflung arm and shook Eldritch, at the same time shouting his name, but there was no response, no let up in that frantic struggle.

Aidan pulled back. It was clear that he wasn't reaching Eldritch. Probably the man was beyond reacting to anything but the pain of the avatar's presence. If that was the case... Aidan took a deep breath and slapped Eldritch hard across the face.

'Eldritch! Put your shields up!' But Eldritch twisted away from him with a whimper of pain, his body curling into a foetal position. Aidan raised his hand again, but the utter vulnerability of that turned back, its pale flesh tracked with the papery silver of old scars, stopped him and he lowered his hand, unable to bring himself to do it.

But what could he do? He couldn't just leave Eldritch as he was. He had no idea how long the avatar could sustain its attack, but purely from his own experience he didn't think Eldritch could survive much more of this. If he chose to do nothing, he would sit here and watch Eldritch die.

Use your own shields, boy.

The voice spoke out of the stillness in the back of his mind. Aidan froze. Use his own shields. Was such a thing possible? It was a simple idea, but the thought of doing anything that might disrupt that fragile protection was terrifying. Having blocked out the avatar's rage once, he didn't think he could stand to be subjected to it again. Aidan felt his palms go clammy with fear. *I can't*. But beside him Eldritch's body stiffened, his back arching as the avatar's influence seethed over him, sending him twisting backwards and forwards, like a fish on a hook. The sleeping bag tangled around his hips and the lamplight caught on a thin trickle of blood that ran from the corner of his mouth. Aidan saw it and looked away in shame knowing he had done that.

'Oh God...'

It was more prayer than blasphemy for the thought of what he was about to try scared him more than he could have said. Yet whatever the consequence he knew he had no choice; he couldn't leave the wizard to suffer. Aidan swallowed against the sudden tightness in his throat, wishing with all his heart that there was some other way but knowing that there wasn't. There was nothing for it; he would just have to make this work.

His mind made up, Aidan settled himself cross-legged beside Eldritch, as close as he dared to the thrashing body, and closed his eyes. He wished it was as easy to shut out the sound of Eldritch's strained, panting breaths and the small, animal noises of pain that were beginning to be torn from his throat. Aidan gritted his teeth and tried to put such considerations out of his mind, but it was very hard. It was one thing doing this as an exercise in Gwyn's lounge, but it was very different when a man's life depended upon it.

Relax and focus.

Once more that half-heard voice in his mind steadied him and again he had the feeling that someone older and wiser stood just behind him, one strong, callused hand resting lightly on his shoulder. The sensation was somehow comforting and disconcerting at the same time.

'Steady, son, don't crack up now,' he muttered. For a second he wondered what he would see if he turned his head, but decided he didn't want to know. *One thing at a time*, he told himself. His imaginary friend could wait. He caught a thread of amusement then and for a second he could have sworn the phantom grip tightened on his shoulder as though in approval.

Nervously Aidan rubbed sweating palms along his thighs. He balled his hands into fists and then shook them out, consciously forcing himself to relax. Right. One thing at a time, indeed. He was already aware of his shields, so reaching out and connecting with them took little thought. It was what he had to do next that frightened him. When he had first tried extending his shields with Gwyn he had managed to move them less than an arm's length before they had started to fade. If this was to work he would have to extend them further and keep them strong. Aidan swallowed convulsively. He understood he was a raw novice when it came to this fantasy of working with shields and energy, but he had to believe he was capable of doing that. Either way he knew that if he focussed on the alternative he and Eldritch were as good as dead. So, he would do what he told every beginner to do: do it the way I've shown you and concentrate on the basics. It worked in karate; he could only pray it would work here too.

Just as Gwyn had taught him, Aidan took a deep breath, focussing on it, following it down into his body, using it as a path to find his centre. He put away all thoughts of success or failure. Nor did he let himself listen to the sounds made by the man in front of him or try to judge if there was any change that might suggest Eldritch was losing his battle with the avatar. Ruthlessly he blocked out everything except his contact with his shields and the soft flow of his breath and gradually he relaxed and found his way to the quiet place that Gwyn's exercise had shown him. In the stillness between one breath and the next he felt the air around him change and he knew that if he reached down he would feel the grittiness of sand beneath his fingers, rather than the worn boards of the cabin floor.

Feeling the familiar sense of lightness and strength stealing over him, Aidan began to extend his shields outwards, expanding the little sanctuary they created around him. In his mind's eye he could see those glorious feathers sweeping away from him and he forced himself to breathe steadily as he watched them begin to spread apart, just as they had on that first evening at Gwyn's. Now, as then, he noted the shimmering iridescence beginning to form between them and he consciously directed some of his energy into that gauzy light, warming it and brightening it as he continued to push them outwards. As his ribcage expanded with each breath so he envisaged his shields expanding, mirroring that movement. In his mind he spread his arms wide and his shields spread with him lengthening out until the space bounded by them was sufficient to take a man's prone body.

There was a sudden sense of resistance and Aidan realised the edge of his shields were brushing up against Eldritch. He thought he could almost see that sprawled shape, etched in starlight and blue fire, through the curtain of his shields. Eldritch lay still now, twisted half out of the sleeping bag, his good arm flung wide, the other draped across his chest. If he was still breathing, Aidan could not tell, but he pushed the thought aside almost impatiently. There was nothing more he could do for the man now. He was either in time to save him or he was not. Rushing now would only damn the pair of them. The cold, dusty air stung his nostrils as he filled his own lungs, preparing himself for one final effort and then he reached out with his shields and wrapped them around Eldritch's crumpled form.

CHAPTER 20

It was a curiously intimate sensation having someone else physically within his shields and, certainly in this instance, not a comfortable one. Aidan felt the grey muffling of leaden exhaustion swamping his own flesh, almost as though it rolled off Eldritch in waves. It covered even the hot red agony of his shoulder, which Aidan now realised Eldritch had used as a goad to keep himself going; a risky game to play, and one that had ultimately taken him beyond the limits of his strength and then deserted him, leaving him drained and defenceless when the avatar struck. There was something else there as well, something alien that Aidan had no name for. He felt it as he lifted Eldritch, pulling the sleeping bag once more around those cold, pale shoulders. He sensed it, running like a thread of black ink in water, spreading out from the avatar's bite and seeping into Eldritch's flesh. Even as he became conscious of it, it slipped away from him. A heartbeat later it was gone and Aidan could not have said what it was he thought he had sensed.

But there was no time to dwell on such things for something else was becoming clear to him. As he cradled Eldritch's body, he was aware of a hollow emptiness, as though more than consciousness had been drained from the man. He had no idea how the knowledge came to him. Perhaps – like the shared intimacy of Eldritch's pain – it was because Eldritch lay within his shields, but whatever the reason Aidan was aware that deep within Eldritch's body there was a sense of faltering, of weakening. He could sense it as though he watched a flame guttering in a lamp too cracked and broken to sustain it. In the flesh under his fingers he felt that ebbing like a second pulse, fading and then momentarily strengthening again, but each time just a fraction less than it had been before. The understanding went through him like a knife.

'No, that's not right! We beat off the avatar. You can't give up now.'

He pulled Eldritch closer, pressing his hands to the too cold flesh and wrapping his arms around him as though by doing so he could hold the fading spirit within its body. Anger flared, brief and unreasonable.

'Damn it, you're not dying on me now. I won't let you.'

But he had no idea what he could do to stop it. He chaffed at Eldritch's hands then cuffed him lightly on the cheeks, little love taps compared with his earlier attempt to rouse him, but Eldritch remained unresponsive in his arms.

'Damn you,' he whispered, looking down at that pale, slack face. In the patchwork of lantern light and shadows, its frame of hair seemed no darker than the thread of blood that had spilled over those colourless lips and clotted in the stubble along his jaw. 'You said you'd be alright, that all you needed was rest,' he reminded the unconscious man, as though those words could somehow stop that fatal weakening. But that had been before the return of the avatar had drained the last of the wizard's strength from him. Rest would not be sufficient to save Eldritch now.

Aidan felt Eldritch's breath catch and falter and then steady once more. He could breathe for him, but what good would it do when there wasn't enough energy to keep his heart beating? Wearily Aidan raised his hand from Eldritch's chest and pushed the hair back from his face, his own body aching with tiredness that wasn't just an echo of Eldritch's collapse. Was it only that evening he had confronted Eldritch on the moonlit hillside, the pair of them facing off like sworn enemies about to do battle? He would never have guessed that scant hours later he would be holding the man as he lay dying. And there was nothing he could do to stop it.

Unless… something Eldritch had said earlier teased at Aidan's mind.

No, he thought, but the memory refused to be buried.

I don't need healing… Eldritch had said. It had turned out to be a lie, but the assumption behind those words was that Aidan was a healer. Why would he have said that?

I can't heal anyone. Aidan swallowed and shook his head.

'I wish it were true, but I'm not a healer. I tried once, dear God, I tried…'

He broke off, a feeling of sick dread in the pit of his stomach. This was ridiculous. He had no healing ability! It had been proven beyond doubt nine years ago. He licked his lips, his mouth suddenly gone dry, pushing the associated memories away, but his mind stubbornly refused to give up the tiny seed of hope that had been uncovered.

This is stupid, he told himself. *There's nothing I can do.* But what if that weren't true? Something had given Eldritch the idea. He looked down at the still form in his arms, but could find no answers there; nothing he could think of would have led Eldritch to see him as a healer, yet it hardly mattered. The man was dying. If he tried and failed it couldn't make the situation any worse. Besides, surely anything was better than sitting in the semi-dark, measuring the seconds between each small movement of Eldritch's chest, holding his own breath after each slow exhalation as he waited for that awful moment when he would know that the stillness was final.

Aware from the sudden pounding of his own heart that he had made his decision, Aidan closed his hand briefly on Eldritch's arm.

'If this doesn't work I'm writing "Told you so" in big letters on your coffin.'

Feeling like Pandora, with her hands upon the lid of the Box, Aidan closed his eyes and reached back into his memory for everything Gwyn had ever told him about healing. He had spent so long burying those memories he was surprised how easily they answered his call, each one dragging with it a tangled knot of emotions. Carefully he sorted through them as they surfaced, refusing to acknowledge anything but the knowledge he sought. He concentrated only on hearing Gwyn's voice; the gentle, matter-of-fact way she had spoken of letting energy flow through his hands and into his mother's body. She had talked of feeling that energy, that essence of life, but though he had tried to do what she said he had never been able to feel what she described, no matter how desperately he had wanted to. Now, as he settled his mind once more, going almost instinctively to that still place within him, he wondered for the first time if that inability to feel was because the energy had not been there or because each person experienced it in a different way. Gwyn had tried her best to describe the sensation to him, but was it really possible? Like trying to capture pain or joy; you knew when you felt them, but would your description mean anything to someone who had never experienced those things themselves? He put the thought to one side. He knew there was energy within him now; he had experienced that soft, glowing warmth radiating through his body. It only remained for him to find out if he could heal with it.

Mostly when Gwyn healed, she held her hands directly over the injury or area of sickness, but he recalled that towards the end she had often sat with one hand over his mother's heart and the other over her solar plexus. When she did that she said she was concentrating on sending her strength. Aidan focussed his attention on that image of Gwyn, seeing her as she had been then, her hair grown back to little more than an elfin crop since she had shaved it off, an act of solidarity with her friend when Anne had lost hers to chemotherapy. She had turned up one day with the feathery ends dyed a bright cerise. He had been mortified by her appearance, but his mother had laughed and declared she would do the same as soon as hers had reached a decent length. Of course, it never had.

In the picture Aidan had of Gwyn now, the sleeves of her old plaid shirt were rolled back and he saw how the muscles of her forearms were tattooed with a filigree of cat scratch scars and freckles, like the faded remains of a tribal rite of passage. He noticed for the first time that she had taken off her assortment of bangles and her silver and crystal rings and wondered at how naked her arms seemed, stripped of their usual adornment. He studiously ignored the gangly teenager sat opposite her, copying her moves, and absolutely refused to acknowledge the fragile figure lying in the bed between them. Instead he concentrated on Gwyn's hands, noting how her fingers were slightly curved as though she was focussing that unseen energy, sending it from her in precise streams into his mother's body.

Keeping the picture of Gwyn firmly in his mind, Aidan brought his awareness back to the present. He shifted position, letting Eldritch's head drop back against his shoulder, catching the unconscious man under the arms so he could steady the weight of him against his chest while leaving his hands free. Though it might have been easier, instinct told him not to break the physical link between himself and Eldritch by laying the other man down. There was reassurance in that simple human contact and after the brutality of the avatar's attack he felt it was important for Eldritch to know that, in whatever darkness he wandered, he was not alone.

That at least he could do. As Aidan cupped his left hand over the side of Eldritch's chest, there where he would have leaned his head to hear the slowly beating heart, and settled his right hand over the man's solar plexus, doubt assailed him once more. Though he filled his mind with the image of that gently shifting tide of energy, though he could picture his body filled with its warm golden glow, he could not touch it. It was as though it lay on the other side of a glass wall and he did not know how to reach his hand across that barrier and make it real.

Desperation welled up in him and with it came anger. He threw himself at that invisible barrier, battering at it as though it could be overcome by strength of will. At the same time he realised he could no longer feel any movement from the man he held, but even the sharp pain of that realisation was not enough to shatter the glass wall. *Damn it*, he raged; he could do this! Gwyn had shown him this the very first night they had worked on shielding together.

And then it came to him. It was as though he had stepped out of himself and was looking over his shoulder at the still body in his arms. He knew Eldritch was close to death, but he put the knowledge to one side as though it no longer concerned him. He would do this because he chose to do it; there was no need for any other reason. In this disembodied state he felt as though he had all the time in the world. He curled himself around Eldritch, pulling him as close as possible against his body, bowing his head so his cheek rested on that matted hair. As he did so he felt his shields flex and tighten, folding themselves like angels' wings around the pair of them. A sense of calm filled Aidan. He took a deep breath and as he exhaled, the barrier melted away like mist. As though it were the most natural thing in the world, Aidan reached across and let the energy flow through him. He filled the space beneath his shields with warm, honey-coloured light, pouring it like a libation over the other man's skin and gradually in response he felt the tiny core of life that remained within Eldritch flicker and then strengthen.

Changing his focus, he felt the stirring of Eldritch's breath as he drew back from the boundaries of death and sometime later – Aidan couldn't have said how long it took – the gradual deepening as he passed from there into the realms of sleep. For a while Aidan continued to watch him until he was sure the crisis was over then slowly he let the light fade from around them, bringing it back within the shell of his body. He felt utterly exhausted as he came back fully into his physical body, yet at the same time curiously warm and peaceful. He had done it. Too tired for exultation, he was satisfied just to sit and let that simple fact sing across his soul. Triumph was the warmth of a living body in his arms and the steady beat of Eldritch's heart under his hand. There was no need for anything else. Carefully, so as not to disturb him, he lowered Eldritch to the floor and then stretched out alongside him. He was asleep almost before he had closed his eyes.

CHAPTER 21

In the chill dawn light Aidan hiked up to the top of the plantation, where he knew he could get a signal on his mobile, and phoned Gwyn. Standing with the vista of the reservoir below him, tendrils of mist rising from the silvery waters and the sky changing slowly from dove grey through peach to lemon and then to the palest sapphire, he wondered at the fact that he had come through the night. It scarcely seemed possible.

He stood for a while to catch his breath. Lightheaded from hunger and with his body aching from tiredness and a night on a cold floor, still he savoured the way the cold air made his nose sting and how the earthy scents of the forest were underlain with the far off sweetness of water. The sun was just showing above the horizon, leaving a trail of fool's gold across the pewter surface of the reservoir. All the signs promised a beautiful day, mild and generous and harking back to the memory of summer, as though trying to make up for the wildness of the night before. It was good to be alive.

Despite it being so early, Gwyn answered her phone on the first ring. Though he knew she must have been worried, she hid it well, only her initial 'Aidan. Thank the Lady!' gave away just how concerned she had been. Typical Gwyn though, there were no questions as to why he hadn't contacted her sooner. As straightforward as ever she contented herself with a simple, 'Are you both alright?' for which Aidan was hugely grateful. He had neither the energy nor the inclination to embark on long explanations now, having yet to come to terms with the night's events in his own mind. He pushed the hair back from his eyes and glanced back the way he had come, aware as never before of the depth of shadows under the trees. *It could*, he thought, *have been very different.*

'More or less, yes. I'm fine. Eldritch got a bit munched.'

There was silence at the other end of the line as Gwyn digested this, weighing his casual phrasing against all that might have happened. Of course, she knew of old how he tended to downplay any physical injury.

'Exactly how "munched"?' she asked carefully.

'He'll get over it. I patched him up, but he could really do with having a professional look him over.'

'Hmm.'

There was another pause. Aidan could almost see Gwyn twisting one hand in her hair as she mentally debated how much patching up had been necessary, but once again she resisted asking for details. 'And the avatar?'

'Oh, I should think that it's just fine.'

'Ah.'

'I'll tell you later. Just come and get us, will you? I don't think either of us is up to walking back to the cars.'

Gwyn must have heard the weariness creeping into his voice for all she said was, 'Where are you?'

'We're at the ropes course; we ended up spending the night in the hut there, but we'll meet you in the car park.'

'You're sure you're alright?'

'Yeah. It was a long night, Gwyn.' His voice faltered as some of the darker memories bobbed to the surface.

'Save the details for later. I'll be with you in half an hour.'

'Thanks, Gwyn.' Had he been able to he would have hugged her. He hoped she heard the gratitude in his voice. 'If you don't see us when you get there we'll be on our way down from the hut,' he added, conscious that it would take him most of that half-hour to get back and he wasn't sure just how mobile Eldritch would be.

'Don't worry.' Her tone conveyed a small reassuring hug of its own. 'I'll find you.'

By the time Aidan returned to the hut, Eldritch had managed to struggle into his clothes although he looked a mess. He sat propped against the back wall, the sleeping bag draped around his shoulders partly concealing the bloody remains of his shirt, its slit sleeve hanging loose from his shoulder. His t-shirt still lay on the floor; too shredded to bother with, but he had somehow managed to get his jeans on one handed and his boots were on his feet although the laces had defeated him. As Aidan opened the door he raised his head, but did not speak.

'The cavalry's on its way. Time to go.'

The news elicited a wan smile that spoke volumes about just how little that idea appealed to Eldritch. Though the man hadn't said as much, Aidan guessed he was feeling sick and shaky and disinclined to any form of movement. From the look of him the brief exertion of dressing had taken all his energy.

As he dropped to a crouch, Aidan noticed the slab of Kendal mint cake he had left beside the sleeping bag was untouched, despite the note he had wrapped round it bearing the instruction 'Eat this. It will make you feel better'. He picked it up, turning it over in his hand and then handed it to Eldritch.

'You need to eat something.'

Eldritch took the bar from Aidan – it was that or be poked in the chest with it – but he did so without any show of interest and, once he had it, he made no move to take even the smallest bite. He regarded the younger man balefully, his grey eyes very dark in their charcoal-dusted sockets.

'You sound like my mother.'

'And you're behaving like a sulky brat,' which was hardly fair. It was only the recent memory of Gwyn standing over him forcing him to drink beer and how much better he had felt as a result that had convinced Aidan to ignore his own nausea and choke down a couple of mouthfuls of the sugary confection himself. But it had made him feel better and he was certain it would do the same for Eldritch if he could be convinced to give it a go.

'Holding it and waiting for it to diffuse into your bloodstream's not going to work. You have to physically eat it.'

That provoked the expected scowl, which at least was better than the look of flat exhaustion that it replaced.

'Yes, Mother.'

'Carry on like that and I'll hold your nose until you have to open your mouth, just like I do to get Sula to take her worming tablets.'

Never having been threatened with such treatment before, Eldritch seemed at a loss for a suitable rejoinder. Finally, he settled for, 'I bet you would as well.'

Aidan treated him to an evil grin and nodded. 'Yep. Trust me, when I woke up I felt as bad as you look. Well, maybe not quite that bad,' he corrected himself, cocking his head to one side as if to study Eldritch more closely. 'But pretty grim anyway. I know your shoulder's giving you gyp.'

Eldritch raised an eyebrow in comment on this level of understatement, but the look in Aidan's eyes acknowledged that he had a very good idea just how much 'gyp' that shoulder was giving and he wasn't unsympathetic.

'But it's got to be what – eighteen hours – since you last ate anything and since then you've hiked across half of Wales, gone ten rounds with the avatar and then used what was left of your energy to keep us safe for the night.' Again Aidan's eyes said more than the bald statement of his words. 'Your blood sugar's going to be lower than a snake's belly and that alone will make you feel pretty sick. You don't even have to chew it,' he coaxed. 'Put a piece in your mouth and just let it dissolve. You'll feel a lot better, I promise.'

Eldritch balanced the sugar bar on his knees and rubbed his forehead with his good hand. He grimaced as his fingers encountered the tangled matt of his hair and he dragged his hand through it, causing strands to stand up in random spikes. It did nothing to improve his appearance, but Aidan doubted that he looked much better himself, so he forbore to comment. Instead he looked pointedly at the mint cake until Eldritch picked it up again with an exaggerated sigh.

'I suppose it's the only way I'm going to get you to stop nagging at me.'

The chipped bark surface of the path squelched wetly underfoot as together Aidan and Eldritch came down the hill, stepping out from the dappled shadows of the trees and into the morning sunshine. Below them, Gwyn's old blue hatchback was just pulling into the car park. It was, thought Aidan, possibly the most beautiful thing he had ever seen. As Gwyn emerged from the car he had a sudden urge to run the last twenty yards, pick her up bodily and swing her round in celebration, he was so pleased to see her, but he wrestled it down, contenting himself instead with lengthening his stride, hurrying towards her without too undignified a rush. Behind him he heard a huff of breath from Eldritch, which might have been a smothered laugh – perhaps his eagerness was more obvious than he had thought – but he chose to ignore it and the man made no other comment, dropping back as Aidan strode down the path. Although he had surprised Aidan by managing the walk down from the hut unaided – no mean feat for someone whose appearance suggested he had all the strength of chewed string – Eldritch wasn't going to manage a sprint finish. Aidan guessed it was largely a matter of stubbornness and carefully husbanded strength that had brought him this far.

The second sweetest thing Aidan had seen that morning was the whirlwind of russet fur that bounded from the car the moment Gwyn opened the passenger door.

'It's alright, Gwyn, let her go. Sula! Here, girl!'

He needn't have bothered calling her. As soon as Gwyn took her hand from her collar, Sula streaked away from her, hurtling across the intervening ground and bounding up at him as though they had been separated for months rather than for a single night. Laughing, Aidan grabbed the front paws that planted themselves in the middle of his chest and hugged her. Normally he wouldn't allow her to jump up at anyone – normally she wouldn't do it – but right now he was willing to overlook such a breach of discipline and simply rejoice in being alive. He nuzzled his head into the soft russet of her fur, rubbing her ears while she yipped joyfully and attempted to twist round and lick his face.

'Behave, you daft mutt,' he protested, jerking his head back out of reach of the slobbering tongue. 'I don't need a wash. Well, not from you anyway.'

He ruffled her ears again and put her down, aware that he was grinning like a lunatic and not caring. Down by the car he could see that Gwyn was also smiling broadly, amused by their reunion antics. She looked up at him and shook her head as though to say, *You're mad.*

'Don't worry, you're next,' he shouted back at her. 'Come on, girl.' He glanced round for Sula. A low growl stopped him in his tracks.

Sula stood in the middle of the path behind him, stiff-legged, every hair along her spine standing up in bristling defiance. She did not respond to his call. Instead, every ounce of her attention was focussed on the path back through the trees. On it stood Marcus Eldritch. Sula took one stiff-legged, bristling step towards him.

'Sula! No!'

Aidan dived forward and grabbed her collar, hauling her back. Under his hand he could feel her throat vibrating, the low, angry viciousness of her growl more unnerving than any bark. The sound was primeval, welling up from some dark and feral ancestry, some long dormant part of her that had never submitted to domestication. He had never heard its like before and it made the hairs on the back of his neck stand up. He glanced up at Eldritch, offering up a little prayer of thanks that the man had had the sense to stand absolutely still.

'She was alright with you the other day at the sailing club. You don't normally have this effect on dogs, do you?'

If Eldritch's face had been pale before, it was several shades whiter now and his eyes were wide and shocked. He looked scared, as well he might, thought Aidan; the sight of Sula must be triggering a nightmare cascade of memories of the avatar, but somehow he kept that from his voice.

'Not usually, no.'

He paused and licked his lips, breathing shallowly. His eyes flicked to Sula and then back to Aidan, but he was careful to make no other movement.

'She can probably smell the avatar's blood on me,' he said in that same calm, level voice, the inflection not varying. 'Easy, girl,' he added, low and soothing. 'I'm not going to hurt you. I'm not going to hurt your dad, either.'

Sula leaned forward against her collar, the malevolence in her growl undiminished.

'I don't think she's listening to me.'

Eldritch lapsed into silence. Aidan could see the fine film of sweat standing out on his face. Enough was enough.

'Sula!'

Aidan wrapped his free hand round her muzzle, clamping it tight, and shook her. The growl stopped abruptly, replaced by a surprised whine. Immediately Aidan slipped his hand from her muzzle and rubbed the barrel of her chest reassuringly.

'Good girl! There's a good girl. It's only Eldritch.' He looked up at the man and grinned, figuring he was in need of reassurance too. 'He may not smell so good at the moment, but it's okay, he's not going to hurt us. You've met him before. He's a friend.'

Sula gave a sharp bark as though unconvinced. Still holding her collar, Aidan reached out towards Eldritch.

'Okay, give me your hand.'

Eldritch looked at him doubtfully.

'So I can get this arm bitten as well?' But he was already extending his arm, trusting that Aidan knew what he was doing. Aidan took his hand, guiding it down towards Sula's nose so that she could smell their two scents intermingled.

'There. That's okay, isn't it?' Aidan might have been reassuring Eldritch as much as Sula. 'This is Eldritch. You remember him,' he said, as though making an introduction to a forgetful maiden aunt. 'He's not so bad after all. Are you okay?' he asked as Sula sniffed again at Eldritch's hand and whined anxiously. He could feel a slight tremor, of tension or fatigue, in Eldritch's arm.

'Yeah.'

A trace of weariness had crept back into Eldritch's voice.

'Are you *really* okay?' he asked again, the narrowing of his eyes telling Eldritch that he wanted the truth, not heroics. Eldritch managed a small smile.

'I'll be glad to sit down,' he admitted. 'Preferably somewhere quiet with no one shouting or growling or attacking me.'

Aidan smiled sympathetically. 'I can't guarantee that just yet,' he said, glancing over his shoulder to where Gwyn was still waiting beside her car. She was watching them closely, the expression on her face unreadable, and for the first time it occurred to him that there might have been other reasons why she had brought Sula with her, not just to keep her out of the way of the cats. Yet if what had just happened had been some sort of test, had it been passed or failed? Eldritch followed his gaze and an expression close to pain tightened his face. Aidan remembered the intensity of his own feelings on meeting Eldritch last night. It seemed like a lifetime ago, but this was the man who had tricked and deceived Gwyn and then left her alone and unconscious. Despite all that had happened since, he felt an echo of that anger rekindle itself deep in his gut. If he could still feel that way, how was Gwyn going to react to the man who had betrayed her trust? In a colder voice than he had intended, he said, 'Come on. Let's get this over with.'

Gwyn's first words were not encouraging.

'You bastard,' she spat as Eldritch approached her. She stepped out to meet him, her arms folded across her chest as though she couldn't quite trust her hands not to betray her. 'If you ever – ever – try and pull a stunt like that again, I will kill you.'

She didn't raise her voice, but that only made her words more frightening. There was enough vitriol in her tone to flay skin raw, but there was also an underlying coldness that let Aidan know that this was no idle threat. Like the viciousness of Sula's growl, this was something new, a side of Gwyn he had never been aware of. It was like drawing a familiar knife from its sheath and seeing there was blood along its edge, that it was, in fact, a killing blade.

'And I will do it in ways that make you wish you'd let the avatar finish you off.'

Aidan couldn't begin to imagine what those were, but he knew with utter certainty that Gwyn did. So, he suspected, did Eldritch.

The man looked dead on his feet. From the way he was standing, Aidan could see he was locking his muscles against the exhaustion that was already stealing back over him. The sugar high from two mouthfuls of Kendal mint cake was never going to last very long. He felt a twinge of sympathy, but he knew better than to try and intervene. This was between Eldritch and Gwyn. He doubted that either of them was even aware of his presence.

'You'd have every right,' Eldritch said. His eyes closed briefly and he made a half-hearted attempt to push the hair back from his face. It was neither tacit apology nor an attempt at reconciliation, just a statement of fact. He made no attempt to justify what he had done by laying out his reasons for her. Perhaps he realised that none of them would make the slightest difference, but the softly spoken, 'I'm sorry,' that followed held the same ring of truth that had underlain Gwyn's promise of vengeance.

Gwyn snorted as though dismissing his words. She stood silently, weighing him up; the grey-eyed Judas who had betrayed her. Yet Aidan remembered her conviction that Eldritch's help would be essential if they were to defeat the avatar. He watched her take in the sling and the bloodstains and his ashen face. Finally, when the silence had been stretched to an almost unbearable length, she broke it.

'You look terrible,' she said.

'You should see the other guy.'

There was a touch of the devil in Eldritch's reply and the faintest trace of a smile. Gwyn, however, wasn't quite ready to let him escape into levity.

'Oh really?'

Sarcasm heated the air between them. The brief-lived smile faded from Eldritch's eyes. He dipped his head, acknowledging her point.

'No, I guess not.'

'I didn't think so.'

Again there was silence, but something passed between them, though Aidan couldn't have said what; an apology perhaps and – just possibly – its acceptance. He read it in the slight softening of

Gwyn's stance and in the subtle change to the set of her shoulders. They would come back to this later, she seemed to say, but now was not the time.

'Come on, get in the car before I change my mind and leave you here, like you deserve.'

CHAPTER 22

'Rise and shine, Aidan. We're home.'

Aidan jerked into wakefulness at the sound of his name and stared in surprise at Gwyn's face peering at him over the seatback. He remembered closing his eyes, relaxing as the warmth and movement of the car made him feel drowsy, but surely he hadn't slept through the entire journey? Gwyn's amused smile suggested otherwise.

'The pair of you went out like lights,' she said, as if in answer to his thoughts. 'We'll go back and get your car later. Sleeping Beauty's too, I suppose.' She cast a sideways glance at Eldritch, her mouth quirking in wry amusement. Aidan took that as a sign that the armistice between them was still intact. 'I didn't have the heart to wake you.'

Aidan rubbed the sleep from his eyes with the heel of his hand. All he could see of Eldritch was a few spiky strands of hair between the seat and the side window where his head had somehow come to rest. He must be tired to be managing to sleep in that position.

'Shouldn't we have taken him to hospital first?'

Gwyn rolled her eyes.

'It's Sunday morning, Aidan. Llancathan doesn't have an A&E department anymore. There'll be one emergency doctor on call covering the whole of Newtown and Welshpool and I don't intend driving all the way to Aber or Shrewsbury. Not before I've taken a look at him first.'

Her expression softened, showing more compassion than her words might have implied and Aidan swallowed his protest. 'A hot meal and bed will do him more good than spending the morning in a hospital corridor, waiting for a junior doctor to dab on some iodine and a few steri–strips and tell him to take paracetamol if it hurts. I can do better than that myself.' She looked back at the sleeping man. 'That's assuming we can wake him up for long enough to get him out of the car.'

She reached across to give Eldritch a shake, but froze as her hand touched him. Aidan saw shock register on her face.

'What? What is it?'

Gwyn stayed where she was, looking intently at Eldritch, and for a second she didn't answer. When she did, it was almost as though she were talking to herself.

'I thought he was shielding.'

Then she seemed to register Aidan's question and turned back to him, an expression of puzzled concern replacing the outright fear that had momentarily haunted her face.

'I'm pretty good at reading power levels and he,' her eyes darted back to Eldritch, 'normally radiates energy. But not this morning. I thought he must have upped his shielding, but he's not. In fact, I'm not sure he's even capable of shielding right now. He's completely drained.'

She stared at Aidan as though seeing him for the first time and her frown deepened. 'And your shields are tighter than they were. A lot tighter. What the Hell happened to you last night?'

Aidan laughed, although the sound was devoid of humour.

'What the Hell didn't happen to us last night?' he threw back at her. He shook his head, denying the memories. 'You really don't want to know.'

Gwyn's look hardened. 'No, Aidan, I do want to know. I'm going to need to know.' Her eyebrows quirked down. 'You've been using power too,' she said, her tone somewhere between observation and accusation. Aidan shrugged noncommittally.

'Okay, it will wait until after breakfast.' Gwyn glanced briefly at Eldritch who was still showing no signs of waking. 'But then we need to talk.' She turned back to her other passenger and shook him gently. 'Eldritch, come on, wake up.'

The man grunted, shifting slightly as though trying to bury his head into a non-existent pillow. She shook him again, somewhat harder, eliciting some mumbling that Aidan translated as 'Go away', or at least a rough equivalent. Gwyn's eyes rolled heavenwards and she turned back to Aidan.

'Tell you what, you keep trying to wake Sleeping Beauty here, while I go open up and put the kettle on.'

Aidan peered at Eldritch. With his long, matted hair and a heavy shadowing of stubble darkening his cheeks and jaw, he looked like a tramp sleeping off one too many bottles of meths.

'I don't have to kiss him, do I?'

Gwyn shot him a venomous look.

'Personally I'd start with a good slap,' she muttered under her breath, then shrugged and added, 'You're a consenting adult, you can do what you want.' Her eyes softened slightly as she got out of the car. 'Just don't blame me if he turns into a frog.'

In the end it took neither kisses nor slapping to rouse Eldritch. Aidan opened the passenger door and the cool morning air combined with a small amount of shaking sufficed to bring the wizard back to a reasonable level of consciousness. While nothing less than a hot bath and a good going over with a razor were going to make him look presentable, the sleep, and probably the warmth, had clearly done him some good. Aidan was pleased to see that some colour had crept back into his cheeks. He might still resemble a tramp, but at least not one who had been dead for three days.

'Food,' prompted Aidan as Eldritch unfolded himself from the car and got used to the idea of being vertical again. 'Warmth. A hot shower… coffee…'

Eldritch perked up visibly at that final suggestion.

'You mean she's not going to tear me into little bits and feed me to the cats?' he asked as he and Aidan walked slowly along the path towards the open front door. Sula lingered, sniffing purposefully at the gate posts and then trotted over to investigate a sprawling hydrangea and the contents of the bird table.

'What makes you think she'd do that?' Aidan grinned at the look Eldritch shot him. 'She loves those cats.'

He turned to call Sula to heel so he didn't see exactly what happened next, but the sound of Eldritch's cry – sharp and high like a man in mortal agony – went through him like an electric shock. He spun round in time to see Eldritch crash to his knees in the doorway, his good hand clutching at his shoulder, his eyes rolled back in his head. He made no attempt to catch himself as he toppled forward and it was only Aidan's diving lunge that stopped him going face first into the slate threshold. The pair of them fell together, Aidan managing to get his shoulder down first so he rolled with the impact rather than having it knock the breath from him. He found himself lying on his back with Eldritch sprawled on top of him. Through his arms he could feel the muscles of Eldritch's body lock rigid.

'Gwyn!' Aidan was shouting for her even as he rolled over, pushing himself to his knees and taking both himself and Eldritch out of the cramped space of the doorway and back into the garden.

'Gwyn, he's fitting!'

He already had his jacket off and was wadding it protectively under Eldritch's head, but as he did so he paused, realising that no longer seemed to be the case. The convulsion-like tautness of Eldritch's body had slackened and he lay still but for the frantic heaving of his chest as if, for a moment, all he could do was struggle to drag air into protesting lungs. Gwyn was there a second later, appearing beside Eldritch's prone form as though she had materialised from thin air.

'I'll call an ambulance.'

Gwyn's hand grabbed him, pulling him back even as he scrambled to his feet. Aidan was shocked by the strength of her, her hand like an iron cuff around his wrist.

'No!'

He would have twisted free, but some small, calm corner of his mind registered the fact that Eldritch had spoken at the same time as Gwyn, his voice little more than a desperate rasp of breath, but the incongruity of that joint command shocked Aidan into compliance. As Gwyn released his wrist, he stayed where he was, a reluctant participant in the uncomfortable scene playing out before him.

Though Aidan had known Gwyn all his life, the woman kneeling beside Eldritch now was a stranger to him. She made no move to touch or comfort the stricken man; if anything her presence seemed almost to threaten him. There was a fierceness about her wholly untempered by mercy or compassion. Looking at her face, Aidan glimpsed the same fey wildness that he had seen in Eldritch when they had met in the pale circle of moonlight, under the ancient trees. Now, as then, some instinct told him that death was less than a heartbeat away. Eldritch seemed to sense it too for he stared up at her, a mixture of shock and desperation in his pale face.

'What harm do you mean, Marcus Eldritch?'

Gwyn's voice rang with an undercurrent of authority that seemed to come from beyond her small frame. There was the power of ritual in her words, invoking a force that compelled the listener to answer. Eldritch fought to get his breathing under control, slowing the shuddering breaths until he could speak.

'None!' he gasped; his voice grated as though the word was torn from his throat. He shook his head weakly, the dark strands of his hair tangling across his forehead. Aidan thought he seemed more shocked than Gwyn by what had just happened. The wizard made a small movement with his hand as though reaching out to her, but the strength eluded him and his hand curled back across his chest. Gwyn watched all of this dispassionately. Her face could have been carved from alabaster for all the emotion she showed. Watching the pair of them, Aidan could sense Eldritch's desperation as he sought for some way to convince her of the truth of his words.

'I swear it. By—'

Swift as a striking snake, Gwyn's fingers were on his lips, silencing him.

'Best not say such things,' she said, 'however well intentioned.'

Her voice echoed with the weight of other worlds; deadly and strange. She continued to eye him up, judging him in some way that Aidan could not understand, though she could hardly miss the shivers that were starting to rack Eldritch's body.

'Gwyn, for God's sake.' Aidan's protest died half-formed as she turned that medusa stare on him.

Stay out of this, her eyes seemed to say. She turned back to Eldritch and Aidan knew he had been dismissed from her thoughts as though he no longer existed.

'Would that it never comes to that.'

Aidan had no idea what she was referring to, but he felt terror stir deep in the marrow of his bones at the weight of feeling underpinning her words. He wondered what oath Eldritch had been about to offer and for what stakes. *The usual ones, boy; body, life and soul,* whispered a small voice in the back of his mind and Aidan knew it for the truth.

'Look at me.'

Gwyn's hand slipped from Eldritch's lips to his jaw, forcing his obedience, though in truth he lacked the strength to turn away. It was no gentle touch either. Aidan saw Eldritch's skin whitening as her fingers dug into the tender flesh, yet the man made no whisper of complaint. He stared back unblinking, fear evident in those grey-ringed irises. Yet as he watched Eldritch surrender to that pitiless scrutiny, Aidan realised with a shudder that it was not Gwyn that the man was afraid of.

How long that strange examination went on Aidan could not say. Afterwards he thought it must have been less than a minute, but at the time it felt like hours and for Eldritch it must have seemed an eternity. Then, as suddenly as it had started, it was over. Aidan felt a shift in the energies boiling around Gwyn and in that moment she opened her hand and released Eldritch's jaw. Aidan saw how the blood flowed back into the spots where her fingers had been, blotching the pale skin. Eldritch was going to have an interesting set of bruises there, but Gwyn offered neither apology nor explanation.

'Be you welcome in my house for as long as that intention remains true.'

Once more her words held the power of an invocation. Eldritch looked like a condemned man who had felt the executioner strap the electrodes against his skin and then seen him inexplicably walk away, leaving him unharmed. He shuddered once, his eyes closing and Aidan thought he had fainted, for the tension drained from his body, but after a second the charcoal-dusted lids opened again and his eyes sought Gwyn's. In a voice barely louder than a breath he murmured, 'Thank you.'

Gwyn brushed the tangled hair back from his temples as absently as she might have stroked one of her cats. She sucked in a breath as though she might say something, but then she shook her head, leaving whatever comment she might have voiced unspoken. Whatever power had ridden her it seemed she was herself again. She looked at Aidan.

'Help me take him inside.'

CHAPTER 23

Propped against the sturdier of Gwyn's two armchairs, with his long legs splayed out in front of him, Eldritch regarded Gwyn warily from beneath eyelids the colour of bruises. How much of that wariness was attributable solely to Gwyn and how much to the large pair of scissors she was brandishing Aidan didn't like to guess. Certainly her behaviour so far this morning was enough to give Eldritch cause for concern, but Aidan was reasonably confident that Gwyn wasn't about to do anything rash. He suspected any means of vengeance she selected would be far more subtle than a pair of scissors through the chest, or indeed any other part of Eldritch's anatomy. Then again, it wasn't his anatomy that said scissors were currently pointing at.

Yet for all his innate wariness even Eldritch's endurance had its limits and it seemed to Aidan that the events of the last half-hour had pushed him very close to them. Even as he watched Gwyn's approach, his eyelids were drooping, though he jerked them open again almost immediately, straightening slightly as though such small measures could hold back the inevitable. Of course, the whisky tumbler full of brandy and hot water that Gwyn had forced down his throat a few minutes earlier wouldn't be helping his level of alertness, even if it had eased the trembling that had racked his body as they brought him inside. Mixed with sufficient glucose powder to sustain a marathon runner it must have been almost unbearably sweet, but Eldritch had swallowed it with none of the protests two mouthfuls of Kendal mint cake had elicited from him earlier. Taken on an empty stomach, Aidan judged it would be hitting his system just about now.

'How come I only got beer when I went all wobbly on you?' he had asked as – somewhat to his surprise – Gwyn had produced a packet of Java coffee, pointed him at the kettle and told him to make the strongest brew he thought he could stomach.

'Because I assumed you wanted to drive home that night.'

Stirring a second spoonful of glucose into the tumbler she had glanced at the wall between kitchen and lounge as though she could see through it to her problematic house guest, stretched out white-faced and shaking in the middle of the room.

'He's not going anywhere for quite some time.'

Threat or promise? Aidan wondered. Even the most casual observer would be hard pushed to declare Eldritch fit for anything more taxing than prolonged bed rest, yet Gwyn's tone suggested she wouldn't give him the option to leave even if that weren't the case. Aidan pondered the possible reasons for that as he watched her steady Eldritch's shaking hand on the glass so that he could drink. He hadn't realised that he too was beginning to shake until Gwyn had pushed him down into her desk chair and told him not to move until she said so.

Now, as he applied himself alternately to the heavily sugared coffee and the doorstop of peanut butter and jam sandwich that Gwyn had placed in front of him – purely as a stopgap until a 'proper' breakfast could be constructed – Aidan realised just how rough he had been feeling. It gave him an interesting insight into how hard Eldritch must be fighting to keep his eyes open as Gwyn knelt down beside him. As Aidan had anticipated, she did nothing more threatening than add the scissors to the assortment of first aid equipment beside him, but for a second Eldritch's face held the look of a prisoner watching the torturer laying out his tools.

'That's a very neat sling.'

Gwyn's voice was just a fraction too bright for the comment to be anything other than a deliberate attempt to lighten the atmosphere. Eldritch made no response, but, like Sampson feeling the cold blade of Delilah's shears, he stiffened as Gwyn's fingers brushed the back of his neck, parting his hair so she could get at the knot and untie it. Intent on what she was doing, Gwyn couldn't see the expression on Eldritch's face, but Aidan could and it surprised him. Eldritch looked like a wild animal ready to bolt. *Surely he can't be shy,* Aidan thought. *She's undoing a sling, not his jeans.* Maybe it was what Gwyn might do next that was worrying him. Aidan took a hasty swig of coffee to hide his smirk. Gwyn could charm the birds out of the trees, but she was having a decidedly less positive impact on Eldritch.

'Are you okay?'

The seductress in question looked round at Eldritch, but if seduction was what was on her mind it didn't show in her face. She cocked her head to one side, a concerned frown creasing the skin between her brows as she studied him. For a moment Eldritch did nothing but stare back at her, his face bleak, his grey eyes haunted by pain that went far beyond the physical, but at length he nodded, as though he didn't quite trust his voice to answer. It was – very obviously – a lie and Gwyn's expression showed quite clearly what she thought of it, but then she shrugged and let it pass, shifting her attention back to the knot. After a moment Eldritch's lids closed, shutting out the world once more.

'In my time we used safety pins.'

It was more small talk, but this time there was genuine

amusement in Gwyn's voice as she eased the sling free, revealing the strips of grey duck tape holding the slit edges of Eldritch's shirt together.

'Inventive though,' she conceded, throwing Aidan a swift grin.

'Didn't have safety pins,' Aidan mumbled through a mouthful of sandwich and coffee. He had been quite pleased with his impromptu repair. At least Eldritch had had a shirt to wear this morning. Gwyn shook her head.

'I always knew you had hidden talents, Aidan. Sadly though I think your first attempt at fashion design is destined for the bin.'

'That's my favourite shirt you're talking about,' Eldritch joined in quietly. He didn't bother to open his eyes.

'Time to start thinking of it less as a favourite shirt and more as a favourite duster.'

What Gwyn saw as she carefully cut through the blood-stiffened rag that had once been Eldritch's favourite shirt shocked her. It wasn't so much the fact that his shoulder and upper arm were heavily bandaged; she had expected that, given the state of his shirt. It was the bruising, spreading like an ink stain from beneath the white gauze and out across the muscles of his chest and arm, that made her pause. On his left arm the faint trace of a suntan ended in a clear line mid-bicep. On his right arm the mottled purple and black spread halfway to the elbow.

Gwyn put down the scissors and studied her patient. Where he wasn't tanned Eldritch's skin was very fair and a tracery of old scars stood out like nacre against the pallor of his chest and shoulders. Her lips narrowed as she studied them. She had a fair idea what had caused them and it was not a comfortable thought.

She looked again at Eldritch's face and was surprised to find that she herself was being scrutinised. Eyes that shaded from the colour of melt water to a dark storm cloud grey stared into hers and for a fleeting moment Gwyn felt a curious sense of intimacy with this man whom she barely knew. *The enemy of my enemy is my friend,* she thought, and then, *With friends like these...* and wondered at the cold shiver of precognition that threaded down her spine.

'Those scars are old,' she said.

'I've been told they're quite impressive.' His voice was little more than a whisper, but it still held an echo of the deep velvety tones that had charmed her on their first meeting.

'Really? Well, I suppose that's one word for them,' Gwyn agreed, letting her tone make it clear that it wasn't the adjective she would have chosen. Eldritch managed a pained look. A few minutes ago it might have made her laugh.

'They're not, though.' She nodded at the four parallel marks that raked his chest, refusing to be distracted. *Less than two years,* she guessed. They were darker than the rest, the skin still slightly pink around their edges.

'No,' he agreed. 'They're not.' And something in his voice suggested that not all the wounds acquired alongside those scars had healed. He leaned his head back against the armchair, fastening his gaze on the ceiling and Gwyn had no need to be told that this was territory he would not venture into with her.

She watched him as his lids drooped and his eyes slowly closed. They jerked open again as she touched his hand and his head came up, his eyes wide and startled. For a moment he seemed to have difficulty focussing on her. Gwyn sighed. She would have preferred not to disturb him, but this had to be done and the sooner it was over the better. Only then would he be able to rest properly and rest was what he needed most.

'Okay,' she said, her fingers resting lightly on the back of his hand as though she might ground him through that contact. 'I'm going to take a look at your shoulder. Then I think you'd best get some sleep. You look about ready for it,' she added. Bruised and bloodied, his arms and sides a mess of small abrasions and grazes, he looked very different from the man who had stood in her garden yesterday. Yesterday itself seemed like a lifetime ago. She squeezed his hand and turned to Aidan.

'I don't suppose you were able to clean this, were you?'

He answered with a quick shake of his head, hastily swallowing a mouthful of sandwich.

'All I had was a couple of sachets of eye wash and some steri-wipes.'

He scratched a hand through the stubble on his chin. 'I cleaned enough blood away so that I could see what I was doing, but there wasn't much else I could do.'

His expression suggested he felt he should have been able to do more, but Gwyn was unperturbed.

'It doesn't matter. Even if you had I'd still have wanted to clean it properly now to be sure.'

She turned back to Eldritch. 'Are you ready for this?'

He said nothing, but he nodded, looking up at her with bleak eyes. Under the dark shadow of his stubble, his skin had turned a peculiar, greenish-grey. Suddenly he looked very sick.

'Gwyn!'

Aidan was shouting a warning, but she was already reacting, grabbing Eldritch as he toppled sideways. She heard the sharp stab of his breath as she caught his arm, swore and muttered a hasty

'Sorry' as she steadied him. From the way his head rolled against her shoulder she doubted he could hear her, but she spoke to him anyway.

'It's okay, I've got you.'

Aidan was out of his chair and crouched beside her with a speed that belied how shaky he had been five minutes ago, shoving furniture out of the way for her so she had space to ease Eldritch down to the floor.

'Thanks, Aidan.'

She bent over Eldritch, feeling the slow pulse beneath her fingers.

'I think he's only fainted; probably the thought of me poking around at his shoulder.'

Aidan nodded. He looked a little pale himself, but his hands were steady as he snagged the little tapestry footstool from beside the radiator and lifted Eldritch's feet onto it. Gwyn stood and fetched her crewelwork shawl from where it hung abandoned over a corner of the nearest bookcase.

'He was out cold when I patched him up last night, which was probably a good thing.'

The catch in Aidan's voice told Gwyn that this was not a pleasant memory. Without speaking she picked up the half-full coffee mug from her desk and handed it to him to finish while she tucked the weight of soft wool around Eldritch. The broad shoulders were cold to her touch, but he looked slightly less green now he was lying down. Unconscious, the pinched look that pain had ground into his bones had slackened, softening the planes and angles of his face. He still had the look of the Devil about him but perhaps a younger, less cynical incarnation; a Lucifer from before the Fall. She touched his cheek thoughtfully and then straightened again.

'I don't think he'd dared look at it himself,' Aidan said softly. He swirled the coffee round in his mug, watching it as though fascinated by the movement of the tarry brown liquid. 'It was only when he keeled over at the hut that I found out how bad it was. If I'd have known—'

'You wouldn't have been able to do any more than you did. But why did you go to the hut? Why not just go back to the cars?'

'We were going to, but…' Aidan paused, looking uncomfortable.

'What?'

'There was something out there… on the hillside. Eldritch sensed something.'

'Not the avatar, surely?'

That wouldn't make sense, not so soon. Aidan shrugged.

'I don't know, but there was definitely something there. I felt it too and whatever it was I sure as Hell didn't want to stick around and find out.'

Gwyn pondered that as she fetched towels and hot water from the kitchen. There were two possible explanations for what Aidan had just described and neither of them was good. Either Eldritch had been unable to inflict significant damage on the avatar or the demon had been able to regenerate the beast far faster than should have been possible. She wasn't sure which scenario worried her more. But perhaps there was a third explanation. Perhaps this thing that Aidan and Eldritch had sensed had been nothing more than a combination of shock and an understandable fear of further confrontation with the avatar on Eldritch's part, magnified by the presence of the shrieks into something far more frightening, something that Aidan had felt too. Outside the light changed as a cloud swept across the sun and for a second she caught a glimpse of herself, reflected in the darkened window. Her mirror self stared back, green eyes dark and cynical under raised brows.

You don't believe that, do you? she asked the image silently. Her reflection shook her head. Gwyn sighed and looked away. 'No, nor do I.'

'So, you headed for the hut,' Gwyn prompted as she cut through the upper layers of bandage encircling Eldritch's shoulder. Aidan nodded.

'It was the nearest place I could think of. He said we didn't have time to get to the cars, but if we could take shelter somewhere he could put a veil round it to keep us safe.'

He cocked his head to one side as though asking for her opinion.

'Hmm…' Gwyn chose to reserve her judgement on that as a strategy. Carefully she unravelled another loop of bandage. 'And he passed out after he'd set the veil?'

'It seemed like hard work and he was already pretty exhausted when I found him above the Bite. Plus we got soaked on the way over and he was going hypothermic. What with that and the shoulder, I'm surprised he lasted as long as he did.'

Gwyn was surprised as well.

'Put it down to pigheaded stubbornness.'

It wasn't a quality she would normally consider admirable, but, as she peeled back the first layer of dressings from Eldritch's arm and shoulder, Gwyn had to admit that there was something to be said for being too stubborn to admit you should have long since given in. Blood loss and pain would have sapped the wizard's strength and while he might have been able to do something about the latter Gwyn suspected he hadn't. Self-healing was difficult – even for an experienced healer – and the worse the injury the harder it became. Sometimes pigheaded stubbornness was all you could rely on.

'He may be stubborn, but the veil saved our lives, Gwyn.'

The defensiveness in Aidan's tone surprised Gwyn. She almost smiled to hear him standing up for Eldritch, but then it struck her that he wasn't talking in terms of some theoretical danger. Her earlier uneasiness returned, turning to fear that stabbed her with an almost physical pain as Aidan added, 'The avatar showed up.'

The flat finality of the statement suggested he didn't want to say anything more.

'That's…' Impossible? It should have been and yet Aidan seemed convinced. 'Are you absolutely certain it was the avatar?'

Aidan said nothing; his expression gave all the answer she needed. The little shred of hope Gwyn had clung to withered and died.

'Do you know what time this was?'

'It was just after two-thirty this morning.'

Damn. So much for wanting to believe it was all down to the shrieks exaggerating their fears. Gwyn's shoulders slumped. Suddenly she felt very tired.

'Gwyn?' There was an edge to Aidan's voice as though he understood there had been a motive behind her questions. 'What is it? What's so significant about when the avatar showed up?'

For several seconds Gwyn chose not to answer. *Why?* she wondered. Wasn't a demon enough for them to have to cope with? Belatedly she realised Aidan was staring at her, waiting for her to explain her reaction. She took a deep breath and let it out in a long sigh, forcing herself to let go of her fears. She even managed a small smile though she could tell from the look he gave her that Aidan wasn't fooled.

'That's too soon for the avatar to have regenerated on its own,' she said simply. She looked down at Eldritch, at the bruising and the bandages covering the Lady alone knew what kinds of injuries and wondered if it had all been in vain. 'Either he couldn't have hurt it as badly as he thought or...' Saying it didn't make it real, she told herself, but still she was reluctant to give voice to what she feared.

'Or what, Gwyn?'

'Or we've got bigger problems than we thought.'

'Bigger than the demon and the avatar?'

'Possibly. I'll need to talk to Sleeping Beauty here before we know for sure. Still,' she forced herself to put that to one side, 'there's no point in borrowing trouble. Tell me what happened with the avatar.'

His scowl told her he hadn't missed her sidestepping his question, but he let it ride. Gradually his expression changed, growing distant and introspective as he considered her request.

'It attacked the veil.'

She hadn't been certain he would answer her. Now she watched him grow still as if he was steeling himself to return to that moment.

'It was...' His voice stumbled as he sought for words to explain what had happened. For a moment he closed his eyes as if doing so would make things clearer and his brow creased as though once gained that clarity was exquisitely painful. 'I...' He stopped again, throwing his head back and drawing in a long, shaky breath. When he finally looked at her, his expression was haunted. 'It was like pure hatred. I've never been so scared in my life.'

The pain in his voice made her ache. Young and strong, Aidan was used to thinking of himself as capable of dealing with any threat or danger head on. Until now. The idea that creatures existed that would snuff out his life with neither thought nor compunction and for no other reason save that it was in their nature to do so was a hard lesson and one Gwyn would have given much to save him from. Crueller still was the understanding that his current defences against them were as much use as a child's mud dam against a spring flood. In the face of such knowledge any reassurance she might try to give would be trite and meaningless. The best comfort she could offer was to assume he could cope and to treat him accordingly.

'Didn't Eldritch do anything?'

Even as she asked the question she dipped her head, focussing on the final remnants of gauze and lint covering the man in question's shoulder. Everything so far had come away cleanly, but this layer was gummed together with dried blood. Three broad stripes of it decorated an area wider than the span of her hand. She lifted a corner, but stopped immediately as she felt the dressing snag and pull. The steady rhythm of Eldritch's breath caught slightly as though, even unconscious, he could feel what she was doing. She spoke to him softly, stroking her hand along his cheek and brushing the tangled strands of hair back from his temples until he settled again. Concentrating as she was on Eldritch it came almost as a surprise when Aidan spoke again.

'He didn't seem able to. He was asleep when it attacked and it just seemed to overwhelm him.'

She had thought his voice held pain before, but that was

nothing compared with the agony that underlay his words now. 'To be honest I don't know if it would have made any difference if he'd been awake. I think he'd put all his energy into the veil. He didn't have anything left to fight with.'

His fingers knotted in the fringed edge of the rug beside Eldritch's head, tangling and untangling the cream and blue wool as if doing so could help him sort out the chaos in his head.

'I managed to block it out with my shields, but he was wide open and it just ripped into him. It was tearing him apart.'

Gwyn winced at the image the words conjured.

'I tried to wake him up, but I couldn't get through to him.' Guilt tinged Aidan's voice. 'He just kept thrashing backwards and forwards.'

Like a horse with colic, thought Gwyn, *frantically rolling as though it could leave the pain behind*. That would explain the grazes and scrapes that patterned the wizard's arms and his sides.

'It was like…' He gestured helplessly, his face contorting in pain at the memory. 'Like watching him being tortured, but there was no point to it, no way of making it stop. I just knew it was going to go on and on until it killed him.'

He turned away as though the sight of Eldritch stretched out on the floor was too graphic a reminder of what had happened.

'Aidan, stop it!' Gwyn put all her strength and surety into that command, cutting across the horror of those memories. To be certain she got his attention, she backed her words up with a short psychic tap, little more than a nudge really, but enough to jolt him firmly back into the here and now.

'Yes, it must have been awful, but don't beat yourself about it.'

He swung back towards her, his face shocked and hurt as

though he thought she was belittling what he had been through, but before he could protest Gwyn spoke again.

'You came through it,' she said, her voice calm and level. 'You both survived.' She glanced briefly at Eldritch and her fine brows raised slightly. 'More or less intact. So whatever you did, it must have been the right thing.'

'What makes you think I did anything?' Aidan spoke dismissively as though denying the possibility. Gwyn turned the raised eyebrows on him.

'You must have done. The avatar wouldn't have given up, so if he couldn't help himself, you must have done something.' As she spoke she layered wet cotton wool over the gummed up dressings covering Eldritch's shoulder. 'Whatever it was you did, it saved both your lives.'

She wondered if it had occurred to Aidan that if Eldritch had died the veil would have failed. Had that happened he wouldn't have outlived the wizard by very long. 'So what did you do?'

Aidan sighed, the tension draining from him.

'I put my shields round him.'

He laughed, the sound curiously devoid of humour, but at least the bitterness had gone.

'I didn't know if I could do it. I mean I had no idea if it was even possible to shield someone else, but it was the only thing I could think of to do. I didn't think I had anything to lose.'

'And it worked.' That was not a question.

'Yes. Yes, it did.'

Gwyn watched Aidan as he considered that fact and saw the remnants of despair in his eyes give way to a look of mingled satisfaction and wonder. She was reminded of the night she had begun to teach him. He had worn a similar look then, when he had first discovered his shields. It wasn't exactly disbelief; it was more as though he was afraid to believe lest it be taken away from him. It was a feeling she remembered from when her own power was just beginning to awaken. As her grandmother had begun to train her, taking her through the first simple exercises, very much as she had now started to do with Aidan, she had known that what she held was as precious as life. On the wild nights when the wind howled down the valley, driving rain against the slates, or the nights of crystal stillness when the starlight found every chink in the curtains, edging her room with silver, and the banshee shriek of a vixen rose up from the woods like a lost soul, she would lie curled in her bed, hugging the knowledge to her and alternating between a wild, quivering excitement that would not let her sleep and a sick dread that she wasn't good enough to be allowed to have such wonders. Of course, as the years passed she had grown comfortable with the fact that the power was part of her and confident in her ability to call it at will. She had never considered that there might be limits to what she could do, boundaries beyond which she could not pass with impunity. Looking back at that young woman, self-certain and confident and shining with power, she wondered briefly if it might have been different. Had she retained that childhood belief that her power could be stripped from her, would she have been more careful? Might she not have made that one mistake that had seared the power from her bones? It was a question she had asked herself on many occasions, a flail she was well used to, familiar in all its various guises. Even now, after long years of healing and discipline had brought a measure of power back to her, not effortless and wild as it had been, but steady and quiet, the thought that things could have been different still cut her to the bone. It was a pointless exercise, whatever the answer might be, but she felt the momentary pain of self-flagellation. With an effort of will, she pushed the thought back into the darker recesses of her mind and focussed instead on what Aidan had achieved, for his was a very real triumph. She conjured a smile for him and was rewarded by the tentative smile that grew on his face in return.

'You have sound instincts, Aidan. Don't be afraid to trust them.'

He sat back on his heels and looked at her, eyebrows drawing down as though he would make something of her comment, then he shook his head and laughed.

'So people keep telling me.' And whatever memory her words had conjured was pushed away. 'What happens now?'

'I sort this out and then we have breakfast.'

CHAPTER 24

'When you said he'd got "a little munched" I hadn't realised you meant it quite so literally.'

Gwyn peered at the clotted scabs, their edges white and soggy where she had soaked the dressings free, puckering away from the surrounding flesh, then turned Eldritch's arm so she could look at the wound that ran up its inner edge. The movement elicited a soft groan from Eldritch and he turned his head fractionally. Gwyn watched him closely. She had hoped he might remain unconscious long enough for her to deal with this or at least that his exhaustion might pull him straight down into sleep that she could deepen, sheltering him from the worst of what was to come. But it seemed that was not to be. She felt a moment's irritation as though the man was being deliberately awkward. Of course, she could always do what he had done to her and hit him with a Levin bolt. Briefly she considered the possibility. It would certainly be easy enough. His shields were virtually non-existent; it wouldn't take much to knock him out again. Or, if she wanted to be really nasty, she could put a small jolt through his shoulder; it would have much the same effect. That would keep him out for some time. Gwyn sighed. She wasn't ashamed of the momentary satisfaction that the thought had given her, but she knew she wouldn't act on it. Above all things she was a healer and there were less harmful ways of dealing with this, even if it meant expending more energy on her part.

She watched Eldritch's eyes move under those bruised-looking lids, sensing him fighting to come out of the darkness. Was that because he didn't trust her? Her lips thinned. That would be rich given what had happened when he tried to cross the threshold of her house. He might yet deserve that Levin bolt through the shoulder and more besides. She shivered, *would that it never comes to that…* but, whatever her fears, for now he was under her protection. She would do what she could for him.

Very gently she felt around his shoulder. The flesh was swollen and hot and she could see the telltale flush of red surrounding the wounds, even over the all pervasive bruising.

'I told you he needed a professional to take a look at him.'

The note of challenge in Aidan's voice made Gwyn look up from her patient.

'Yes, you did,' she agreed, guessing what was coming next.

'So are we going to take him to hospital?'

Gwyn took a deep breath, pulling calm around her like a cloak.

'No,' she said, firmly. 'This is messy, but I still don't think they'd do more than clean it up and give him a shot of antibiotics. Trust me, Aidan, when it comes to dealing with this I'm as professional as you're going to get. There's probably only one other person in… I don't know, maybe a hundred miles, who would know how to handle this and sadly,' she cast an exasperated look at Eldritch, 'he's not really up to it right now.'

'So what do we do?'

'Something I probably should have done earlier,' Gwyn admitted. Something she would once have done automatically, but which now she had to consider and justify, weighing the cost against the other things she needed to do and the power they would require.

'I'm going to block the pain in his shoulder.'

As she spoke, Gwyn went around the room lighting the fat beeswax candles placed strategically along the windowsill and the mantelpiece and the squat tealights, in their jewel-coloured glasses, that were scattered over the shelves of the two bookcases. Patterns of emerald and ruby and sapphire spilled over her hands as she pushed them together into little clusters and the warm scents of beeswax and vanilla brightened the air, mingling with the heavier notes of the incense sticks that now smouldered on her desk. 'Not only will that make him a lot more comfortable, so he'll be able to sleep, but it also means I can clean that bite properly without having to worry about hurting him. Once that's done, you can give me a hand getting him into bed and I'll do what I can to start topping up his energy levels.'

'You can really do that? Stop the pain, I mean.'

Gwyn took her time lighting the final candle, adjusting its position and then watching for a few moments to assure herself it was burning steadily before she extinguished the match between wetted fingers. She turned to look at Aidan, a small frown denting the skin of her forehead.

'Of course I can. I've done it for you, don't you remember?'

'Well, yes, but that was before...'

The sentence hung in the air unfinished, but Gwyn knew what Aidan had stopped himself saying. *That was before I singularly failed to cure your mother's cancer. When you decided everything I'd ever told you was a lie.* Gwyn felt a familiar stab of pain. She thought she had kept it from her face, but Aidan looked embarrassed, almost as though she had spoken aloud. She clamped her teeth in her lip, but it did nothing to stop the flow of words through her head. *It wasn't a lie, Aidan, but I was asking you to call upon powers you had no experience of using, hoping that between us we could reach her. And we might have done, if you'd been trained. But you weren't and the irony of it is that it was your mother who'd told me to stop teaching you. Maybe I shouldn't have done it, shouldn't have tried to get you to use techniques you'd not learned, but, bless you, you did your best. It wasn't your fault and it wasn't my fault. Neither of us was good enough.*

'It was a long time ago,' Aidan finished lamely, not looking at her. For a second Gwyn couldn't speak. Her throat was full of suppressed words that had tumbled inside her through the years until they were worn down like sea glass, the sharp, cutting edges blunted and smoothed, transformed from their original shapes and no longer quite recognisable as what they had once been. She could hold them under her tongue now and no longer bleed, but they were still sufficient to choke her. With an effort she swallowed them down, understanding the tacit apology in Aidan's awkwardness, but her hand was still shaking as she dropped the spent match into the wastepaper basket.

'It was,' she agreed.

'Eldritch, look at me.'

The sooty lashes flickered as though he was scraping together the energy to lift his lids.

'Come on, look at me.'

Gwyn put her hand to his cheek, feeling the prickly stubble under her palm contrasting with the surprising softness of the skin under her fingertips. She stroked her thumb along the line of his cheek, tracing the shape of the bone through the skin and slowly his eyes opened. For a moment he stared up at her and Gwyn was struck again by the beauty of those eyes. Rowan had used the right word when she had described them as gorgeous. Or at least that was true while they were unguarded and innocent, as they were now. An impish thought crossed her mind, bringing a smile to her lips that would have been singularly hard to explain had Eldritch been alert enough to notice it. As it was, those grey and silver eyes had yet to focus properly, giving Gwyn a few moments of grace to school her expression into something less mischievous. Quite why her mind had presented her with that particular idea she couldn't have said, although, feeling the tickle of laughter bubbling up inside her, she wondered whether it might not be mild hysteria. After the morning's rollercoaster of emotions Gwyn felt she was entitled to a little hysteria. Besides, she could come up with no better reason for why she had found herself thinking what Rowan's reaction would be when she described this scene to her.

Of course, she would have to edit the details slightly for Rowan's benefit. She eyed Eldritch's prone form appraisingly; dark jeans cut low on his hips, his white shirt stripped off and carelessly discarded – those would be the sort of details to set Rowan's matchmaking heart racing, as would a tantalising description of how his broad shoulders tapered down to said hips and a nicely flat stomach. Not too much muscle; more a dancer's body, lean and strong, than the over-bulked physique of a body builder. Oh, she could have a field day. Of course, she would need to leave out the bandages and the blood and the fact that Eldritch was barely conscious, but with subtle editing she could wind Rowan up beautifully before she had to admit to a more prosaic truth. Gwyn bit her lip to stop the smirk that was threatening to spread across her face. *Thanks, Ro, I could do with a laugh right now.* Not that Rowan need have any real fear of her pairing up with Marcus Eldritch, but it certainly wouldn't stop Gwyn pretending otherwise just to tease her.

Almost reluctantly Gwyn called her thoughts to heel. Amusing though the diversion was, she had work to do. She turned her attention back to Eldritch. A small, puzzled frown creased his forehead as he stared up at her.

'You're smiling.' Even his voice sounded slightly out of focus.

'I have been known to, on rare occasions.'

It seemed that Eldritch wasn't up to recognising sarcasm.

'You should do it more often.'

Oh please, thought Gwyn, *all that Mills and Boon stuff was for Rowan's benefit. Don't go picking that out of my mind or we'll all be in trouble.* She regarded him caustically. *Maybe I would smile more if I didn't have to pick up the pieces of arrogant, chauvinistic idiots…* She stopped short of saying it, reminding herself that it was hardly reasonable to be scoring points off a man who was barely conscious. Yet there was no denying that something about Marcus Eldritch brought out the worst in her. *Just one of his many natural talents*, she thought. Aloud she said, 'There hasn't been much to smile about recently.'

Perhaps he read the feelings behind her words for his forehead creased as if in pain.

'I'm sorry.'

Gwyn snorted and shook her head, torn between irritation and a sudden unaccountable sense of amusement with herself and with this maddening enigma of a man. It scarcely mattered how they had come to this point. They were here now and they would just have to go forward as best they could. The clinking of cups in the kitchen and the drifting ashtray smell of brewing coffee reminded her that there was someone else she should try to go forward with from where they were. There was nothing to be gained by wishing that the past was anything other than it was.

And you, she thought, *you need to go forward too. Let go of what you used to have and live with what you have now. It's not the same, but it's good enough.* She sat for a moment, thinking about the truth in that statement. Before this weekend she would have said that she had moved on, but Eldritch's ridiculous stunt with the Levin bolt and then Aidan's lack of trust in her healing had touched a nerve. She had never thought of herself as a proud woman, but now she wondered how much of that pain had been bruised pride. *Now who's the arrogant fool?* asked a small voice in the back of her mind, and for that she had no answer.

Taking a deep breath she pushed the dark storm wrack of her hair back from her face and focussed once more on Eldritch.

'Do you trust me?' she asked. Eldritch regarded her questioningly. His face still chalky, the finely arched brows stood out as though they had been drawn on his skin with ink.

'Do I have a choice?'

'Not really.' A hint of mischief crept into Gwyn's tone. 'You haven't got the strength to shield a small rodent right now so there's no way you can stop me.'

That wasn't strictly true. If he chose to refuse her help she wouldn't force it on him even though she was physically capable of doing so, given the state he was in. But she hoped he wasn't that stubborn.

'But that's not what I asked. Do you trust me? This will be a lot easier with your consent.'

Eldritch turned his head fractionally towards her and Gwyn saw the shadow of pain settle once more on his face.

'I'd trust you with my life,' he said softly and there was such a mix of emotion in his voice that Gwyn could not tell if he was joking.

'I'm hoping it's not going to come to that.'

Eldritch's lips twitched in what might have been an attempt at his old, wolfish smile, but he made no further response. He lay quietly as though he had indeed placed his life in her hands, leaving nothing more for him to say or do. Even the edgy wariness he had shown towards her earlier had dropped away, leaving only that sense of quiet acquiescence.

Unsure what to make of this, Gwyn reached over and took his hand, covering it with her own, feeling the memory of strength in the intricacy of sinews and bones beneath the cool flesh. Wordlessly she offered comfort, reassurance, perhaps even thanks that, for the moment at least, he had chosen not to fight her. She herself would have been hard put to say just what it was she sought to convey, but after a moment the long fingers turned, lacing themselves with hers. She stroked the palm of his hand where mud and gore had streaked and dried, crusting the lines of his life.

'You used blood to anchor the veil?'

She glanced at him questioningly. He turned his head a little further so he could look at her fully.

'For the south, yes.'

'Ah,' she breathed, understanding. Curious, she asked, 'What signs did you use to shape it?'

Eldritch did not answer immediately. His eyes grew dark and introspective and Gwyn had the sense of him piecing together shards of reality from the cobwebs of pain and exhaustion that were the bulk of his memories of that time. Finally, the grey eyes drifted back to focus on her.

'Keth for Strength, Sho for Protection and Roc for Safety.'

He lay still, eyes never leaving her face as she contemplated the choice of those wardings and all that that choice revealed about him. Gwyn tipped her head to one side.

'Hmm... I would have used Bel for Sanctuary, Mir for Silence and Serreth for Stillness.'

She offered that to him freely, a microcosm of her own world view, in exchange for that brief insight into his own soul.

'Avoid its notice rather than confront it.' One dark brow quirked upwards. 'I wouldn't have thought of that,' he admitted. Still holding his hand, Gwyn shrugged one-sidedly.

'You learn to work within the limits of your power.'

To her surprise she could find no trace of bitterness within those words although that didn't stop her hoping that Eldritch wouldn't ask her what she meant. But perhaps he was conscious of the price he had paid for working beyond his limits for he said nothing. Gwyn changed the subject to spare them both.

'I'm going to put a pain block on your shoulder to deaden the nerves while I clean it up. Don't,' she added quickly, putting her hand to his cheek again to stop him as he automatically turned his head to look at the wounds. Though he didn't fight that gentle restraint, she felt the muscles bunch along his jaw. Questioning grey eyes sought hers.

'How bad...?'

'You didn't look at it after the fight?'

Eldritch swallowed as if his mouth had suddenly gone dry and Gwyn's mind was filled with the image of a dark-haired man kneeling in the mud amongst the tall shapes of spruce and Douglas fir, sweating and shaking and almost physically sick with shock. He cradled his arm to him, his body hunching forward protectively, while around him the air still shivered with the hot metallic stink of the demon. The gradually falling dusk had painted the world in shades of lilac and dove grey before he moved again.

'No, I suppose you wouldn't have,' she answered herself softly, shocked by what she had seen. She looked down at the stricken man, wondering if he was aware of what he had just done. From the slightly feverish look in his eyes she guessed not. Her fingers strayed from his cheek to smooth a matted spike of hair.

'Well, it's not pretty,' she said with a rueful glance at the bruised and torn flesh. She felt a little stab of guilt as Eldritch flinched from her bluntness, but she would have no lies between them now, no matter how well intended. 'But it's not as bad as it looks.'

Her hand returned to cup his cheek, gently reinforcing her reassuring words.

'That's why I'd suggest you rein in your curiosity for now and don't look at it. There's a lot of bruising, which makes it look worse than it is. The wounds themselves aren't deep, but they need to be cleaned before they go septic.'

The muscles under her hand tensed and she guessed he was already feeling the infection that had started to spread through his flesh.

'Which is why I want to put a nerve block on you before I do anything. You may still feel a little of what I do, but I promise it won't be much. What I need to know is, are you willing to let me?'

The look of surprise on Eldritch's face asked clearer than words what had happened to her earlier assertion that he had no choice but to trust her. She looked directly into his eyes.

'There's always a choice.'

His brows drew down fractionally as though trying to gauge

what other meanings lay behind her words, but then he seemed to dismiss the thought and relaxed again and she felt more than saw the slight movement of his head as he nodded.

'Okay.' She squeezed his hand briefly. 'Let's do this.'

As she whispered the familiar litany of protection in her mind, Gwyn drew Eldritch's hand up to rest with hers in the centre of his chest. Around her she could feel the wards on the house, brushing the edge of her senses like subtly shifting veils of energy. Knowing that they were safe within them, still she formed this inner circle of light, invoking the powers beyond her own, linking her senses to the flickering energies of the candle flames and the grounding scents of incense and lavender. These were her anchors, the guides she set to mark her boundaries as she crossed into the borderlands of the spirit.

Beside her she could feel Eldritch straining to follow what she did, very much as she herself would have done had their situations been reversed.

'Just relax,' she murmured, her voice no more than a slight eddy of breath. 'You don't need to do anything, just let it happen.'

His fingers tightened briefly against her own and then his grip loosened. Carefully she extricated her fingers from his and stretched her hands out above his shoulder. His eyes tracked her movement, huge and dark against the chalky pallor of his face. She felt a twinge of exasperation and rolled her eyes at him, treating him to her fiercest mock scowl.

'Relax.'

She shifted her focus then, extending her senses down into the painful mess that was his shoulder. With studied discipline she ignored the aching wrongness of torn muscle and skin and the first cindery traces of infection crying out to her to set them right, seeking instead the trails of red pain that ran along Eldritch's nerves. With infinite patience she slipped along each one, warming and soothing, gently weaving her own energy into the bruised and mangled flesh, shutting down the pathways along which the pain travelled.

There were other, simpler techniques she could have chosen, but this was the most effective and Gwyn wanted to be certain that Eldritch would feel nothing of what was to come. It was a small thing, but she wouldn't have him worn down by further pain when she could prevent it and she had made up her mind to keep him from its wearying grip for as long as possible.

In itself what she was doing wasn't difficult though it took a certain clarity of focus, even without the awareness of his unhealed injuries prickling like a thousand tiny barbs in her own flesh. It was like chasing subtly coloured threads through a tapestry, more by feel than by sight, but there was a deep satisfaction in what she did. As she worked she could feel Eldritch's breathing evening out, his body slowly relaxing as strand by strand she isolated the jagged mass of pain and locked it away from him.

When she was satisfied that she had deadened even the smallest tendrils of pain and he would feel nothing for some hours, Gwyn slowly withdrew, gently pulling her senses back from him. Her patient shifted slightly as she lifted her hands away from his shoulder but did not open his eyes. With the tension swept from his body he seemed far younger, despite his stubble and matted hair. Or perhaps, thought Gwyn, it was the faintest of smiles curving his lips that took the years from his face. Somewhat to her surprise she found herself smiling in response. *Maybe we should both try this more often, Mister Eldritch.*

'Was that real?'

The sound of Aidan's voice made her turn although Gwyn realised she had been aware of him standing there for some time, quietly watching her. Now he leant against the door jamb, two mugs and a packet of biscuits seemingly forgotten in his hands.

'Just now, I got a flash of him in the forest, after he'd been hurt.' He eyed Gwyn accusingly as if he suspected her of some form of trickery.

'You picked that up as well?' Gwyn was surprised.

'So it was real.'

Gwyn nodded.

'Yes, I'm afraid so. It happens sometimes when people are completely unshielded. You find you're picking up thoughts from them, seeing things replayed in your mind that you weren't there to see. In normal people – that is in people who don't have significant amounts of power,' she corrected herself, 'it's a very bad sign. Usually it only happens when someone's critically ill – I mean on the point of death – or in such extreme terror that they truly believe they are about to die. At times like that a person's shields will sometimes fail totally and they'll unwittingly broadcast images or thoughts, perhaps about what they're experiencing right then or maybe something that happened to them earlier in their lives. It might be an image of their childhood, anything. That's why sometimes you hear of people who say they know a dying friend or relative went to Heaven because they had an image of them with their parents just at the moment they passed.'

Aidan's head came up and he looked at her sharply.

'You mean he's dying?' he demanded, his voice a mix of shock and anger.

'No! No, not at all. When you use power it's possible – theoretically at least – to drain yourself to that level, although I'd never known of anyone actually doing it; not until our friend here, that is. It's not something you'd ever want to do, in fact it's downright dangerous.' Her lips thinned as she eyed the unconscious man. 'But he's not going to die. Not while I have anything to do with it.'

Aidan glared at her and in that moment Gwyn could see the ghost of a frightened teenager lurking behind the anger in those hazel eyes. He had heard a similar promise from her before. Yet his next words were not the accusation she had expected. Instead, in a more diffident voice, he asked, 'I didn't break your concentration, did I? He was pretty keen I didn't disturb him while he was putting the veil round the hut last night.'

His eyes flicked to Eldritch's still form and then back to Gwyn.

'Hmm, I imagine he was. Veils are tricky at the best of times and I expect his concentration was a little off, given the circumstances.' Secretly Gwyn was amazed that Eldritch had managed any power working given the state he must have been in. 'A veil isn't something you can stop halfway through. It has to be created in one go so if you'd interrupted him he would have had to have started again from scratch. Frankly I don't think he'd have been able to do it.'

She looked down at Eldritch, imagining the man she had seen in that snatch of vision dragging the last vestiges of power from the marrow of his bones to weave into a veil, knowing he had only one chance to complete it. It was a harrowing thought. No wonder he had told Aidan not to interrupt him. Deliberately she stretched and rolled her shoulders, reining in her natural empathy and grounding herself firmly within her own body. Aidan was watching her closely. She smiled reassuringly at him.

'What I was doing is very different. It is easier to do it in one go, but it's not essential. If you'd disturbed me I could have picked up from where I left off.'

Aidan digested this silently.

'What were you doing, Gwyn?'

'Just what I said I would; numbing all the nerves in his shoulder to stop him feeling any pain for a few hours.'

From his expression she realised that wasn't quite what he had meant. Resting her chin on steepled fingers, Gwyn thought for a moment, wondering how best she could explain this. She felt tired and slightly lightheaded from the energy she had expended and she wanted to finish tending to Eldritch's shoulder, not get involved in a discourse on psychic healing, but she owed Aidan too many explanations already to care to add another to the tally.

'There are a number of ways to deal with pain,' she started, picking her way through something she had known for so long it was more instinct now than knowledge. 'On a very basic level you can use energy to ease it; a bit like putting a hot water bottle on a sore muscle.'

Her hands spread out as though smoothing some invisible limb.

'It's warm and soothing and it just eases the pain away.' She paused and regarded Aidan, something akin to a challenge rising in her forest green eyes. 'It's what I did for you when you cracked your ribs that time at school.'

'The psychic equivalent of two aspirin and a glass of water?'

Gwyn bridled, offended by the disparaging comparison. She sniffed and said slightly pointedly, 'I like to think that it's rather more effective than that.' But then she remembered that Aidan was blessed with almost rabid good health and had an attitude towards physical injury that would put a Spartan to shame. Two aspirin and a glass of water was most likely a remedy he resorted to in only the direst circumstances. In a somewhat better humour she continued.

'The only thing is it's not much use if you're then going to do something to aggravate the pain again. So, if all I wanted to do was numb his shoulder for a few hours so he could get some sleep then that would be fine, but as soon as I start poking around, cleaning it up, it's going to set off a whole new set of pain impulses and he'll feel everything I do.'

Aidan made a face at the prospect.

'Exactly,' Gwyn agreed with him.

'So what have you done?'

Despite his previous scepticism, Aidan looked intrigued.

'You know how nerve impulses travel, don't you? Well, you can use psychic energy to interfere with that transmission. It's a bit fiddly, but it's very effective because even if more pain signals are triggered they can't actually travel along the nerves. He won't feel anything in that shoulder for a couple of hours now.'

She almost added, 'I can show you how to do it, if you like,' but stopped herself even as the thought took shape. Given the circumstances of her earlier attempts to teach him healing, it was unlikely that Aidan would ever want to revisit the experience. It wasn't something she could blame him for. Regretfully Gwyn pushed the idea away and, conjuring a hopeful expression, looked pointedly at the two mugs in Aidan's hands.

'That wouldn't be tea by any chance, would it?'

Gwyn bent once more over Eldritch's shoulder only to glance back up as Aidan sucked in his breath in a loud hiss.

'Is something wrong?'

Aidan was staring in horrified fascination at the white foam fizzing up around Eldritch's collarbone.

'I thought the hydrogen peroxide was a joke.'

'Why? It's one of the most effective things you can use for cleaning wounds, especially ones like these.'

'It also stings like buggery.'

Gwyn gave her ex-ward a stern look.

'I'll have to take your word on that; it's not something I've tried. But I do know these will do a lot more than sting if they go septic.'

As she spoke she dribbled more hydrogen peroxide over the lower bite mark, stretching the skin between forefinger and thumb as she did so to open it up. Aidan winced as the raw flesh was obscured by white froth.

'Really, Aidan, I'd never have thought you were squeamish. It's honestly not that bad. I use it on the cats' ears all the time when they've been fighting.'

Aidan gave her a black look, which Gwyn deflected with a toss of her head.

'If it weren't for all the fizzing you'd barely notice it was happening. Besides, he can't feel a thing.'

Aidan scratched irritably at the stubble along his jaw, looking as though he would argue the point, but it was true that, contrary to all his expectations, Eldritch did seem oblivious to what was going on. Even when Gwyn repeated the process on the other gouges, making them fizz and foam until she was satisfied they were thoroughly clean, the slow rhythm of the rise and fall of his chest remained unchanged. Watching Gwyn dab Eldritch's skin dry with yet more cotton wool, Aidan asked curiously, 'Why bother with all this if you're going to heal him?'

'That's a very sensible question, but it's not a case of either or. If it works then why not use it? Science, magic, even herbs get a look in today. Comfrey,' she added, selecting a small glass jar and smearing a liberal quantity of its contents over Eldritch's bruises.

'A spot of hydrogen peroxide now should mean that tomorrow I can concentrate on helping the flesh to knit rather than trying to control an infection.'

'Tomorrow?' Aidan waited as Gwyn taped dressings over Eldritch's shoulder and arm. 'Why not today?'

'Because all this takes energy and there's a limit to what I can do in a day. Believe it or not, this isn't the worst of his troubles. It will be stiff and sore for a good few days, but, if we keep it clean, it should heal up perfectly well on its own, whether or not I help it along. Which I will,' she added, 'just not today.'

She rested her fingers briefly on the centre of Eldritch's forehead and then just below his sternum. Eldritch, who might as well have been unconscious for all the reaction he had shown to her earlier ministrations, moved his head fractionally, his lips parting as though he would speak, but he made no sound. A minute shiver ran through his body.

'It's okay,' Gwyn soothed him. 'It's alright.'

Her frown hardly matched the soft words, but fortunately only Aidan could see it. She noticed him looking at her and gave him a rather tired smile.

'What I need to do today is work on his energy levels. They're far too low to chance leaving them to recover on their own. The pain block was worth doing because he needs to rest properly, but I won't have any power to spare for physical healing.'

'Is there anything I can do to help?'

'You can give me a hand getting him into the spare room.

He's likely to sleep for most of the day and I'd prefer he did it in bed rather than stretched out on the floor where I have to keep stepping over him.'

Aidan grinned, not fooled for a moment by Gwyn's offhandedness. He scratched his chin, then ran his hand through his hair and grimaced.

'You're acting as though you've got fleas. I'm going to do a bit of work with him once we've put him to bed and then I'll sort out breakfast. In the meantime, there's plenty of hot water, why don't you have a shower?'

Aidan started to scratch his cheek, realised what he was doing and stopped. Gwyn smothered a grin.

'Give me a hand shifting Sleeping Beauty and then go and have a shower, Aidan.'

'Are you suggesting I smell?'

Gwyn leaned towards him, sniffed pointedly and wrinkled her nose.

'Now that you mention it, yes. Worse than an incontinent yak herder.'

Aidan raised his eyebrows.

'Is that the yaks or the herder that are incontinent?'

'Both. Now help me get him to bed and go. You know where everything is.'

Twenty minutes later and clean of body – if not of clothes – Aidan padded barefoot down the stairs. Thanks to the flowery nature of the toiletries available in Gwyn's bathroom he suspected he now smelled more like a eunuch than a yak herder and was less than convinced that this was an improvement. He thought he might say as much to her, if only to make her laugh, but when he came to the bottom of the stairs and looked across into the spare bedroom, he saw she was still sat beside the bed, apparently deep in trance. Beyond her, Eldritch was little more than a blanket-muffled shape and a tangle of dark hair on the blue and white stripe of the pillow, but Aidan didn't have to see to know that Gwyn's extended hands were spread over the wizard's heart and solar plexus. A cold chill ran through him at the sight. It wasn't just that the scene looked so much like the image he had conjured of Gwyn last night, it was the implication of what she was doing that hit him hardest. A surge of emotions stopped the breath in his throat, making him physically recoil and he wondered what was wrong with him. Every shred of conscience told him he should be thankful that Gwyn was able to help Eldritch – God knew he would have given anything to have had her help last night – but what churned inside him now was not gratitude. What he felt now was a cocktail of pain and rage and jealousy that she could do for this stranger what she had been unable to do for her best friend. Bile burnt the back of his throat and he turned his head, his fists clenching impotently at his side. Unseen, he drew back from the doorway and silently slipped away.

CHAPTER 25

Gwyn found him sat on the old slate bench, head bowed, oblivious to, or perhaps ignoring, the glorious view out across the valley. Tucked in the lea of the garden wall where the laurel and the honeysuckle combined to break the prevailing wind, it was a sheltered spot, ideal for solitary thought. Over the years Gwyn had spent many hours there, so many that she sometimes wondered why she hadn't worn buttock-shaped hollows in the stone. A great many of those hours had been spent thinking – *oh, be honest with yourself, Gwyn, the word's brooding* – about the young man who sat there now, trying to find something – anything – that would unlock their relationship and bridge the gulf between them. It was somehow fitting to find him here now.

Aidan seemed to be in a world of his own and Gwyn paused just to look at him. Freshly washed and tousled from only a rough combing with his fingers, the strands of copper running through his hair were very noticeable this morning. They had been Anne's trademark, she remembered, though her friend had loathed them with a vengeance. Too light to be termed an elegant auburn, by the end of each summer they were bleached to a sandy ginger making her draw comparisons between her hair and a marmalade tom. She had been openly envious of Gwyn's dark mane. 'You wait until we start going grey, then you'll think the opposite,' Gwyn had often remarked, never understanding why Anne should want to part with her glorious fire-streaked hair for something as flat and boring as her own. Today Aidan looked very much Anne's son.

He must have felt her gaze for his head came up and he looked at her, but he said nothing. His face was blank as though he beheld a stranger.

'Breakfast will be about five minutes.'

Aidan nodded then went back to staring at his feet or whatever it was that had held his attention before.

'Mind if I join you?'

He didn't look up this time, but, somewhat to Gwyn's surprise, he hitched along slightly to give her room to sit beside him. It was only a small bench so even though she took care to sit right at the end it still meant they were almost touching. For a while they both sat there, saying nothing. When she judged enough time had passed, Gwyn broke the silence.

'Care to tell me what's wrong?'

She glanced at him briefly and then looked away, her eyes returning to tracing the outline of the hills back to where the flat top of Cadair Cawr could just be seen, diminished by distance but still standing supreme among the lesser slopes. The wind, an almost constant companion this high up the valley, ruffled the honeysuckle, a stray zephyr finding its way through the leaves to whip a few loose strands of hair across her face. She pushed them back and the movement seemed to break Aidan's introspection.

'I healed him, Gwyn. Why couldn't I heal her?'

There was no need to ask who he was referring to. He turned on her with all the bitterness and pain he had held within him spilling over into his voice, accusing her.

'Why couldn't *you* heal her?'

The rawness of his emotion was like a lash and Gwyn felt her eyes blurring as though she had been struck. She turned away, but not before Aidan had seen the pain on her face, livid and real as the imprint of a fist.

'I'm sorry,' he said, after a moment, his voice still ragged. She wasn't certain he meant it, but at least, she told herself, he had had the grace to offer her that much of an apology. There had been times when she would have rejoiced to have had that much from him. His head was down again, but just as she thought that was all he would say, he straightened and shifted to face her.

'Damn it, Gwyn, why could I do it for him when I couldn't make it work for her?'

The pain was still there, but she sensed that it wasn't just a rhetorical question. He genuinely wanted to know. Gwyn sighed and wiped a hand over eyes that were gritty and tired. She had a feeling that Aidan wouldn't like what she was about to say. *Oh well.*

'It's not the same, Aidan. Yes, you saved his life, but you didn't heal him. Not as such. It worked this time because essentially Eldritch was – is,' she corrected herself, feeling the tall, gaunt presence there on the edge of her consciousness without her even having to seek it out, 'a perfectly healthy individual. Yes, he was dying, but it was because his psychic energy had been drained to a point where there was too little of it left for him to live, not because his body was riddled with cancer that neither I nor the doctors could stop from spreading.'

Aidan looked at her with something very akin to hatred in his eyes.

'But you still tried energy healing with her. You still encouraged me to try it with her. Why? What was the point if you knew she'd die anyway? How could you make me think we were helping her, that I could help her, when you knew that wasn't true?'

Somewhere in the midst of the sentence the hatred ran out and his voice cracked with sorrow and a deep and aching regret. It was the first time they had spoken of this thing that had lain between them.

'But we did help her, Aidan,' Gwyn insisted. '*You* helped her. People do recover from cancer, they go into remission. Sometimes they do it when they've been treated with chemotherapy and radiotherapy and everything else Western medicine can offer. Sometimes they do it when they've been on weird wholefood diets, or had prayers said for them, or they've stopped walking on the cracks in the pavement. And some people,' she continued softly, her own voice blurring with unshed tears, 'too many people, die despite everything. The truth is we're a long way off understanding why; what it is that makes that difference.'

They sat in silence then, sharing the wind and the pale autumn sunshine. Gwyn stared out across the valley noting automatically that there were sheep grazing up at the top of the ridge so the day would remain fine. Beside her Aidan was still, his head bowed once more, his hands clasped in his lap. Had they been in church, she might have thought he was praying. Very quietly Gwyn spoke again, seeming to address her words to the hills and the sky as much as the young man beside her.

'I desperately wanted your mother to live. I would have done anything I could to help her. So yes, I tried healing her, and yes, I encouraged you to do the same. I tried to stop the tumours growing. When I found I couldn't do that I tried just to slow them down and I hoped and I prayed that with the extra energy we could give her that she'd be one of the ones whose bodies could fight back, that we could help her to keep going until the chemo and the radiotherapy finally worked. And perhaps that wasn't fair on you. Perhaps I should have told you that the chances of our succeeding were so slim that really there was no hope and told you not to bother, because I knew that was the case. But you trusted me and she trusted me and she wanted so much to live. I couldn't take that hope away.'

'She hung on much too long.'

'I know she did. She didn't want to leave you.'

'So all we did was to help her to cling on? While her body was eaten away by the tumours?'

'No!'

That was not a thought that Gwyn would countenance.

'We helped her, Aidan. She was pain-free for far longer than would have been the case otherwise, and she was active and able to do things that she wouldn't have been able to. That was something she wanted. Every extra day she had was a gift that she seized with both hands. She could have told me to stop at any time. Sweet Lady, I asked her to let me stop, but she wouldn't let me. She begged me to carry on, to keep fighting with her. She paid a horrible price in those last months, but to her it was worth it. She loved you so much.'

The last was a truth she held out to him as a gift, a reminder of something precious he had kept locked away for so long that he had almost forgotten its existence.

Gwyn might have said more. Aidan turning towards her, his eyes suspiciously bright, might have said something, but at that moment the strident tone of a smoke alarm split the air, just before the acrid smell of burning reached them. Gwyn jerked upright, startled, and swore furiously. Aidan stared at her and then, against all expectations, threw his head back and laughed.

'Let me guess – breakfast's done.'

'Gwyn? What's a blood mage?'

Breakfast finished with, they were sat once more in the lounge with Gwyn perched on the windowsill and Aidan sprawled across the 'human' chair, the other being taken by Kali. There had been very little of the bacon to be recovered and Aidan hadn't even bothered trying to scrape the carbon off the toast. Given that he had had to put it out before he could touch it there had seemed little point – it went straight in the bin. Not even starving birds would be tempted by such leftovers and, judging by the number of bird feeders in Gwyn's garden, there were few of those around. The eggs at least had been salvageable by dint of the fact that they were still safe in their shells, waiting for Gwyn to come in from the garden and fry them. By the time four fresh rounds of bread had been toasted, watched ostensibly by Gwyn and surreptitiously by Aidan, he had scrambled them and recycled the remains of the bacon as a garnish.

Gwyn regarded Aidan over the rim of her second mug of tea.

'Who's been talking to you about blood mages?' she asked curiously.

'Would you believe the avatar?'

With a degree of reluctance, Aidan described the conversation that had taken place through the cabin door.

'Could he be one?'

'Eldritch?'

Gwyn's eyebrows soared skywards, all but disappearing into her hair.

'He's the most opinionated, bloody minded, chauvinistic… What are you laughing at?'

'You like him then,' Aidan managed to choke out, dissolving into howls of laughter at the look of disgust on Gwyn's face. Gwyn's gaze turned venomous.

'It doesn't matter whether I like him or not,' she huffed. 'Sometimes you just have to work with people regardless.'

'But could he be?' Aidan persisted, swallowing down his laughter. 'You – I mean the avatar – said the scars on his body were proof.'

The tight line of Gwyn's lips softened slightly.

'Yes, I saw those. Our friend has encountered demons before, I think, but a blood mage?' She pushed the thick plait of her hair back over her shoulder and shook her head.

'No, he's certainly not.'

After a moment she asked curiously, 'So, why didn't you let me in?'

'I very nearly did.' The thought of how close he had come to doing so made Aidan's heart pound, even now. 'But before he created the veil, Eldritch said that no matter what I saw, or heard, or whoever I thought was outside the door, I mustn't open it.' Aidan's eyes darted to Gwyn's. 'And I guess I chose to trust him, rather than you. I'm sorry,' he added sheepishly, as though it really had been her standing in the night.

'I'm not!' Gwyn declared vehemently. 'Thank the Lady you did. Don't go making a habit of it though; taking his side against mine.'

Aidan's mouth quirked in answer to Gwyn's mock basilisk glare.

'What are we going to do, Gwyn, about the demon?'
'We'll fight it. It's the only thing we can do.'

'But I felt it. I felt its anger, its strength. What chance do we stand going up against something like that?'

'Demons can be beaten, Aidan. If Eldritch and I had been together last night, between us I think we could have taken the avatar.'

She glanced at the door of the spare bedroom, but said nothing. Following her gaze, Aidan commented, 'It was stupid of him, trying to take it out alone.'

Gwyn did not respond immediately. She sat there on the windowsill, knees tucked up to her chin, both hands wrapped around her mug, gazing into the slowly cooling depths.

'I might have done the same once,' she mused.

'You?'

Aidan's forehead creased as he tried to picture this and failed. Now it was Gwyn's turn to laugh at him.

'I was young once, you know. And reckless. Maybe not as much as our friend, but then again, you don't always see what you're doing as reckless, especially not when you're doing it to keep other people safe.'

She swirled the tea in her mug thoughtfully.

'I was very different when I was younger. In those days I had real power.'

She glanced up, but if she noticed Aidan's expression of mingled fascination and amazement at this unexpected candour she did not let it deter her.

'Oh, I'm not saying I wouldn't have been scared – of course I would have been – but I'd have gone up against the demon on my own rather than put someone else's life at risk, no question about it. It would have been a matter of pride too. When you have power it makes you a bit cocky. You get used to dealing with things yourself. So few people have it, to any usable degree, that having it sets you apart. You don't mean it to, but it does. You become very self-reliant. It doesn't feel right to ask other people for help, it's as though you have no right to do so, almost as though doing so makes you indebted to them.

'Maybe if they were family,' she mused, 'or your partner, maybe then it would be different.'

She pursed her lips, thinking about what she had just said. 'I don't really know. I've never had that sort of relationship with anyone who's had power. It must be like finding the other half of your soul…'

Her face grew pensive and then she visibly gathered herself, choosing not to stray any further down that path. 'But ask help from strangers? No, it wouldn't be right.'

'What happened, Gwyn? What happened to your power?'

It was something that had been intriguing Aidan since their first conversation in the Shepherds' Rest; an untold prologue to the story they were now engaged in and several times he had been on the verge of asking her, but had never quite found the courage to do so. Now, in the light of what she had already revealed, it seemed the time might be right. Even so, he half-expected her not to answer.

For her own part, Gwyn was also unsure. Was it time for him to know? Not all of it perhaps and certainly not about James. It wasn't just that it was a promise to Anne she didn't feel able to break, however reluctant she had been at the time to give it. She simply couldn't face that particular revelation now and she wasn't at all sure that Aidan could either. But there were things she could tell him that perhaps he had a right to know, seeing as he had, in a way, been involved.

Putting her mug to one side, Gwyn wrapped her arms round her shins.

'It was the autumn before you were born,' she said, her eyes becoming distant as though she was flicking back through some mental photograph album to an image of that time.

'Your mother had a horse, Monty. I don't know if you'd remember him.'

Aidan thought for a moment. Gwyn's words conjured a dozen fractured images of a tall brown creature – chestnut, he supposed, considering those images now – that seemed to be all legs and a long, swishing tail. Harder to understand was the other memory that came at Gwyn's words. More vivid than his recollections of the horse, this was of his mother standing in the dusk by the paddock fence, dashing ill-concealed tears from her cheeks. There seemed to be no reason why his mind should have conjured such an image until it came to him that this had been the day that Monty had been sold.

'I called in to see her one morning and found her going frantic.'

Gwyn's words called Aidan back from the contemplation of his mother's face and he focussed anew on what she was saying.

'She'd been riding in the field behind the cottage and Monty had put a foot down a rabbit hole. She said the bone breaking had sounded like a pistol shot.'

Over a quarter of a century later Gwyn could still call the images of that day in her mind, scrying them across the years, as clear and sharp as if it had been yesterday that she had stood in that loose box and seen a horse that was as good as dead if she didn't intervene.

Monty stood utterly motionless, his head hanging. Even his normally restless ears made no attempt to telegraph an awareness of the two women

*entering the stall. Gwyn would have known from the sight of him that
something was terribly wrong, even without an awareness of the pain that
rolled off him in waves. That excruciating stillness was something she
recognised from long experience and her stomach twisted to see it in the
normally spirited gelding. Seemingly peculiar to animals, Gwyn wondered
if humans had ever had that ability for absolute stillness in the face of
pain; certainly she had never seen it demonstrated. What experience she
had had of sick and injured humans had left her with a very definite
preference for treating animals.*

*As Anne took another look at her stricken horse and bolted for the
house, Gwyn caught her friend's arm.*

*'No! For the Lady's sake, don't call the vet,' she cried, rightly guessing
where Anne had been headed.*

'Why not?'

*Anne was almost too frantic to hear anything she said and when
Gwyn didn't immediately let her go she struck out at her. Gwyn caught
her other arm and shook her hard enough to make her head spin.*

*'Because if you do, you'll end up having to have him put down. Let
me deal with this first. Then you can call whoever you want to.'*

'I knew from one look that the vet wouldn't be able to do a
thing.' Gwyn pulled herself back from her memories and
addressed Aidan once more. 'But I knew that I could.'

She saw the scepticism that he couldn't quite keep from his
face and accepted it without rancour, understanding that, after
what she had described, such a claim must seem impossible. But,
having only ever known her in this semi-crippled state, Aidan
could have no idea how brightly the power had burned within
her. She smiled at him.

'The good thing about healing injuries is that you're essentially working with the body. It remembers what it is to be whole and unharmed and that's the state it naturally tries to return to.'

Scepticism gave way to disbelief on Aidan's face. Now he was sure she was trying to kid him.

'Don't look at me like that, Aidan. You know about muscle memory and how it takes less effort to build a muscle back to strength than it does to make it strong in the first place. Well, all the body's tissues have an equivalent of muscle memory and when you're healing an injury, that's what you work with. Of course, if a lot of tissue's been destroyed you may have to compromise on what's achievable and it takes an awful lot of psychic energy to speed up the healing process significantly, but this was a fresh, straightforward injury – catastrophic, but straightforward – and in those days,' her lips kinked into a wry smile, 'I had power to spare.

'Even so, it took me nearly two hours to stabilise the leg, getting the bone cells to start to knit together across the break, and then taking it to the point where it wouldn't all come apart again the moment any weight went on it. Of course, it wasn't by any means fully healed at that stage, but I'd done enough to make sure he wouldn't have to be put down.'

Gwyn made no attempt to disguise the note of pride that crept into her voice. For all that it had eventually cost her, that healing was still a success that couldn't be taken away. She flushed slightly, remembering the satisfaction she had felt when she finished. At that point she had been so tired she had had difficulty standing herself, drained by the magic – yes, what she had done warranted that name – that she had just worked. Working automatically, she dismissed her protective circle, releasing the energies she had harnessed to keep her and the horse safe and then, because she was young and confident and she wanted to revel in the horse's discovery that he was free from pain, she made one small error of judgement. She let her shields down completely.

'I don't get it, Gwyn.'

Aidan was looking at her quizzically. He gave a one-sided shrug.

'You healed a horse. What does that have to do with you losing your power?'

What indeed?

'In itself, very little and, if it had ended there, it wouldn't have been a problem.'

She spoke calmly, almost indifferently, as though what they discussed was inconsequential. After almost twenty-six years she could manage that. She could keep the pain from her voice, but she knew, from the change in Aidan's expression, that she hadn't kept it from her eyes.

'I'd used a huge amount of power to perform that healing. Though I'd never have admitted it at the time, I'd taken myself to the limit of what I was capable of. I had nothing left. By the time I'd dismissed the circle and all my protections, I was shaking like I'd run a marathon. But that was okay. Monty was safe and with a few hours' rest and a decent meal inside me I'd have been alright too.'

She sighed and her fingers strayed to the crystal bracelets round her wrist; amethyst and turquoise and a deep, clear peridot that matched her eyes. Without looking up she said, 'Unfortunately, that was when your mother collapsed.'

She heard, and ignored, Aidan's shocked intake of breath, continuing on over his startled, almost involuntary, question as though he had not spoken. The words had a life of their own now and she had little choice but to let them come before her courage and her composure deserted her.

'She hadn't told me she'd been thrown when Monty went down. I think she was too concerned about his leg to give it any thought or to realise that the reason she was feeling so sick had nothing to do with fear. All the time I was healing him she stood there, one hand on his head collar just talking to him all the time, telling him that everything was going to be fine, that I was going to make everything right.'

She gave an odd half-smile at the memory.

'I have no idea whether she believed it herself, but that's what she did. Then, when I'd finished, Monty just shifted slightly, like horses do when they're half-asleep and she realised he had his weight on that foreleg without any problems. You should have seen her face. It lit up like a candle. She threw her arms out and I swear she was going to grab me and dance a jig round the stable –'

For a moment Gwyn's voice had been warm with the memory of the laughter and that ecstatic jubilation that had welled up in her friend. Now there was a sudden break in the laughing voice and it was as though a cloud had passed in front of the sun.

'She took one step and sort of staggered and as I made a grab for her I felt her pain rip through me. I didn't have the strength to hold her. We both went down and I knew something was desperately wrong. I could feel something tearing inside her and I reacted instinctively. There was no time for niceties, for redoing my circles or lighting incense or candles to give me my boundaries. I just grabbed for whatever energy sources I could find.'

Amethyst chips slipped through her fingers like beads on a rosary as Gwyn's voice changed yet again, switching from her narrative to a footnote of magical theory and then back once more.

'There are channels of energy that exist naturally. They're not the sort of thing you should touch unless you know exactly what you're doing and you're very well prepared. I might just have got away with it if I'd been fully shielded and grounded, but I wasn't. Hell, I hadn't even been aware of this channel until then, it was that deep. It can only have been adrenalin that let me reach it.'

The restless movement of her fingers stopped as she faced again the horror of what she had done. She looked up at Aidan.

'I tapped straight into it, wide open and totally unprepared. It's a wonder it didn't kill me.'

Gwyn's whole body tightened as she remembered the energy surging through her. It had been like plunging her hands into fire, the molten rivers of it blasting up through her bones and searing the flesh from them. She had thought she heard Anne cry out and then realised it was she herself who had screamed, the sound ripped from her as she pitted her puny abilities against that maelstrom.

'It went through me like acid. I still don't know how I managed to channel it and I've no memory of using it to stop the haemorrhaging, although somehow I must have done because, when I came round, your mum was fine and I'd survived something I really had no right to. There was only one problem.'

She dredged up a small, bleak smile.

'It had burned out every power channel in my body.'

Silence followed Gwyn's words. There was little that could be said in the face of that admission, no words of comfort or of thanks seemed appropriate. In the end Aidan settled for simple fact.

'You saved her life.'

Gwyn shrugged, the small gesture somehow suggesting that anyone would have done the same in those circumstances.

'She might have survived, if we'd got her to hospital in time, but in all probability, yes.'

'In the Shepherds' you said you'd saved one life, probably two,' Aidan recalled. 'So it was her and Monty.'

'Not exactly.'

Gwyn paused and looked at Aidan with a curious softening of expression.

'There was something else your mum hadn't told me.'

When she had come back to herself she found she was slumped against the stone manger. Anne was crouched beside her, her face pale and scared, but showing no trace of pain, only deep concern for her friend. Gwyn shifted slightly and a look of relief crossed Anne's face.

'Are you alright?'

Gwyn considered shaking her head and thought better of it. Her body felt numb, as though all her nerves had been cauterised, but she could take a shrewd guess that it was going to be infinitely worse when the shock wore off and she started to feel again.

'You didn't tell me you were pregnant.'

Anne's pale cheeks stained crimson.

'Have you told James?'

'No! I mean, not yet…'

Anne looked away quickly.

Gwyn reached out and took her friend's hand. The effort of doing so nearly made her sick. Very quietly she said, 'It's not his, is it?'

For a moment there was silence. Even the horse was still. Anne bit her lip, her blue eyes suspiciously bright. After a moment she shook her head.

'No.'

Her voice sounded very small. Gwyn leaned her head back against the hard stone and wondered fleetingly if the Lady was mocking her. Had she just intervened to stop something that Anne might have preferred to let take its natural course? Almost afraid to know the answer she asked, 'Have you decided what you're going to do?'

On the other side of the small lounge, Aidan leaned forward in his chair waiting for her to speak.

'Anne was pregnant. She wasn't just haemorrhaging, she was having a miscarriage.'

Gwyn looked at Aidan to see if he understood.

'The one life I definitely saved that morning wasn't Anne's and it wasn't the horse's. It was yours.'

CHAPTER 26

Surely he had only closed his eyes for a moment? He had been trying to make sense of the protective wards Gwyn had been placing before she started work on his shoulder. They were quite different from anything he would have set and his curiosity had been roused for all that it was his body that they were being used on. Of course, she had sensed what he was trying to do and had told him to relax and let her get on with it, but somewhere he remembered thinking that Gwyn was more amused than annoyed at his curiosity. Even so, he hadn't meant to close his eyes, not even in feigned obedience, but as warmth spread through his shoulder and down into his bones, they had slid shut in spite of all he had intended. Just a few seconds, he had told himself; then he would open them again. Now, feeling the smooth weight of sheets and blankets along his body, Eldritch realised he had been fooling himself.

He had a vague recollection of the boots being pulled from his feet and of Aidan all but carrying him in here. Then once more he had found himself being helped out of what remained of his damp and muddy clothing, only this time it had been Gwyn doing the helping. Eldritch felt a wave of heat wash down his body at the thought. The woman had no shame. Not that there had been anything in Gwyn's straightforward touch to echo Helen's intimate caress, but it had shocked him nonetheless to feel the warmth of a woman's hand brushing his skin, just as it had earlier, when she had parted the hair on the nape of his neck before untying his sling. Then it had reminded him of how Helen's hand would slide up under his hair and the strength of her as she used to pull his head down while he pretended to resist, insisting that he didn't want her kisses. The muscles of his neck and shoulders had locked rigid with the memory, causing his right shoulder to blossom into a starburst of red agony and he had gritted his teeth and concentrated on the pain, grateful for the way it wiped everything else away, from the unwanted intensity of that oh so innocent touch to the warm notes of the witch's perfume as she knelt beside him.

His body leaden and heavy, he lay there, his mind drifting. He thought he could feel clean bandages swathing his shoulder, but he didn't have the strength to lift the covers and find out. Even the effort of turning his head on the pillow left him exhausted, but the pain that had ridden him since his ill-fated meeting with the avatar was gone. Gwyn had been as good as her word. Whatever she had done to clean those wounds he had felt nothing of it and the whole area was still curiously numb. Were it not for those half-felt bandages – and in truth Eldritch wasn't sure whether he could actually feel them or if they existed purely in his imagination – and the bone deep weariness that pinned him to the bed, he could fancy the whole encounter a particularly unpleasant dream. Even the whispering of the demon had fallen from his brain the moment he had crossed the threshold of the cottage, its absence like the passing of a migraine.

The thought brought his mind circling uneasily back to Gwyn and he found himself thinking of the strength of her hands and the unexpected gentleness of her touch. Eldritch knew he did not deserve such generosity, not after the way he had behaved towards her and certainly not when he considered what might yet come to pass. Yet he had seen the knowledge of those things in her eyes and still she had chosen to help him. The idea that she understood what was happening and had knowingly stepped into danger at his side overwhelmed him. He had no right to such support from anyone, yet he knew now he could not do this alone. Would she have time to learn to hate him if the demon rose? Had he the strength he would have buried his face in the pillow. As it was, Eldritch closed his eyes in despair, remembering only too well what had happened the last time a healer had met with a demon. The pain of that memory followed him down into his dreams.

Aidan was very quiet as he considered the implications of what Gwyn had told him. She saw it in his eyes, the way he worked his way round the fact that she had been crippled saving his life. First came the wash of guilt she had hoped, but not expected, he might avoid, but gradually, as she let the silence grow, making no demands upon him, the realisation dawned that it was his mother's life she had acted to save, not his. His had been incidental. In one way his very existence was down to her and yet he owed her nothing. It took a lot of considering and she could see him approaching the idea from different angles, a small frown dinting the skin between his brows. Eventually he looked at her directly, his expression thoughtful but not defensive.

'I don't know what to say,' he admitted.

'You don't have to say anything. I told you because you asked, not for any other reason. It's not as though you had any choice in what happened.'

Gwyn saw a hint of surprise in Aidan's eyes as she gave voice to the same conclusion he had come to himself. He hadn't expected it to be that simple. Gwyn smiled to herself. She would have thought he might have realised by now that she was the last person who would make demands upon him.

Aidan seemed to reach a decision. Smothering a yawn, he stretched the tension from his shoulders and ran his fingers through his hair, ruffling it into unruly spikes.

'If you don't need me for a while I'm going to head for home,' he said, pushing himself out of the chair. Halfway to the door he stopped and swore softly. 'The Land Rover's still in the forest.'

He turned back to Gwyn, but did not put his question into words. She shook her head, a wealth of regret in that small movement.

'We can go and pick it up later, but I'm sorry, I daren't leave him. Not yet.'

She reached in her pocket and flipped her own car keys at Aidan. He caught them one-handed and stood for a moment, fingering them thoughtfully as he looked at her.

'Why can't you just take him to hospital, Gwyn?'

It was no longer a challenge. He accepted there were good reasons, but he wanted to know what they were. Gwyn sighed.

'Because putting him in hospital would be a death sentence. His energy levels are more stable now, but there's still a strong chance he could go into psychic shock. If he crashed, they wouldn't be able to do a thing about it. Hell, they wouldn't even know what it was they were dealing with.'

She laughed, a short, sarcastic sound, then continued in a softer voice.

'He was desperately lucky when it happened last night that you reacted the way you did. The thing with psychic energy is that it isn't an added extra. We all have it because it's what keeps us alive. It *is* our life. Without the energy you gave him, he would have died, just as surely as if he'd lost too much blood. Even if that weren't the case, at the moment he couldn't shield to save his life – literally. He doesn't have the strength. What do you think would happen if the avatar attacked him now?'

Aidan scowled. There was only one possible outcome.

'He'd be dog food.'

Gwyn didn't so much as smile at the pun, intentional or otherwise.

'Precisely. The demon knows him; it's marked him through the avatar. Even if it can't attack him directly – which might be difficult,' she conceded, 'I don't know for sure that it couldn't influence him. What I don't want is to be taking a call from the hospital later this evening to say he's just thrown himself from a third-floor window.'

Aidan looked shocked.

'Do you think that's likely?'

Gwyn shrugged helplessly.

'Honestly? I don't know. It's not a chance I'm willing to take. But there's something else you should know as well. Even if it can't touch him, I think the demon's already found someone it can influence. Assuming Eldritch did manage to damage the avatar – and Lady bless us, let's hope he didn't get that chewed without doing it some serious damage – it shouldn't have been able to re-manifest as soon as it did. The only explanation I can think of is that someone deliberately worked a power raising last night and channelled that energy to the demon.'

Aidan sat down heavily on the arm of the chair. He stared up at Gwyn, his eyes wide and troubled.

'So that's what you meant when you said we've got even bigger problems than we thought. Is it possible that someone would do that?'

'Unfortunately, yes. As to who it was and what they did to raise the power, well we might see something in the paper in the next couple of days, then again we might not. But if someone is enough under the demon's influence to do that then I'd hate Eldritch to get a visit from them while he's flat on his back in hospital.'

Unconsciously they both glanced at the bedroom door and then back at each other.

'You're talking murder.'

'That would count for nothing in someone under the demon's influence – especially if they'd given themselves willingly.'

There was a weight of sadness in Gwyn's voice. Aidan could only stare at her, appalled.

'I'm sorry, Aidan. At the moment it's only a theory. I don't know for sure.'

Her eyes said otherwise. Aidan flicked the leather key fob thoughtfully.

'Do you want me to stay?'

'No, there's no need. There are sufficient wards on this place to keep us perfectly safe. Nothing that intends us harm can cross them unless I invite it in.'

Aidan was opening his mouth to ask her just how certain she was about that when something in her words struck her. *Nothing that intends us harm...* He looked across at Gwyn, his brows drawing down as he struggled to remember something else she had said, something similar. Haltingly, groping for the words, he said, 'When we were outside you asked Eldritch what harm he meant and then later you said he would be welcome in your house "for as long as that intention remains true".'

Gwyn nodded.

'Yes, I did.'

She looked decidedly uncomfortable; perhaps as uncomfortable as Aidan now felt.

'You also said that when he collapsed outside he hadn't fainted, it was something different. What happened?'

Gwyn sat back on the windowsill. For a long time she was silent, looking first at her bracelets and then at the floor, anywhere it seemed rather than look at Aidan. When she did finally raise her head there was something akin to sadness lurking in the depths of her eyes.

'What you saw was what happens when someone walks unshielded into a warding,' she said slowly. At first Aidan refused to understand what she was saying.

'But nothing happened to me. I didn't have to be invited inside.'

Gwyn's lips tightened.

'Technically my asking you to help me get Eldritch inside was an invitation although I don't think it would have been sufficient to protect you if you were possessed by the demon.'

'But Eldritch isn't…' Aidan proclaimed angrily. He stopped abruptly as he saw the shadow deepen in Gwyn's eyes. If he hadn't been sitting down, his legs would have folded under him.

'Possessed by a demon?' Gwyn finished for him, quietly, when it became apparent that Aidan could not, or would not, complete his sentence. The upward slant of her brows seemed to ask how sure he was of that assertion. She took a deep breath. It seemed an eternity before she released it again.

'No, he's not possessed; I'd have been able to read that.'

Aidan remembered all too vividly Gwyn's hand clenched on Eldritch's jaw, forcing the wizard to meet her gaze, and the fear in Eldritch's eyes as to what she might find. It also explained one other thing that had happened that morning.

'Sula,' he breathed. In her customary place by the door, Sula's ears pricked at the sound of her name. She looked up expectantly, but then returned her head to her paws when Aidan made no move to rise.

'Yes, Sula. She's another reason to believe that he's not possessed. She wouldn't have let him past her if he was.'

'So?'

Aidan shrugged helplessly, uncertain what all this meant. Surely it had to be a good thing that Eldritch wasn't possessed? Yet Gwyn was looking about as happy as if her doctor had told her not to worry about the chest pains because the brain tumour would kill her first.

'Something has happened to him. Something that triggered the wards.'

'Can't you tell what?'

Gwyn gave Aidan a scathing look, which softened as she realised he wasn't questioning her ability but had simply assumed she would have some way of finding out. She shook her head sadly.

'It's not as though there are guidelines for this, Aidan. I can't pull a copy of *Black's Medical Demonology* off the shelf and look up the symptoms of demon influence. I'm fighting to work this out blind.'

'So what do we do?'

'Keep him behind protective wards until he can shield himself and keep an eye on him. I don't believe for an instant that he would willingly submit to the demon or that he really has any intention of harming us. He was as shocked as I was that he'd triggered the wards.'

'He was frightened too,' Aidan said, remembering the energies that had seemed to boil around Gwyn and the otherworldly presence that had burned within her eyes. He didn't add that Eldritch hadn't been the only one.

Gwyn nodded.

'He had every reason to be, but I read him as deeply as I could outside and again while I was working on him just now, and I couldn't find anything definite.'

'Could it just be that he'd been tainted by the avatar? In the forest he said he thought maybe Sula was reacting to the smell of the avatar's blood on his clothes,' Aidan suggested hopefully. Gwyn shrugged noncommittally.

'Maybe,' she said, but her eyes suggested she didn't believe it possible. 'We'll just have to wait and see what happens.'

'Are you sure you don't want me to stay?'

The smile on Gwyn's face was like the sun coming out after an autumn storm.

'No. He couldn't magic his way out of a paper bag at the moment and you've got better things to do with your day than play bodyguard. Go on, go home. The cats and I will keep him out of mischief and if you come back this evening we'll go and pick your car up.'

When Eldritch opened his eyes she was standing by the bed, as beautiful as moonlight. Helen! The sun had found a chink in the curtains, illuminating dust motes and falling like a mantle over the honeyed silk of her hair. For a moment he dared not even breathe, lest the smallest movement might break whatever enchantment had wrought her, but something must have betrayed him for she turned towards him and her face brightened as she realised he was watching her. It was not the cynical mockery of a smile he had come to know in their last days together, but an expression of love; tender and warm as a kiss. His Helen then, not the demon mistress she had become. Oh God – he felt his whole body begin to tremble – how he had missed her!

She reached down and took his hand and he focussed on the long, slender shape of her fingers, surprisingly solid and warm on his. He did not trust himself to speak around the lump that had risen in his throat, but simply wound his fingers with hers as they had always done. Her smile deepened and her voice, when she spoke, was husky and sweet.

'Hello, El.'

It was the pet name she had had for him. How long had it been since he had heard it said like a caress and not a flail? Eldritch's eyes blurred and he blinked rapidly to clear them, afraid that when he opened them again she would be gone or worse, that she would change again. Helen seemed to understand him, as she always had, for the hand tightened around his as if to reassure him.

Movement behind her drew his eye as a tall shape stepped from the shadow and up to the bed. It was Paul.

'So I'm dead then?' He finally found his voice.

The fingers stirred against his and Helen shook her head, sending the corn silk fineness of her hair shimmering. Paul draped an arm around his sister's shoulders. A hand's width taller and with hair that tended more towards mouse than Helen's warm blonde, he had the same fine features as his sibling although the delicacy of his jaw was disguised by a closely cropped beard and the line of an old scar that ran across his chin. The same deep blue eyes regarded Eldritch with compassion.

'No. Not this time. You're safe.'

Somehow Eldritch found the strength to turn his head away so neither of them would see the tears that burned in his eyes.

'Safe?' Even to his own ears his voice sounded raw. 'There's no such thing as safe. Not anymore.'

He swallowed down bitterness and the angry choke of words that came in place of the tears he would not let himself shed. He wanted so much to believe them. More than that, he wanted to believe that they were there beside him. The violence of the emotion surprised him. He thought he had buried it deeper.

A hand brushed the sweat-dampened strands of hair back from his forehead and he felt the softness of Helen's lips brush his cheek. He was conscious as never before of the warm scent of her skin filling his senses and his heart lurched as though it might burst against his ribs.

'I've missed you.' The words were almost a sob.

'Sshh.' Her fingertips pressed gently against his lips, silencing him. 'We're here now. We're always with you. We'll never leave you.'

'I daren't let them get involved.'

Eldritch fought down his emotions, concentrating on something other than the aching void that had been left by their loss.

'You can't stop them.'

Paul's voice was matter-of-fact, cutting to the heart of the matter. Helen's was gentler, offering him reasons but the same end result.

'If you weren't here to help them, they would have to face the demon anyway. Isn't it better that they do it with you? That they know what it is that they face?'

Neither of them had asked who he meant.

'That's just it. They don't know. They don't know what it can do.'

Sitting on the edge of the bed, Helen took his face between her hands. Her palms felt warm and her fingers very strong, cupping his cheeks as much as forcing him to look at her.

'El.' The look she gave him was the one she reserved for when she considered he was being particularly dense. 'It was the young man's friend who died. They're not stupid. They deserve to be given the choice.'

Her hands lingered for a moment on his cheeks and then, sinuous and graceful as a cat, she stretched out on the bed beside him, matching her body to the length of his and holding him close. Eldritch was aware that Paul had moved to the foot of the bed where he stood like a guardian, watching over them both.

'Trust them.' Paul's light tenor made it sound so simple. 'They're involved anyway. The healer is strong. She can help you. The young man…' He hesitated for a fraction of a second as though something puzzled him. 'There's a power that links to him, though where it comes from I don't know. He could even be a Child of the Covenant.'

The comment made no sense to Eldritch and he wanted to ask his brother-in-law what he meant, but the weight of exhaustion pressed down on him and he felt Helen's arms tighten around him, cradling his body even as her presence soothed the aching wounds in his soul. Before he could so much as frame the question, sleep claimed him once more.

Aidan was back shortly before six, just as the first stars were starting to show in the darkening sky. With him he brought two carrier bags. The first he dropped casually by the door, the second he presented to Gwyn with all the pride of Cro-Magnon man bringing home half a woolly mammoth to the cave.

'Aidan, you're an angel. You're going to make Jane a wonderful husband one day.'

Aidan growled under his breath, but otherwise chose not to rise to Gwyn's teasing.

'I wasn't sure if Gandalf would be up to eating, so I got him some soup and there's an extra portion of sweet and sour chicken just in case. How's he doing?' he asked, casting a glance towards the spare room as he followed her into the kitchen.

'He's still asleep.' Perhaps she felt his concern, for she added, 'That's not a bad thing. It's giving him time for his core energy to stabilise. If he hadn't been sleeping naturally I'd have put him under.'

Aidan's eyebrows raised, not so much at this statement of what Gwyn could do, but at the casual way in which she said it.

'Wasn't that what the brandy was for?'

'It helps,' Gwyn admitted and Aidan wondered if he imagined the edge of amused satisfaction that he heard in her voice. 'But I wouldn't want to overdo it. He'll be sore enough when he wakes up without having a hangover to deal with. How are you feeling?'

'Me? I'm fine. I'm used to yomping around hills in the dark.'

'But not fighting demons.'

A long appraising look accompanied the plate she passed him. Aidan did his best to return it with an expression of open innocence rather than the guilty squirm that felt the more natural response. Not that he thought he had anything to feel guilty about, but with Gwyn it wasn't always easy to be sure. The stare continued for a few moments more before Gwyn relented, but the thin smile she gave him said clearer than words that while she would accept that for now, if he started feeling less than fine she wanted to know about it, sooner rather than later.

Satisfied he had been let off the hook, Aidan busied himself with the takeaway, heaping fried rice onto his plate. Gwyn put down her own carton and stared at him.

'Sweet Lady, have you been fighting?'

Aidan looked up quizzically and then, following her gaze, realised she had noticed the dark russet bruise spreading out across his knuckles.

'Training, Gwyn. The word's training.'

He pulled his hand back as she reached to touch it, embarrassed not so much by the injury but by the fact that it had been a sloppy technique that had caused it. Not that the bruise he'd caused on Graham Tiggs' elbow was any smaller, but that was hardly the point.

'You went to karate?'

He shrugged, not sure what else she would expect him to do on a Sunday afternoon.

'The state you were in?'

Aidan looked at Gwyn oddly, unable to understand why anyone would consider mere exhaustion a reason for not training.

'I was fine,' he protested. 'Until Sensei made me do a line up and told Keith, Martin and Tigger to go for me all at once.'

It was in the resulting melee, when he was dodging out from under a flurry of Keith's roundhouse kicks whilst doing his best to keep the other two from piling over the top of him that he had caught Tigger's elbow with a poorly placed back knuckle strike. Neither of them had given it a moment's notice until the end of the lesson when they had, quite good-naturedly, compared bruises.

'Had you annoyed her?'

'Who, Sensei? No, she often does things like that with the seniors.'

And if you don't tell her about any injuries or illness before the lesson then you've only yourself to blame if you can't cope with what happens when you're in the dojo. He didn't say that out loud though. He had found that very few people outside the world of martial arts understood that particular element of the karate psyche. He knew he should have admitted to being a bit slower on his feet today and said so before the lesson. Sensei knew exactly how hard she could push her students, but if they didn't bother to tell her about a problem then she wouldn't bother to take it into account. Her argument was that she wasn't psychic so she couldn't know unless they told her. Aidan wasn't so sure about that, but he accepted he had only himself to blame for his ragged performance.

'You're completely mad,' Gwyn commented despairingly, her eyes rolling heavenwards as though invoking the judgement of some higher power.

'That's rich coming from a woman who considers demon hunting to be a perfectly normal occupation. Talking of which, what do you want to do about Gandalf's food?'

'Put it in the oven. He can have it later if he's awake enough, but for now we'll leave him to sleep.'

CHAPTER 27

Eldritch's personal belongings made a small pile on the bedside table. As Aidan peered over Gwyn's shoulder at the still, blanket-wrapped form inhabiting her spare bed he noticed them; the watch, wallet and car keys, a handful of small change and a door key and the thin copper band he wore around his right wrist. The plastic bag with its contents reduced to a nightlight and box of matches was there too, as was the small, black-handled knife and the antique sapphire ring on its chain. It could have been accidental, but Aidan rather thought that Gwyn had put those items at the very front of the pile deliberately so that their owner had but to open his eyes and he would see them there, waiting for him.

Eldritch lay slightly turned onto his good side as though he had shifted in his sleep. Blurred by the weight of blankets and quilt, the shape of his right arm showed folded across his chest while his left arm was stretched along the top of the covers, the palm turned up, the fingers curled, almost as though he were holding something. A small strip of sticking plaster showed on the ball of his thumb. Very quietly, Gwyn stepped forward and pulled the blanket back up over that outflung arm.

'I'm surprised he can manage to sleep after what happened last night,' Aidan said as she rejoined him by the door. 'I'd have thought he'd be having nightmares. That pain block of yours must be really something.'

Gwyn shook her head.

'No, that will have worn off some time ago. At the moment he's simply too tired to dream, but they'll come soon enough.'

Aidan couldn't help the shiver that edged up his spine. Judging by the questioning look she shot him, Gwyn had seen it too.

'I'm not looking forward to that myself,' he confessed. Gwyn's face softened, understanding showing in her green eyes.

'You could stay here tonight,' she suggested gently.

'Thanks, but I'm not sharing. With either of you.'

'Don't be daft.'

Then she realised he was joking and gave him a stern look before continuing with her original train of thought. 'I'll change the sheets and you can have my bed. I'm quite used to sleeping in a chair.'

Somehow Aidan did not doubt that. He wondered if Gwyn intended to do just that tonight; camp out beside the wizard's bed in case of any crisis in the night.

He looked again at the blanket-muffled shape. Though still undoubtedly pale, sufficient colour had returned to Eldritch's face that his brows and lashes no longer stood out in absolute monochrome. While it would have been stretching the truth to say he looked well, at least he no longer looked as though he was dying.

'It really was stupid of him, thinking he could take on the avatar on his own.'

'Not stupid.' Gwyn's face was thoughtful as she turned and looked up at him. She leaned back against the door jamb, her arms crossed, her head tilted to one side in that characteristic way she had when she was seeking out the right words to explain herself. Somehow she still managed to look serious despite the schoolgirl pigtails she had pulled her hair into before they had sat down to eat.

'Arrogant. He knew what he was facing and the implications if he couldn't defeat it, but he didn't think he needed help.'

'No.'

They both turned at that soft exhalation of sound. Grey eyes regarded them from beneath a tangled black forelock.

'You're vulnerable.' Eldritch's voice was quiet but steady. 'I couldn't ask you to take that risk.'

Gwyn pushed herself off the doorframe and went back to the bedside. After a moment Aidan followed her.

'What do you mean we're vulnerable? Vulnerable to what?'

'To the demon. Both of you. You're vulnerable to its influence.' The grey eyes swung from Gwyn to Aidan. 'Oh, you may say you're not a healer, but you're just as much at risk.'

This was news to Aidan. He looked at Gwyn for confirmation, wondering why she hadn't mentioned this, but if anything she looked more confused by Eldritch's assertion than he was. There was genuine puzzlement in her voice as she asked, 'What makes you think healers are more vulnerable to a demon than anyone else?'

A look of weary anger flickered briefly in the back of Eldritch's eyes as though he felt Gwyn was being deliberately obtuse. He had no strength to hold it but its echo was there in his voice as he answered her.

'Because I've seen it happen.'

He looked at Gwyn as though to ask why she was fighting him when they both knew he was right, but when she said nothing even that drained away. His eyes drifted from them and he seemed to sink back into the blankets as though something

375

else had been lost along with that spark of antagonism. Then, like a man backed into a corner and arguing for his life, he spoke again.

'We didn't realise at first. Paul and I thought we were both going a little crazy or perhaps, after what had happened, it was understandable that she'd become withdrawn and edgy. But everything changed that day. Everything. And by the time I knew for sure, it was too late. I'd lost them both.'

His voice was quiet, but somehow its very lack of emotion left Aidan in no doubt that what Eldritch spoke of had ripped the heart from his world and taken him to the very edge of madness, yet he had no idea what that thing was. But Gwyn knew. Compassion filled her voice.

'Someone you knew was possessed?'

Perhaps it was a measure of how near he was to the end of his reserves or perhaps he had finally decided to be honest with them, but, for whatever reason, Eldritch answered her directly.

'Helen.' He swallowed heavily as though his throat had closed on the name. 'My wife.'

'But you said…' Aidan stopped as he saw the pain etched on Eldritch's face. When Gwyn had confirmed Eldritch's real identity he had assumed that everything the man had told him when they had met on the sailing club jetty was as much a fabrication as his Ph.D. and his interest in lead mining. Now he recalled the aching grief that had haunted the tall man's voice as he spoke of the woman he had lost and he realised in that, at least, Eldritch had not been acting.

As though he had read Aidan's thoughts, Eldritch's eyes sought his. Desolate and grey as the Atlantic, they held an acknowledgement of what he had tried to do that afternoon and something that might have been an apology.

'It happened eighteen months ago. But it wasn't cancer.'

And just for a second, beyond either acknowledgement or apology, Aidan glimpsed the agony of loss that had torn across Eldritch's soul. He had said it was ancient history. Aidan thought eighteen years might pass and that would still be a lie.

'There was a demon in Southwark. You may have read about it in the papers – it made all the nationals for a day or two – a hedge fund manager who came home one night and killed his kids, his wife, the nanny...' Eldritch's voice was stronger now, though it would have been hard to describe it as normal. Beneath the fall of dark hair, his pale features were calm, the grief pushed back into some private corner of his mind where no one else would have to see it. What he spoke of meant nothing to Aidan, but Gwyn nodded slowly as though it had struck a chord with her.

'Wasn't he the one who committed suicide afterwards? They found his body – or at least what was left of it – on some wasteland out towards Vauxhall where he'd set himself alight.' She paused, frowning as she dragged her memory for the details of an eighteen-month-old tragedy that had barely cast a ripple on the national conscience before being displaced by the next horror story. Aidan was reminded of why he rarely bothered to read the papers. But Gwyn did and she clearly remembered. 'Only there was some question as to whether or not it was suicide – the burns weren't right or something – and the coroner ended up recording an open verdict. Some of the tabloids were claiming that the wife's family had connections and they'd had him killed, although it seemed rather far-fetched.'

'Not as far-fetched as the truth. The coroner had every right to be concerned. It wasn't suicide. He'd been blasted apart with

Levin fire. Every cell in his body was reduced to charred carbon.'
He looked again at Aidan. 'It's what I nearly did to you last night.

'His name was Nigel Granger. We never did find out how he
came to be taken as a host. There was some talk of his taking drugs
or having a drink problem, but how much of that was down to
the papers trying to find a reason for him caving in his family's
skulls with his son's cricket bat, I don't know. Not that it really
matters. Helen had sensed a weakening in the boundary and we
knew something was trying to cross. From then it was a race to
pinpoint exactly where the weakening was. When the papers
reported what had happened we knew a demon had come
through and had taken a host. We'd lost round one.'

'You make it sound as though you had done this before,'
Gwyn noted, sliding into the chair at the end of the bed.

'We had.'

For a moment Eldritch's composure slipped, but he swallowed
and gave a small, one-sided shrug, effectively dismissing anything
else he might have said. He pushed himself up the bed, propping
his shoulders on the pillows.

'Not often, thankfully, but when it was necessary.'

'Why would you do that?'

After the previous night's encounter, Aidan couldn't imagine
why anyone would deliberately go looking for a demon. The black
brows rose and there was a trace of amusement in Eldritch's tone
as he answered.

'The same reason you'd risk your life finding people who've
got themselves lost on a mountain.'

'No way,' Aidan snorted. 'You can't tell me that mountain
rescue's like playing Rentokil with demons. Nobody's trying to
kill you when you go on a shout. You're up against the weather

and the hill, nothing more. It's not inherently dangerous. It's about knowing what you're doing up there and having the skills to cope with the conditions.'

The hint of a smile threatened the corners of Eldritch's mouth.

'Believe it or not that's what you do when you set out to deal with a demon. It's just that the skills we use... that I use,' a wince replaced the smile as he corrected himself, 'aren't something that just anyone can choose to learn. You have to have the power in you to start with.' He paused to push the ratty strands of his hair out of his eyes. 'Why are you part of the mountain rescue team?'

'Because even though the mountains round here aren't particularly high, they have a reputation...' Aidan paused and laughed as he realised what he was about to say. 'Actually, they have a reputation for being evil, for catching people out. Bogs, hidden hollows, the sorts of things that get people into trouble, we have them in abundance. People go up and they get lost or they're not as prepared as they thought they were, then the weather closes in and suddenly they're in real trouble. Somebody has to get them down.'

'And you'd rather risk your life...' Eldritch raised his hand to forestall Aidan's protest. 'In a controlled and calculated way – by going up and helping them, than leave them to try and cope with something they don't have the ability to deal with?'

Aidan gave a little shake of the head as though the answer was so obvious he couldn't see why Eldritch was bothering to ask the question.

'You can't just leave them to it. People would die.'

He saw the look on Eldritch's face and stopped, his own face flushing.

'Exactly,' Eldritch said quietly. Amusement danced fleetingly in his grey eyes, but rather than press the point he returned to his story.

'Once a demon has taken a physical body it becomes almost impossible to trace. The energies that mark it as having crossed from the Unseen Realm are masked by the host, but the papers all carried pictures of Granger so we used them to scry for him. He grew up in Vauxhall and for some reason the demon took him back there. We tracked him to an old industrial estate.'

The lightness that had come back into Eldritch's voice died away as he spoke, his tone flattening once more as if the only way he could deal with the memories crowding in on the back of those words was by stripping all emotion from them.

'You can never tell with demons. Sometimes, when they first take a host, they seem to be overwhelmed by the sensations of this world, almost drunk on it, and they go berserk, as the one in Granger did, killing everything around them. Others seem more controlled and instead of going for the immediate gratification of inflicting physical pain, they go for more subtle pleasures. A demon can wield despair and misery like a knife and with far less chance of being uncovered. They can mimic a host so well that even the people who know them can't tell what's wrong.'

A flicker of pain breached the wall at the back of Eldritch's eyes.

'Even the ones who know about possession. But one thing we were confident about was that if you attack demons with magic that's how they fight back – with magic. Granger was a big man – powerful, a body builder – not what you'd expect from a hedge fund manager.' Eldritch's lips curled into the briefest of smiles, rueful and self-mocking, but his left hand bunched in the quilt until his knuckles were white. 'We'd have thought twice about going up against him physically, but that was never the idea. We planned to trap the demon with magic, the three of us coming from different directions, surrounding it in a web of power, before driving it out of the host and destroying it.'

'What happens to the host when you drive a demon out?' Aidan asked the question without thinking.

'Aidan!'

Gwyn, who had listened quietly to Eldritch's story, uncurled from her chair, coming upright with a look of mixed horror and embarrassment on her face, and the implications of what he had said hit Aidan like a punch to the stomach. He coloured and looked away, unable to face Eldritch.

'I'm sorry. I didn't mean...' he muttered, breaking off shamefaced, but there was no way he could take the words back. Eldritch's face drained of what little colour it had held yet of the three of them he recovered fastest.

'It's alright.'

It was obviously a lie and for a moment the mask slipped and the aching void of grief opened up in his eyes. He smothered it down, but the cost of doing so grated in his voice as he turned to Gwyn.

'He should know. You both should.'

Even so, the silence stretched thin between them before he continued, but neither Gwyn nor Aidan thought to break it. When Eldritch finally spoke it was with casual brutality as though the words meant nothing to him. Yet somehow that very offhandedness only emphasised the tragedy that lay behind them.

'Once someone's been taken by a demon they're dead,' he said harshly. 'The presence of the demon destroys the mind and the body becomes nothing more than a suit of clothes that the demon inhabits. Sometimes when the demon is driven out the body dies, sometimes it doesn't, but to all intents it's the same thing – the host is dead. All you're left with is a shell.'

Aidan swallowed heavily, feeling grief rise in his own chest and settle like an iron band around his heart, knowing that Eldritch was describing what must have happened to his wife. Not looking at either of them now, Eldritch went on.

'We completely misjudged what it would do.'

Pain slid into his voice again, despite all his efforts to keep it out, and puzzlement as though even now he was trying to work out how they could have foreseen what would happen, as if in hindsight they could have avoided the tragedy that had been waiting to claim them.

'Demons fight magic with magic. Magic is their element. It's what they do. But not this one. This one fought back physically. I suppose it could have gone for any one of us, but Paul was the closest. Granger split his head open with a piece of angle iron. If Helen and I had been a second later it would have killed him. Instead we killed Granger. Normally you drive a demon out of its host, trap it in a power net and then destroy it, but with Granger we had no choice. Helen and I drove him off with Levin fire and then I finished him while she worked on Paul.'

There was no emotion in Eldritch's voice now, nothing in his flat intonation to convey the horror of what he had done or what he had been through and if he cared what Gwyn or Aidan thought there was no indication in his face or in his voice. He could have been oblivious of their presence for all the notice he paid them.

'Helen was a powerful healer.'

Aidan was aware of Gwyn leaning forward in her chair at those words, her green eyes focussed on Eldritch like a hunting cat, her expression intense.

'She saved Paul's life, but the demon took her while she was healing him. I cast a binding over Granger to hold the demon within his flesh and then I reduced every cell in his body to ash. The demon should have been destroyed along with his body, but it wasn't. I don't know if the binding wasn't strong enough.' For the briefest second he faltered, crippled by the weight of guilt indelibly linked to that possibility. 'Or if the demon had already left him before I set it, but while Helen was exposed in her healing trance, it took her.'

Eldritch's voice cracked on those last words and he shifted roughly in the bed, turning away from them, his face to the wall. If doing so hurt his shoulder then the pain was nothing compared with the torment that came from sharing those memories. As silence descended upon the little bedroom, Aidan sagged back against the pale chambray wallpaper, uncertain what to do or say. Eldritch's turned back was an eloquent demand to be left alone with his grief, yet Aidan was torn between the feeling that he had no right to intrude and a genuine desire to offer comfort, though he couldn't imagine what he might say that could possibly help. As he wrestled with the two conflicting desires, Gwyn slipped quietly from her chair and came and sat on the bed beside Eldritch's turned back. Aidan thought she would take his hand or try to comfort him in some way, but all she did was place a hand lightly on his arm. The contact was neutral, almost to the point of being impersonal, yet it was sufficient to let the man know that she would not allow him to withdraw from them and bury himself in his suffering alone. Aidan saw Eldritch quiver at the touch and Gwyn must surely have felt the tremor go through him, but she did not withdraw her hand and, to his intense surprise, Eldritch made no move to shrug off that contact.

'Now I understand why you did what you did yesterday.' Gwyn's voice was gentle as she addressed herself to Eldritch's turned back. She paused for a second, looking down at him, but if she had hoped for a response she showed no surprise when none was forthcoming. Her voice, however, was a good deal more caustic as she continued. 'Not that that makes what you did any less idiotic.'

Eldritch's back stiffened under Gwyn's hand, the sheer unreasonableness of her comment piercing the layers of his grief in a way that no amount of sympathy could have done. He was tired, he was hurting and, just possibly, he had expected better of her than that. Very slowly, the movement grinding knives into his shoulder, he heaved himself over to face her, his sharp features dark with anger.

'You…' Words failed him.

'Witch?' supplied Gwyn, helpfully, something akin to mischief dancing in her green cat eyes. For a second Eldritch could only glare at her as he realised he had risen to her bait.

'Witch,' he finished, between gritted teeth. The way he said it made it clear it wasn't the word he had almost used; similar perhaps, but not quite. Yet even though he knew she had provoked him deliberately, now he had responded to her he could not simply turn away again. Whether he liked it or not she had pulled him back from the edge and it was not a place he would retreat to deliberately even if his adversary would have let him.

'I was trying to save your life,' he ground out.

This time Gwyn did catch hold of his hand, taking it between her own as though it were something infinitely precious, and her voice was very different as she spoke again.

'I know. I'd just rather you didn't throw your own away at the same time.'

Eldritch seemed unsure what to make of that. He said nothing, but the rage seeped away from his face giving Gwyn space to continue.

'I can't judge what happened to your wife because I don't know how she approached her healing, but I promise you that when I heal I keep my shields up. Whatever happened to Helen, it doesn't mean you need to worry about me.'

Still Eldritch regarded her with no discernible expression on his face, but Gwyn seemed unbothered by his lack of response. She squeezed his hand briefly.

'We need to talk, but first, you need to eat something.'

Deftly she tucked his hand back beneath the covers as she rose from the bed. Casting a glance across at Aidan, she added, 'And then you and I have a couple of cars to retrieve.'

The story of Aidan, Gwyn and Eldritch's fight to find the demon and stop its manifestation continues in:

Child of the Covenant

Book Two of the Dark Places sequence.

Author's Note

In telling this story I have taken a few liberties with the landscape of mid-Wales. Not all the features I describe – most notably the cliff known as "the Bite" – exist outside the murky realms of my imagination. Likewise the names I have ascribed to them are my own creations. My purpose in all of this has been solely to entertain and I hope that those who know and love the area will forgive me.

Some real places are referenced to set the context in which my story takes place but the town of Llancathan and the village of Caeglas are both fictional and any resemblance to real locations – or to the businesses or individuals associated with them – is coincidental.

Any errors in the Welsh I have used are entirely down to me. Linguists will undoubtedly note that the name Gwyn – spelled with a "Y" – is a man's name. Gwen is the feminine form. However, in the case of my character, Gwyn is short for Gwynyfa – another of my linguistic creations. Those who are interested can read an explanation of how she came by her name in *Child of the Covenant*, the sequel to *The Demon's Call*.